'Full of well-handled forensics and the brooding atmosphere of the Essex coast, this is an impressive second episode in a very promising series' *Mail on Sunday* on *Shot Through the Heart*

'*Shot Through the Heart* demonstrates that Isabelle Grey has all the command as a crime novelist that she has channelled as a television writer' *The Independent*

'Isabelle Grey has already distinguished herself with a series of police procedurals that combines attention to detail with compassionate intelligence' *Sunday Times* on *Shot Through the Heart*

'An unusual police procedural . . . beautifully written, full of interesting insights, and atmospherically set' *Literary Review* on *Shot Through the Heart*

'Grey's credentials as a television writer shine though . . . the inner working of the Major Investigation Team are just as enthralling to read about as the serial killer they are hunting' Clare Mackintosh, author of *I Let You Go* on *Good Girls Don't Die*

'Assured, convincing and especially good on . . . the delicate – and often dodgy – nature of the relationship between the police and the press' Laura Wilson, author of *The Wrong Girl* or ·····

'Combines clever plc ····· feeling' *Sund* ·····

Isabelle Grey is a television screenwriter whose credits include over thirty-five episodes of *Midsomer Murders*, *Casualty*, *Rosemary and Thyme*, *The Bill* and *Wycliffe*. She has also written non-fiction and been a magazine editor and freelance journalist. Isabelle's previous novels include two psychological thrillers, *The Bad Mother* and *Out Of Time*, and the first book in the DI Grace Fisher series, *Good Girls Don't Die*. Isabelle grew up in Manchester and now lives in north London.

Also by Isabelle Grey

Out of Sight
The Bad Mother

DI GRACE FISHER

Good Girls Don't Die
Shot Through the Heart
and coming soon
The Special Girls

Isabelle Grey

SHOT THROUGH THE HEART

A D I Grace Fisher Thriller

Quercus

First published in Great Britain in 2016 by Quercus
This paperback edition published in 2016 by

Quercus Editions Ltd
Carmelite House
50 Victoria Embankment
London EC4Y 0DZ

An Hachette UK company

A CIP catalogue record for this book is available
from the British Library

PB ISBN 978 1 78648 001 9
EBOOK ISBN 978 1 78429 282 9

10 9 8 7 6 5 4 3 2 1

Typeset by Jouve (UK), Milton Keynes

Printed and bound in Great Britain by Clays Ltd, St Ives plc

SHOT
THROUGH
THE HEART

1

Russell Fewell's white van skirted the raised area of green that fronted the old stone church. A middle-aged woman was waiting for her Jack Russell to finish sniffing around the base of the metal pole that bore the heraldic village crest. The woman looked up and watched as his van turned left into the long, meandering High Street. Russell wondered if she, like him, was spending Christmas Day alone and, if so, how she felt about that.

Several of the front doors of the crooked old Essex houses had been decorated with evergreen wreaths brightened with red berries or chevroned ribbons, and lights shone from many of the casement windows. As he cruised along the narrow street, he could see Christmas tree lights twinkling in one or two of them. He thought the houses themselves, painted pink, yellow, pale green or white and packed tightly under their overhanging gables, looked like wrapped presents. The gifts he'd chosen and carefully wrapped for his two kids were in the back of the van. On top of the rifle.

Russell lowered his window. He'd imagined that he'd almost be able to smell the aroma of roasting turkey, but all he got was the biting metallic tang of impending snow. The news programme on the radio this morning had banged on about the bookies' odds on it being a white Christmas, and already a few stray flakes were drifting down and melting on his windscreen. He had a vivid mental flash of jolly Santa Claus colours, fresh scarlet against unblemished white.

At the end of the High Street he passed the turning to the lane where his grandparents had once lived. That's where he always used to go for Christmas dinner when he was a kid, much the same age as his son Davey; all the family together, uncles, aunts, cousins packed in around two small tables pushed together even though they were of different heights, everyone flushed and laughing and waiting for his grandmother – the only one able to get in and out of the room unless people climbed over one another – to bring in the plum pudding, eerily alight with a flickering blue flame of poured brandy. Every year the same. Family. Family didn't change. At least not until people got old and died. That was the whole point of family, wasn't it?

The chill air stung his cheeks and made his eyes smart. No wonder so few people were out and about. He brushed away the tears and closed the window.

Last year, even with the divorce, he and Donna had managed to spend Christmas together. That's the one thing they'd firmly agreed upon: they might no longer be married, but they'd always be family. That's how they'd treat one another. Not only for the kids' sake but because it was true.

Not any more.

He speeded up. Then slowed down again: no rush. Important to do this right, just as he'd planned. He passed the primary school on his left. It was deserted, closed up for the holidays, but it was the school he'd attended and where he'd taken each of his kids in turn. This was his home town. His mum had been able to trace her kith and kin back through generations of local agricultural labourers; his dad's family, from the neighbouring county of Suffolk, were much the same, impoverished and probably illiterate workers. This was the soil to which he belonged. To which he'd return. He didn't mind. Better to lie in the new burial ground than allow himself to be cast out, tormented, humiliated in the eyes of his own children. That was a life not worth living.

His was the only vehicle on the road, but nonetheless he indicated before turning right into Fairfield Close. Neat houses built of brick with white woodwork and picture windows. Driveways for two cars. Front gardens that weren't enclosed by hedges or fences, leaving space for kids to kick a ball about or circulate on bikes. Here the front windows had fairy lights looped across them and it was possible to glimpse more of the rooms inside, to see animated television screens, Christmas trees, colourful decorations, people sitting together. It wasn't that he was jealous of the people in these houses or envious of what they had and he didn't: it wasn't that. It was the injustice of it all. It burned like acid, ate away at him, shrank him until he could bear it no more.

Fairfield Close capillaried into three cul-de-sacs. Russell drove to the end of one of them and turned the van round. He was aware that he might be drawing attention to himself, but he wanted to be pointing in the right direction. He wasn't sure what would happen afterwards, whether he'd get back in the van or would simply walk away. That bit wasn't so important. Besides, whether he walked or drove, he didn't foresee anyone making a serious attempt to stop him, not when they'd be all slowed up from booze and second helpings of turkey and stuffing and roast potatoes and he had a rifle in his hands.

He parked outside the house, positioning himself so he'd be able to cover the front door from the back of the van, and got out. He could see them all indoors, sitting around the festive table. He opened both rear doors and lifted out the presents he'd wrapped with such love. As he placed them on the ground beside him, a couple of snowflakes landed gently on his bare hands. He glanced up at the sky, which looked pulpy and malignant, before reaching in to pull the rifle into position. He closed one of the doors so that he could turn smoothly, take hold of it, raise it to his shoulder and fire, just the way he'd practised out on that deserted country lane. Then he leaned back against the closed door, pulled up the hood of his black anorak, stuck his hands in his pockets and waited.

The dogs – black Labradors, mother and son – were threshing around, wagging their tails and scenting fresh air. The heat of the Aga, which had been on full blast all day, had warmed even the quarry-tiled lobby where Robyn Ingold and her parents hung their coats and cleaned their boots. None of them had dressed up for the day; it was enough to put on the silly paper hats that came out of the crackers, and she was wearing her everyday jeans and a warm sweater. There would be enough roast goose to keep the three of them going all week. Just as well really. Her mum and dad would be busy tomorrow with the Boxing Day shoot. With the wildfowling season finishing at the end of January, the sportsmen would be wanting to make the most of the holidays; among them would be some of her dad's best clients, the City types who'd spend tens of thousands on a single gun and then bring it to him for hand-crafted alterations. And meanwhile she'd be stuck into her revision, preparing for the mock exams she had to sit as soon as term started in the New Year. The minimum fuss of cold meat and leftovers would suit them all fine.

The moment Robyn opened the back door the dogs were through it and off, lolloping down towards the line of poplar trees at the end of the garden where they could sniff around for rabbits or other creatures in the long grass beside the fence. She grabbed a jacket and followed them out. It was beginning to get dark, but she could see the snow swirling in over the fields from the marshes beyond the sea wall a quarter of a mile away. She'd already fed the hens and made sure the two donkeys had water and fresh hay, but she made her usual circuit, checking they were all safely locked up for the night. The grass was speckled white and, though it was mushy underfoot, she hoped it would settle. It certainly felt cold enough. She loved waking up to the deep snow-clad silence which always seemed so mysterious and full of promise.

She whistled to the dogs and, when they came immediately, let them know they were released: it was important with gun dogs never to slack on enforcing their obedience, even when it didn't seem to matter. Martha was getting old, maybe a little deaf too, and didn't always come as quickly as she should. That wouldn't do in the field; there was no room for sentiment, not when the guns had paid a lot of money for their day out. But Bounder was a good dog, trained partly by Robyn's father and partly by his own mother, Martha.

She looked east towards the estuary but the gathering snow obliterated the view. The Ingolds had no immediate neighbours and the only visible lights were at least half a mile away. She caught the muffled cry of a curlew carried on the wind. The sound rose, repeating, questioning, wild and lonely like the cry of the wind itself. She loved it, had always loved hearing it, especially at night when she was all tucked up warm in bed. She wondered again what it would be like to leave this place, to go away to university and be constantly with other people, to lose that unconscious absorption with the cast of the sky, the shivering leaves of the poplar trees, the morning's dewy animal tracks in the grass, all the accumulating details that defined the little kingdom of her childhood. The thought was strange but also exhilarating.

She turned to look back at the house, a rather lumpy extended bungalow at right angles to two solid brick-built Victorian barns, one the garage, the other where her dad had his workshop. Her mum hadn't yet drawn the curtains and Robyn could look right into the living room, aware that, as darkness fell, her parents wouldn't notice her watching them. The red candles on the dining table still shone amid the remains of their traditional dinner. Burning logs smoked on the open fire. Coloured lights on the Christmas tree went on and off in pattering sequence. Her parents stood with their backs to her, watching the television, the news probably, or maybe the Queen's speech. Her dad, in worn jeans and a soft Viyella shirt, was stocky, still with a full head of resilient sandy-brown hair. Her mum was about the same height, round and comfortable in a denim skirt and striped blouse, with a practical bob of blonde-highlighted hair. Robyn felt a wave of deep affection. An only child, she'd never been tempted to indulge in teenage angst: every day she saw how hard her parents worked and knew how ready they were to share the rewards with her, so why should she give them any grief?

The dogs brushed against her legs, and she felt a cold dribble of melting snowflakes run down the side of her neck. Time to go in. As she started to move towards the house, something about the way her parents stood within the cosy frame of the window – leaning forward, intent on the TV screen, her mum's hand clasping her dad's arm – made her stop and look again. Somewhere in the world the news could not be good. A dreadful road accident? Some awful terrorist act? Whatever it was, it didn't really affect her. She knew she ought to feel more pain, more empathy, more involvement with what went on in the wider world, but the honest truth was that she didn't. She leaned down to pat the two dogs. They needed no urging now to run back indoors, and she followed them across the whitening grass.

They stopped optimistically in the kitchen to check their empty bowls, so Robyn entered the living room before their bois-terous presence alerted her parents to her return. Although Nicola immediately switched to a more neutral expression, Robyn had just enough time to catch the troubled look in her eyes. Leonard, as always, appeared imperturbable.

'What's the matter?' she asked.

'Some madman over Sudbury way has gone on a killing spree,' he said. 'I suppose all the pressures of Christmas are too much for some people.'

Still alert to some vestige of concealed tension between her parents, Robyn picked up the remote control and flicked through to a twenty-four-hour news channel, which cut from a studio newscaster to library stock shots of sunny summer streets and an ancient church.

It's reported that five people have been shot dead and three more have been taken to hospital with what are described as life-threatening injuries. No motive has yet been estab-lished for the killings, but unconfirmed sources suggest that the gunman, who has yet to be identified, has turned the gun on himself. The nightmare in the historic Essex village of Dunholt began shortly after half past two this afternoon when . . .

Robyn let the newscaster's voice wash over her.

'Dunholt?' she asked in alarm.

'Yes,' said Nicola. 'But it's all right. I mean, we don't know anyone there, do we? Thank goodness.'

It was clear from her mother's question that Nicola hadn't remembered the casual conversation a week or so earlier with Robyn's best friend at school. 'But that's where Angie and her family were spending Christmas,' Robyn told them. 'With her grandmother. She's got one of those quaint old houses in the High Street.'

3

The call from HQ to say that the Major Investigation Team was urgently required thirty miles away in Dunholt, followed by a look at the breaking news story, gave Grace Fisher the kind of heart-sinking moment that made her wish she had a different job. She and Lance Cooper had no choice but to sober up and drink black coffee until a driver came to pick them up. She had never been even peripherally involved in an incident of such tragic scale before, and realized how very glad she was that Lance was here with her so she did not have psych herself up to face it alone. She knew it would be easier to deal with the potentially overwhelming human cost once she was able to start concentrating on the details, making lists and accomplishing straightforward achievable tasks, but the waiting was unbearable, especially when only minutes earlier they'd been laughing over a chaotic game of Scrabble and finishing a second bottle of wine.

Plus she felt terrible for Lance's boyfriend, Peter Burnley, who, as they got ready to go, was decent enough to accept their apologies and make light of his abandoned Christmas. Grace assured him he was welcome to stay for as long as he liked and should make himself at home, even though she knew it would be the middle of the night before she got back – if then.

She and Lance had become good friends over the past few months. She was well aware that he'd been with the Colchester Major Investigation Team longer than her, yet he had been genuinely pleased for her when she'd been made back up to detective inspector after the successful conclusion of the Polly Sinclair case. At work he remained discreet about his sexuality, and she was touched to be one of the very few in whom he confided, and been delighted when he and Peter had accepted her invitation to Christmas lunch in her new home. If they were all now technically over the drink-drive limit, it was thanks to the delicious wine that Peter had brought. She'd only met him one or twice before, and, despite an inbuilt prejudice against financial advisers, had liked him instantly: he was self-deprecating and observant, and also kind and considerate towards Lance, which was all that really mattered. She disappeared upstairs to change into warmer, more practical clothes – offering Lance the chance to express his own more tender regrets for a ruined afternoon – cheered by today's revelation of how truly happy and in love they seemed.

Pulling on a warm jumper, she thought how unbelievable it was that, this time last year, she had still been married to Trev and living in Kent. Last Christmas she and Trev had gone to stay a couple of nights with her sister and her rowdy young family, and Grace was well aware that this year Alison had been rather offended that she'd turned down the annual invitation. But Grace had longed to create a holiday tradition of her own, and wanted to mark her first winter in Wivenhoe by planning and cooking a full Christmas dinner, which, if she said so herself, had been a success.

Her mobile buzzed with a message to say that the car had arrived and was waiting for them in the street outside, so she went downstairs to fetch Lance.

They spoke little on the forty-minute drive, conserving their energy for what was to come. The Dunholt church clock was already striking five as they arrived at the compact modern vicarage that would serve as an emergency meeting point until the village hall could be set up as a temporary incident room. The falling snow muffled much of the noise of other cars arriving and doors slamming. The police driver opened her car door. As she stepped out, she noticed several faces at windows, neighbours staring out at the commotion as if, by missing nothing, they could come to terms with their brutally altered world. She and Lance walked up a longish garden path from where, through shadows of thick shrubbery, she could make out a row of elegant windows belonging to the original eight-bedroom Georgian rectory next door. She thought wistfully how useful such facilities would be at a time like this.

Even though she suspected that quite a few of the team squashed in around a teak dining table that appeared to double as the vicar's desk had partaken of a good measure of Christmas cheer, there was none of the usual banter and catching-up gossip. Everyone was relieved when Detective Superintendent Colin Pitman, looking as spry as ever, quickly and efficiently got down to business.

'We are awaiting verification,' he began, 'but two eyewitnesses have identified the gunman as a local man, thirty-one-year-old Russell Fewell. In addition, a body has been found in the churchyard, the victim of an apparently self-inflicted gunshot. Death has been confirmed, and we believe the body to be that of Russell Fewell. All the witnesses so far have described only one shooter and one weapon, so it's probably safe to assume there's no further immediate danger.'

'How many dead, sir?' asked Grace. 'The news reports say five.'

'So far we have six confirmed fatalities, including the suicide, three people in hospital and eight separate crime scenes,' said Colin grimly.

'Has the weapon been recovered?' asked Lance.

'Yes, from beside the body,' said Colin. 'A Heckler & Koch G3 rifle. Russell Fewell did not hold and had not applied for a Section 1 firearms certificate, and the weapon appears to be unlisted.'

'Isn't that the same type of gun that police marksmen use?' asked Grace.

'Yes,' said Colin. 'Although it, or a variant, has also been military issue in Iraq and Afghanistan, so there's likely to be plenty of them knocking about. And let's not forget that Colchester – a garrison town – is not that far away.'

'Was Russell Fewell ex-military?' asked DC Duncan Gregg.

'Not as far as we know,' said Colin.

Duncan looked relieved, and Grace remembered that he was himself ex-army.

'Our first objective,' Colin resumed, 'is to formally identify all the victims and inform next of kin. Then, while it appears that we have our perpetrator, we still need to build up as detailed a picture as possible of the day's events ready for the coroner's inquest. So we want formal statements from all the witnesses who've already come forward, and we'll need to identify any other potential witnesses. Uniform have already begun house-to-house. And we must find out all we can about the shooter.'

'Sick bastard!' Grace caught the whispered curse from the other end of the table.

Colin did his best to ignore the accompanying murmur of revulsion that passed through the packed vicarage dining room and carried on. 'First task is to secure his home and any related properties. We've already recovered his van, which he used for his work apparently. We think he repaired washing machines, dishwashers and the like.'

'Was he self-employed?' asked Grace.

Colin consulted his notes and shook his head. 'No. On short-term contract to one of the big appliance companies. No criminal record, but I want to know everything there is to know about who he is, why he's done this and what, if any, relationship he has to each of the victims. Any other questions?'

'Do we know anything else about his mental state?' asked Lance. 'I mean, he can't have been normal. Who'd do a thing like this? And on Christmas Day?'

Several people muttered and nodded in agreement. 'We're waiting for access to his medical records,' said Colin. He held up his hand to halt the fresh wave of disgust. 'Listen up. As if things aren't already bad enough, you need to know that the first victim, Mark Kirkby, was a serving police officer. One of our own.'

Colin allowed time for the outrage and hurt felt at the killing of a fellow officer to ebb away, then looked at Grace. 'DI Fisher, I want you to deal with the family.'

Grace nodded, aware of the general feeling that sending an officer of senior rank would show proper respect. 'I understand, sir,' she said. 'One question, though: the fact that Mark Kirkby was the first victim, does that suggest he was top of Fewell's list in some way?'

'Yes, very much so, unfortunately. The gunman's ex-wife, Donna, and her two kids were spending Christmas with Mark

Kirkby. They were all inside when Fewell shot and killed Kirkby outside his house.'

'Bastard!' This time the curse wasn't whispered. Grace swallowed down her repugnance. Fewell was already one of the damned, consigned to the hell that history reserved for mass murderers, but he could have her hatred to top it off, and welcome.

'His wife and children weren't among the victims?' she asked.

'No, thank goodness. They were unharmed.'

Grace let out a sigh of relief: at least the investigating officers were spared the horror of a family annihilation. However pitiful the physical carnage when children were involved, it was the sheer vindictive futility of such violence that proved hardest to bear. 'But they saw what happened?' she asked. 'They're witnesses?'

'Absolutely,' said Colin. He remained silent for a moment as the team absorbed this new aspect to the day's reality. 'It's possible that Fewell could have set out intending to shoot them all, but either missed the opportunity or lost his nerve. Donna Fewell and her two children have been taken back to her house and we've got a family liaison officer with them now. DI Fisher, I want you to be the one to talk to them too. Find out what history there is of domestic violence, the circumstances of the divorce, anything she can tell you. This hasn't just come out of nowhere.'

'Do we know if Fewell deliberately targeted any of the other victims?' she asked. 'Or was it only Mark Kirkby?'

'From what we've got so far, which isn't much, it appears his only direct connection was with his ex-wife's new partner. But we can't rule out grudges against the others.'

'So otherwise he might just have been shooting at random?' asked Lance, the bafflement clear in his voice.

'It's starting to look that way,' said Colin. 'But it could have been very much worse. In experienced hands the G3 can fire several hundred rounds a minute, so I suppose you could say we've got off lightly. Two Home Office pathologists are attending and a third is on her way from London. All leave for scene-of-crime officers has been cancelled, although, with the continuing snowfall, there's probably very little they can usefully do now until daylight, which won't be until eight o'clock tomorrow morning. Ten centimetres of snow is predicted by then, and overnight temperatures will be below freezing, so wrap up warm.'

'Has a refreshment van been organized?' asked Duncan. 'Hot drinks and bacon butties are not going to be a luxury on a night like this.'

'As long as traffic isn't held up by the snow,' Colin said with a smile, 'then Teapot One's ETA is half an hour.'

The team laughed, relieved to break the tension.

'Even though it's not yet official, we know the perpetrator is dead,' Colin continued. 'We're not looking for anyone else in connection with these crimes. So our investigation has to be a *how* and a *why*, especially the *why*. And, I promise you, we are going to get answers. However, I cannot emphasize enough that the chief constable intends Essex Police to control the flow of all intelligence about the shooter. All information is to be passed to me, every scrap, and no one speaks to the media, on or off the record, for any reason. We give them information as and when we decide to, not the other way round.'

'It may be that some people will choose to approach the press rather than us,' said Grace hesitantly. 'The media are bound to dig up information we'll miss.'

'Very possibly,' agreed Colin. 'But I don't want to be ambushed by any vital details we don't already have. I want you all to make sure there are no loose ends for the media to unravel before we've got the full picture. Got that?'

Everyone nodded, their faces sombre, all well aware that, for a police officer, aiding and abetting the press was a hanging offence. Grace sighed, envisaging how quickly the world's media would engulf this rural backwater. The intrusion would be not only physical – satellite vans, camera crews, journalists scavenging for 'colour' – but also emotional, with raw grief filmed and served up on an endlessly rolling loop and with talking heads repeatedly asking stunned friends and neighbours how they felt about what had happened. How did anyone feel? How did anyone even begin to make sense of such pointless and random horror? Except, she reflected, the causes of human evil all too often turned out to be banal and rooted in the most unspectacular of resentments and woes. She'd seen her share of wives and girlfriends savagely beaten or even murdered for allegedly undercooking the bacon or forgetting to record a TV programme. The worst tragedies often had the most paltry motives.

'And finally' — Colin once again held up a hand as the team sensed the end of the briefing and began to shift around and murmur to one another — 'I've been informed that the chief constable has already had Number Ten on the phone, and that the prime minister wants to put in an appearance here tomorrow on behalf of the nation.'

'No pressure then,' said Duncan wryly.

'It is Christmas,' said Colin, deadpan. 'We should also expect a message of condolence from Sandringham. And with that in mind I want you all to remember that, with the gunman dead, the media will be rooting around to find someone more news-worthy to blame. Our job is very simple: to make quite sure they don't pick on us. So if Fewell does have any prior history of domestic violence or any other unsavoury practices, I want us to be the first to know about them.'

4

It was around 6 p.m. on Christmas Day when Grace rang the doorbell of Donna Fewell's box-like little house. Lance had gone to secure Russell Fewell's rented flat, and to check whether he'd left a suicide note or anything else that might help explain his actions. Grace hoped that, if he had, it wouldn't say anything to cause his family yet more pain. She was pleased she'd managed to secure Duncan as her wingman; his presence would offer an unthreatening manliness that she hoped might be comforting for Donna and her kids.

The snow had stopped falling, but the lowering sky promised more to come, and, with darkness, the temperature had dropped by several degrees. Grace was glad when the family liaison officer – a constable from the local station whom Grace did not know – opened the door and let them into the brightly lit shelter of the narrow hallway. The FLO, a plain young woman with badly cut short hair and intelligent eyes, introduced herself as Ruth Woods.

'How are they?' Grace asked her quietly, nodding towards the living-room door, which Ruth had sensibly shut behind her.

'Very shocked. I said you might want to speak to Donna alone, but she refuses to be separated from the kids.'

'Understandable. If we have to, we can wait to take a formal statement in the morning.'

'She thinks it must all be her fault. She wanted to go and say sorry to everyone.'

'You explained why that's not possible?'

'Yes. Luckily the vicar called round. She's well liked, the vicar. Exactly what you need at a time like this. Said she'd make sure that people understand how Donna feels about what her ex-husband has done.'

'Had Donna been concerned about Fewell's violence before today?'

'No, I don't think so. I didn't want to start asking questions before you got here.'

'Good, thanks. What about Fewell's relationship with Mark Kirkby? Has Donna said anything to shed light on what was going on there?'

Ruth shook her head. 'Not really.'

It occurred to Grace that Ruth would have known Mark Kirkby. 'Everyone at the local nick must be pretty shocked,' she said.

'Dreadful business,' echoed Duncan.

The FLO nodded but showed little emotion.

'And the kids?' asked Grace. 'How are they?'

'Ella's only six. She doesn't really understand. I think she was more scared of the blood than anything. Davey's that bit older. He's clammed right up. At least the vicar's visit provided a bit of welcome distraction.'

'OK. Do you want to go in first? Make the introductions?'

The room was too small to hold six people comfortably. Donna took her daughter onto her lap, and Ruth disappeared to the kitchen next door and came back with two upright chairs for her and Duncan. Grace took the armchair opposite the two-seater couch on which Donna sat with her children. Still dressed in a Primark Christmas jumper with a holly-sprigged plum pudding on the front, Donna had a pleasant face with inquisitive eyes and straight shoulder-length dark hair tucked back behind her ears. Grace had been informed that she worked part-time behind the counter in a building society, and could imagine her being helpful and concise. It was less easy to see her as perhaps a battered wife, but then Grace knew she didn't look like the stereotype of one either.

'I'm very sorry for your loss,' Grace began, once the formalities were over.

'*My* loss?' asked Donna sharply.

'The children's father,' said Grace mildly. 'And your partner, Mark Kirkby.'

Donna shook her head as if trying to shake off the bewilderment hammering at the inside of her skull. It didn't seem to work.

'When had you last seen or spoken to Russell?' Grace asked.

'Not since last week, when the kids broke up from school for the holidays. Mark said . . .' Donna broke off but determinedly recomposed herself. 'Mark thought we should all take a little break from each other. A breather. Let things settle down again.'

'Why was that? Had something happened? An argument?'

Donna shook her head, absent-mindedly stroking her daughter's hair as she spoke. 'Russell was never very good at coping when things got on top of him, but everything had been fine between us until I met Mark, and then Russell just seemed to lose it. Like it was OK for us to split up, but not OK once I met someone else.'

'Was he jealous? Controlling?'

'I don't know what it was. Maybe not so much over me, but the kids, you know? He kept saying he didn't want Mark taking over his kids.'

'Mark didn't have children?' asked Grace, although she already knew the answer.

'No. He's not been married. But he loved having all of us over to his place. There's a nice big garden, and he went out and bought a trampoline and stuff for them.' She ruffled Ella's hair. 'You liked that, didn't you? Going over to Mark's house.'

Donna's whole body crumpled, and she began to sob, clinging tightly to her daughter, who twisted herself free, looking up at her mother with a mixture of alarm and curiosity. Beside Donna, Davey seemed to shrink even further into himself, while Duncan and Ruth sat silently, doing their best to look at nothing in particular.

'Why would he do this?' Donna cried. 'No one was out to get him. It was all in his head. How could he do such a thing?'

Grace sat quietly until Donna calmed herself. She glanced around the room as unobtrusively as she could: there was little in it apart from the couch, armchair, TV and a box of toys and children's DVDs in the corner, but it was clean and tidy, and framed school photographs of both kids adorned the little mantelpiece over the gas fire. All the same, she wondered what rows or fights these two young children had seen or overheard in this house.

'You said the divorce had been amicable?' Grace asked once Donna seemed ready.

'We married too young,' said Donna. 'We just, you know, fizzled out.' She wrapped her arms around Ella. 'This makes no sense. No sense at all. Russell wasn't like that. He was a pushover really, a right softie.'

'You said he thought someone was out to get him. What made him think that?'

'Russell was afraid he was going to lose his driving licence,' said Donna. 'He was really stressed out about it.'

'Why was that?' Grace knew that Russell Fewell had recently been charged with a drink-drive offence, but she wanted to hear what Donna would say.

'It was really bad luck, but he'd lose his job if he was banned from driving. Probably have to pay a big fine too.' Donna sighed. 'He blamed Mark.'

'Why would Mark be to blame?'

'He wasn't; it was Russell being stupid,' said Donna. 'He'd got a bee in his bonnet. Accused Mark of getting one of his mates to follow him and pull him over.'

Duncan cleared his throat, making Grace aware that he was signalling his protest at such an accusation against a murdered fellow officer. Out of the corner of her eye she also noticed Davey, who until now had appeared not even to be listening, turn to look at his mother beside him on the couch. Realizing that Grace was watching him, he swiftly reverted to blankness.

'Did you think that might be true?' Grace asked Donna carefully.

'Of course not!' said Donna. 'Why would he?'

'Did Russell often get ideas like that about people?'

Donna wrapped her arms around Ella once more. 'No, not really. It's just, since I got together with Mark, he really lost it.'

Grace decided to let it go for now. She had yet to tackle the hardest part of why she was here. She pulled a sheet of paper out of her bag and unfolded it with trembling fingers. Never in her entire career had she faced such a list, the deadly roll-call of forty minutes of sheer madness. *Sick bastard!* That whispered curse had been right. And there was no point trying to protect Ella and Davey from these harsh realities: they'd been there; they'd seen Mark Kirkby die, knew their father was a killer. Grace licked her dry lips before speaking.

'Donna, I need to ask you something very difficult. And I need to include Davey too, in case he knows any of these people from school.'

Donna took the proffered piece of paper and scanned the list of names. Uncomprehending, she stared at Grace. 'What is it?'

'All the people he shot,' Grace said gently. 'I need to ask you if you're aware of any connection that Russell had with any of them, however slight. Did he know them? Do you? Or were they . . .' Grace stopped, not sure, in front of Davey and Ella, how best to finish the sentence. 'Or were they just in the wrong place at the wrong time?' she ended lamely, feeling at that moment that all her skills and experience were woefully inadequate for such an event. She caught Duncan's eye and he gave her an encouraging nod: she was doing the best she could.

The colour drained from Donna's cheeks as she once more read down the list of names of dead and wounded.

Davey stirred and craned to look over his mother's shoulder. 'After Dad shot Mark, he shot a man who came out of one of the houses opposite.' He spoke matter-of-factly. 'The man wanted to know what was going on, and he wouldn't go away. Then Mum made us go indoors.' He pointed to the paper. 'None of them are to do with my school.'

Donna covered her mouth with her hand, her eyes widening in shock. She shook her head in disbelief and then pointed reluctantly to the last of the names. 'She works in the Co-op. Her husband died last year. Her son is training to be a teacher. But I doubt that Russell would've known who she is.'

'Thank you. She's one of the three in hospital. She was in her car. She drove past him at the end of the High Street.'

'Will she make it?' asked Donna.

'I don't know.'

'Russell grew up in Dunholt,' said Donna. 'Why would he want to hurt these people?'

Grace steeled herself to remain professional. 'Do you recognize any of the other names?'

Donna shook her head and handed back the sheet. 'No. Sorry.'

'Thank you,' said Grace, trying not to shy away from the hurt and confusion she saw in Donna's eyes.

'And you're absolutely certain that it was him?' asked Donna. 'There's not been a terrible mistake?'

'There's no doubt at all,' said Grace. 'We have a handful of eyewitnesses who saw pretty much his whole rampage.'

Donna hung her head in exhaustion.

'If it helps,' Grace added, 'two of the eyewitnesses described him as panicked, frightened almost, as if he was firing in self-defence.'

While Donna nodded as if this made some kind of sense to her, Davey sat up straight. 'What does it matter, anyway?' he asked belligerently. 'Your job is to catch people, isn't it? But Dad's dead. You know who did it.'

'That's right, Davey,' Grace answered softly. 'But sometimes it's also important to understand why things happen, especially when something is so sad and will affect a lot of people.'

'You think he's a nutter!'

'No, Davey,' Grace said gently. 'I'm not saying that. But he must have been very, very upset, don't you think? Not his usual self?'

'Everybody's going to hate him anyway,' the boy said fiercely. 'So what does it matter why he did it or what was wrong with him?'

'Hush, Davey,' said Donna. She reached out to soothe him, but he jerked away from her, shifting to the far edge of the couch. His sister stared at him with big grave eyes.

'I'm so very sorry that you've lost your father in such terrible circumstances, Davey,' said Grace. 'And I think we owe it to you and your sister to find out what happened. Not only to learn if we could have done anything to prevent it or to stop such a thing happening again, but to find out if anyone could have helped your dad. Don't you think that's a good idea?'

Davey shook his head, refusing to be consoled, and then swung his legs over the arm of the couch, hunching his back against them.

Grace turned back to Donna. 'Do you know where Russell might have got the gun?'

Donna looked perplexed, as if she had not yet even considered that question. 'No idea,' she said. 'He was never interested in guns. An air gun, perhaps, when he was a kid. Shooting rabbits on his dad's vegetable patch. And those things cost money too, don't they? We've both been skint since the divorce, so where would he get the cash to buy a gun?'

'We don't know yet,' said Grace. 'Though it seems that the firearm has never been listed, so it's probably not come from a legitimate source. We're working on it. Did Russell have any friends it might've belonged to?'

'No,' said Donna firmly. 'Russell was never into, like, playing those online war games or military-type stuff. He liked a bit of fishing with his mates sometimes, otherwise it was a spot of darts down the pub. I know no one's going to believe it now, but . . .' Donna stopped, embarrassed. She glanced at Duncan and then at Ruth, who gave her a sympathetic smile. It seemed to give her the courage she needed, for she lifted her chin defiantly and wrapped her arms around her daughter. 'Their dad was a nice guy,' she said. 'The very last person on earth you'd ever dream could do such a dreadful thing.'

Ella began to cry. 'I want my daddy,' she wailed into Donna's plum pudding jumper. 'Where's Daddy?'

Grace concentrated on some scribble or other in her notebook so that she didn't have to speak. She wasn't sure she'd ever find the words to explain to herself, let alone to this family, what had happened here today.

5

Ivo Sweatman, chief crime correspondent of the *Daily Courier*, hated this kind of news. There was no good to be had from it, no fun, no tricky leads to chase, no competition for a fresh angle, just woe and misery and then more of the same. And at fucking Xmas too. Not that he minded being called away from Tiny Tim and the Yuletide log, whatever the hell that was supposed to be.

He hated Christmas, always had, ever since he was a kid. Especially when he was a kid. All that playing happy families when he knew damned well that almost as soon as he'd unwrapped his presents they'd be packing his trunk to send him back to prep school, and then he'd have to leave most of his gifts in an empty bedroom and wouldn't get to play with them again until the February half-term, by which time he'd hate the very sight of them. It was all a show, a pantomime to avoid revealing why they'd sent him away to boarding school and how they really felt about that. Ivo had longed to beg them to tell him straight: they might manage to fool themselves, but they sure as heck weren't fooling him.

Still, at least he'd had the good sense, before racing from London to cover the Dunholt slayings, to secure a room in one of the town's few B & Bs. He rather enjoyed the thought of there being no room at the proverbial inn for his fellow cowboys from rival titles. Although, quite frankly, he'd much rather have stayed at home. He should've given the story to one of the junior reporters and hunkered down to finish his M & S turkey dinner and sparkling elderflower water. Christ, he must really be feeling his age.

As he expected, all roads leading to the High Street had been cordoned off, the police cars' flashing blue and orange hazard lights warning him that, even with a press pass, he wasn't going to get anywhere near the heart of the action. Not that there would be any action, merely a bunch of police constables getting chilblains while guarding nondescript patches of snow where helpful neighbours and a hapless rubbernecker had each been dropped by a single bullet.

And, if there was a story building, then that was it: the bullets. It was a shocked young paramedic who had attended one of the victims who survived, who had then called his older brother, who had tipped off a reporter at the local paper, who had tipped off the *Courier*'s news desk. From what the paramedic had said, it sounded like the shooter had used a type of ammunition that would cause maximum physical damage. Which made the weirdo loner bastard a *real* sicko.

Information about the victims had been coming in constantly since the story broke: the first fatalities were a thirty-two-year-old police constable along with one of his neighbours, a forty-seven-year-old manager with a road rescue service. The gunman had apparently not encountered anyone else until he entered the High Street, where he shot dead an elderly woman and her teenage granddaughter, visiting with her family for Christmas. They'd been on their way to check on an elderly neighbour. A few doors down, two brothers (both married with young kids) who had left their mince pies half-eaten to go and investigate the commotion outside were both felled on their doorstep. A motorist who'd been approaching from the other end of the High Street and made the mistake of slowing down to see what was going on, and a middle-aged couple who had peered out of their window, had been badly injured, but luckily it appeared that the shots had lost velocity as they went through glass, diminishing their power to kill.

For once Ivo took no pride in possessing such arcane forensic expertise, but he knew enough to work out that the shooter must have used soft-nosed expanding bullets. The ammo of a hunter, a sniper, an assassin. If that *was* the story, then he'd bet the farm on his editor creaming it at the mere thought of the proliferating pages of explanation, with diagrams, and before-and-after photos of spent bullets, and endless speculation about whether the massacre was revenge or punishment, a warning or a desire to make some kind of twisted statement.

Ivo had already obtained Fewell's address from the electoral register and downloaded a map. It was too dark and wet to bother getting that out of his pocket now, but he'd memorized enough of it to skirt round the police cordon and start trudging in what he was pretty sure was the right general direction. Lights were on in the little houses he passed, but curtains were tightly drawn; entire streets seemed to be holding their breath. As quickly as it popped into his head, he committed the line to memory: he could probably use it later when he filed his copy.

But his heart wasn't in it. It was an effort to get the adrenalin flowing over such sorrow and waste. What did an execution-style slaying have to do with some sixth-former and her granny who were unlucky enough to be in the wrong place at the wrong time? Right now he simply wanted to bolt back to the pink scatter cushions and patchwork bedspread of his overheated B & B and get annoyed about ordinary things like how impossible it was to open those dinky little UHT milk portions piled in a saucer next to the child-size kettle without making a mess.

But he had a job to do, no matter how much it wearied his soul. Better buck up. Spotting an old-fashioned red telephone box, he took shelter and used the meagre light to consult his printed-out map. The shooter's gaff was just round the corner, and he prepared himself to start knocking on doors, ready to blag his way in with the neighbours to find out where Fewell worked, who his mates were, where he might track them down for a little chat, and where on earth he might lay his hands on some photos. Fewell might be dead, but nevertheless he was tomorrow's MOST HATED MAN IN BRITAIN, and the punters would want to see for themselves THE FACE OF EVIL.

As the questions Ivo needed to ask began to form in his mind, he could feel the familiar tingle of anticipation kick in after all. Russell Fewell – what drove him? Had he planned it and, if so, for how long? Had the bastard been waiting for Christmas Day, making sure, like John Lennon's murderer, that no one would ever forget him? Was it the special day that had pushed him over the edge, or had he spontaneously woken up this morning to find his sad little existence so unbearable that he had picked up a rifle and got in his van?

Fewell's atrocity happening on Christmas Day unquestionably made for unbeatable headlines, but it also made Ivo's job a whole lot harder. No corner shop was open for gossip; there was no possibility of mingling with the mums outside the school gate or the patients waiting in the local GP surgery; even the one pub that had offered Christmas lunch had now closed out of respect. It was frustrating because, in a town of three or four thousand people, everyone was connected somehow to everyone else, yet he wouldn't be able to start gleaning any decent local colour until everything finally reopened, which probably wouldn't be until after Boxing Day. At least by tomorrow some politician or other – the home secretary at the very least – would be wheeled out to express shock and horror and then wash the current government's hands of all responsibility. That would fill a few column inches. But everyone would have that, and Ivo liked to pride himself that any story going out under his byline had its own unique slant.

Reluctant to leave the relative shelter of the phone box, he wondered if he ought to call Hilary Burnett, the Essex Police communications director. He liked to think she'd have a soft spot for him after last summer when he'd done his best to stop DS Grace Fisher – Detective Inspector Fisher now – getting the chop. Hilary should be able to provide some hard facts on the weapon by now, as well as the timings and the fatal route Fewell had taken through the little town.

What Ivo would like most of all would be a cosy fireside chat with DI Fisher. The Ice Maiden, he'd dubbed her when he first encountered her, but he felt differently about her now. With her clear gaze, soft brown hair and slender grace, she certainly suited her soubriquet. While she was definitely a survivor – and he was glad of that – she was also passionate about what she did, and vulnerable too. He looked forward to seeing her again, and to working alongside her. He wasn't going to bother asking himself how she might feel towards him.

He speculated about her promotion. Especially given how that slimy boss of hers, Colin Pitman, had taken over as head of the MIT in Colchester after Ivo's old mate Keith Stalgood had retired. It was Keith who'd told him over a cup of coffee that a deal had been done, that the sweetener for Colin accepting a reprimand for his failure to pursue a complaint against one of his officers on the Kent force was a fresh start running the show in Essex. Keith had more than hinted that he'd personally had a hand in finessing Grace's reinstatement as DI as the necessary quid pro quo for the whitewash on Colin. He was a good bloke, Keith. Old school. There weren't many like him left.

It was blokes like Keith who brought a glimmer of integrity and hope to Ivo's job. Back in the day, long before the Leveson Inquiry, it had been an honour in a big case to be taken into the confidence of the senior investigating officer, especially when the case wasn't going to plan or when the SIO needed help to flush out a suspect. Those were the days when there was mutual respect. Sure the police and the media each played by different rules, but they were rules that, while they could be very crea-tively bent, *were* rules. Now, instead of a code of honour, there was bureaucracy. And profit.

Ivo heaved a sigh. Nostalgia wasn't going to get this job done. Better shift himself, get back out in the snow and start thinking how best to schmooze Fewell's neighbours. As he was pulling his gloves back on, his mobile vibrated in his pocket. He fished it out: not a number he recognized, but he took the call.

'Mr Sweatman?' asked a chirpy but determined voice. 'I'm Bobbi Reynolds, head of communications at the Police Feder-ation in Leatherhead. Just a courtesy call to check whether you need any further information about Constable Mark Kirkby.

I've already emailed you his CV and some photos, but if I can be of any other assistance, please don't hesitate to let me know. We're obviously sensitive to the need to show the utmost support for his family, friends and police service colleagues at this tragic time.'

Ivo wondered whether she was reading from a script, and how many times she'd already delivered this same spiel to his esteemed colleagues on other newspapers. 'Thank you,' he said. 'I might well come back to you later.'

'Any time,' Bobbi assured him. 'One of my assistants will be available 24/7 until further notice.'

Ivo was impressed, although hardly surprised, at such profligacy: everyone knew how the Police Federation squatted on a huge mound of cash. He'd once visited the Leatherhead HQ – which doubled as a hotel, with restaurant, bar, heated pool, gym and leisure suite, all heavily subsided for Federation members – and had admired the sheer chutzpah of its heroic no-expense-spared bling. He could certainly imagine Hilary Burnett envying their ability to so blithely offer a round-the-clock service, but kept his views to himself, thanked Bobbi again and hung up. Yet he felt irked by her breezy assumption that he would lead with the story of her choosing, and suddenly wanted to show her what a contrary old bugger he could be. If the party line was to have Mark Kirkby, the fallen hero, as the front-page lead, then it was up to him to buck the trend. Ivo Sweatman would find his own story to tell, thank you very much.

6

It was well past midnight when an equally exhausted colleague dropped Grace home after a slow journey through falling snow. She let herself in and found that, in her absence, Lance's boyfriend had done all the cleaning up: the table was cleared, the Scrabble board put away and, in the kitchen, the dishes had been washed up and piled neatly on the draining board. Opening the fridge, she saw that Peter had found cling film and done his best with all the leftovers. Christmas Day had been and gone.

She took a festive satsuma from the bowl and, peeling it, wondered how Peter felt about his day, abandoned in the house of a virtual stranger and left to go home alone. But then she thought about Davey and Ella and their mother, about the relatives of the two brothers who had been killed who had turned up at the vicarage as Grace and the team were leaving, in search of some kind of respite from this sudden onrush of terror and pain, and about all the other families coping as best they could. She sat on her little sofa, on which kind and thoughtful Peter had even straightened the cushions, and began to cry. She wept for the tragedy she'd witnessed; she wept for herself that she'd had to steel herself to walk into people's lives at such a moment and yet remain calm and professional, and, knowing it was pathetic, she wept that her first Christmas here in her own little house in Wivenhoe had been spent watching someone else be happy in love.

Tears at bedtime. That's what her dad used to say when she and her sister were little, when it was the three of them, before he remarried. *Dry your eyes. It'll all look better in the morning.* Her mum had died when Alison was born, yet their dad had coped. Or appeared to. But maybe he'd cried like this when he was on his own at night. *Tears at bedtime.* Well, she wasn't going to let that be the story of her life any more than he had.

Grace almost wished that Peter had left her something practical to do, but on the other hand getting out of bed at six in the morning was going to be enough of a struggle, given that there would still be a couple of hours before it got light. She blew her nose on a piece of kitchen roll, switched off the downstairs lights and went up the narrow staircase. There were three tiny bedrooms, and when she'd moved in four months ago she'd chosen the one at the back, using the two front rooms as an office and spare room. She liked looking at her neighbours' little courtyard gardens and the irregularly tiled roofs of the old houses in the next street. The view was magical now, with just enough moonlight to illuminate the falling snowflakes. She realized suddenly how cold she was – the heating must have gone off hours ago – and pulled the curtains, deciding she'd get undressed after she'd washed her face and brushed her teeth. She could shower in the morning.

It had been Colin's debrief back at the vicarage that had kept the core team so late. Lance had reported on his visit to Russell Fewell's modest one-bed flat on the outskirts of Dunholt's small post-war council estate, where media satellite vans already lined the road. Most of Fewell's shocked neighbours were elderly or retired and had said that he'd been friendly and polite, kept himself to himself, a bit shy perhaps, and given absolutely no sign of what had been to come. The flat was spotless, bed made and not even a dirty teaspoon in the sink. Scene of crime had already arrived, but had turned up nothing so far except an empty rubbish bin and, neatly laid out on the kitchen worktop, all the paperwork for his drink-drive offence, on which Fewell had opted to go to court. There was no suicide note and nothing to indicate why he had left there early that afternoon intent on committing mass murder.

As Grace got into bed and pulled the duvet around her, she thought about what Donna Fewell had said about her ex-husband believing that Mark Kirkby had arranged for him to be followed and pulled over for a breath test. That kind of self-exonerating paranoia often became the final straw in a life already going downhill and was almost certainly no more than a symptom of whatever had driven him to his final terrible violence.

Once Donna's children had fallen asleep, Grace had been able to speak to her more freely. Donna had once again dismissed her ex-husband's belief that his arrest had been somehow fixed, insisting that it would simply never occur to Mark to do such a thing, and it was all in Russell's head. Grace knew she mustn't let her own bitterness colour her judgement, and she had no reason to doubt Donna's sincerity, but she knew all too well that there could be two sides to this kind of story. Back in Maidstone her fellow officers had blamed her for a popular colleague's arrest on drug charges. They'd sent her to Coventry and put dog shit in her desk drawer. When she complained, they laughed and told her that it was all in her head. She shouldn't entirely rule out the possibility that Fewell's accusation against an apparently exemplary police officer might possibly have been true.

If she was honest with herself, she'd have to admit she'd found it hard to warm to Mark Kirkby's father or his younger brother, Adam. It's not that she hadn't felt for them, especially the stricken father. A former custody sergeant, John Kirkby was tall and well built with a close-shaven head; although coming up for sixty he remained fit and imposing, and it was hard to watch a man like that humbled by grief. Yet he was clearly one of those officers who had got a bit too used to being obeyed, and he still carried his authority as though it belonged to him personally, rather than to the job he'd retired from three years ago. His surviving son, a prison officer, appeared to be a silent carbon copy of his father, and Grace couldn't help wondering whether Mark too had been one of those men – like her ex-husband, Trev – who enjoyed the power of a uniform a little too much. She wished Lance had been with her when she'd gone to talk to them; he'd have been able to separate guilt over her lack of sympathy from what was perhaps a valid insight.

But Lance had been busy elsewhere, digging into Fewell's background, searching for anything that might help explain his actions or shed light on his thinking. Grace didn't envy Lance having to stay one step ahead of the reporters and camera crews, who were all in hot pursuit of the same information. On the other hand, she thought drowsily, as sleep finally seemed to be claiming her, at least Lance had Peter in his life, had a shield against the reality they'd all wake up to in the morning.

But sleep wouldn't come. She wasn't happy with herself for disliking a man whose son had just been shot dead. She really hoped that her past difficulties weren't going to turn her into someone who'd lost her ability to be objective, forever blind to how her reactions had been warped by what had happened. Bottom line: however strained the relationship between Mark Kirkby and his new partner's ex-husband, he most certainly hadn't deserved to die.

Especially not when the pathologists' preliminary findings were that the gunman had used a type of bullet chosen by snipers who wanted to make sure the job was done properly. The results had been brutal, and Grace recalled from a ballistics training course she'd done a few years ago how hollow-point bullets broke apart on impact, causing such devastating internal damage that they'd been banned from use in warfare under the Hague Convention. She didn't want to imagine the distress knowledge of such injuries would cause the victims' already traumatized families. Including John and Adam Kirkby.

The rifle Fewell had used had been sent to a forensic weapons examiner. The Essex police armourer who had joined them at the late-night vicarage debrief had pointed out that rifles and hollow-point ammunition were used for deer hunting, and that although there wasn't much of that around here there was plenty of sport a little further north, in Suffolk. It's possible the rifle had been stolen in a domestic burglary and then sold on. The rest of the discussion had ranged over whether Fewell had specifically chosen hollow-point bullets in order to inflict particularly dreadful injuries and, if so, what that suggested about his state of mind. Far from cruel and sadistic, the profile they'd gathered so far suggested a man out of his depth. Whatever the truth, the prime minister's statement on the ten o'clock news that the UK had one of the lowest rates of gun homicides in the world had brought little comfort.

Grace rolled over in bed, tucking up her knees to get herself warm, yet the events of the day – yesterday now – refused to flee her brain. Despite her meeting with Mark Kirkby's father and brother, despite watching some of the other victims' relatives arriving at the vicarage, despite even the impact that little Davey and Ella had made upon her, her thoughts remained stubbornly with Russell Fewell. Even his ex-wife said he was the last person on earth to do such a thing. Why did that seem to hold the key to the tragedy? It was the voiceless and dispossessed who 'went postal'. She was a police officer, a detective; it wasn't often her job to have to explain why things happened, only how, and who was responsible. Right now the hope that there was some way to make sense of Fewell's motives seemed futile.

7

It was still dark when, next morning, Robyn heard her father's light tread move along the hall. She opened her eyes and listened for the familiar bustle and scrabble of the dogs as Leonard opened the boot-room door to let them join him in the warm kitchen. For a moment she felt cosy and safe in bed, but then she remembered: Angie was dead.

Angie Turner, clever and athletic, able to cut through any nastiness with her droll humour, had been the first to welcome Robyn when she'd started at the private girls' day school in Colchester nearly five years ago. Although Robyn, moving from her local state secondary school, had been determined not to be awed by her new classmates' big houses and their parents' expensive cars, she had desperately wanted to fit in and do well because she knew what a sacrifice it was for her parents to pay the fees, and she wanted them to see how happy she was. It was Angie who had made that happen. Angie, a friend to everyone, who was now dead.

Robyn had cried herself to sleep and now felt more tears coming, so swung her legs out of bed, grabbed her slippers and a dressing gown and went through to the kitchen to find her dad. The moment he saw her, he opened his arms and drew her into a wordless hug. At seventeen, she was now as tall as him, but he was wide and strong and smelled like all her best childhood memories. The hug didn't last long: Leonard kissed the top of her head and pushed her lightly away.

'Porridge?' he asked. 'Bacon? Cold roast goose?'

She laughed in spite of herself, grateful for his customary composure, his instinctive understanding that too much sympathy would break her. 'Porridge,' she answered, going to sit at the kitchen table, from where she could watch as he lifted the lid on the Aga hotplate, selected a pan and a wooden spoon, and took out oats and milk. She liked watching him work: he was a craftsman, meticulous and patient in the way he chose his tools and placed the necessary materials within reach. It wouldn't get light for another hour at least, yet, unlike the effort and rush of a school day, the warmth and electric light felt restful this morning. She noticed though that her dad hadn't put on the radio, as he usually did.

'What time are you off?' she asked him.

'I'm not going. I asked Robbie to stand in for me.'

'Why?' She spoke before the reason occurred to her; she didn't want to hear it spoken aloud.

'Seemed best to stick around today,' he said, intent on stirring the porridge. 'Bowls?'

She got up and handed him two blue and white striped bowls from the cupboard. He took them without looking up from the pan, leaving her to find spoons and place a tin of Lyle's Golden Syrup on the table. Leonard had already made a pot of tea, and she poured out two mugs. The tasks distracted her somewhat from the tears that threatened to return, but it was no good: she wasn't going to be able to think about anything else today.

Neither spoke as Leonard poured the thick steaming porridge into the bowls and they each twisted their clean spoons into the syrup. She waited until he had, from working habit, placed the lid neatly back on the tin before she broke their customary silence.

'Do you mind if I take mine through, so I can watch the TV news?'

Leonard sighed and looked steadily at her. 'Are you sure that's a good idea?'

'Maybe they'll have found out more about him and why he did it. I need to know what's going on. Please, Dad?'

She could see him making an assessment, weighing the pros and cons, as he did every decision, large or small. He nodded. 'OK.'

Robyn picked up her bowl and mug of tea and made her way through to the sitting room. She felt comforted when her father followed her, drawing back the curtains before coming to sit beside her on the sofa. And it was soothing to watch out of the corner of her eye how he concentrated, as he always did, on eating his porridge from around the rim of the bowl, where it was cool, before working his way into the hot centre. She felt a slight chill from the uncovered window; outside a low sliver of moon made the snow appear to give off a light of its own, a pure radiance that was instantly diminished by the jewel-like colours of the television screen.

She didn't need to select a channel; the same twenty-four-hour news they'd been avidly watching last night came up automatically as she turned on the set. The mass shootings in Dunholt remained the lead story, although apart from images the media had not had the night before there was little new. The gunman, Russell Fewell, was now revealed to be a slight wiry man in his early thirties, described as a domestic appliance engineer, divorced with two children. Were it not for the new context in which he had placed himself, the photograph shown most often might have suggested that he was reticent and embarrassed by having his picture taken: now he appeared shifty, resentful and malevolent. Of all the victims, the channel had the most information about the first, Mark Kirkby, with numerous photographs of him in police uniform at his passing-out parade, with his father and brother at a family wedding and, rugged and heroic, on a sponsored climb of Kilimanjaro, raising money for a kids' cancer charity.

There was better news of the survivors, all still in hospital: two were recovering and although the condition of the third, the woman Donna knew who worked in the Co-op, remained critical she was now thought likely to pull through. A talking-head expert then explained that their injuries had been mitigated by the gunman's choice of ammunition, which, after passing through window glass, had been unable to cause the kind of devastating injuries inflicted on the people who had died. With a fresh pang of anguish, Robyn recognized Angie's father in a short clip from the night before, making his way into some unnamed building, pursued by reporters repeatedly calling out his name. Robyn thought he looked as if he were in hell. Mercifully, the segment cut to a reporter standing in brightly-lit snow as he read out the royal message of condolence.

Leonard put his half-eaten bowl of porridge down on the coffee table. Robyn hadn't yet touched hers.

'Why don't you turn it off?' he said. 'Go and get dressed. Take the dogs for a run. Nothing to be gained from moping.'

'He must've used hollow points,' she said, turning to him, trying not to imagine Angie sustaining the kind of wounds she had seen when hunters shot deer or, once in the West Country with her dad, a wild boar.

'He was a madman,' Leonard said firmly. 'A lunatic. Probably high on something or other. Why don't you and your mum write to Angie's parents? A letter of condolence. You have to think of it like a terrible freak accident. Put it behind you. It's not what life's really like. You mustn't start thinking like that.'

Robyn knew her dad was right: he was always right – a sensible, reassuring and dependable sort of right. But the horror of her grief and shock felt too raw for her to be able to believe his words. She was sure she would in time, but not yet. 'I'll go and have a shower,' she said. She glanced at her untouched bowl on the coffee table. 'Sorry about the porridge.'

When, an hour or so later, Robyn returned to the house with the dogs after giving them a long icy run along the grassy bank of the sea wall, she was surprised to see a van backed up to the door of Leonard's workshop: someone must need a delivery pretty urgently for the courier to turn out so early on Boxing Day. But then, she supposed, her dad was a regular customer. She knew most of the drivers by name – it was a small company with only two or three properly certified staff and vans secure enough to transport firearms – and she waved to Kenny as she shooed the dogs indoors. She paused by the back door to observe a skein of Brent geese flying in along the estuary. The sky was now a pale cloudless blue, making the snow almost unbearably bright where the low sun shone across its crisp surfaces.

Her cheeks tingled with the cold, and the house felt stuffy, the air still rich with yesterday's cooking smells but no longer in a good way. Martha and Bounder rushed to their water bowls, then looked expectantly from her face to the door, imploring to be let back out. She called to her mother, but there was no reply. Nicola, who acted as office manager, must also be over in the workshop, double-checking the paperwork for whatever order was going out.

Robyn had been trained since childhood to respect the invisible line between home and business, and beyond a smile or occasional helpful response to a question never engaged with any of Leonard's visitors. He took his legal responsibilities extremely seriously, and even though she was now old enough to handle all the weapons and ammunition, she was very seldom allowed in the secure workshop, and never unsupervised. When he was working, she knew to remain obediently invisible.

'Sorry, guys,' she said to the two dogs. 'You'll have to wait until Kenny's gone.'

She was hungry now but, helping herself to a cold roast potato from the fridge, was immediately assailed by guilt at the thought of the luxurious feeling she'd had yesterday afternoon, stretching her toes towards the fire, her stomach full, laughing with her parents at the Christmas movie on television, while all the time Russell Fewell was loading his rifle and setting out to kill Angie and her grandmother, who she now knew had merely popped down the street to check on an elderly neighbour. She threw the remains of the potato into the compost bin.

Robyn didn't want to be alone with this leaden lump of grief lodged under her heart. Last night her parents had made her turn off her phone, not wanting her to be deluged with texts and calls from grieving school friends until she was ready to deal with them. Now, though she craved company, she was scared of everything becoming too real; once she turned on her phone and began to listen to her friends' tears and disbelief, she wasn't sure she would cope. She went to look out of the window to see if the green courier van had left yet. She was relieved to see it trundling carefully off up the snowy drive: now she could go in search of her father.

8

Grace spotted Lance across the half-empty car park at police HQ and stood waiting for him to join her, watching her breath turn cloudy in the cold air. She reflected that his relationship with Peter was certainly having a positive effect on his appearance: he'd recently cut his brown hair a bit shorter and she was sure the well-tailored suit that made the most of his trim figure must be new. It had been a very long while since she'd gone out to buy new clothes with a particular man in mind, but her little pang of longing was swiftly buried beneath a rush of almost-panic that told her she wasn't yet ready to open herself up again to that kind of emotional risk.

Lance greeted her with a warm smile. 'We never thanked you for lunch.'

'Peter did,' she replied, returning his smile as they crunched their way across the snowy car park. 'He did all the washing-up.'

Lance coloured with obvious pride and affection and, after entering the security code, held the entrance door open for her. Upstairs, the big open-plan MIT office was abnormally quiet, even for Boxing Day. Some desks remained unoccupied, and those who had come in were unusually subdued. As a detective inspector, Grace got a corner spot with a half-partition that gave her if not exactly enhanced status then at least some privacy. The team hadn't had a female DI before, and although some of the team like Duncan had happily transferred their loyalty from their old boss, DCI Keith Stalgood, others had remained sceptical and quick to judge, so she was still glad to have Lance watching her back.

She was surprised to see someone sitting in her chair. John Kirkby, half-turned towards the window, made no move to get up, leaving her no choice but to stand in front of her own desk. Seeing how grey and weary he was, she could hardly begrudge him; indeed, given that the spare chair was home to a pile of accumulated files, if she had been sitting there when he'd walked in, she would have instinctively offered him her seat. And yet his occupation of it felt like an invasion.

Admonishing herself for her pettiness, she quickly cleared the files off the other chair and dragged it closer to her desk. 'How are you today, Mr Kirkby?' she asked, hearing immediately how trite a question it was.

'No parent expects to outlive their child,' he answered.

'No,' Grace agreed. 'Is there anything I can do for you, anything I can help you with?'

'I realize it's not kosher for me to be privy to your investigations,' he said. 'Not now I'm retired.' Grace fought down the sense that, in making this admission, he was somehow both granting her a favour and assuming she'd make an exception. 'But I'd appreciate it if you'd keep Curtis Mullins up to speed. He's a uniform PC here in Colchester and was a close friend of Mark's. I suggested he come up later and introduce himself. You can trust his judgement on what he does and doesn't pass on to me.'

It was a statement of fact not a request, but Grace nodded. 'I don't know him but I'll be glad to meet him.' She smiled and met Kirkby's gaze, not acquiescing and making no promises while wishing he didn't make her feel so antagonistic. She had no intention of allowing PC Mullins to run around MIT being John Kirkby's private bagman.

'Thank you.' He pushed himself up from her chair and held out his hand across the desk. She shook it and then watched him walk to the door of the main office, the poignant dignity of his bearing forcing her to chastise herself for her prickliness.

She waited until he was gone, and then went to tap on the door to Detective Superintendent Pitman's office. Colin looked up and beckoned her in.

'Yeah, I know,' he said, inclining his head towards the door through which John Kirkby had departed. 'But I reckon we're going to have to cut him at least a little slack. He was a local branch chair of the Police Federation, which makes him a popular guy. Not only will he have helped a lot of rank-and-file officers and their families, but he also no doubt knows one or two funny handshakes into the bargain. So, all in all, it means he's well in with people whose cages you do not want to rattle unless you really have to.'

Grace sighed. She knew Colin was right. Best not go looking for trouble. The Police Federation was loyal to a fault and, as the nearest thing to a trade union that the police service was allowed to have, that was its brief. Yet it still rankled that the Federation had paid all of her ex-husband's legal fees when he'd gone to court on assault charges even though she – the victim – had been a fellow officer.

'Mark Kirkby's a police hero, so let's just keep his father happy, OK?' said Colin, as if he were reading her thoughts.

'Sure.' She forced a quick smile. 'Anything new come in?'

'Not really. Doesn't look like the post-mortems are going to throw up any surprises beyond what's already evident. The gun was unlicensed, not reported stolen, and there's no match on the unsolved crime index. Wendy and the other scene examiners have managed to recover spent bullet casings from most of the scenes. They've been sent to a ballistics expert for examination, although it's doubtful that rifle rounds are going to yield links to other criminal activity.'

They both knew that criminals preferred handguns or sawn-off shotguns, making a rifle unlikely to come up on any forensic databases.

'If the rifle was borrowed from someone without a firearms certificate,' said Grace, 'then there might be someone out there right now with a very guilty conscience. We could put out an appeal for information on where the gun came from. Offer an amnesty, perhaps?'

'Good idea,' said Colin. 'People are often more willing to hand over illicit weapons after this kind of tragedy. I'll have a word with Hilary, get her to sell it to the chief con as a positive initiative.' He looked at his watch. 'And, speaking of our ever-popular communications director, I'd better go and smarten up ready for her press conference.'

Grace thought he looked smart enough already. Her boss was good-looking and knew it. He kept in shape, always wore a pristine white shirt and had a full head of dark hair that was beginning to turn a distinguished grey at the temples. The fact that he was a self-serving hypocritical coward was not evident in a single line of his face.

'Sir,' Grace called after him as he headed off. 'Perhaps John Kirkby would like to be included in the press conference?'

Colin smiled, a smile that, however well she knew him, could still make her feel like she'd won a prize. 'Hilary's already ahead of you,' he said. 'She's prepping him now.'

Grace went back to her own desk – and her own chair – feeling wrong-footed and dissatisfied. The hushed world outside her window, still blanketed with snow and with none of its familiar traffic noise thanks to the rest of the population sleeping off its Christmas Day excesses, made her feel even more surreal. She'd had three or four months in which to master the knack of not letting it get to her that she once again had Colin Pitman as a boss, and now she mustn't let John Kirkby's high-handedness rub her up the wrong way either. She'd dealt with plenty of overbearing officers in her time, and most of them turned out to be totally decent by-the-book reliable family men. There was nothing to suggest that John Kirkby wasn't among them, so she should simply pack away her cat-and-dog antipathy to the poor man.

Maybe it was the nature of the investigation itself that was bothering her: apart from doing their best to line everything up for the coroner's inquest, there was little to do. The perpetrator was dead. Whatever they discovered about Russell Fewell's balance of mind as he set out yesterday afternoon on his killing spree, and however he'd come by his weapon, none of it would bring back his victims or prevent further harm – it was too late for that. But, she reminded herself, some semblance of knowledge and understanding, however superficial, would help the victims' loved ones to let go of their anguish, however slightly. She could imagine all too well how firmly grief would anchor itself to one single question: *why?*

The balance of Russell Fewell's mind was likely to be of most concern to the coroner, so Grace checked through any new information that had come in since last night. Lance had been tasked with finding out everything he could about him; local doctors, teachers and others had already come forward with offers of help, so they knew that Fewell had not visited his GP in several years, had no recorded history of mental health problems and was not known to have abused either drugs or alcohol. He'd left school at sixteen with a few good-enough qualifications and had been in more or less continuous work since. Eyewitnesses to the shootings said he had appeared calm and controlled. One woman thought he'd been crying but that it might also have been the cold stinging his eyes. The tiny flat he'd moved into after the divorce had been clean and tidy. Unless someone higher up had the clout to gain holiday access to the banking system, they wouldn't have his financial records until Monday, but as yet there was nothing to suggest hidden gambling debts or a nightmare payday-loan scenario. The only clue to his state of mind was the one he'd chosen to leave for them: the summons to appear in court on a drink-drive charge.

Grace typed in the relevant details, curious enough to check out the background to Fewell's arrest for herself. He had been pulled over soon after leaving a pub on the outskirts of Colchester when a patrol car had spotted a broken rear light. He refused to be breathalysed, but a test taken later at the station showed him to be minimally over the limit. Something about the date caught Grace's eye, and she realized it was the same day and month as his date of birth. If he'd been out celebrating with some mates, it would've been all too easy go over the limit. Sheer rotten luck. No wonder he felt fate was victimizing him. Then she read the name of the arresting officer. It was Mark Kirkby's friend, PC Curtis Mullins.

9

Ivo had covered all the usual bases – as had all his esteemed colleagues: it was like the queue to climb bloody Everest, with
everyone chasing the same small pool of interviewees – but so
far he had come up with nothing worthy of a front page, let
alone a headline. He needed to box a bit more clever. A couple of
the Dunholt pubs had reopened, offering at least some sense of
community, but then it turned out that the staff had barely
known Russell Fewell. The bastard seemed like a model citizen,
neither a drinker nor rabble-rouser, not a ladies' man nor a wife-
beater. Ivo felt like quoting that old *Monty Python* sketch about
the accountant who wanted to be a lion-tamer. Could yesterday's tragic rampage really be as banal as that?

Ivo mentally shook himself: he had a reputation to protect
and the rest of the afternoon to dredge up an angle that none of
the others would think of.

It was brass-monkey weather out there, and he'd retreated to
his B & B to pick up his gloves, which in a senior moment he'd
taken out of his coat pocket and left on the bed. His widowed
landlady was as loquacious as he'd often found B & B owners to
be – they must do it for the company as much as the cash – so
he made his way down to the kitchen for a chat. Mrs Cotman

had a good heart and was keen to tell him that Dunholt really wasn't a bad place, as if the little town somehow shared responsibility for Russell Fewell's sins. She was also happy to answer his questions about what people around here did with their spare time. Twenty minutes later he'd gleaned a couple of suggestions worth following up, and retreated to the patchwork and frills of his room to google angling clubs: fishing, according to Mrs Cotman, was a popular local sport, and the website of the club nearest to Dunholt very helpfully supplied the home phone number of its membership secretary.

Ten minutes later Ivo was following exceptionally precise and twice-repeated directions to Gable End Cottage in an outlying village. The trip would probably be a total waste of time, but he reminded himself that he'd stumbled across some of his finest stories merely by asking a few random people a few random questions. Plus he'd immediately detected in Martin Leyburn's voice an eagerness to be helpful tinged with half-smothered excitement at being brought, however tangentially, into the spotlight that was both familiar and faintly dispiriting. On the other hand, he had no brighter ideas for spinning this story across two columns.

Ivo rapped the dolphin-shaped knocker on the pale-blue front door, and moments later Martin Leyburn welcomed him in, offering tea or coffee, both of which Ivo declined. A man his age had to show some consideration for his prostate, and he'd just drunk two industrial-strength cups with Mrs Cotman. The Dunholt Angling Association membership secretary, who wore a Viyella shirt under a green sweater, with trousers, socks and shoes in more or less the same shade of grey, led him into a small black-beamed sitting room with an open fire. Martin winced as he sat down, explaining that he was on the waiting list for a hip replacement. Ivo took a quick look around. It appeared from the limited-edition framed prints of Spitfires and Hurricanes on the walls and the books on bidding conventions in bridge on the table beside the armchair that he was dealing with a man who appreciated method and structure.

If there was a Mrs Leyburn, she must be busy elsewhere, and Ivo hoped that was where she'd remain. Maybe it was because women better understood the power of gossip, but they tended to be warier and less cooperative than men, who were generally easier to draw out. Or perhaps it was simply innate male arrogance about the soundness of their own judgement that blinded them to the possibility that they were being milked. Ivo took a weary pride in his ability to win and retain people's trust. It was an art, one he was sure that the world's greatest fraudsters must possess in trumps. Not that Ivo regarded himself as a con man, far from it: he and the *Daily Courier* were after all the very bastions of truth. It was simply that, when people were dazed, struggling to comprehend and desperate to go over and over every tiny detail, well, then there were no limits to the time and patience he was prepared to offer.

Ivo had already explained on the phone that he was after the human-interest story – what kind of man Fewell was and what might have propelled him towards such a terrible act. Now Martin was at pains to make clear that, although he wouldn't describe himself as a friend, he'd known Russell Fewell for well over ten years and – he stressed this – had always liked him. Ivo admired Martin for that, especially after speaking to so many others who were only too keen to disown the rogue gunman.

Martin must have used Ivo's journey time to search out Fewell's club membership records, for he now handed over a couple of printed-out computer entries, explaining that Russell had joined as a teenager and taken part in a fair number of matches over the years, although he'd only ever won three or four.

'He wasn't one to put himself forward,' said Martin. 'Not really bothered about competing. He just liked to be out and beside the water. I knew his father better. He passed away three years ago, so I was pleased as punch when Russell started to bring his own boy, Davey, along with him.'

Ivo already knew that Fewell had two kids, Davey and a younger sister, Ella. He couldn't help a natural curiosity about Davey: Ivo had lost a parent at much the same age. 'Did Russell get on well with his son?' he asked.

'Very well. Both of them quiet types. Russell seemed to enjoy showing him the ropes, watching him learn.' Martin shook his head sorrowfully. 'I wish I'd done more. Wish I could've helped him. It should never have come to this.'

'What do you think went wrong?' Ivo held his breath.

'He'd started to come on his own, without Davey. Then he stopped coming altogether. I hadn't seen him for a couple of months.'

Ivo was pretty sure he could detect a rider to that statement, and nudged as gently as he could. 'So you hadn't seen him recently?'

Immediately Ivo detected the small and familiar tussle of conscience he'd expected. Now it could go either way. Martin might clam up, unwilling to break a confidence, even that of a murderous dead man. Or the temptation to play his part in the drama, that illicit thrill of contributing his unique perspective to the debate, would prove irresistible, in which case Ivo knew how little prompting it would probably take to get him to spill whatever he had to tell.

'You wanted to help him?' Ivo prodded.

Martin nodded, and Ivo couldn't help feeling a stab of disappointment that yet again thrill won out over conscience.

'He hadn't responded to my annual renewal reminders,' said Martin. 'I knew his dad, remember, and we don't have that many memberships that span three generations. So I called round to see him.'

'How was he?'

'In a bad way. I knew his marriage had broken up a while back, but he'd seemed to take that in his stride. It hadn't stopped his days out with Davey. But that last time I saw him he looked . . .'

Martin broke off, and Ivo waited, genuinely curious now to gain some insight into what had happened to push a pleasant-sounding bloke who cared about his kids right off the edge and into the abyss.

Martin sighed. 'I didn't know how seriously to take it. I mean, no question, he was wound up, but how much of it was real? And now you read in the paper that the guy he was accusing of all these things was a policeman, so then you don't know what to think, do you? I mean, the local bobby is hardly likely to behave like that, is he?'

'You mean Constable Mark Kirkby?'

Martin nodded, clearly now having uncomfortable second thoughts. This was the moment when it became vital for

Ivo to cut off all retreat and extract every last crumb of information.

'Russell must've been relieved to have someone to talk to. Sounds like he was in a pretty bad way. And you were a mate of his dad's, after all. A father figure even.'

Martin looked relieved, grateful almost for Ivo's absolution. 'He was in a terrible state,' he agreed. 'He said his wife's new boyfriend was turning her against him, trying to steal his kids, making his life a misery.'

'Was he ill, do you think?' asked Ivo. 'Mentally?'

'He didn't strike me that way at the time. But then I'm no expert. He was angry and upset, but mainly about losing his kids. Scared more than anything. It's hard to tell, isn't it?' He gave a nervous chuckle. 'What is it they say? Just because you're paranoid doesn't mean they're not out to get you.'

'I'm not quite sure what you mean,' said Ivo.

Martin hesitated. 'Russell was saying that his wife's boyfriend had fitted up his arrest, was trying to get him sacked. Then he clammed up, wouldn't say any more about it.'

'What was your reaction?'

'I suggested he talk to Citizens Advice. My sister-in-law volunteers there. They're pretty clued up.'

'Very sensible. I don't suppose you know if he took it up?'

'No, I don't.'

'And when was this?'

'About ten days ago. I've been wondering whether I ought to go to the police, but then I don't want to waste their time. What do you think?'

'Sure. Why not?' Ivo paused long enough for Martin to notice his hesitation. 'But Mark Kirkby did win a police medal, climbed

Kilimanjaro for charity. There'll be officers on the inquiry who knew him.'

'I know. That's what I was thinking. And I don't want to go stirring up trouble, speaking ill of the dead. But it doesn't square with what Russell said about Kirkby being so gratuitously mean and nasty. I liked Russell. You couldn't meet a less aggressive or violent man. I simply can't see him ever contemplating such an act unless . . .'

Martin broke off again, shaking his head in perplexity at it all. Ivo thought about the ammunition Russell had used, the kind you'd choose if you were out for revenge, to make a point, to leave absolutely no doubt about your intentions. Either Russell was one really sick fuck or Mark Kirkby was no hero.

He wondered what kind of response he'd get if he called Bobbi Reynolds at the Police Federation for a comment: a pretty dusty answer, he imagined. None of his usual police cronies would want to play Secret Santa on this one either. Fair enough. Couldn't blame them for sticking together. A fellow hack was probably the last person Ivo would ever rat on.

'I only wish I'd done more,' said Martin, giving him a look that was almost beseeching. 'Maybe, if I had, then none of this would have happened. I hoped, when you rang, that maybe you'd know the best thing to do.'

'Let me dig around a bit,' said Ivo, already enthusiastically blocking out a front page in his head. 'See what the general opinion of Mark Kirkby is. I mean, even if he was a bit of a bully, he still didn't deserve to die, did he?'

'I was thinking of young Davey,' said Martin with quiet dignity. 'He deserves an explanation, if there is one. The truth.'

Bingo! thought Ivo. *That's my angle!* The victim no one else will be thinking about because no one ever fucking thinks about the kids. While every other newspaper and international media outlet would be busy demonizing the boy's father, Ivo and the *Courier* would fearlessly champion his innocent children!

10

Grace didn't need to go looking for Curtis Mullins; he found her, presenting himself at the opening to her cubicle around three o'clock that afternoon. He was in civvies and must have come in specially, since he was clearly not on duty. He was tall with golden hair and very blue eyes, almost Nordic-looking, and she recognized him as a familiar face about the station. He introduced himself respectfully and seemed genuine enough when he said that he hoped she wouldn't object to keeping him updated on anything that might help Mark Kirkby's family come to terms with their loss.

'Of course I understand how desperate they must all be for answers,' she assured him. 'It's impossible to comprehend such a tragedy. Which is why, actually, I'm really pleased to see you. Do sit down.'

Curtis sat, his back straight, feet apart and planted firmly on the floor, a posture that signalled tactful respect for her rank.

'I'm preparing our submission to the inquest and wanted to clarify the circumstances of Russell Fewell's arrest for drink-driving.'

'Why?' Curtis's interruption was sharply spoken.

'I'm looking into his state of mind.' Surprised at his immediate defensiveness, she spoke as mildly as she could. 'It was you who pulled him over. Can you talk me briefly through the arrest?'

'He had a broken rear light. When I spoke to him, I could smell alcohol. He admitted that he had been drinking but refused to be breathalysed, so I arrested him in order to test him at the station.'

'Did you have any other reason to believe he was over the limit?'

'I didn't require any other evidence.'

'But had he been driving erratically? Slurring his words or unsteady on his feet?'

'No, ma'am.'

'How did Fewell react to being stopped and then arrested?'

'Well, he wasn't happy. Who would be?'

'Was he cooperative, belligerent, abusive?'

'He was all right to begin with. Claimed he hadn't realized the light was broken.' Curtis's voice rose slightly and his mouth set in a stubborn line. 'He could've just consented to the breath test.'

'You didn't consider letting him off with a warning?'

'Are you questioning my judgement, ma'am?'

'Not at all.'

'He admitted he'd been drinking. I'd've thought you'd be happy to see a dangerous driver taken off the road?'

There was a glint in his eye, and Grace wondered if Curtis was one of those officers who was calm and friendly enough when they were in charge but who quickly became injured and resentful when their authority was questioned. Especially by a woman of senior rank. She decided to change tack.

'You may not be aware that the nearest thing to a suicide note was Fewell's court summons on this charge.' She spoke as neutrally as possible. 'So the coroner may well regard Fewell's own perception of the circumstances of his arrest as directly relevant to his state of mind.'

Curtis looked shocked. 'I don't understand. What do you mean, a suicide note?'

'Fewell's flat was spotless. The only thing left out on display, where it was certain to be found, was his summons.'

'I didn't know that.'

'No reason why you should.'

Curtis had gone quite pale, making Grace curious about the intensity of his reaction.

'No one is saying this is your fault,' she told him. 'You were quite correct in doing your duty. But if Fewell had lost his driving licence, he'd have been unemployed. And he'd have found it difficult to pay a big fine. He was already under a lot of pressure. This seems to have been the final straw.'

Curtis nodded. His blue eyes looked at her with concern and also, she was sure, a certain amount of calculation. *What was he thinking?* she wondered. *What was he not saying?*

He sighed and got to his feet. 'I'm sorry not to be of more help, ma'am. It was a routine stop. I'm surprised I even remembered the name, to be honest.'

'OK. Well, thanks.' Grace too got to her feet. 'And you have my condolences. I understand you and Mark Kirkby were good friends?'

He nodded miserably. 'Since school. A long time.'

'That must be hard. I'm sorry.'

He stopped on the threshold of her cubicle and turned back. 'Is it likely that I'll have to give evidence at the inquest?'

'That'll be up to the coroner.'

He nodded again, his eyes troubled, then said goodbye and walked across the MIT office to the door. She watched him go, experiencing that itchy feeling that meant she'd missed something. Maybe she should have asked him outright about Fewell's paranoia; after all Donna had seemed to suggest it was common knowledge. Why hadn't she? Was she starting to believe it wasn't simple paranoia, that Mark Kirkby *had* asked a mate to follow Fewell and pull him over? She was almost relieved to be distracted from her suspicions by Duncan bringing her a sheet of paper.

'Preliminary ballistics report, boss.'

'Anything I need to know?'

'Maybe. The spent bullet casings recovered in Dunholt have military head stamps.'

Grace frowned. 'The army's not going to be using hollow-point ammo.'

'Precisely. Which means that someone reused the brass casings.'

'Why would anyone want to do that?'

'Quite a few sportsmen make their own ammunition,' he said. 'It's a popular hobby. Home-loading, it's called. The precise way the cartridge is loaded with the primer, powder and bullet affects the accuracy of a shot. Plus, if you're going to make your own, it's a lot cheaper to pick up spent brass cases.'

'You seem to know a lot about it!'

Duncan smiled. 'A little. The Police Federation organizes the occasional day's duck shooting with a club out on the marshes. It's good fun. Just shotguns, but some of the guys there also go after deer up around Thetford. They'll be using rifles, and I've heard them talking about home-loading.'

'So it's possible that an enthusiast who makes his own bullets passed some along to Russell Fewell?'

'Yes. Except rifle ammo is very strictly controlled, including home-loaded. Especially hollow-point bullets. They should all be accounted for on the firearms certificate of the person who takes possession of them. It's against the law to supply rounds to anyone who doesn't hold a certificate with the appropriate conditions.'

'So it's not going to be that one of Fewell's mates simply gave him a handful, no questions asked?'

'Not if the mate is legit, no.'

'OK, that's a big help, thanks,' said Grace. 'Can you inform the firearms liaison officer? And maybe do a bit of asking around yourself. See if the military head stamps on the brass casings ring any bells.'

'I can get a list of the registered firearms dealers within striking distance of Dunholt,' said Duncan, 'Talk to those who keep a good ear to the ground. And to some of the guys from the wildfowling club. But I doubt I'll find many sportsmen at home on Boxing Day. It's traditionally a big shoot day.'

'Well, I guess it can wait until tomorrow.' As Duncan turned to go, Grace was reminded of her earlier visitor. 'Tell me, do you know Curtis Mullins at all? A uniform PC.'

'Not well. Only by sight really. Why?'

'John Kirkby wants him kept in the loop. I need to know if he's discreet, that's all.'

Duncan shrugged. 'Never heard anything against him.'

'OK, that's good. Thanks.'

Grace decided not to waste any more time worrying about Curtis Mullins. Fewell's arrest had been a fair cop – his subsequent breath test had proved he was over the limit – and on a quiet winter's night you might very well pull someone over for a broken light merely to break up the monotony. She might not want to be best pals with John Kirkby, but she knew nothing about his son to suggest such a daft conspiracy.

An hour or so later she was taken aback to hear the reason Colin had summoned her to his office. 'I told you not to upset John Kirkby!' he exclaimed.

'I didn't!'

'Then why have I had a call from him, complaining that you are harassing PC Mullins over the circumstances of Fewell's arrest?'

'Harassing? That's nonsense!'

'So you did question him?'

'It wasn't exactly water-boarding! I just asked him about Fewell's reaction to the arrest. It goes to his state of mind.'

Colin waved aside the air in front of him. 'Well, there's no reason for Mullins to be on the witness list for the inquest. It's irrelevant who arrested Fewell. All that matters is that Fewell went postal over it. That in itself says all we need to know about his state of mind, don't you think?'

'Yes, sir.'

'So leave PC Mullins alone.'

'I didn't chase after him, sir. He came to see me. John Kirkby's messenger boy.'

Colin softened. 'OK. Fair enough. But I don't want John Kirkby throwing his toys out of the pram again. Or not in my direction. It may not be very politically correct to say so, but between you and me he's a pain in the arse.' Colin grinned boyishly. 'Look, I'm already getting an earful from the missus about working over Christmas. What I don't need is a former branch chair of the Police Federation belly-aching in my other ear about the insensitivity of my senior officers.'

'Understood.' Grace made herself smile, though she didn't much like the waspish sting in the tail of his fake appeal to camaraderie.

'Why don't you go on home?' said Colin. 'I am.' He got to his feet, sighing and shaking his head. 'It's not surprising this is getting to everyone.' He looked at her ruefully. 'I shouldn't have spoken about John Kirkby like that. Not even to you. Poor man. Can you imagine what he's going through? I was right out of order.'

'We're all upset,' Grace echoed dutifully.

'I'll be glad to get it all wrapped up and off our desks. Start the new year with something a bit less emotionally challenging.'

'It's hard on everyone,' agreed Grace, following him out of his office. 'You go on. I need to gather some stuff together first.'

As Colin left, she realized that she was the last person in the office. At least until the cleaners came. They had to work Christmas too. She suddenly realized how exhausted she was. Colin was right: all murders were tragic, but Fewell's actions – so extreme, so pointless – had been particularly affecting. So many grieving families tonight, so many old friends and colleagues wondering how such a thing could happen to the ordinary, harmless, unassuming people they knew. Donna and her children too: it was important not to forget they were victims as well.

She almost wished that Lance's background checks *would* show that Fewell was the only one who could in any way be held responsible for this bloodbath, so that it was irrelevant what kind of man Mark Kirkby had or hadn't been, or what kind of friends he had. People needed Fewell to be an evil monster so they could put what he had done into a box of incomprehensible aberrations and move on. The last thing anybody wanted was moral ambiguity, and Grace knew she'd never be popular for even so much as raising the notion that the truth might not be as clear-cut as the tragedy demanded. Especially when all she had to go on were the delusions of a mass murderer.

As she closed down her computer and gathered up her bag and coat, she asked herself if she *had* been insensitive towards Curtis Mullins. A police force was a strong community, and she understood the impulse to look after one's own, yet she just wasn't sure that Colin was correct in deciding that the best thing to do was bag it all up and get it off their desks. And whose cause did John Kirkby imagine he was serving, calling up a detective superintendent and expecting his concerns to carry such weight? She might be very tired and very naive, but it didn't feel right to her. She wished, not for the first time, that she had a boss she could trust.

11

Trying to get hold of the Ice Maiden had all been a bit Deep Throat, but the subterfuge was necessary: Grace Fisher would be badly compromised if her phone records ever revealed contact with a tabloid crime reporter, however unsolicited. Ivo hadn't been at all certain that she would agree to meet. He hadn't seen her since all the chaotic coming and going around the final discovery of a body last summer, and, although they hadn't spoken about it then or later, he liked to think they'd shared a moment of silent understanding, and that perhaps afterwards she'd regard him as an ally, as someone in whom it would be safe to place her trust. Jesus, he should listen to himself! Anyone would think he had a schoolboy crush on the woman. And they'd probably be right.

He'd been asleep when Martin Leyburn had called late the previous night. He'd had to struggle awake, up out of a nightmare in which he stood in the study of his prep school housemaster and had to account for his dismal results in a maths test. Ivo had dealt with late-night calls like this many times before. They went with the intimacy he forced upon the relatives, witnesses and other survivors of the tragedies about which he wrote. The calls came from people in pain and shock, for whom the ground beneath their feet had, apparently without effort, opened up to reveal the true horror of the emptiness below. Often those most troubled were at the periphery of events, as Martin Leyburn was, but their sudden comprehension of the precariousness of their beliefs, of their very existence, was no less real or intense.

Sure enough, since Ivo's visit to Gable End Cottage, Martin had been crucifying himself over why he had failed to recognize the depth of Russell Fewell's distress, over whether he could and should have done something different to divert the unseen but impending catastrophe. He'd wanted to talk about all the things he now imagined he ought to have done, and Ivo had let him talk. He'd learned over the years that the quickest way to get back to sleep was to let people get everything off their chests. His job, after all, was to coax and cajole people into talking to him, so who was he to shut them up when that's what they actually longed to do?

It had taken Martin twenty-odd minutes to work his way through the familiar tropes: disbelief, regret, horror, vulnerability, loss of innocence and back to disbelief. *I can't get my head around it. I just can't.* How many times had Ivo heard that? And, frankly, he wasn't sure he'd ever really got his own head around some of the stories he'd reported. He thought of the notorious murder trials he'd sat through, watching the jurors' faces as they passed around the scene-of-crime or post-mortem photos it was their duty to look at. It was real but couldn't be real. How could it be real? In their town, or the next street, or their children's playgroup? That's what every citizen of Dunholt would be thinking for the next few years if not for ever. Young Davey Fewell and his kid sister most of all.

Martin had tired eventually, thanked Ivo and hung up. Ivo had known there was little chance of going back to sleep and had waited for the cravings to kick in. *What he wouldn't give for a bottle of brandy!* But this too would pass. Booze was about oblivion, and the trick, he'd learned at these moments, was to face head on all those ugly, leering, shameful thoughts that he'd prefer to forget. So he had, though it hadn't been much fun. And now here he was on a Sunday morning in the horrible cafe of a ring-road superstore, surrounded by desperate-looking couples in quest of bargain white goods in the pre-January sales, waiting for DI Grace Fisher to join him for an undrinkable cup of coffee. Not that he was any great gourmet, but never had he seen a place less conducive to the joys of breaking bread with a friend.

He spotted her now, weaving her way gracefully between baby buggies and fractious children. He raised a hand to attract her attention and was surprised at his own delight when she immediately smiled and then, reaching his table, greeted him with what appeared to be a modicum of genuine warmth.

'Ivo,' she said, holding out her hand.

He took it. 'DI Fisher.'

'Grace, please.' She sat down opposite and, glancing from his cup to the queue at the self-service counter, waved away his offer of a beverage.

'Good choice,' he said and was rewarded with another smile. Maybe his wish that she'd allow him to be her self-appointed champion wasn't so utterly ridiculous after all. Nor perhaps his conviction that she'd take seriously what he had to say.

'I'm afraid I don't have long,' she said.

'I'll cut to the chase then. Yesterday I had a story all ready to go about the relationship between Fewell and his first victim prior to the shooting.'

Her grey eyes regarded him steadily. 'Go on.'

'Someone who knew Fewell and liked him says he was absolutely fine until his ex-wife began dating Mark Kirkby.' Ivo paused, waiting to see how much of this she was prepared to hear. She gave a tiny nod, so he continued. 'According to my source, Fewell complained that Kirkby was nasty and mean, victimizing him and doing everything he could to try and take his kids away. Even claimed he'd tried to fit him up in some way.'

'Fit him up?'

'Fewell then clammed up, apparently. My source wasn't sure what he meant.'

'OK.'

Ivo was content to sit and watch her as she digested everything he'd said. He could happily watch her all day.

'But you didn't run the story?' she asked at last.

'It was spiked. The bosses wouldn't have it. Said that monstering a victim who was a good-looking young police officer with a glowing record wouldn't sell newspapers.'

The tiny cynical curl at the corner of her mouth seemed at odds with her response. 'It wasn't Mark Kirkby who killed five people and wounded three others,' she said.

'No, but if he tormented Fewell until the poor guy got into such a state – well, it's not quite as goodies-wear-white-hats and baddies-wear-black as people would like to think, is it?'

'And what use would it be to vilify Mark Kirkby now?'

Ivo had enjoyed an almost identical conversation on the phone with the editor who'd informed him his story was dead in the water. 'It might help Russell Fewell's kids,' he said, crossing his fingers tightly under the table that she would understand how important this was.

She looked down and ran a finger along the edge of the table before looking back up at him. 'All the same, you can't expect us to turn on one of our own.'

'No,' he agreed. 'And, as my editor reminded me, Mark Kirkby was a member of the Police Federation, which represents 140,000 officers in England and Wales. Plus it controls a war chest out of which it funds libel actions on behalf of officers who are less than enchanted by what newspapers write about them. And has enjoyed an almost unbroken run of successful cases, I might add. Given those odds, and even though you can't libel the dead, my editor didn't feel my story had legs.'

From the lift of one delicate eyebrow she didn't seem to like that any more than he did.

'So why are we here?' she asked, and now he detected a genuine warmth in her curiosity.

'My source doesn't care about Mark Kirkby,' Ivo told her. 'He's concerned about Fewell's kids. He knows young Davey. Saw how close he was to his dad.'

'Ah.'

She looked hurt, and he waited for her to say more, but she just kept looking at him with those lovely grey eyes of hers.

'You and I both know what it's like for the families of murderers,' he urged her. 'Donna Fewell's not going to be able to stay in Dunholt. She'll probably have to change her name. Even then those kids will be stigmatized for the rest of their lives.'

'They won't need other people to do that to them,' she said with a sigh. 'They'll do it to themselves.'

Ivo pushed home his advantage. 'Davey and Ella aren't to

blame. They're as innocent as everyone else. Their dad did a terrible, terrible thing, but I don't believe he was evil.'

'You'll be a lone voice in the wilderness.'

'Do you have anything I can use? Something to make my story stack up?'

Ivo watched as she thought about it, thought long enough for him to be certain she had something. But would she share it? Finally she blinked a few times and licked her lips. 'Tell your source to contact the coroner's officer. Tell him he can ask to speak at the inquest. Then you can report what he says.'

'That's likely to be months away.'

She spoke carefully. 'Unless you can show that Mark Kirkby misused his official powers, it's not a police matter.'

Ivo wondered if this was a hint. 'Did he?' he asked.

She looked a little flustered. 'No.'

Ivo didn't entirely believe her denial and guessed from the tiny frown that creased her forehead that she didn't either. But then she shook her head in dismissal of whatever idea had occurred to her. 'No,' she repeated more firmly. 'He didn't. There's no evidence whatsoever to suggest that.'

Ivo was surprised at how bitterly disappointed he was. He must be getting old and gullible, but he'd simply never doubted that the Ice Maiden would feel as strongly about championing the underdog as he did. Seemed he was wrong.

'I have to go.' She pushed back her chair yet made no move to stand up. 'Your source?' she asked. 'Is he reliable?'

'Solid gold. He's known Fewell since he was a teenager. Knew his dad too.'

She nodded slowly, considering what to say, then took a deep breath and leaned forward across the table towards him.

'What will also come out at the inquest – and absolutely not before,' she added with heavy emphasis, 'is that although Fewell left no suicide note, he did leave out on deliberate display the court summons for a drink-driving charge. It related to an incident outside Colchester when he was initially pulled over because of a broken rear light. It was his birthday.' She paused to push back the hair that had fallen across her cheek. 'The arresting officer was at school with Mark Kirkby. There's absolutely nothing to suggest that it's more than a coincidence, but it may not have looked that way to Fewell. And it may help his kids to know that, to understand one of the building-blocks in their dad's fixation.'

Ivo grinned with relief: he had not misjudged her! 'Thank you!'

She nodded, unsmiling. 'Goodbye. And good luck.' Almost impetuously, it seemed to him, Grace held out her hand to him again. As he held it for a moment he suddenly became aware of a middle-aged couple at a nearby table looking at them with idle speculation. What did they make of this overweight over-the-hill specimen gazing with such adoration at a clear-skinned, bright-eyed young woman dressed in an elegant fitted dark business suit and pale-blue shirt? Not lovers, certainly. Father and daughter was the best he could hope for. What the hell, he'd be more than happy to settle for that.

12

Robyn laid the surplus eggs in their corrugated cardboard tray in the passenger seat footwell of her mother's Suzuki four-by-four, ready to be dropped off at the farm shop. The owner, who liked a Sunday morning chat with her regular customers, had called to say she'd be open as usual. It had rained in the night, and most of the snow had melted, leaving icy puddles and an uninviting mist of grey drizzle. Robyn stood for a moment watching her mother's four-by-four as it set off along the rutted track leading up to the line of high hedges that hid the road. It had to pull up onto the muddy verge to allow a silver Volkswagen saloon to slide carefully past. Leonard was inside the house, so Robyn wrapped her arms around herself to keep warm and waited for the silver car to draw up outside the workshop. A balding, overweight man in an ill-fitting grey suit got out and made no secret of taking a good look around.

'Morning!' he called. 'I'm looking for Leonard Ingold. Is he about?'

'He's indoors. Let me fetch him.'

Assuming the man was a client, Robyn left him standing outside. Clients never came into the house. Leonard was obviously not expecting a visitor, but he left what he was doing and went out to greet him. Robyn went to the sink to wash her hands after handling the eggs and idly watched out of the kitchen window as Leonard and the man shook hands.

They seemed to know one another. They walked together over to the workshop, where the visitor waited for Leonard to unlock the door to the reception area, the only room where customers were permitted. He didn't look like a sportsman: he wasn't dressed in jeans or corduroys, with a tweed or waxed jacket, like the wildfowlers and other shooters who came – usually by appointment – to have guns cleaned and repaired or, more often, to buy the specialist ammunition that Leonard made and supplied for deer-stalking. A perfectly balanced bullet for a sporting rifle could make all the difference, and her dad's reputation brought sportsmen here from far and wide. Occasionally someone in a suit would come before or after work to drop off a valuable gun or antique weapon for alteration or restoration, but men like that drove much more expensive cars, and, besides, this guy was unlikely to be on his way to work two days after Christmas. Robyn thought he looked more like a supplier of some kind or a burglar-alarm salesman.

Anyway, she didn't really care who he was or what he wanted. Even her mum, the authorized 'servant' listed on Leonard's firearms dealer's licence who did all the meticulous bookkeeping, generally left the men – for it was nearly always men – to talk in private. However much Nicola respected her husband's craftsmanship, she said she found endless discussions on the intricacies of shooting boring, and Robyn didn't disagree.

Robyn wasn't really interested in anything today. She felt as if she were waiting to pack up ready for some huge journey, or to move house, or something. Not that she ever had moved. She was trying not to think about Angie, yet the sense of crushing weight and impending catastrophe remained, along with a strange sort of guilt over whether she was feeling what she was supposed to be feeling. She'd spoken to two of her school friends on the phone this morning, and they'd said pretty much the same thing. In a way it had helped, but she also wished she hadn't spoken to them, because afterwards none of them had known what else to say to one another. It felt wrong to start chatting about normal stuff, like whether Sally would still hold her New Year's Eve party, or about the start of term the following week, as if life could simply flow onwards again as before. Yet what else were they to do? Angie was not going to be at the party, not going to be in class when term started, would never be there to chat on the phone again, and yet the rest of them had to carry on as if nothing had happened.

Robyn felt she ought to do some revision, but knew she wouldn't be able to concentrate. She regretted now that she hadn't gone with her mum to deliver the eggs and pick up some more feed for the hens; small practical tasks seemed to take away some of the flu-like feeling that weighed her down. She looked around the kitchen: plenty of little jobs she could usefully get on with here.

When Leonard came into the kitchen half an hour later, she was absorbed in scraping limescale off the old mismatched saucers beneath the haphazard collection of potted plants along the windowsill, and finding solace in replacing dullness with shine.

'Fancy a walk, Birdie?' he asked.

'Two seconds,' she said. 'Just want to finish this.'

Leonard called to Martha and Bounder. They had already

been out this morning and came reluctantly from the fireside, stretching and yawning and wagging their tails in an amiable demonstration of obedience. Robyn neatly lined up the geraniums, cyclamen and Christmas cacti along the freshly wiped windowsill and stood back to admire her handiwork, looking to her father for approval, but he was at the back door, pulling on his coat and shooing out the dogs. She grabbed her own jacket and joined him outside.

'Down to the creek?' From beside the door he picked up a bulging cloth bag tied firmly with knotted string. He held it up. 'A batch of casings I reckon are counterfeit. Chinese, probably. One or two of them split when I was loading, and I don't want them finding their way to some idiot who thinks it's OK to take a chance. Best drop them where they won't be found.'

Robyn nodded. She knew that, while gun parts had to be strictly accounted for, her dad occasionally disposed of worn-out tools and other bits and pieces by weighing them down with a stone or old brick and sinking them deep in the river mud. She'd heard him joke that he liked to imagine he was leaving a nice puzzle for some future archaeologist to find and interpret.

They set off together across the grass. The drizzle had cleared, and there was nothing she liked better than to be out with her dad. Not that they necessarily talked much, other than to call the dogs, and usually she enjoyed his silent presence, loved sharing the details that caught his attention – an unusual migratory bird, the way the wavelets scudded against the wind, the first purple flowers appearing on the sea lavender. Today though she craved distraction, wanted a bit of idle chat.

'Who was that guy?' she asked.

'I know him from the wildfowling club,' said Leonard. 'Wanted advice about security and stuff.'

He sounded bored, so Robyn did not pursue it. Instead she settled into the familiar rhythm of his footsteps as they skirted the low-lying fields and reached the grassy ridge of the sea wall, where they could look out across the pools and lagoons of the salt marsh. In between the interconnected islands of khaki-coloured seablite, some still bearing patches of snow, the water was a startlingly intense blue. She looked up at the sky, pleased to see tiny patches of matching blue emerging from behind the cloud cover. A strong wind blew in from the distant North Sea, and she stuck her hands in her pockets and turned to walk into it, knowing without being told that they would be heading along the sea wall to the spot where a winding route led – if you knew where you were going and had done it before – down the other side and out across a linked zigzag of muddy islets to a part of the main creek a little way further out.

'It's going to be strange going back to school,' she said.

'But you're happy there?'

She heard strain in his voice and realized with a pang that, though he had barely met Angie, he must feel for her parents and be experiencing that wing-tip brush of another father's loss. She tucked her arm into his.

'You know how brilliant it's been in the sixth form. The teachers are right behind us, and the girls are fine. But Angie was special. Just so lovely. And she understood all this.' Robyn swept her free arm out towards the water. 'Not everyone understands why I love it here, why I'd rather have this than endless shopping and parties.' A moment of clear recognition of the finality of death hit her, and she breathed in sharply. 'I'll miss her.'

'It's been a shock,' said Leonard. 'But you're young. You have plenty to look forward to.'

She understood her dad's pragmatism. It wasn't dismissive; quite the opposite, it stemmed from a deep and instinctive desire to shield her from unhappiness.

'I know,' she said, giving his arm a squeeze. 'And I do.' Ahead of them the low sun broke through the cloud, its light picking out the white sailing boats anchored over on the far shore of the estuary. 'But it makes me feel really selfish. I mean, Angie's not going to have any of that. Her parents will never see her go to uni, have a career, have kids. Yet none of that stuff feels real. If I'm honest, all I really feel sad about is how much I'm going to miss her, how she won't be there, sitting next to me in the biology class next week.'

'That's not selfish, Birdie,' said Leonard. 'It's a compliment to her memory.' He let go of her arm as they reached the vestigial path – a line of worn and flattened grass – which meandered across the salt marsh towards the channel of deep fast-flowing water, and turned his head to speak over his shoulder. 'When my father died, I don't remember thinking about anyone else at all.'

Robyn held her breath. She knew that her grandfather had died when Leonard was six years old, and he seldom spoke of his childhood, making this a rare moment of intimacy.

'It was years before it even occurred to me that my mother might have felt the same as me. And I certainly never considered all the things in life that my father had missed out on. All I cared about was that I hated us being left alone, hated my mother not being the same, because she was worrying about everything all the time. I hated it. That was my grief.'

'But you were so little,' she said, taking his hand to scramble down the steep side of the sea wall.

'I know Angie was your friend, but you mustn't let this business get you down. You've got your exams this year. Then you'll be off to university. No one in my family has ever got a degree. You've a whole lifetime of opportunity in front of you. And we'll do all we can, financially. You know that, don't you?'

'I do know I'm not alone, Dad.' She gave him a smile, trying not to cry. 'Thank you.'

Leonard nodded gruffly and then turned to lead the way, the heavy cloth bag swinging by his side.

13

Ruth Woods, the family liaison officer, opened the door when Grace rang. Grace had called half an hour earlier and explained that, if possible, she wanted Donna Fewell's permission to speak to Davey alone.

When Grace had got into her car in the superstore car park after meeting Ivo Sweatman, she was shaking with anger at the thought of Mark Kirkby and very probably his oldest friend Curtis Mullins conspiring to persecute Davey and Ella's father for no apparent reason other than that Mark fancied taking over Russell Fewell's family. Grace knew that some of her rage stemmed from her own demons; the image she was building of Mark Kirkby as a bully who loved the uniform because it gave him licence to swagger and throw his weight about reminded her uncomfortably of her ex-husband. But she was also aware of how the intolerable and terrifying helplessness that resulted from such bullying could drive someone essentially compliant and unassertive right over the edge. As Fewell, alone outside, witnessed his kids sitting down to Christmas dinner with his oppressor, had it been merely the work of minutes, seconds even, to progress from the red mist of wronged victim to mass murderer?

Having listened to Ivo, she refused any longer to believe it had been merely bad luck or coincidence that it had been Mark's best friend who had arrested Fewell on his birthday, a date Mark could easily have picked up from Davey and Ella if they'd drawn their dad a card or phoned him during the day to sing 'Happy Birthday'. She even speculated about the broken light: it wouldn't be at all difficult to smash a rear light in the darkness of a pub car park.

She'd tried hard to reason with herself – was she being as paranoid as Fewell himself? – until she recalled Davey's swiftly suppressed reaction when Donna had talked about how Russell had blamed her new partner for all his misfortunes and had accused Mark of getting his mates to follow him and pull him over. Had Davey's glance been a signal that maybe he'd believed his father? If so, how did the boy feel now, when no one had listened to his dad when they had the chance? She hoped that maybe, without his mother present, Davey might open up to her, if only to lay this whole thread of supposition to rest.

'Donna would like me to be there too,' Ruth now explained quietly in the narrow hall. 'She's OK with it unless Davey gets really upset. Then I'm to fetch her immediately.'

'Of course,' said Grace. 'And thanks. Donna must trust you. That's good. God knows, she needs someone she can trust right now.'

Ruth nodded, her expression serious, as if this assignment was too tough to allow compliments. 'Davey's upstairs. I'll let Donna know we're going up.'

Grace waited for Ruth to come back out of the lounge and followed her upstairs. The FLO tapped on the bedroom door. 'Davey? Detective Inspector Grace Fisher is here. You met her the other day. She'd like to talk to you.'

Grace approved of the way that Ruth spoke to Davey as she would an adult. From what she'd seen the other evening, he was a sharp kid, not one who'd appreciate baby talk. The door opened and for a moment Grace was taken aback that she had to look down from the point between the door and the jamb where she'd been expecting to see Davey's face. He was, after all, barely ten and slight for his age, taking after his father, who had not been particularly tall – just a child, looking back up at her with big serious eyes.

Instinctively Grace crouched down on her heels to bring her head slightly lower than his. He faced her squarely, still holding on to the door.

'I'm sorry that I can't leave you all in peace,' she said. 'But I'd like to know a bit more about your dad and what he was like. Ruth is going to be here with you. Where would you like to talk? Here or downstairs?'

Davey thought for a moment and then opened his door wide. Turning away from her, he went to sit on his bed, knees up and his back against the wall. Grace sat on the end of the bed and Ruth remained standing by the door. The duvet cover was printed with blue and red Spider-Man figures, and there was a scatter of dinosaur toys on a low table under the window mixed in with Lego pieces and a couple of plastic dragons. A big poster of a scary Tyrannosaurus rex was Blu-tacked to the wall. The paintwork was scuffed and chipped, and the windows dripped with condensation, but it seemed like a warm, safe little room.

'So you like dinosaurs?'

Davey nodded.

'Was your dad into that kind of thing too?'

The boy nodded again, and Grace decided she'd have to be direct. 'How often did you see your dad, Davey?'

'Weekends. Used to, anyway. He'd take me fishing and stuff.'

'When you say you *used* to see him at weekends . . .?' Grace left the rest of the question unspoken.

'We started doing stuff with Mark instead.'

'And was that fun? Did you like that?'

Davey shrugged. Grace didn't sense much enthusiasm.

'You heard your mum talk about how she and your dad were taking a little break from one another,' she said. 'Did your dad talk about that?'

'Not really.'

'If you could have chosen, would you rather have spent more time with your dad?'

Davey looked down, gave a tiny nod but said nothing.

'Can you remember if your dad was upset about anything in particular – about how things were with Mark?'

'Doesn't matter now.'

'Well, it does to you and your sister. To understand what made your dad so unhappy.'

But Davey looked down, twisting his hands, making shapes with his fingers, saying nothing.

'You missed your dad when you didn't see him at weekends?' Grace asked.

He nodded, still not looking at her. 'He had to spend them all by himself.'

'And was he upset about that?'

Another nod. 'He wanted to see us. I didn't like him being on his own.'

'And when you were together, what kind of things did you do, besides fishing?'

Davey shrugged again. 'Just telly and stuff.' He thought for a moment. 'He liked making things.' Grace heard the pride in his voice as, for the first time, he looked at her directly. 'We built a go-kart once.'

'That's a good memory,' she said, smiling at him.

'He was really upset,' said Davey abruptly, 'because of what I said.'

'What did you say, Davey?' she asked gently.

'I told him about the gun.'

Grace hoped she hadn't betrayed her surprise and didn't dare glance at Ruth, who remained preternaturally still. 'The gun?' she echoed softly.

'About Mark showing it to me.'

'Mark had a gun?'

'It was Mark who liked guns, not Dad.' His answer was un-equivocal, and he stared at her fiercely.

'He liked to shoot?' Grace asked as casually as she could. 'I know a lot of people around here shoot duck or go clay-pigeon shooting.'

But the boy hugged his knees tightly and looked away, evidently feeling he had said too much. Grace racked her brain to try and remember if anyone had checked to see whether Mark Kirkby had a firearms certificate. She didn't think anyone had. Why would they?

'You know, Davey, a lot of police officers are trained to use firearms.' He looked at her anxiously, and she smiled a friendly smile that she hoped wasn't too obviously encouraging. 'A lot of police officers learn to be familiar with different guns. Is that what you mean about Mark?'

Davey nodded warily. 'Maybe. He showed me once. It was big and really hard and heavy. I didn't like holding it. Mark told me not to tell anyone, but I told Dad and then Dad got upset.'

'What did your dad say?'

'He was going to speak to Mark about it.'

'And did he?'

Davey shook his head. 'I asked him not to. Mark said it had to be a secret. Just us, or I'd get into trouble. That Mum and Ella weren't to know. Besides . . .'

'What, Davey?'

'There only would've been another row.' He hung his head. 'So I told Dad I made it up,' he mumbled, lowering his head onto his clasped knees. 'That he'd make me look stupid if he said anything.'

'Can you describe the gun you held?'

'I don't remember.'

'You said it was big and heavy.'

'I don't remember. Maybe I did just make it up.'

Grace wished she'd paid closer attention to her young nephews as they charged around her sister's house, shooting one another. 'Was it a handgun?' she asked. 'Like a water pistol? Or longer, like a droid blaster? A shotgun or a rifle, maybe?'

'It wasn't a toy!' His voice rose as he became upset, and Ruth took a step forward.

'No, it was real, I know,' said Grace, moving to make way for Ruth to sit beside the boy. 'I'm only trying to think of ways to describe it, that's all.'

'It wasn't real,' he said angrily. 'I just imagined it.'

'There's nothing to be frightened of,' said Grace. 'No one's cross with you. You're not letting anyone down.'

'I don't remember!'

'It's all right, Davey,' said Ruth. 'You don't have to think about it any more now. You've been fantastic. Do you want to go downstairs and find your mum?'

Davey nodded and, straightening his legs, slipped off the bed. He stood for a second, hesitating, then looked directly at Grace.

'He's still my dad.' The note of defiance quavered slightly.

'Of course he is,' said Grace, moved by his courage. 'And I really don't believe, deep down, that he was a bad person.'

'Can you tell people that?' he begged. 'Please?'

Grace nodded. 'I will. I'll do my best, I promise.'

The boy held her gaze for a moment longer, then took Ruth's proffered hand and went out of the room with her.

Grace remained where she was. Taking out her mobile, she called Lance, who picked up almost immediately. 'You in the office?' she asked.

'Yes.'

'Can you check something for me? Whether Mark Kirkby had a firearms certificate or ever received firearms training.'

'Will do,' said Lance. 'Any special reason?'

'Can't speak now,' she said. 'Are you still gathering background on Fewell?'

'Yes. Want me to change tack?'

'No, you're fine as you are. Talk to you later.'

She hung up. Whatever Davey tried to claim about making it up, she believed that Mark Kirkby had shown him a gun and that Davey had told his father about it. The obvious explanation was that the gun was legally held and fully accounted for, and, childless himself, Mark had naively imagined that a bit of mystery and drama would be fun for the boy. But all Grace's instincts screamed that this wasn't what had happened.

Hearing the doorbell ring, she went quietly out onto the landing. She saw Ruth Woods come out of the lounge and go to open the front door, but was unable see who was there. Hearing a deep male voice, she was taken aback to realize it was John Kirkby, come to offer his condolences to his son's girlfriend and her children, and to enquire whether they needed anything, if he could help them in any way. Grace ducked back out of sight as Ruth led the visitor into the lounge. John Kirkby was the last person she wanted to see with these dark new perceptions fresh in her mind. She sent Ruth a short explanatory text and then, as soon as she heard the lounge door close safely behind them, slipped downstairs and out of the front door.

14

Grace sat with her back to her desk, looking out of the window, considering how she was going to handle Davey's revelation. First, she wanted to be certain that Lance had discovered nothing about Russell Fewell that would lead her to question Davey's faith in his dad – like, for instance, if Fewell's computer browsing history turned out to be full of searches for violent far-right groups or armed militia fantasies. She knew that wasn't likely to happen, but she was anxious to have someone she could safely discuss this with and was pleased when Lance finally came and tapped on the cubicle partition.

'Shift those files and sit yourself down,' she told him. 'Bring me up to speed, and then I want to run something past you.'

Lance drew the chair up to the side of her desk. 'The good thing about the Sunday after Christmas is that nearly everyone's at home,' he said. 'So I've been able to track people down and look under every possible stone I can think of. But there's nothing on Fewell to predict what happened except his growing obsession with his ex-wife's new partner.'

It was as she had expected, although a tiny part of her was nonetheless disappointed. 'Do you know when that started?' she asked.

'Donna Fewell and Mark Kirkby had been seeing each other

for about eight months. The relationship only began after the divorce had gone through, and there's no reason to doubt what she says – that the divorce had been amicable, with no one else involved. All the people that have been spoken to – work colleagues, friends – said Fewell barely mentioned Mark Kirkby until about three or four months ago. But around that time he became increasingly bitter and paranoid about him.'

'He may have been right to be paranoid. Curtis Mullins was the arresting officer on the drink-drive charge. He and Mark had been friends since school.'

'Bit of a coincidence,' remarked Lance drily.

'Yes. And, two hours after I asked Curtis some absolutely routine questions about the arrest, Superintendent Pitman gets a call from John Kirkby complaining of insensitivity and harassment.'

'That's not mincing his words, is it?' Lance frowned. 'Peter and I ran into Curtis in a bar just before Christmas.'

'You know him?'

'Only through work. We were waiting for some friends at the Blue Bar when he came in with a group of guys, and, well, Peter reckoned we were likely to get hassle from them. One of them kept looking over in our direction, kind of aggressive, you know? You develop a sixth sense about that kind of stuff, so we just had a quick drink and went on home.'

Grace shook her head at the pointlessness of such aggro. 'Still,' she said, 'if you and Peter are serious—'

'We are.'

'Then your sexuality is going to become common knowledge around here eventually. Surely the sooner people know – and are happy for you – the better?'

Lance laughed without much humour. 'And when I get pulled over for a broken rear light?'

'Curtis wouldn't dare do that to a fellow officer.'

'Really?'

Grace was about to argue, but then thought better of it. 'There's more to tell you.' She spoke in a low voice, so Lance had to lean forward to hear her clearly. 'I just spoke to Fewell's son, Davey. He said Mark showed him a gun. A big, heavy one. Told him not to tell anyone.'

'Wow,' said Lance. 'So that's why you asked me to check whether Mark Kirkby had a firearms certificate?'

'And did he?'

'No.'

Grace was shocked. For a police officer to be in possession of an illegal weapon showed a streak of recklessness – and arrogance – beyond what she'd so far allowed herself to imagine.

Lance's voice cut into her thoughts. 'However, he did receive police firearms training, although he never qualified as an authorized officer.'

'So what the hell did he think was he doing? If he'd been found with it, he was risking a prison sentence.'

'And what was he doing showing off like that to a kid?' said Lance contemptuously. 'So, when's Davey coming in? You'll want to get him on video.'

'Yes, I know, except I'm not sure it'll work. I'm scared he'll clam up completely if we put too much pressure on him. The moment I pushed him to open up a little bit more, he back-tracked.'

'What about his mother?' asked Lance. 'Why hasn't she mentioned Mark having a gun?'

'I'm not sure Donna knew,' said Grace. 'Davey said he told his dad, who was furious about it. I mean, you would be, wouldn't you? His son is ten years old. You don't put a bloody great Heckler & Koch assault rifle in the hands of a ten-year-old and then order him not to tell either of his parents. Especially not if you're a police officer!'

'But you do believe Davey?' asked Lance.

'Yes, I do. And so did the FLO, who was there the whole time,' said Grace. 'Davey said he was scared there'd be a row between his parents and asked his dad not to say anything.'

Lance was silent for few moments. Grace waited for him to consider the implications, hoping he'd arrive at the same conclusion as her.

'Do you think it's possible that Fewell used Kirkby's own gun to kill him?' asked Lance.

'I've no idea,' said Grace, relieved. 'But it is another rather large coincidence, isn't it?'

'And, if Fewell had somehow got hold of the weapon, Mark Kirkby could hardly report it stolen, could he?'

'Well, could be that Fewell took it in the hope it would cause trouble for Mark if the gun went missing,' suggested Grace. 'And then, when Mark didn't report it stolen, there it was, begging to be used.'

Lance whistled through his teeth. 'If you're right, then it's a lead we have to follow up. But you'd be opening up a box of snakes.'

Grace glanced towards the closed door of Colin Pitman's office and lowered her voice. 'What do I do, Lance?'

Lance too spoke more quietly. 'You've not brought the boss in on this yet, then?'

Grace shook her head. 'I'm waiting until I've spoken to Donna.'

'Don't wait too long.' There was a clear note of warning in Lance's voice.

'I won't. But John Kirkby turned up just as I was leaving, so I haven't had a chance yet. And I wanted to speak to you first. I mean, all I've got so far is the word of a traumatized ten-year-old. And it's Davey I want to protect. Believe me, I know how hard it is to speak up when no one wants to hear you. Unless we can get some kind of evidence to support him, it'll be his word against some pretty formidable adults.'

'I guess we could get a search warrant for Mark Kirkby's house and car,' Lance suggested dubiously.

'Can you imagine how that would go down? Besmirching the good name of a fellow officer who's been viciously gunned down on his own doorstep on Christmas Day? Davey wouldn't stand a chance.'

Lance thought for a few moments. 'OK, so even if Mark Kirkby wasn't shot with his own gun, where did he get hold of an illicit weapon and, presumably, ammunition?'

'And *why*?' asked Grace. 'If he'd wanted a firearms certificate to join a shooting club or whatever, he'd have got one, no trouble. Why on earth take such a risk? What did he want an illegal gun for?'

'Ballistics haven't come up with anything on Fewell's rifle?'

'Not yet. We've been given priority, but we're still waiting for the full report. And Duncan is asking around about the ammunition. He thinks we might get a lead on that. So can we just keep this between us for now?'

She knew this was asking a lot, and she wouldn't have blamed Lance for backing away. But he nodded. 'Sure,' he said. 'After all, it's not like we're looking to take any dangerous villains off the street.'

'True. And, whatever we find, it's not going to bring any of Fewell's victims back, either.' As Lance got up to go, Grace recognized the depth of her relief that he hadn't rejected her conjectures as outlandish. 'Thanks, Lance. Really.'

Lance returned her smile before heading off to his own desk. Grace sat back, realizing how comforted she was by his support. Lance's ready acceptance of what Davey had said reassured her that her innate dislike of John Kirkby and his dead son hadn't led her to totally unreasonable and unfair conclusions. Lance would probably never realize just how much that meant to her.

15

It was the following morning before Donna Fewell could be approached. After some discussion with Ruth Woods, Grace had decided it would be better if the family liaison officer sounded her out first, and they had agreed that Ruth would ask Donna whether Mark had ever shown any interest in guns. The response was disappointing: Donna had said no, and Ruth was sure that her lack of reaction was genuine. Which meant that, if Davey *had* told his dad, as he said, then Russell Fewell had not brought the issue up with his ex-wife.

Ruth had also warned Grace against returning too soon to the house to speak to Davey. Ruth continued to believe that he'd told the truth the previous day, but reported that he was evidently distressed and overnight had become even more withdrawn. Pushing him too hard before he was ready would, she felt, be counterproductive.

Grace trusted the FLO's judgement, yet their conversation made it no easier to decide when and what to say to Superintendent Pitman. All morning she'd been in two minds about whether to speak at all, yet she knew she'd have to inform him at some point of what Davey had said, however reluctant he'd be to hear it. If only Keith Stalgood had still been sitting in the black leather executive chair that went with the role, then she would have had no such hesitation. But nostalgia was useless. She had to deal with what was in front of her. Nevertheless, she was happy to be reprieved for a little longer by Duncan, a big smile on his face, bringing her the follow-up to the preliminary ballistics report.

'We have a match,' he said.

'You mean the rifle has been fired in other incidents?' she asked, very much surprised at such a development.

'Not the gun,' said Duncan. 'But there's a match on the ammunition. Or, to be absolutely precise, the tool used to load the primers inside the spent casings.'

'You'll have to explain. That's way too specialist for me.'

Duncan grinned. 'Whoever reloaded the rounds used by Russell Fewell has a repriming tool that left microscopic, slightly off-centre, scratch marks on all the primers recovered from the spent casings. There are identical marks on primers recovered from other incidents, including four murders.'

'You're talking about rifle rounds?' asked Grace, confused.

'No, that's what's so interesting,' said Duncan. 'These other bullets were fired from different types of handgun all using different calibre ammunition, but all reloaded using the same repriming tool.'

'So we have a single armourer making and supplying ammo for criminals right across the UK,' said Grace. 'Is that what you're saying?'

'That's what it looks like,' Duncan agreed cheerfully. 'His handiwork is linked to four separate, unrelated murders – a drive-by gang shooting in north London, another gang shooting in Manchester and two armed robberies in Birmingham – plus four other non-fatal incidents across London.'

'Does the National Crime Agency have anything on this?' she asked eagerly.

'Not a lot. Usually ammunition is supplied along with an illegal weapon as part of a package. But it can be difficult to obtain extra ammo, and it doesn't come cheap, so could be that our chap specializes in supplying that market.'

'But he could also be handling firearms as well?'

'Sure.'

Grace mentally reviewed what she knew about gun crime: well over a thousand shots had been fired last year in London alone, and the vast majority of firearm fatalities were young. She longed to share with Duncan what Davey had said, to ask if he had any idea why on earth a serving police officer would have connections to such a criminal trade. 'Surely, this armourer could be absolutely anywhere?' she said. 'Poland, Russia, Albania. He could be dealing through the dark web, getting paid in Bitcoin.'

'Except that the rounds Fewell used had spent casings with British military head stamps,' Duncan reminded her.

Grace frowned. 'Easy enough to obtain from any war zone where our troops are serving.'

'True,' said Duncan. 'But I've been speaking to few of the local firearms dealers. There's a guy called Leonard Ingold who's always been very cooperative. Tips us off if he's offered firearms not held lawfully on a certificate, that kind of thing. He suggested that if the home-loader of the rifle rounds used by Fewell *was* local, then the brass casings would probably have come from STANTA.'

'What's that?'

'Stanford Training Area, just north of Thetford. Leonard says he's occasionally reused spent casings from there himself. Although the army are pretty thorough at clearing up after themselves, there's a civilian guy, a range warden, who must be pocketing some of the brass and selling it off for beer money. He shouldn't be doing it, but there's a lot of deer in Thetford Forest, so he'll find plenty of ready customers nearby. Deer-stalkers are really into home-loading; a perfectly balanced bullet makes a big difference.'

Grace shook her head. 'And how many thousands of rounds do the army get through? I'm not sure how this helps us.'

Duncan smiled in obvious delight. 'Ah, but it does, boss. You just have to be a bit of a geek. The head stamp has the manufacturer's name and the year of issue. So I checked with STANTA. No reported thefts of military ammunition, but one of the units using the firing range had a batch matching those stamps. It's not definitive, but it does potentially link to the rounds used by Fewell.'

'You're saying our armourer could be local?' Grace was impressed.

Duncan nodded in satisfaction. 'Yes. I realize it's still a needle in a haystack, but I'd like to follow up with the range warden who's been selling the brass. Get a list of his customers.'

'Good idea.' Grace worked back through everything Duncan had told her so far. 'You told me before that hollow-point ammunition had to be listed on a firearms certificate. Are details of the head stamps recorded?'

'No. Sorry, boss. That would make it way too easy.'

Grace laughed. 'Yeah, I guess so.'

'But it's still worth a chat with the range warden, don't you think?'

'I do, yes,' she said. 'This is really good work, Duncan. Keep on digging, and let's see where it takes us.'

She was happy to watch him return to his desk with a spring in his step. All too often the most intractable cases were solved by dogged legwork and number-crunching, and Duncan was a proper old-style copper used to getting results through sheer hard work. She remembered some quip from a championship golfer that her dad used to quote when she grumbled about finishing her homework or wanted to abandon a task that was proving trickier than expected: *The harder I practise, the luckier I get.*

The comforting echo of her dad's voice in her head provided the final push she needed to go and speak to Colin Pitman. Rising from her desk, she reminded herself that, while she might have little respect for Colin's moral courage, he was nonetheless shrewd and realistic, and had always been adept at cutting through swathes of intelligence so a team could home in on what mattered. Perhaps, after all, he would surprise her?

'Come in,' he said when she tapped on his door. He smiled wearily. 'I'm just going over the protocol for Mark Kirkby's funeral next week. Hilary wants an immaculate police presence. Luckily John Kirkby is only too keen for his son to be buried with full ceremony, and given that the Police Federation is picking up the bill we can really go to town.'

Grace's heart sank as she closed the door and came to sit opposite him: he really wasn't going to want to hear what she had to say.

Colin must have sensed her misgivings, for he gave her a very direct look. 'John Kirkby has specifically asked for Curtis Mullins to be one of the bearers,' he said pointedly. 'White gloves.

Guard of honour. A service drape with the Essex force insignia. You get the picture?'

'I understand perfectly, sir.'

He pushed the paperwork away from him and sat back. 'What happened to *Colin*?' he asked with a wry smile.

'You're a superintendent now,' she said lightly, trying not to clench her teeth and changing the subject as swiftly as she could. 'I've had the follow-up ballistics report. It links Russell Fewell's ammunition to multiple incidents, four fatal. It suggests a single armourer supplying ammunition and possibly also weapons to criminals right across the country.'

'Right.' He scanned the copy she handed him, but she could see from his expression that he wasn't very interested. 'How do you intend to action this?'

'There's a possibility that the armourer is local. Duncan Gregg is looking into it.'

'You've been busy.'

His tone suggested a reprimand, probably because Grace had not kept him informed. But she was a detective inspector now, and wasn't expected to keep him abreast of every separate line of inquiry.

'It seemed worth putting some effort into tracking down where the gun and ammunition came from,' she said carefully.

'Well, if it goes somewhere, fine,' said Colin airily. 'But I think we've got enough for the coroner now, don't you?' He tossed the report back onto his desk. 'Hilary reckons the media will be eager to move on. Her advice is that Dunholt isn't the kind of horror story people want to hear much more of, not at this time of year.'

'Sure,' said Grace. 'That's only natural. But if, further down the line, we can show that in the wake of this tragedy we're taking illicit weapons off the street and putting the people who supply them behind bars, that would be a real PR feather in our cap, wouldn't it?'

'Of course. But I don't want officers tied up on non-urgent investigations when they could be at home with their families. It's bad for morale. All those who worked on Christmas Day and Boxing Day are getting time off in lieu. That includes you, Grace.'

'The troops will really appreciate that. Thanks.'

She knew she was allowing herself to be sidetracked, but what she could do about it? There was no way she could tell Colin now that Mark Kirkby, an officer about to be eulogized with full police honours, had been in illegal possession of a firearm and had possible links to a criminal armourer.

She returned to her desk hoping that maybe Ivo Sweatman's investigations, whatever they were, would turn something up, although in the light of Davey's revelation she worried that she should never have given him the lead about Fewell's drink-drive arrest. It had been madness ever to agree to their meeting in the first place. While she despised the tabloids for their methods and for the glee with which they set out to shame people, deep down she couldn't help believing that she and Ivo were on the same side. And she liked him. All the same, should she now warn him off investigating Curtis Mullins? If any of this got out before she could prove that Davey was right, it would be a total PR disaster for the police, for which she was unlikely ever to be forgiven. She could cope with that if she had to, but not with the negative emotional impact on the boy, which would be incalculable.

Davey had told her the truth, his truth, and it was her task to investigate, even if it meant defaming fellow officers. She had done it before and been punished for doing her duty by those she trusted. But if she let that stop her doing her job, she might as well pack up and go home.

16

The Cricketers was a large cosy-looking pub about half a mile north of the main Colchester bypass. According to the statement made by Russell Fewell after his arrest it was where he'd met up with a couple of friends to celebrate his birthday last November. Now, early on a Tuesday afternoon between Christmas and New Year, there were only three other cars in the car park. Grace doubted the pub would be busy. Not that she intended to go inside. She parked in a corner of the large tarmacked area at the side of the building and wondered what on earth she thought she was doing here.

She had just spent several hours – time that should have been spent on far more justifiable tasks – leaning on people to search databases for any record of Russell Fewell's van that night. An image from a number plate recognition camera close to the turn-off he'd have taken to get here showed that, on his journey to the pub, both his rear lights had been working.

In his statement Fewell had accepted that a light was broken, but said he hadn't been aware of it before PC Mullins drew it to his attention. It was, of course, perfectly possible that someone had reversed into his van in the car park and broken the light while he was inside with his mates, but might he not then have noticed the broken glass on the ground when he came out of the pub?

Grace began by walking the two diagonals across the car park, scanning for any specks of red: nothing. She then skirted the perimeter, still looking across the gritty surface. There were cigarette ends, a couple of discarded chocolate wrappers and an empty cigarette packet. The planters, although the geraniums looked frosted and wilting, were well tended, and she suspected litter was regularly cleared. She stood still, trying not to shiver as the cold seeped through her clothes. *I'm Curtis Mullins*, she thought. My best friend Mark has told me that Fewell's going to be here. I know his vehicle registration. I need an excuse to pull him over later. I park in front of the pub, tell my partner I need a leak, slip out the back and, when there's no one about, smash one of the back lights on his van. *Then what?* Well, I wouldn't leave the evidence here on the ground. I'd sweep it out of sight, wouldn't I?

At the back of the car park was a thick evergreen hedge, planted to shield the neighbouring houses from the nuisance of slammed car doors and carousing customers late at night. A car drove in and parked as Grace slowly walked the length of the hedge, carefully inspecting the earth around its sturdy stems. The middle-aged couple who got out stared at her in bemusement, so she gave them a friendly smile and carried on with her search. As they walked away she spotted what she was looking for: rough pieces of broken red plastic brushed in among the roots of the hedge. She took out her phone and photographed them, stepping back to take a series of contextual images, and then went to her car for plastic gloves and an evidence bag.

As she sealed the bag and wrote in the necessary details, she knew she was running too far ahead of herself. The broken pieces could come from any vehicle, and even if forensics matched the pieces to a light from the make of van driven by Russell Fewell, it still meant nothing. How many of those white delivery vans had been in and out of this car park in the past month? What she thought she'd found simply didn't matter enough in the face of the inevitable and wholly understandable demonization of Russell Fewell. Truth was, no one would want to give a toss what had happened here.

And yet, and yet . . . the coincidences were starting to mount up, which must be what Fewell had thought too. If he'd been paranoid, then she was equally so.

Maybe she was just jumping at shadows, building conspiracies, over-identifying with a mass-murderer. Yet what if Curtis Mullins also knew that Mark had an illegal weapon? Was that why he'd seemed so jumpy about having to give evidence at the inquest?

Grace got into her car and started the engine to generate some warmth. The image of Davey with his toy dinosaurs and Spider-Man duvet came into her mind, and she felt like crying.

What Russell Fewell had done was appalling, unthinkable, the worst incident she'd ever had to deal with. Each time he pulled that trigger, he had been a monster. And yet Grace had a tiny inkling of how he must have felt. It was how she'd felt back in Maidstone. She'd done nothing wrong but had been victimized and forced out of her job by the very people from whom she expected help and protection. It had nearly driven her mad. And here, in an evidence bag in her lap, was proof that Fewell might have been driven mad too. Evidence enough for Davey Fewell and his sister, anyway.

She faced an implacable wall. Mark Kirkby. Curtis Mullins. John Kirkby. Colin Pitman. Probably Hilary Burnett too. And even if she persuaded Colin to listen, she had no real evidence, and he'd be right to dismiss everything she had as mere conjecture.

She thought of the middle-aged couple that had watched her poking around in the scrubby roots of the hedge. They had certainly thought she was crazy. Maybe she was.

17

Despite the damp chilly air a large crowd had already gathered outside the fourteenth-century church in Dunholt when the coach transporting those of Angie Turner's classmates who wanted to attend her funeral arrived from Colchester. A single service was being held for all five victims, and it seemed to Robyn as if the entire population of the little town had come to pay their respects to their neighbours and their families. A cluster of satellite vans was parked around the village green. Keeping the reporters, photographers and television crews in check were two long lines of police officers, all in full dress uniform, presumably a mark of respect for their fallen colleague.

The January term had begun two days earlier, and the atmosphere had been overheated and intense, with even the teachers appearing to encourage sometimes hysterical displays of grief. It had all been too much for Robyn, who longed to escape back to the peace and seclusion of home. Today, Wednesday, the school party had been asked to arrive and take their places early and, all equally immaculate in their sixth-form uniforms of grey or black suits, they processed in line up the path. Robyn looked to either side, hoping to spot her parents among the sea of faces, but she reached the knapped-flint porch without seeing them. Entering the church, her group was ushered to a pew right at the back of the nave and asked to squeeze up as tightly as they could. Rows of extra chairs had been placed behind them as well as down both aisles. As she took her place she was dimly aware of arches and high stone walls covered with marble memorial plaques.

There were massive arrangements of white flowers in front of the altar and around the pulpit to one side and the brass lectern on the other. The five coffins, three of dark varnished wood, one white and one draped with a dark cloth embroidered with some kind of crest, had already been brought in and lined up in a row. Each bore an identical floral arrangement of hellebores, also called Christmas roses. Robyn tried not to picture what they contained. She knew she was among the tiny minority of those here today who had actually seen the reality of gunshot wounds, who understood the difference between a shotgun and a rifle, or hard-point and soft-point ammunition. It was her father's trade, so she had grown up with such knowledge, but in her world this was focused on killing animals and game birds in the most efficient and humane way possible. It was about lessening cruelty and suffering, not about . . . about *this*.

She was also well aware that none of her school friends agreed with her about shooting game. Once or twice she'd tried to argue that if you cared about animal welfare then eating a wild duck cleanly shot out in its habitat on the marshes was infinitely preferable to buying some intensively reared chicken pumped full of polyphosphates and water. But it was impossible to convince them that their mum's roast chicken was more morally questionable, or that gutting and skinning a bird yourself was a whole lot more honest than paying a fortune for plastic-packed organic chicken breasts in Waitrose. And anyway they weren't interested, not really. They went 'Ew' and 'Yuck' and started talking about who was going to so-and-so's party at the weekend.

And why should they be interested? All the girls packed in alongside her on the pew were the daughters of people who worked indoors – lawyers, doctors, company executives. As was Angie. Robyn realized that her friend's parents and older sister must be sitting somewhere in front, amid the rows of bent black-clad backs. Angie's grandmother had also died, so presumably aunts, uncles and cousins must be here too, though Robyn didn't know any of them. The organ was playing some quiet, soothing music, but neither it nor the background susurration of people crossing their legs, coughing, whispering to each other or rustling their orders of service could entirely drown out the few raw sobs coming from the pews nearest to the coffins.

To distract herself, Robyn looked up at the stained-glass windows, but there wasn't enough light to illuminate them, and they looked pretty dull to her anyway. She had no idea who the saints depicted in them might be. Her family had never been religious. The natural world was enough for them – the big ever-changing skies, the stars at night, the beauty and power of the sea out beyond the estuary, the local birds, plants and animals. Their endless variety had fascinated her for as long as she could remember and was why she hoped to study for a degree in conservation biology. She wondered what Angie had believed in, or whether the faith contained within these stone arches and walls brought any comfort to her family, and where in heaven or earth the god symbolized by the big cross up on the altar had been hiding himself on Christmas Day.

Robyn had never lost anyone close to her before. Her dad seldom saw his mother, who lived in Canada with her second husband, and her other grandparents were infrequent visitors. One of Leonard's friends had dropped dead of an aneurysm about a year ago, but while she'd been curious about her dad's reaction to the news it had not really touched her. She could scarcely believe that Angie wasn't about to throw back the lid of her coffin and come dancing down the aisle any moment, laughing at everyone for being so gullible as to think she'd vanish and leave them like this.

And of course she hadn't vanished. Physically her body was here now. Lying there boxed up in her white coffin. It was horrific, intolerable, made Robyn want to push her way past her school friends and run out of the church, find her dad and hug him as tightly as she could. But she forced down her panic with the thought that everyone here must feel the same. That's why the decision had been taken to hold one service for all five victims, so that no one need go through this alone.

The missing coffin was of course that of the gunman; she'd heard at school that he'd already been discreetly cremated after a very small, very private service. Robyn thought about how he had ended his life right outside this church, in a snowy corner of the old burial ground. In the two weeks since the shootings all visual traces had gone, either cleaned up and repaired or melted away. But Robyn had seen blood on snow many times. She loved working with the dogs on a shoot, and it was always cause for encouragement and praise when they dropped a bird they had retrieved at her feet. The mental image of fresh blood on snow – if she thought about it at all – brought sensory memories of blue skies and bluer water, fresh, sharp, invigorating cold, of the dogs' bright eyes and steamy breath, of the camaraderie of a successful day's sport. The catastrophic damage that a 7.62 x 51 mm soft-point rifle round could cause to a human heart or skull at almost point-blank range literally did not bear thinking about.

Robyn wished that she'd been able to be with her parents, who would follow the service with hundreds of others outside, but entry to the church had been tightly restricted. The place was full now, and the vicar in her cassock and gown was climbing up into the pulpit. After that the service took on the atmosphere of a school assembly, or some longer and more symbolic event like Founders' Day, and Robyn stood, sat, sang hymns, listened to readings and eulogies, knelt and pretended to pray along with the rest, as required. Afterwards, only a few lines from a W.H. Auden poem that someone read stayed in her head: *The truth is simple. / Evil is unspectacular and always human, / And shares our bed and eats at our own table.* Something in them struck horror deep into her heart, and she was glad when at last the congregation stood and watched in silence as the five coffins were carried slowly out of the church and down the path to the flower-filled hearses.

By the time Robyn and her school friends came out into the misty air the first of the cars was already driving away. The police officers in their buttoned tunics who lined the road stood stock-still in eerie disciplined silence. As the hearse bearing Angie's white coffin set off, one of Robyn's classmates gave a wave of farewell and suddenly they were all waving and crying and hugging each other, simultaneously bereft and relieved that this part was now over and they could get back to school, back to a semblance of their normal lives. Never had a science lesson seemed more inviting.

Detaching herself, Robyn looked around one last time for her parents. At breakfast she'd begged them both to come, even though Leonard had barely known Angie, and Nicola had only stopped for tea a couple of times when picking Robyn up from Angie's house. Robyn finally spotted her mother standing with a small group of people over by the brick wall that ringed the churchyard. There was no sign of her dad, but a familiar-looking overweight balding man in an ill-fitting black suit was introducing her mother to a tall, slim, serious-looking woman with neatly cut straight brown hair. As Nicola turned to shake the woman's hand, she caught sight of Robyn and soon afterwards excused herself and came over to join her daughter.

'Hello, love.' Nicola looked at her anxiously. 'You all right?'

Robyn nodded. 'Who were you talking to?'

'They're the detectives in charge of the case.'

'Detectives?'

'Yes. Have you never met Duncan Gregg?' said Nicola distractedly. 'We've organized events for him occasionally, for some police social club he's involved in.'

'He came last week to talk to Dad.'

'Did he?' said Nicola. 'Well, they were probably doing the rounds of all the local firearms dealers.' She sighed. 'They have to do something, I suppose. Can you imagine?'

Robyn nodded, trying to remember what it was her father had said about the man who visited the workshop. 'Where is Dad?'

Nicola looked down at the scuffed toes of her black boots. 'He couldn't make it,' she said. 'Look, is that your school coach? You'd better get moving.' She pecked her daughter on the cheek and gave her a little push. 'See you later.'

Robyn turned to follow her classmates, feeling suddenly as if each footstep was too heavy to take. She hadn't realized how tightly she'd been clinging to the comforting thought of seeing her dad, hearing his voice and feeling his reassuring hand on her shoulder. *Family*, he always said. *First, second and last.* Right now she could really do with that impregnable little wall around her. If she had any kind of faith, then that was it: family.

18

At nearly two in the morning on a damp Friday at the end of the first week of January the commercial side street near the centre of Colchester was deserted apart from two squad cars parked either side of a taped-off area of pavement. On the corner, about fifty yards beyond the police barrier tape, was a late-night bar that Grace knew to be a popular gay venue. Usually it would be brightly and invitingly lit, but now the exterior was almost entirely dark and the bar didn't look at all appealing. What light did emerge made the pavement look slick and greasy.

Grace left her own car a few yards away and went to join Dan Evans, the sergeant from the homicide assessment car, who stood rubbing his hands together in a futile attempt to keep warm. The original Victorian buildings had been rather messily adapted to current use, and she saw that the blue and white tape closed off a narrow entranceway leading to a small yard, now used as a parking area.

Waking her out of a deep sleep, a civilian call handler had rung forty minutes earlier to inform her, as duty DI, that there had been a suspicious death in Colchester. An IC1 male had been found with head injuries and taken to hospital, where he had been pronounced dead. The assessment car at the scene had requested MIT support.

'Morning, ma'am,' said Evans. 'Sorry to drag you out at this hour, but we need a strategy for the scene preservation.'

'No problem.'

'There's not much to see.' He shone a torch over the barrier tape onto a red-brick wall that rose along one side of the entrance. 'The victim was on the ground there. A couple of guys leaving the bar on the corner found him, a little before one o'clock. They called an ambulance, said he was unconscious and bleeding from pretty serious head wounds.'

'Any other injuries?'

'Not that we know of so far. But there was more than one blow to the head, apparently. It wasn't simply a bad fall. When the paramedics got here, they reckoned he was already dead, but didn't want to take chances so took him to hospital. I got them to bag his hands as a precaution and asked them, if possible, not to disturb his clothing until they heard from you.'

'Good, thanks. The guys who found him, you've got their details?'

'Yes, ma'am. They said he wasn't known to them.'

'Had he been at the bar?' Grace looked around the deserted street. 'There's not much else going on around here this late at night. Unless he's got a car parked nearby.' She nodded towards the darkened yard. 'Any vehicles in there?'

'Uniform says one, a silver Audi, but I didn't want to contaminate the scene. We weren't called until the hospital had confirmed death,' he explained. 'I've already notified the coroner.'

'Thanks. Where are uniform now?'

'In the bar taking names and addresses, though I think most

of the punters have left by now. Just as well that uniform decided not to wait for us and got stuck in. There's never enough man-power these days, is there? Don't know how the great British public expects us to run a half-decent service with all these cutbacks.'

Grace ignored the sergeant's grumbling. 'Who's there now?'

'The manager, if you want a word.'

'Please.'

Their footsteps echoed in the empty street. Evans pushed open the door and held it for her to go ahead of him. The place was empty except for a burly man of about forty unloading glasses from a dishwasher behind the bar and, standing talking to him, PC Curtis Mullins.

Colin Pitman had organized for those who'd worked over Christmas to take different days off over the New Year holiday, and so Grace hadn't crossed paths with Curtis since she'd searched the pub car park. She had welcomed the break and tried to push all her suspicions and concerns to the back of her mind – until the funeral two days ago. Then she'd felt such a terrible hypocrite watching Curtis Mullins at the front of the white-gloved bearer party carrying Mark Kirkby's coffin past the honour guard to the waiting hearse. Poignant images of John Kirkby stepping forward to place Mark's custodian helmet on top of the draped coffin had been beamed around the world and had adorned most of yesterday's front pages. Mark Kirkby was a fallen hero and Curtis Mullins his grieving comrade.

'Ma'am,' Curtis addressed her respectfully. 'This is Derek Slater. He's been here all night.'

Avoiding eye contact with Curtis, Grace showed the manager her warrant card and introduced herself. Apart from three earrings in one ear, Derek looked to her like a former regimental sergeant major, the kind with a twinkle in his eye and a soft spot for the lads who might end up at the sharp end in some war zone. She doubted that much would go on in here unobserved by him.

'Any reason to fear trouble tonight?' she asked. 'Notice any arguments that might've got settled outside later?'

'Nothing.' The manager nodded towards Curtis. 'And I've said I'll ask around the regulars tomorrow. Tell them to get in touch if they saw or heard anything, even if they didn't realize at the time what was going on.'

'We've got details of everyone who was still here when we arrived,' Curtis told her.

'Good, thanks.' Grace recalled what Lance had said about sensing Curtis's hostility at the Blue Bar before Christmas, but she could discern no trace of homophobia now, and the manager seemed perfectly relaxed in his company. But stuck in her head was a mental image of Curtis looking around a darkened pub car park before using his baton to smash the glass of the rear light of Russell Fewell's van. She turned to face Derek. 'Have you had any recent problems with harassment or homophobic abuse?'

'Nah, not really. We get the odd scallywag once in a while, thinks it's clever to show off his vocabulary. But we get on very well with our neighbours, on the whole.'

Grace turned reluctantly back to Curtis. 'What was the victim wearing?'

Curtis consulted his notebook. 'Grey suit and tie. Navy scarf. Black leather shoes.'

'No coat, even in this weather?'

'Not with him, no,' said Curtis.

'We often get people dropping in for a late drink after work, or whatever,' said Derek. 'I don't remember noticing anyone in particular tonight, though. But that doesn't mean he wasn't here. We were fairly busy.' He shook his head, clearly upset by the night's events. 'Poor bloke.'

'He may not have been in here,' said Grace. 'Hopefully tomorrow someone will be able to bring over a photograph of the victim. That might help jog a few memories.'

'Of course.'

'You can close up now, if you want to.'

'Right you are.'

Grace followed Curtis and Dan Evans back outside. 'Who was the first officer attending?' she asked.

'I was, ma'am,' said Curtis. 'My partner went with the paramedics, for continuity of evidence. They took the victim to the General. I secured the scene and got details from the two men who found him. One of them had stopped to light a cigarette right by the entrance to the yard, and spotted him slumped on the ground.'

'They didn't see anyone else?'

'No.'

'Did you check out the car park area?'

'Empty apart from a single car, registered to a company in London. The yard is surrounded by buildings. No way out.'

'Any CCTV?'

'Not here. There will be on the approach roads, though. Want me to get started on that?'

'Please.' Grace turned to Evans. 'Have we got scene of crime organized?'

'No, ma'am. Waiting for you.'

'OK. Let's see if we can get someone down here first thing. Meanwhile keep it taped off and put someone on duty.' She looked at her watch. 'Not too long before the town gets moving again. So what's your view?' she asked them both. 'Robbery? Attempted carjacking? A sexual encounter gone wrong? Hate crime?'

Evans shrugged. 'I never saw the body.'

'There have been a couple of muggings in the past month,' said Curtis, 'but nothing to suggest a hate crime. And, as you say, we don't know if there's any connection to the bar.'

'True,' said Grace. 'Well, I'd better get over to the hospital. See if we can get him identified. Thanks, both of you. I'll catch up with you at the station later.'

As she walked to her car, wondering if she'd be able to get any drinkable coffee at the hospital, she heard footsteps behind her.

'Ma'am?' It was Curtis.

'Yes?'

He looked over his shoulder to check that Evans was out of earshot. 'I wanted to apologize.'

Grace was taken aback. 'What for?'

'John Kirkby kicking up a fuss. I mean, I don't blame him for being upset right now, but I hope you don't think I went running to him like I had any kind of problem.'

'He's lost his son,' said Grace. 'Think no more of it.'

'OK. Thanks.'

He stepped back to give her room to open her car door. Before she got in, she scrutinized his face, trying to make out what he was really thinking. 'Tell me,' she said. 'With the benefit of hindsight, would you have handled Russell Fewell's arrest any differently?'

Curtis looked at her in a way she found impossible to deci-pher. 'I could've not turned up for work, I suppose,' he said, his tone hovering on the edge of insolence.

It was obvious he wasn't going to elaborate, so, already regret-ting that she'd spoken without forethought, she got into her car. Driving away, a glance in her rear-view mirror showed him standing in the street, watching her.

The Accident and Emergency Department was enjoying a three-in-the-morning lull, and Grace quickly located the young medic who had pronounced the victim dead. He confirmed what Sergeant Evans had reported, that the victim had suffered serious and multiple head injuries. 'Looked like he'd been attacked with a baseball bat,' said the doctor. 'Never knew what hit him, I'd say.'

'So an unprovoked attack rather than a fight?'

'I'm no expert,' he said. 'He was dead when he got to us, and we were requested not to remove any of his clothing, but I didn't see any signs of other injury.'

'OK, thanks,' said Grace. The doctor directed her to the hospi-tal morgue, where she found the uniform constable who had accompanied the ambulance paramedics waiting in the ante-room. He stood up as Grace came in, and from the way he blinked and opened his eyes wide she suspected that he had been asleep. She wasn't too concerned: the body was secure enough in here for continuity of evidence not to be an issue. However, while there was no pressing need for her to disturb a Home Office pathologist in the middle of the night, she did need to make a decision about whether to wait or go ahead and search the pockets for anything that would help establish the victim's identity.

The low background institutional hum and buzz of the hospital building seemed preternaturally loud, and the artificial lighting seemed to have acquired an almost invisible flicker. She was aware that her own lack of sleep was making her mind play funny tricks, jumping about and losing her train of thought. She'd have preferred to go home for a couple of hours' sleep, but the idea that somewhere this man might have a family or friends wondering why he hadn't come home and what had befallen him made the decision for her.

She'd brought a forensic suit with her from her car, having learned from prior experience that one of the night-duty mortuary attendants tended to be less than helpful. She pulled it on over her clothes and, with the uniform constable present to record her actions, unzipped the body bag. There would be ample opportunity to study the full extent of his injuries later at the post-mortem, so she tried not to look too closely at the head as she slid a gloved hand carefully into each of the jacket pockets, hoping to find a wallet or mobile phone. Yet something familiar drew her eyes to the face. Despite the matted hair and terrible black mash of bone and blood that had been his left eye socket, she recognized him. It was Peter Burnley.

19

Grace and Duncan sat together in an increasingly cold car out-side Lance's Lexden Park flat. It was seven in the morning and barely light. The trees that in the spring and summer gave a glossy richness to this part of Colchester now looked like bony fingers reaching out to a colourless sky, promising another dreary, dank January day. They were waiting either for a light to go on or for Lance to open the shutters on his living-room win-dows so they would know he was up and about. This was the worst death knock she'd ever had to do. Dreading it, she was glad Duncan had been available to share the task. It was essen-tial to have another member of the Major Investigation Team with her in case Lance suddenly and unexpectedly confessed to murdering his lover or later turned out to be a suspect, and Duncan was discreet, observant, thorough and, above all else, kind.

Grace had left the hospital telling herself she was going home for a quick shower and some strong coffee, but really it was to give herself time to prepare for this. Poor Lance, in that first flush of love; Lance, a very private man whose relationship with a murder victim would have to be disclosed and investigated, whose relationship made it necessary to exclude him as a suspect;

her friend Lance, whose heart she was about to break. She longed to get on with it, but held back, reluctant to barge in and rouse him from sleep merely to relieve her own need for action.

Lance would want to know everything that had happened to Peter, but there was little Grace was allowed to tell him until he had accounted for his own whereabouts last night. Only six or seven hours had passed since Peter's death and her team was still gathering evidence. Nothing that it was in her power to do would be overlooked, yet she was acutely aware how family and loved ones were nearly always left with unanswerable questions about what had taken place. Lance knew as well as she did that this could be the worst part of a murder case, yet knowing it would not protect him from the devastation of possibly never fully understanding why this had happened or – perhaps worse – from unsubstantiated hints of unsuspected lies or betrayals.

'He's up and about.' Duncan's voice interrupted her thoughts, and she looked over to see a line of artificial light appear above the tall wooden shutters.

'Give him time to get the kettle on,' she said.

They sat a few minutes more before Grace sighed and opened her door. Duncan followed her to the imposing entrance porch of what had once been a commodious Victorian family home. She pressed the bottom bell and, after a moment, heard Lance's voice on the intercom.

'It's Grace. Duncan's with me. May we come in?'

The front door buzzed open immediately, and she led the way across the hall to Lance's flat. He opened the door wearing an old-fashioned paisley-patterned dressing gown. His face showed alarm. 'What's the matter? What's going on?'

'I'm so sorry, Lance, but we have bad news. Can we come in?'

Lance stood back, and Grace waited for him to close the door and show them into his living room. It had a high ceiling with deep plaster mouldings, bare floorboards and a comfortable brown leather sofa and armchair. An old upright piano stood against one wall, and there was a homely scatter of books, magazines and a laptop on the floor beside the sofa.

'What's happened?' he asked. The slight tremor in his voice anticipated how his world was about to be divided by the sharp line of before and after her reply.

'It's Peter. He was found earlier this morning with serious head injuries and was taken to A & E.'

'But he's OK? I can go to him?'

'The ambulance got to him very quickly, and everything possible was done, but I'm afraid he was pronounced dead on arrival at the hospital.'

'Dead?'

'Yes. I'm so very sorry.'

'I don't understand. What happened? Some kind of accident? A car crash or something?'

'We're treating the death as suspicious.'

'Someone attacked him?'

'We'll know more in due course.' It was abundantly clear to Grace that Lance's shock was genuine, that he had nothing to do with Peter's death, but there was no room in a murder inquiry for personal loyalty or compassion. She was determined to do this absolutely by the book so there could be nothing for a slippery defence lawyer to catch them out on later, and could only hope that Lance would eventually appreciate her reasons for remaining professionally detached.

'What about next of kin?' she asked gently. 'Are his parents alive? Does he have siblings?'

'Yes, I think so. He never really talked about them.'

'Do you know where they live, where he grew up?'

Lance shrugged. 'London.'

'OK, don't worry. We'll track them down. Do you know where he was last night?'

'Out with clients.'

'You didn't go?'

'Why would I? It was work. Some boring financial management company.'

Grace licked her lips, psyching herself up. 'Where were you? I'm sorry, Lance, but you know I have to ask.'

'Sure,' he said without any bitterness. 'I was here.' He looked down in bewilderment at the previous evening's distractions on the floor beside the sofa. Only now did he sit, dropping down onto the leather seat as if all his strength had gone.

'Alone?'

'Yeah.'

Grace took the armchair so that she remained on a level with him. Duncan pulled out the piano stool and perched on that.

'Did you call anyone, speak to anyone?' she asked.

'Only Peter. He rang to say goodnight.'

'Did he say where he was?'

'Just leaving the restaurant, some country-house hotel in Dedham Vale.'

'Did he say where he was heading?'

'That he might go for a quick drink to wind down, then home.'

Feeling her release of tension, Grace recognized how scared she'd been that, if Peter had been at the late-night bar, he'd kept his visit a secret from Lance.

'Home here, to you?' she asked.

'No, his place. He said it was too late to disturb me. Oh God!' Lance rubbed his face, clearly realizing that the call he was describing had been his final contact with his lover.

Grace gave him a moment or two to recover sufficiently to continue. 'And after his call,' she asked. 'What did you do?'

'Watched the end of a film on my laptop, then went to bed.' He took a deep breath and let it out in a long, juddering sigh. 'You can check my browser history. And confirm what time I shut down the computer. That's all the alibi I have.'

'You realize we'll have to bag it?' Duncan spoke for the first time. 'We'll get it back to you as soon as we can. You do understand, don't you, mate? Trust me, we're going to dot the i's and cross the t's on this one. Do our best to get the bastard.'

Grace had no idea how many people at work knew or cared about Lance's sexuality, and she was touched by Duncan's heartfelt avowal of support.

Lance smiled wearily. 'Thanks. Do whatever you have to do.' He turned to Grace. 'I don't suppose they'll let me see him?'

'Not yet.' Grace was glad she didn't have to spell it out: Peter's body was evidence, and it was vital to avoid contamination.

'We're obviously going to have to exclude you from the investigation, but we also need to build up as full a picture of Peter as we can. Anything you can tell us will help.'

'Of course. I'll have a think. Later.'

'That's fine. But one question meanwhile. Had Peter mentioned any recent problems or threats of any kind? Anything he'd been concerned about?'

'Nothing. Life was fine. He was happy. We were happy.'

'Can I get you something, mate?' asked Duncan. 'Tea, coffee?'

Lance shook his head, the confusion of grief beginning to take hold. 'No, thanks. I can manage. I think I'd like to be on my own now, if you don't mind.'

'Are you sure there's nothing we can do?' asked Grace. 'Is there anyone you'd like me to call?'

'No, really.' He looked at her beseechingly. 'And there's nothing more you can tell me? Nothing at all?'

'Not at the moment. I'm so sorry, Lance. Peter was such a lovely man. A really, really lovely man.'

Grace looked at Lance in his old-fashioned dressing gown, hunched forward on the sofa, elbows on knees and head in hands. It had been a long time since she had felt quite so helpless.

20

Robyn found Leonard waiting outside school on Friday afternoon to give her a lift home, as he had promised. The high roof of the muddy Land Rover was easy to spot even among the other parents' glossy SUVs, and she climbed up into the passenger seat with relief: never had the clattering bang required to close the door sounded more welcome. It had been a long, exhausting week, and tough enough to struggle with the weirdness and hysteria surrounding Angie's death without post-Christmas torpor and the threat of impending exams. She really needed the escape offered by the weekend.

'OK?' asked Leonard once he had manoeuvred the rugged vehicle safely through the school-gate traffic.

'Yes,' she said. 'Exams start on Monday. No one will have time any more to write sad poems or huddle in corners and cry.'

He glanced across at her. 'Didn't know you were such a cynic.'

'I'm not. But Angie would've hated all that. And it's the people who barely knew her making the loudest fuss.'

'Fair enough.'

They drove in companionable silence through the outskirts of Colchester. It took a while to clear the suburbs, but finally they were on the familiar B road with fields and trees on either side. It was not until Robyn glimpsed the distant blue glitter of the reservoir that the tension of the school day slipped away and she could feel her shoulders relax. The sun was low in a clear sky, and it would be starry and cold again tonight. She leaned back into the seat, watching out of the passenger window for the occasional opening of the view across to Mersea Island and the surrounding wetlands. That was her landscape, her world, her place of refuge.

But as the suffocating pressure of school released, another anxiety took its place. This was a new undercurrent that she'd tried and increasingly failed to banish from her thoughts. It had to do with the overweight balding man in the badly-fitting suit who'd come to talk to her dad the day after Boxing Day. At the funeral her mum had said he was a detective, but that hadn't been what Leonard had told her, and she had lain awake that night trying to work out why something so trivial bothered her so much in the midst of possibly the worst thing that had happened in her life. She had decided that maybe that was precisely it: the mind seizing upon the least significant detail to chew away at as a way of protecting itself from something too big to comprehend. But then why had it risen to the surface again now, right when she could leave the cares of Angie's funeral and the school week behind her?

She shifted in her seat to glance at her dad. His eyes were on the road, his hands relaxed on the steering wheel. He knew this road backwards, could probably negotiate every twist and turn with his eyes shut. She wondered what he was thinking about and with a jolt realized suddenly that she couldn't ever recall asking herself that before. Leonard had always been so pragmatic, such a steadying influence, that she'd never had reason to speculate about his inner life. But he must have one:

everybody did. What did grown-ups think about? Her parents got on well. Robyn wasn't aware of any pressing business or financial or practical issues. He always seemed to be occupied with something or other in a calm, contented sort of way. She'd always assumed that he was thinking about what he was doing or was about to do next.

It might be due to the grief and stress of the past two weeks, but the notion that she had no clue to her dad's inner existence was frightening, as if a chasm of uncertain depth had opened at her feet right when she already felt herself on slippery ground. And all because of a pointless discrepancy between what he and her mum had each said to her about DC Duncan Gregg! She wasn't even sure that it was a discrepancy, for both had mentioned the wildfowling club. But why had Leonard not simply said, when she'd asked, that the visitor was from the police? She had already worked out the answer: because he didn't want to upset her any more than necessary about Angie.

The Land Rover looped down the gentle hill towards the bridge spanning a narrow point of the reservoir and bumped across the giant concrete-aggregate slabs that made up the roadway. Several birdwatchers with binoculars leaned against the fencing on the nearside of the road, looking up the main body of water, stubbornly staying put until it was too dark to see. The setting sun reflected back off every ripple and wavelet, making the water almost too bright to look at. A swan was making its final effort to rise into the air, madly beating its wings and kicking its webbed feet against the water until it won free and rose magnificently into flight, its wings steadying almost immediately to a more lyrical rhythm. No doubt the birdwatchers were interested in rarer species, but no matter how many times she watched a swan take wing, the sight never failed to impress her. She turned to look at Leonard, who must have seen it too, for he smiled at her.

'The guy who came to see you last week,' she said impetuously. 'Who was he?'

'Which guy?'

It was true there must have been several visitors over the past week while she was at school, yet a nagging suspicion whispered that her father knew exactly whom she meant. 'He was at the funeral too,' she said. 'Mum said he was a detective.'

'Oh yes.' Leonard sounded unconcerned. Robyn allowed herself to be reassured: maybe the omission, or obfuscation, or whatever it was, was unimportant.

'Why didn't you tell me he was from the police?'

'Dunno. Can't remember. Didn't want to worry you, probably.'

'Why would I be worried?'

'Well, because of Angie. You were already upset. I didn't want you thinking about it more than you had to.'

'Why did he come to see you?'

'The police were talking to quite a few registered gun dealers. You know, had we heard anything? Did we know the gunman or have any idea where he might've got the rifle? That sort of thing.'

'Did you?'

'What?' Leonard laughed at the question.

'Did you know the gunman?'

'Of course not.' Leonard checked his mirror and pulled the Land Rover onto the grass verge and stopped. He switched off the engine then turned to face her. 'What's up, Birdie? This isn't like you.'

She looked into his face, into his familiar, friendly, loving eyes, muddy green with tan-coloured flecks, and saw something she'd never seen before, a flash of something calculating and misleading as if there were another person hidden behind them. The sudden wave of vertigo that swept over her made no sense – her parents' accounts of the police visit seemed both innocuous and entirely plausible – but it wasn't about facts, it was something that struck far deeper than that.

She reminded herself that she already knew he could be an actor when he needed to be. When she'd been out beating on a big shoot day with wealthy clients she'd seen how he'd act the part of the *Downton Abbey* family retainer. It was part of the job – to flatter men who expected to be flattered – but what if the secret element to that performance also gave him a kind of edge? What if knowing it was all an act, one they happily accepted at face value, stopped him feeling inferior about being in the service of these more powerful men? If that were true, then what other secrets lay behind the friendly and familiar mask?

Robyn had no idea why, but at that moment she knew – just *knew* – that a certain kind of lying came naturally to him, that, far from being awkward or embarrassed about it, he did it fluently and without a second thought, that he did it all the time.

A car drove past them, rattling the loose-fitting windows of the Land Rover. Time seemed to stop. Her world went backwards. She felt sick.

'I think maybe I picked up a bug at school,' she answered. 'Can we just go home?'

21

Dr Samit Tripathi, the Home Office forensic pathologist, regarded Grace sympathetically over his rimless glasses, yet she still felt as if she were making excuses for herself as she explained why her team had not managed to locate Peter Burnley's next of kin or medical records in time for the prearranged Monday morning autopsy.

Peter's passport, found in his flat, established his identity, and other ID in his possession confirmed what Lance already knew, that he was a consultant employed by a financial services company in London named Buckingham Gate Associates. Buckingham Gate had a stylish website with photos and potted biographies of its principals, but the shocked and helpful woman to whom Grace had spoken on Friday had been unable at that point to provide any further useful information. She had promised to email a copy of Peter's CV, but Grace had not yet received it. Peter had given his employers as his referee for the rented flat in Colchester, and his phone and car – the silver Audi found in the yard where he was killed – were both registered to Buckingham Gate. Neither his phone nor laptop revealed any contact details or recent communications with family or, it would seem, any non-professional friends other than Lance.

Grace wondered if perhaps Peter's sexuality had encouraged him to be hyper-discreet, just as Lance himself was at work – so much so that, until Lance told her, she hadn't previously guessed that he was gay, although of course it had then made complete sense. Even in this day and age, might that explain why Peter had apparently not been in touch with family or old friends? It was unusual for a life to be quite so tidy, and experience had taught her that extreme discretion all too often turned out to conceal the kind of secrets that were potential motives for murder.

Still, maybe Peter was someone who simply preferred a tidy life. Her instincts about the man with whom she'd eaten lunch and played Scrabble on Christmas Day rang no alarm bells at all: she'd liked him, pure and simple. She couldn't recall any moment when he'd appeared evasive or opaque, and the warmth of his affection for Lance had seemed entirely genuine. She hoped poor Lance wasn't about to have his grieving heart crushed by whatever secrets the investigation might bring to light.

'The body is that of an adult male, of slim build, height five foot eleven. He has been identified to me as Peter Burnley, thirty-four.' Dr Tripathi began his post-mortem examination just as Colin slipped into the viewing gallery beside her. Grace was surprised to see her boss: he hadn't mentioned that he would attend, and the presence of a detective superintendent wouldn't normally be deemed necessary. She assumed he was here as a courtesy to Lance and, even if this were merely to do with appearances, she was grateful for his sake.

As Samit ran through the circumstances of how and where the body had been found, and catalogued all the marks and injuries, old and new, Grace tried not to think too hard about the careful dissection and evisceration that was to follow, and to view the naked body on the stainless-steel mortuary table not as a previously warm and vivid human being but as physical evidence. Listening carefully as Samit described each of his findings, she focused on the specifics that would influence her investigation: no defensive wounds, no skin or other tissue under the fingernails, bruising to the backs of both knees and multiple blunt-force injuries to the head, the first blow to the head probably administered from behind as he went down following the strike to the legs, and three further blows inflicted while he was on the ground; the attack was likely to have happened where the body was found; the weapon had been smooth and rounded, possibly something like a police baton.

The gory remainder of the autopsy, apart from the detailed examination of the skull and brain, did not add anything of significance, and Grace was relieved to be able to walk about and stretch her limbs once Samit had concluded his work and recorded the time. Leaving the pathologist to strip off his gloves and protective clothing and then go to get changed, Grace and Colin went downstairs to wait in his office.

'Next of kin have been located,' Colin told her quietly.

'Oh good. Did that come from Buckingham Gate?'

'In a manner of speaking.' He paused, a slight smile revealing an odd frisson of excitement. 'We're to step back on this one. Do what we're requested and no more.'

Grace frowned. 'I don't understand. It's early days. There's still every chance that a witness will come forward, or that we'll find new evidence to point to the identity of the perpetrator.'

'Maybe,' said Colin. 'But the Essex coroner has agreed to transfer the case to London.'

'But why? That hardly ever happens.'

'It does when there are special circumstances,' said Colin. 'There are other agencies involved. They'll take over the inquiry.'

'What's going on?'

'Peter Burnley was working undercover. But not a word of this to Lance,' he warned. 'Or to anyone. Just you and me. And Hilary, obviously.'

Grace shook her head at why it had to be 'obvious' that the communications director should be informed when a team of experienced detectives couldn't be trusted. Not that she cared about whose turf this was; for her the only priority was to catch the person who had beaten to death the considerate man who at Christmas had left an immaculate house for her to come home to after a long and traumatic day. But that thought gave her pause: who was the real Peter Burnley? Was that even his name?

'So how much can you tell me?' she asked. 'What was he up to? What was he investigating?'

Colin shook his head, clearly enjoying the secrecy. 'There's nothing I can say. Only that the spooks will take it from here.'

Grace suspected that Colin himself had been told nothing more, but she didn't push it: if he liked the supposed glamour, let him have it. 'But what was Peter, or whoever he was, doing in Colchester?' she asked. 'Apart from the garrison, what on earth is there here to spy on?'

'No idea,' said Colin. 'I genuinely don't know. But it was impressed upon me that absolute discretion is required. The family will not be identified.'

'So Burnley wasn't his name?'

'I assume not. As soon as the coroner releases the body, it will go to them. Up to you what story you choose to tell Lance. You know him better than me. But it had better be a good one. It's got to stick.'

Samit, now dressed in chinos and a fleece jacket, came to join them in the office, preventing Grace from asking Colin any further questions.

'It all looks pretty straightforward,' he said. 'I'll be giving cause of death as skull fracture and laceration of the brain consistent with blunt-force impacts to the head.'

'Great, thanks. If you can send me a copy of your report as soon as it's ready?'

'Of course.'

Grace was suddenly pleased that she had witnessed the postmortem and seen for herself that Samit's matter-of-factness was entirely genuine. For him this was a run-of-the-mill case with no mysteries or unexpected complications. Precisely why a man calling himself Peter Burnley had been murdered in a yard off a side street in rainy Colchester at one in the morning was not a question the pathologist was required to answer. Now it would seem that Grace would not be permitted to answer it either. Except that she owed it to Lance to do everything she bloody well could.

22

This had been billed as the Old Bailey trial with a story to die for – a woman accused of murdering her husband by way of a poisoned microwave curry. Rumour had it she'd also done away with two previous partners in a similar manner. But today the lawyers – all on whacking great fees – had spent hours arguing over some tedious legal point. No wonder the judge looked fit to nod off; Ivo was close to narcolepsy himself. And it wasn't even as if the dowdy middle-aged woman in the dock was your archetypal black widow. In fact she looked almost as bored as he was. Ivo had a horrible feeling that, through sheer tedium, the defence counsel would at any moment bludgeon the prosecution into abandoning the case. Unless Ivo chose to fritter away his newspaper's resources on the queen of the ready meal's personal story – not a very beguiling option, in his view – an acquittal would leave him with no fucking story and a completely wasted two days.

It had been his editor's idea for him to attend the trial. Not that he minded the odd few days hanging around the Central Criminal Court. Back in the day the basement press room had always been as useful as El Vino's for picking up gossip, and this week had been no exception. Besides, the atmosphere at one of the more notorious murder trials could often be as buzzy and testosterone-charged as finals day at Twickenham. Not that the outcome was generally much in question, but the spectacle of wide-awake judges, strutting QCs, eager solicitors and the parade of expert witnesses was like being backstage at a Tudor joust, all the highly paid nabobs there to perform for one another. To be fair, it wasn't much different down in the press room, waiting to see who'd win the sweepstake on how long the jury would be out and, in the good old days, racing for a landline to dictate the story to the copy-takers back at the ranch. A good trial raised everyone's game.

But the trial of this mousy widow was not one of them. Which was probably how she'd got away with it more than once. It was Friday afternoon, and Ivo was tempted to leave, but he had a sense that, where his editor was concerned, he ought to mind his P's and Q's for a while yet. He didn't blame the man. He'd been leaned on from above, that was plain enough; and not only his editor either but the newspaper's lawyers too. What Ivo wasn't sure about, and would give a lot to learn, was how the Police Federation had been informed that he'd been sniffing around Dunholt trying to flesh out Martin Leyburn's portrait of PC Mark Kirkby, fallen hero, thug and controlling bastard.

Truth was, it had probably been Ivo's own blundering that had tipped them off. Once DI Fisher had explained about the drink-drive arrest that had provoked Russell Fewell to complain to Martin Leyburn about how he'd been fitted up, it hadn't been difficult to put together enough of the rest of the story and to believe that Mark Kirkby – along with his chum Curtis Mullins – could add 'corrupt cop' to his list of honorary titles.

However, if the pressure on his editor had come from the Police Federation, their efforts to silence Ivo had achieved the contrary effect, and he'd been keeping his nose stubbornly to the ground for any titbits of information on what had become of young Davey and his family since the New Year. After a cleverly managed midnight flit from the town, Donna Fewell appeared to have gone totally off the radar, at least until yesterday, when Ivo had been rewarded by some idle chat in the Old Bailey press room. One of the agency guys had heard from a stringer that Mark Kirkby's father, himself a retired copper, had fixed it through the Police Federation for Donna Fewell and her kids to move into one of the numerous picturesque holiday homes owned and maintained by various local Federation branches, though it wasn't known exactly where.

Ivo had got onto that straight away and, after calling in a couple of favours he'd been keeping in his back pocket for a rainy day, discovered that Donna, Davey and Ella presently occupied an apartment in a new luxury development in Weymouth, where Davey, under a new name, was now attending the local primary school. According to the Federation website, the apartment (heavily discounted for the benefit of members and entirely free to any officer in need of a welfare break) had stunning views and was fitted with every conceivable amenity, from a widescreen TV with surround sound to an American-style fridge-freezer.

Not that Ivo begrudged Davey and his family a bit of comfort and security – God knows, back in his drinking days he'd been more than happy to get bladdered at the Federation's expense when the opportunity presented itself – but he couldn't help wondering if John Kirkby had really gone to such trouble for the family of his son's murderer purely out of the goodness of his heart. Call him a cynic, but Ivo would rather put his money on Kirkby senior having both a guilty conscience and something to hide. And he wouldn't object to finding out exactly what that was.

If Ivo had been desperate for a story, then Donna Fewell and her grieving kids could easily qualify as THE MOST HATED FAMILY IN BRITAIN, at least for a day or so. The great tabloid-reading public loved nothing better than to point the finger and create enough distance to disengage themselves from a reality that veered uncomfortably close to home. Easier to demonize and tie enough garlic around the door to keep the devil at bay. Ivo had always reckoned he usefully combined the roles of witchfinder general, exorcist and whatever the job title was of the guy who supervised the village stocks. He probably ought to be doorstepping Donna and her kids right now except they were on Police Federation property and he didn't much fancy stirring up a hornets' nest, not given the many and glorious ways in which his life would subsequently be made difficult.

Besides, if he were honest, uppermost in his reluctance to approach the luxury development was the thought of ten-year-old Davey, not only starting out at a strange school in an unfamiliar town, having to remember his new name and strictly forbidden to mention his father, but also having to be grateful to John Kirkby for his worldly blessings. That last thing rankled somewhere deep inside him.

It wasn't that Ivo's own father had been a bully, merely introverted and unimaginative, but Ivo had been at boarding school with enough little boys who'd been terrorized at home and, as soon as the trunks were unpacked, had become bullies in turn.

He had little doubt that Mark Kirkby had learned his winning ways at his father's knee, and the idea of Kirkby senior now playing a benevolent Scrooge to Davey's oblivious Tiny Tim made Ivo's guts squirm. The kid had quite enough suffering to face from his real dad's heinous legacy; he didn't need Kirkby moulding and deforming him like the biblical vessel marred in the hands of the potter.

Ivo hardly saw himself as the guardian angel type, yet he was sorely tempted to get himself down to the Dorset seaside and keep a weather eye on young Davey, if only for the hell of it. And if this poisoning trial didn't perk up and there was no other mayhem to distract him this week, maybe that's what he'd do.

23

Grace kept half an eye on the main office door all the time Duncan was talking to her. Although Lance had been given compassionate leave, he had called yesterday evening to insist he'd rather come back to work, and she was dreading the moment when she would have to lie to him.

'The range warden guy at STANTA was as helpful as could be,' Duncan was telling her. 'Probably because that's the only way he's going to hang on to his job now he's been caught skimming off the shell casings. But he couldn't provide any leads. Or, rather, too many. Most people's licences only allow them two hundred and fifty rifle rounds at a time, so the guy had a lot of customers to whom he sold small bags of brass casings every so often. He either had no idea who they were – just people in the local pub – or they were regulars, members of local Thetford Forest clubs or licensed gun dealers like Leonard Ingold – the guy that put us on to him in the first place. And they all check out.'

'No local villains, no names you recognize?' asked Grace.

Duncan shook his head. 'Nope. Short of gathering up as many rifle rounds from as many different sources as possible and sending them all off to ballistics, it's a dead end.'

'I bet the SIO tasked with matching Cinderella to the glass slipper never had to worry about how much it cost,' said Grace.

'No.' Duncan smiled. 'And even if we got a lead on our man's workshop, it's unlikely to be enough to get a search warrant, which we'd need if we want to examine his repriming tool for whether it leaves the telltale marks.'

'Well, thanks anyway. Let's leave the file open, and keep putting the word out for information.'

'Will do.'

Duncan had already turned to go when she called him back. 'Just a thought, but I wonder if the Christmas Day massacre wasn't enough to shock your honest, decent armed robber into sharing a bit of intel? What do you think? Worth chatting to the post-sentencing interviews officer to see if anyone might tell us where they'd go to buy unregistered ammo?'

Duncan looked dubious. 'Happy to give it a whirl, boss. But if he's smart, our man will be using a firewall of fixers and couriers and middlemen. The end user may genuinely have no idea where the gear comes from.'

Grace sighed. 'Quite right. But have a word all the same, will you? We might get lucky.'

Duncan nodded. 'I'll also check with the Met, see what they're doing their end.'

'Good. Thanks, Duncan.' She watched him return to his desk, stopping beside Lance, who must have slipped in without her noticing, to place a friendly hand on his shoulder. She watched as Lance looked up at the older man and gave a ghost of a smile; his face was pale and his brown eyes sad and hopeless. How was she going to look into those eyes and not tell him the truth?

Not wanting to ambush Lance in the open-plan office, she waited for him to come to the relative privacy of her cubicle, which he soon did.

'How are you?' she asked. 'You know you don't have to be here if you don't want to.'

He shrugged as if he didn't care either way. 'Any news?'

'You understand that I can't yet share any operational details with you. I'm so sorry, Lance, but my hands are tied. But there is one thing you need to know.' She knew she was rushing, gabbling, exposing her nervousness at wanting to get this over and done with before she weakened. She took a breath and tried to slow down. 'Sit down, please.'

Lance sat, his shoulders bent, his hands between his knees but his eyes fixed on hers.

She took another deep breath. 'His employers at Buckingham Gate Associates have contacted Peter's family.' She paused – even his name was possibly a lie – but the rest still had to be said. 'His body will eventually be released to them. They want a private funeral and have said that they do not wish any details to be made public. At least for the moment.' Those last words were wishful thinking, but she had to throw Lance some morsel of consolation.

He stared at her, and she couldn't divine whether his utter dismay was incomprehension, anger or desolation. He sighed and seemed to deflate physically in front of her. 'You keep thinking that people have stopped being like that, you know?'

Grace fought back the longing to assure him that the door closed in his face had nothing to do with the denial and distaste that accompanied prejudice and ignorance, but she had no choice but to let him think that. 'I'm so sorry, Lance. If there's anything I can do.'

'If I write a letter, will Buckingham Gate forward it?'

'Yes, I'm sure they will. I honestly don't know if you'll get a response, but I promise to make sure that it reaches Peter's family.'

Lance placed a steadying hand on each knee and pushed himself to his feet. 'And cause of death?' he asked, looking at the floor.

'Blunt-force trauma to the head.' Grace no longer cared whether protocol ruled that she shouldn't divulge this information. 'He would have died almost instantaneously. Probably literally never knew what hit him,' she said, echoing the tired young medic in A & E.

Lance sat back down slowly, his head in his hands. Grace got up from behind her desk and went to kneel beside him, putting her arms around him as best she could. 'Go home, Lance,' she whispered. 'Or take my keys and go to my house, if that's any better for you. I can make up the bed in the spare room. Stay as long as you like. I'm here. I'll do whatever I can to help you get through this. You're not alone.'

He pulled back from her, briefly pressed her arm and then let go in order to drag a cotton handkerchief out of his trouser pocket. He wiped his face. 'I'll go home,' he said. 'I'll call you later.'

'Shall I get someone to drive you?'

'No, I'll be all right.'

Powerless, she had to watch him go. In those few moments she became aware of the bowed heads and careful hush around him, and was glad for his sake that the reaction to his lover's death had been not gossip but respectful sympathy.

As soon as Colin returned to the MIT office, she knocked on his door. 'I've sent Lance home,' she said. 'I told him the family want no contact.'

'How did he take it?'

'I imagine he thinks they're homophobic.'

'That may be all to the good,' said Colin. 'The less mystery he suspects the better.'

Grace wasn't sure which she hated him for the most – his heartless pragmatism or his detestable complacency.

'So where are we up to with the investigation, such as it is?' he asked, clearly oblivious to her thoughts.

'The clients who took Peter Burnley to dinner are from the local office of a big wealth-management company called Oakmoor. They were networking in the hope he'd bring in new clients, new business. They said he'd been perfectly relaxed and the evening was uneventful. I wasn't able to access his mobile phone records because they've been blocked, but Lance's phone shows that Peter Burnley called around the time the clients say they all left the hotel. He and Lance spoke for three or four minutes. Lance's computer also checks out. Unless he was in two places at once or had an accomplice, he was at home watching the end of a film around the time of the killing.'

'What about the bar in Colchester?' asked Colin.

'Nothing,' said Grace, well aware that the more time passed, the less people would remember noticing anything or feel moved to come forward with new information. 'However, we have got a more precise timeline from a couple of guys who remembered chatting to him in the bar. He had one beer and said he was off home to bed. None of the customers that night has any relevant previous or gives cause for concern. No one remembers seeing him leave the bar, and, apart from a camera that picked up his car en route from the Dedham Vale hotel, we've nothing else so far on CCTV. Nothing at all to show how the offender arrived at or left the scene. And there are no obvious links to similar crimes.'

'Fine,' said Colin. 'You've been very thorough. We can file it as a Category B homicide, and no doubt our friends will be relieved to write it off as an attempted mugging gone wrong.'

Grace suppressed a fresh wave of hatred. 'So what do they think *did* happen?' she asked sharply. 'Do they have a hand in the lack of evidence?'

'I doubt we're going to be taken into their confidence,' said Colin. 'Chalk it up as one less thing for us to worry about. I assume you have plenty of other work to get on with?'

Grace, appalled, looked at him in amazement. Was that even a glimmer of amusement in his eyes?

'Come on, Grace,' he chided. 'Lance will get over it. They'd not been together all that long.'

'Long enough.'

'Well, I'm sorry. But it's not like we're agreeing to some dreadful cover-up. This really does look like a mugging gone wrong, and, for all we know, that's all it was. Just bad luck. The wrong place at the wrong time.'

Grace could feel the phone in the pocket of her suit jacket vibrating and pulled it out to look at the screen. 'Sorry, sir, I have to take this.'

Colin waved her away, and she was careful to shut his office door behind her before she took the call. 'Lance?'

'I've just got home,' he said. 'Can you come over? Something's not right. I think someone's been in here while I was out this morning.'

24

Grace had been tempted to take Duncan with her: he had a good eye for detail and, given that Lance himself seemed uncertain on the phone whether anything was actually missing, it would be helpful to have a second opinion. But it was cowardly to use someone else as a shield. She had to go alone.

Lance buzzed open the outer door and stood waiting inside his flat. His skin was clammy and his eyes had a febrile brightness. 'Someone's been in here,' he said without any greeting. 'I just know it.'

'Do you think you've been burgled?' asked Grace.

'Not that I can see. But, you know, I sensed the air was different the moment I walked in. Then I noticed a drawer that always sticks was properly closed, and I got the jitters. So I took a proper look around. The stuff on my desk isn't the way I left it. It looks arranged. And my kayak's been moved, no question. Come and see. There are marks on the carpet that shouldn't be there.'

He led the way quickly into a small room that Grace hadn't really taken note of before. There was a chair and a small desk with a metal cabinet beside it and bookshelves above, but most of the space was taken up with a red kayak, paddle, life jacket and helmet.

'I didn't know you were into kayaking,' she said.

'It's how Peter and I met,' he said tersely, already squatting down to point out a dusty ridge on the carpet. 'Look. I haven't moved the kayak since September. My cleaner just vacuums around it, and anyway she hasn't been here since last week. You can see here where it's been shifted. Someone's moved it. Someone's been in here.'

Standing in the doorway, Grace had a mental image of someone from MI5 or Special Branch or even a police anti-corruption unit, for all she knew, moving furtively around Lance's home. She sympathized fully with the panic that had crept into his voice. What should she do? Encourage him to ask questions, to ferret out the truth for himself? Or divert him?

'But there's nothing missing?' she asked. 'Nothing obvious, anyway?'

'No. But then I don't know what they were after, what they wanted.'

'Did you put the alarm on when you left?'

'Yes. I mean, I must have. I'm pretty sure I turned it off with the fob when I came home. You know what it's like. You do these things on automatic pilot. I don't consciously remember.'

'You are still in shock,' she said gently, hating herself for such blatant gaslighting. 'You're sure you're not just being hypersensitive, aware of things you normally wouldn't notice?'

'My cleaner comes every Wednesday,' he insisted. 'That kayak has been moved since then. And not by me.'

'Who else has keys? And an alarm fob?'

Lance shook his head as if trying to clear his thoughts. 'Only my cleaner,' he said. 'And Peter, of course.' He dropped down onto the desk chair.

Grace's heart sank. 'But Peter's keys are safely bagged up with the rest of his things.' She tried to inject as much dismissive authority into the statement as she could while a scenario unfolded in her head in which the organization Peter had worked for had access to all his belongings and so its people would have no trouble letting themselves in and out of Lance's flat. They must also have been monitoring Lance's movements, to know when the flat was unoccupied. She felt repulsed by the notion of one service spying on another when they were all supposed to be on the same side.

She realized that Lance was staring at her as if she'd suddenly turned into an alien. 'How about a cup of tea or something?' she said, turning away to head for the kitchen.

She already had the kettle on and had found two mugs in a cupboard before he joined her, though he remained standing by the doorway. 'Who did the post-mortem?' he asked.

'Samit,' she answered, surprised by the question. 'Why?'

'You are telling me the truth?'

'About Peter's death?' she asked, relieved that she could find one bit of safe ground. 'Yes, of course. And no one's more straightforward and independent than Samit Tripathi.'

Lance licked his dry lips and nodded, looking at the floor rather than at her. 'OK.'

The kettle came to the boil and switched itself off, but she ignored it and went over to him, taking hold of his arms. 'If you want to report this as a burglary, you go ahead. I can make sure it's prioritized. Maybe your alarm box has some electronic record of being turned on and off. If you want to get to the bottom of this, we will.'

Lance took a deep breath and raised his eyes to her. 'No, it's fine. I must've just spooked myself.'

'Are you sure? Really sure? If you want it followed through, it's not a problem.'

'No,' he said decisively. 'I don't even know what day it is, let alone whether I shut a drawer properly. I'm sorry I dragged you over here.'

Grace fought the impulse to tell him he was right, to apologize and beg his forgiveness for encouraging him to distrust his own instincts. Lance was the closest friend she'd made here in Essex, and it was dreadful to look him straight in the face and not tell him what she knew. And yet she had to assume that unknown officers in a parallel service had good reason to do what they were doing. Surely it would be unforgivably stupid to stumble blindly into someone else's operation without any idea of what she was meddling with? After all, she knew nothing about Peter beyond that he wasn't who he'd claimed to be. And that alone might devastate Lance. Even if she told him what little she knew, was that really going to help him get over his shock when they had no way of finding out the rest?

'Have you got time to stay?' Lance's query broke into her thoughts.

'Yes, of course.' She was damned if she'd compound her bad faith by abandoning him because right now leaving seemed a much easier option. She let Lance make some coffee and followed him through to the sitting room.

'Have you got your laptop back yet?' she asked, now feeling guilty that she'd never thought about how he'd have to manage without it right when he probably needed it most.

'Yes, thanks. Duncan had it sent over.'

'Good. That was kind.'

'Yes.' He sipped his drink thoughtfully. 'He mentioned that I could go away. That he could sort somewhere for me to stay, a welfare break, through the Federation.'

'Would that help?' Grace despised her reactive sting of relief. 'Do you have someone to go with?'

Lance shook his head. 'My sister offered, but maybe I'd be less lonely on my own, somewhere where there are no associations with anything. And it's not as if I've got funeral plans to keep me busy.'

'We could hold a private service, a memorial, if that would help?'

'No. Thanks. Or later, maybe. I'm just so *hurt*, you know? I can't get my head around what's happened. All I want to do is run away.'

'I know it's not the same, but I felt like that when my dad died. But you can't outrun it. Not in the end.'

'I know. But how else am I to get through the next days and weeks?'

'Then go,' said Grace. 'Let Duncan get it all organized for you. You can always come back if it's not right.'

'I'm not leaving you in the lurch at work?'

'Lance, please, do whatever's best for you. That's all I care about.'

'Thanks, Grace.' He leaned across the brown leather sofa and kissed her cheek. 'Sorry, but do you mind if I ask you to go now?'

In her car driving back to the office Grace felt worthless and ashamed. She had no idea whether she'd done the right thing in lying to Lance – and she wasn't going to attempt to dress it up: her deliberate withholding of the truth *was* a lie. She tried to comfort herself with the notion that she could tell him later, when he was less raw, less volatile and could begin to handle the notion that even the truth was a dead end. He'd despise her later for having lied to him today, but that was her problem.

She parked behind police HQ and got out of her car into the chill January air feeling that she was accomplishing nothing and letting everybody down.

25

Robyn couldn't quite acknowledge to herself why she had 'forgotten' to mention to either of her parents that she had a half-day at school and would be coming home unexpectedly early. Once the idea had entered her head that her father was capable of lying to her, she had watched him carefully. She wasn't even sure what she thought he might be lying about. That wasn't what really mattered. And anyway the only actual lie she knew for certain he had told her was small and insignificant, told only for her sake, to spare her feelings. Everybody told that kind of lie. It meant nothing.

What was frightening and had gnawed away at her all the time she'd been busy memorizing her chemistry and biology was the ease and fluency with which he'd done it, his relaxed smile and clear gaze. For him to be so convincing a liar that no thought of possible duplicity had ever previously entered her head meant that she could no longer take a single word he said at face value. Everything he'd ever said to her could be a lie. He could be a lie. Or she could be totally wrong, blowing something trivial up out of all proportion because she was in a state about Angie and exams and leaving home for the first time in the autumn.

It wasn't that she wanted to think such thoughts about him. She hated it, hated herself. But now that the idea had taken root, she couldn't seem to find a way to kill it, to prove to herself that she was wrong.

Robyn told Sally's mother she was happy to be dropped at the end of the track, and she waved goodbye to them before shouldering her school rucksack and setting off down the gentle slope towards home. Along the road, even in a four-by-four, the high hedges shut off the view of the spreading water, and only after turning onto the track did the view open up. Seeing it now, she felt she could breathe again and hoped perhaps her dark thoughts would simply blow away in the clean, sharp wind. But she was not to have the view to herself today: a familiar green van was slowly approaching, and she could soon make out her favourite driver at the wheel.

She stood waiting on the verge for Kenny's van to come past. He stopped, wound down his window and greeted her with a smile.

'Packed it in for the day?' he asked.

'Yes. It's exam week.'

'Ah well, I was never too hot at exams. But then look at me now!' He banged the flat of his hand against the metal door, laughing at his own joke.

Kenny's customary friendliness cheered her. She realized she knew nothing about him despite the fact that he had been picking up and dropping off for her dad for almost as long as she could remember. She felt impelled to ask him something, it didn't really matter what. 'Where are you off to now?' she asked. 'Long drive?'

'Nah, not really,' he said. 'And at least there's no more snow.'

He put the van into gear. 'Don't work too hard!' He waved out of his window as the van trundled carefully on up the track.

Kenny often grumbled about the state of the track, although he knew as well as she did that Leonard chose not to improve the surface because the ruts and bumps helped deter any intruders tempted to try breaking into the secure workshop. As she set off again, she had a fleeting insight into how an outsider might view her home: it had never before occurred to her that there might be anything odd about its isolation or its need for discipline and discretion.

She rounded the last curve of the track, heard the distant plaintive cry of a curlew and saw Leonard coming out of the workshop. He locked the door behind him as he always did and set off across the garden to the path that led to the sea wall. In each hand he carried one of the large sturdy canvas carriers from the farm shop; whatever they contained, both bags bulged oddly and looked pretty weighty. Intent on his destination, he didn't look round, and although she could easily have attracted his attention Robyn didn't call out to him.

Nicola's car was gone, and the back door to the house was locked, so she must be out somewhere. Robyn let herself in and was greeted ecstatically by the two dogs, which had as usual been shut in the boot room. As she went to the kitchen sink to run herself a glass of water, she watched her father's figure heading away towards the bright blue water. The kitchen was orderly: the plants on the windowsill had been watered, the frayed red and white checked tea towels hung from the rail of the Aga. Everything was normal. Nothing was different or out of place. And yet she knew that everything was wrong.

Her dad returned less than an hour later. If he was surprised to find her with her feet up in the lounge watching daytime television, he didn't show it. Nor did he offer to explain where he'd been.

'You turning into a student already?' He pushed her legs aside so he could sit beside her on the couch. 'What is it, *Countdown*?'

'No, some stupid film. American heroines with big hair and shoulder pads.'

'How did the chemistry exam go?'

She was touched that he remembered. It was always Leonard rather than Nicola who kept abreast of what she was doing at school.

'Not great, actually.' She sighed. 'I can't seem to concentrate properly.'

'Well, it's only the mocks this time. But you've got to stay on course for the grades you need.'

'I know. Please. I don't need a pep talk.'

'Fair enough. Look, what do you say to a bit of a break during the Easter holidays? Just a few days, but proper time off before the real exams?' He ruffled her hair as he used to do when she was a kid. 'Rest those brains of yours.'

'Maybe.'

'Shall I see if Jerry can let us have the Vale do Lobo villa again? You loved it there. Sunlounger by the pool, walks on the beach. What do you say?'

'It'd be lovely,' she said doubtfully. 'But I could only spare a few days away from revision. Wouldn't it be too expensive just for a few days?'

'Don't you worry about that. Jerry gives us mate's rates.

Besides, I bet, once you're a student, you won't want to holiday with us at all. So let's make the most of it. Yes?'

'Yes. Thanks!'

He patted her knee and rose to his feet. 'I'll talk to your mum and get it sorted.'

He left the room, but then immediately came back. 'I've been having a tidy-up. Want to have a look?'

Robyn was taken aback. It was taken for granted that she never entered his workshop, except occasionally as far as the reception area or office in order to call him for supper. Recovering from her surprise, she was struck by something in his expression she'd never noticed before: he wanted to please her. It made her feel afraid.

She forced a smile and followed him outside, suddenly aware as he unlocked the workshop door of the security camera mounted above it. Stepping inside, he punched in the alarm code and then held the door for her to enter. The reception area, a deliberate pastiche of a gentleman's club, with dark-green carpet, leather button-back chairs and framed prints of hunting dogs on the walls, along with an incongruous modern coffee machine, was unchanged since her last visit. The tiny office, where her mother worked, opened off this room and had a pleasant view of the garden. Opposite was the door to the actual workshop, and she waited curiously as Leonard punched in another security code to release the locks. The unadorned space, with its whitewashed walls and concrete floor, turned out to be smaller than she remembered, and she realized how much of its exterior footprint must be taken up by the windowless strongroom at the far end.

'I realized it must be a decade or more since I had a really proper tidy-up,' he said. 'Another new year, and you'll be leaving home. Time flies. The number of dead ladybirds and spiders I found in all the boxes!'

He waved a hand towards a wall hung with neat rows of yellow, blue and green plastic box-trays. Robyn remembered her first glimpse inside this room on her fourteenth birthday, the age at which she'd been legally permitted to handle a rifle and ammunition. It was the first time she'd been allowed to see the detail of what her father did for a living, and she had been fascinated by the coloured boxes containing different sizes of casings, primers, die sets, loading blocks and the other paraphernalia required for loading rifle rounds. On one wooden workbench were green metal presses, die plates, a powder dispenser, scales and tumblers, plus, mounted on delineated boards, various drills and other tools; a second bench had lathes and wood- and metal-working tools for repairing, servicing and renovating the weapons themselves. Everything looked spotless and pristine, exactly as it had on her birthday nearly four years ago. She couldn't imagine that her father's tidy-up had taken very long.

'You're the neatest person I know,' she told him, wondering why he'd wanted her to come in here again now, what it was he wanted her to see.

'Some people think the big thing in life is to express yourself, to be creative. Painting, dancing, music, that kind of stuff. I like accuracy,' he said with a laugh. 'Precision.'

'You don't need to tell me!'

'Everything went to pieces when my father died,' he said quietly. 'Whenever I see an earthquake or something like that terrible tsunami on the news, that's how it felt. They probably have some fancy name for it now, but I simply wanted to put everything back the way it was.' Without even being aware of doing it, he straightened a metal punch so that it lined up with the edge of the workbench. 'I wanted to provide properly for you and your mum, so you'd never have to know what it was like to live so precariously.'

'You do look after us!' Robyn went to hug him. Feeling his warmth, the comforting chug of his heart against her ear, a dreadful thought struck her and she drew back. 'Dad, you're not ill or anything, are you?'

'No, of course not. Why on earth would you think that?'

And then his eyes had that invisible screen again, so that, although he was looking at her quite naturally, candidly even, she knew she was not seeing his real self. She took a step back, looking around the workshop, a place that appeared to her not to have changed at all since four years ago. Did that make it ordinary? Was *ordinary* something you should trust? She looked again at her father's face, the most familiar thing in the world and now also utterly strange to her. Could she tell him how she felt? Explain her fears to him? Or might that risk making everything worse?

'It's weird to think that by the end of the year I'll be living somewhere else,' she said. 'I bet I'll be really homesick.'

'I know how much we're going to miss you. But I'm so proud of you, Birdie.' He swept an arm out, gesturing to the whole workshop. 'This is for you. It's all for you.'

She could see how much he loved her. That much was undeniably genuine and true. But, if bringing her in here now to see his work was a demonstration of his loyalty to her, then to what exactly did he expect her to be loyal in return?

26

Looking at the gaudy blue, white and gold statue of mad King George III, Ivo could only assume that His Royal Highness had never visited Weymouth in January; only a balmy summer could possibly have transformed a harbour town into a bling eighteenth-century holiday destination, complete with esplanade, assembly rooms and hotels facing the wide sweep of especially fine sand. The seafront terraces remained, and the resort still made a living from visitors, although the amusement arcades and posters for a Christmas pantomime suggested a slightly less fashionable clientele. Ivo had vacillated between booking himself into one of the haughty-looking Regency hotels, where, totally out of season, he'd be likely to rattle around on his own, or one of the cosier places individualized by coloured awnings over their front doors. In the end he'd gone for something between the two, and now stood looking out of an admittedly rather pretty first-floor bay window at a slate-grey sea across which a vast and incongruous catamaran nosed its way towards the ferry terminal on the west side of the bay.

The light was fading, and the chill coming off the glass of the window promised that as soon as it got fully dark the temperature would drop viciously. For a brief moment Ivo longed to seek

out the familiar snugness of some ye olde English pub, but automatically shook off the lure: the charms of a curry house would
have to do, even without a cold Kingfisher to wash down his
rogan josh. He wondered what Donna Fewell and her kids did
with themselves down here, two hundred miles from anyone
they knew and loved. Where the fuck could they go on a night
like this for warmth or company or distraction, let alone
entertainment?

The first thing he'd done on arriving in Weymouth was check
out the location of their apartment. Even though the block had
no doubt been thrown up in order to cash in on the sailing
events of the 2012 Olympics, a couple of the 'exclusive' one-
bedroom flats had yet to be sold, and its soubriquet of 'luxury'
seemed justified solely by some glossy glass-fronted balconies.
Ivo reckoned that, for all its slick brochures and sea views, it
must be as much of a cage for Davey, Ella and Donna as the modern prison hulk that not so long ago had been moored a little
way along the coast.

Ivo shivered not with cold but with the anger that had carried him down to Weymouth. He wasn't sure why Davey's plight
had got under his skin so badly. Or maybe he was. But so far he'd
always managed to dodge that emotional bullet and, if he hadn't
taken one for king and country to please the expensive trick-
cyclist to whom the *Courier* had sent him to cure his drinking,
then he certainly wasn't about to do so now. No, the real reason
was simple hatred of those in authority who misused their
power. Maybe that's why he'd crossed the line for the Ice Maiden
last year; all that business with her thug of an ex-husband, and
the way her work colleagues – those twisted little Dixons of
Dock Green – had frozen her out for standing up for herself.

Jesus Christ, if you can't turn to the boys in blue when you're in trouble, what can you do?

But at least Grace Fisher had known the people she was dealing with and what she'd got herself into. Davey presumably had no idea; Ella was little more than a baby, and Donna Fewell, well, either she'd been too fuck-struck to want to see the truth about Mark Kirkby, or he'd done his dance of the seven veils so adroitly that she had absolutely no clue as what he and his school chum were really up to in their vindictive persecution of her ex-husband.

What a treasure Mark Kirkby must've been! Ivo was fully prepared, given the chance, to embark on some strategic character assassination at the inquest. He could see that DI Fisher's hands were tied: coppers look after their own – fair enough, so do most professions – and using the uniform for an occasional spot of private enterprise was a time-honoured perk. No one would thank her for daring to interfere in such sport. But there were some rules that mattered more in certain professions. Call him old-fashioned, but Ivo believed that, if standing by a mate meant turning a blind eye to a fit-up, then a line had been crossed. Which is where the clarion voice of the fifth estate was supposed to come into play.

Ivo whiled away a couple of hours in his room catching up on emails and watching the television news until he reckoned it was sufficiently late to go out and select a place to eat. The achingly cold wind off the sea stung any bit of exposed skin it could find and convinced him to stumble into the nearest curry house without even looking at the menu posted in the window. He was glad to see he wouldn't be the only diner – that is until he recognized the rugged-looking bloke sitting at a table towards the back of the restaurant, facing the door. Fuck him if it wasn't John Kirkby.

Ivo quickly took stock, wondering if Kirkby would recognize him. It was over a fortnight since the press conference that followed the shootings, but Ivo couldn't be sure whether John Kirkby would recall his face from the media scrum or perhaps be familiar with his name. For all he knew, it had been John Kirkby himself who'd got the Federation lawyers to lean on Ivo's editor and force him to back off from investigating his son. He decided to play safe, and gave the man a friendly nod, choosing a table diagonally across from him in the otherwise empty restaurant. He concentrated on the overlarge menu, giving the other man time to make the first move.

Once he'd ordered his food and been presented with a glass of tap water, he looked up and found John Kirkby trying to catch his eye.

'Here on business?' Kirkby asked pleasantly. Ivo decided it was a fair bet that he'd not been rumbled.

'Checking out some properties,' Ivo responded. 'Now my dad's on his own, he seems to think the seaside would be bracing.'

'It's certainly that!' Kirkby agreed.

The short exchange gave Ivo a chance to study the man: he looked tired and sick. His jowls and lower eyelids drooped as if he'd lost suddenly lost weight, and he wasn't showing much appetite for the prawn biriani in front of him. Ivo checked himself: don't go feeling sorry for the bastard!

'What about you?' he asked. 'What brings you here?'

'Family business,' said Kirkby. 'Much the same as you.'

So they were both lying, thought Ivo. The best way to get people to tell you what was really on their minds was silence, so he smiled and nodded, grateful to the waiter for choosing this moment to bring poppadoms and pickles, with which he could legitimately busy himself while Kirkby decided how desperate he was to confide in a stranger. After a moment Ivo heard a sigh and deliberately waited just that little bit too long before looking up.

'You wonder sometimes what it's all for, don't you?' Kirkby informed the otherwise empty restaurant.

Ivo gave a smile of encouragement. 'Yeah, well . . .'

'I'm guessing your dad's retired? So what did he do?'

Ivo's father had in fact long ago retired to the cemetery, but he answered the rest of the question honestly enough. 'He was an aircraft engineer. Served in the RAF during the war and fell in love with flying.'

'And now? What's he got to show for it?'

'Not much,' agreed Ivo.

Kirkby shook his head and signalled to the waiter for another beer. 'Can I get you one?'

'No, thanks. I'm off the sauce,' said Ivo. 'Doctor's orders.'

'See what I mean? A man works his guts out, and then what? Can't even enjoy a beer when he wants one. Mind you – don't get me wrong – I loved my job. Police sergeant. Loved the service. Proud to wear the uniform. But now?'

Ivo strove to keep the cynical sneer off his face. 'No respect,' he suggested. 'Political correctness, government cutbacks.'

'And the rest!'

Ivo wondered how much of this he could stomach, coming from the father of a cheap bully, but was again rescued from having to respond at any length by the arrival of his rogan josh. In any case, Kirkby was only beginning to get into his stride.

'I wasn't the only one to sacrifice my marriage to the job.

And for what? You know they don't even have canteens in police stations any more? You come in from a long shift in weather like this after dealing with the scum of the earth, and all they offer you is a microwave to heat up your own food. And what do we get in return? All this human rights rubbish – pink and fluffy welfare visits to granny-bashers, or making sure that some Albanian drug lord who just sold Tinkerbell to a trafficking gang gets free legal advice *and* an interpreter. And after all that, the best the politicians can find to do is give us grief over our pensions. It's taking the piss.'

'At least you've not been privatized,' said Ivo between mouthfuls.

'Not yet, maybe. But all these new ACPO types with their fancy management degrees telling us we have to work smarter when what they really mean is, let petty criminals give us the finger and walk free . . . It's us who has to tell the burglary victims who live next door to a crack den that they'll be taking care of themselves from now on. I mean, all this after the flak my generation took during the miners' strike and the poll tax riots. I ask you! The politicians then were happy enough to shove us into the front line so yobs could throw bricks at us. The government ought to show more bloody respect. We're the ones who defend the most vulnerable in society. We're the service of last resort. And they'd do well not to forget it, in case one day they call us and we're not bloody there!'

'The state should look after its own,' Ivo agreed blandly.

'Too right.' Kirkby seemed to deflate, all his hot air spent. He shook his head wearily. 'Still' – he sighed – 'charity begins at home, right? You've got to try and do what's right by those nearest to you, however hard.'

Ivo speculated whether he meant Donna Fewell and not for the first time wondered precisely why John Kirkby had taken it upon himself to look out for the family of his son's murderer. 'So how long are you down here for?' he asked casually but with keen interest in the answer.

'I go home tomorrow.' Kirkby pushed away his half-drunk glass of beer. 'Home!' he repeated bitterly. 'I lost my son recently.' He pursed his lips together tightly, and Ivo suspected that he was battling not to well up. 'I've two boys. He was my first. Couldn't ask for a more wonderful son. The best. So I'm here, trying to do what he would have wanted.' He shook his head slowly. 'What more can you do?'

Ivo produced a murmur of sympathy as Kirkby looked directly into his eyes, making it hard for Ivo not to feel for the man's distress.

'Oh well,' said Kirkby, reaching into a pocket for his wallet and tossing a couple of notes onto the tablecloth. 'Thanks for listening. I hope I haven't given you indigestion!'

He got up and, passing Ivo's table, held out his hand. Ivo took it. 'Take care,' said Ivo, and was surprised to find that he almost meant it.

As the restaurant door closed behind Kirkby, letting in a freezing gust of air, Ivo's eyes fell on the banknotes left on the table: the man had left a stonkingly generous tip.

27

Grace hated to admit it, but she had felt a tangible sense of release when Duncan proved as good as his word and had whistled up a last-minute flight for Lance to take a welfare break in the Algarve courtesy of the Police Federation. Lance had left the previous evening and would not return for more than a week. Grace had wrestled with herself for the past couple of days: should she have told him the little she knew? Should she argue with Colin to find out more? Or should she shut up and not interfere? Then she'd woken in the middle of the night, gripped by the dread that one of the security services knew precisely why Peter had been killed and the identity of his killer, yet intended to take no further action. Sleepless, she'd lain in bed, imagining herself in Lance's place and telling herself how right he'd be to curse the cowardly friend and colleague who simply sat on her hands and followed orders.

This morning, taking advantage of Lance's absence, Colin had officially informed the team that their first week's work on the Peter Burnley murder was being transferred to London, where the coroner now had jurisdiction over the case. He fielded their questions patiently and skilfully, and although no one was happy – this investigation was close to home, and they wanted to do their very best for a colleague – Grace couldn't help wondering whether there wasn't an undercurrent of relief. The team's inquiries so far had hit dead end after dead end, and no one wanted to be the first to say aloud that they had drawn a complete blank. A thorough examination of the crime scene had yielded nothing of any value; few people had been around so late on such a grim night; it wasn't a residential area so house-to-house had been of little use; and a limited media appeal had failed to bring forward any new witnesses. Grace understood the team's dismay at their inability to make headway, so perhaps morale would rise now that responsibility for solving this case had been lifted from their shoulders.

Every detective had an inquiry like this at some point in their career, in which the assailant just didn't make enough mistakes to be caught. It didn't take a criminal mastermind for that to happen, just dumb luck the victim didn't fight back or cry out loudly enough to attract attention, no passer-by witnessed anyone leaving the scene and no meaningful physical evidence was found. Here the only remaining angle was why the killer had chosen Peter as his victim. In most murders there is some kind of prior association between victim and assailant, but, with the rest of the team working on the assumption that Peter Burnley's cover story was his true identity, that line of inquiry was, unbeknownst to them, a complete waste of time.

And it wasn't only Lance she felt guilty about. There was Davey Fewell too. Grace's last conversation with Ruth Woods had carried a bitter sting: the FLO had informed her that John Kirkby had arranged for Donna Fewell and her kids to be relocated to the south coast. History would be written by the victors: John Kirkby would get to coddle Davey into accepting his version of the truth. However much Kirkby knew or didn't know about his son's corrupt activities, Davey would end up even more undecided about what he had seen, even further from the truth about what had driven his father's actions on Christmas Day.

A date had yet to be set for the inquest into the Dunholt killings, so Grace still had a little time in which to find some evidence to support Davey's story about the rifle, though where that was going to come from, she had no idea. She told herself that was why she hadn't yet said anything to Colin: not only would he not thank her for dumping unwelcome hearsay evidence on him, but she was also certain that he wouldn't be able to suggest anything she hadn't already thought of herself. The even more uncomfortable truth was that no police force liked to wash its dirty linen in public, and Davey's allegation would probably have been investigated very differently had they suspected the lethal weapon had previously been in the illegal possession of one of the civilian victims of the Dunholt massacre.

Her guilt wasn't helped by the knowledge that she'd been avoiding Curtis Mullins, who'd been hanging around the past few days looking for an opportunity to speak to her. For all she knew, it was about the Peter Burnley murder case: he'd been the first on the scene after Peter's body had been found, and many officers would feel that gave them a personal stake in an inquiry and the right to be kept informed. But she just couldn't trust herself to be civil to him, not when she suspected that he was still acting as John Kirkby's eyes and ears.

The hours until lunchtime dragged. Grace had seldom felt so ineffective or useless. Deciding that a breath of fresh air might help, she headed out, intending to treat herself to a brisk walk around Castle Park. At the bottom of the stairs she spotted

Curtis crossing the back lobby and made a snap decision: time to push on, do something, stop hiding! She called to him, curtly suggesting he accompany her to one of the nearby cafes for lunch. He accepted without hesitation.

They stood silently beside one another in the queue at the counter, his height making Grace feel slightly overpowered. She ordered and paid for herself, then made her way to an empty table, leaving Curtis to follow. He soon joined her with only a coffee, nothing to eat. She bit into her ciabatta and waited to see if – and how – he'd open the conversation. He spooned up some of the froth on his cappuccino and took a long look around the cafe – she almost wondered if he were checking whether any-one else from the station was here – but said nothing.

'You've been wanting to speak to me,' she said. 'What about?'

He hung his head, and she found herself staring at the reddish-gold strands of his hair. He and she were more or less the same age, yet he seemed much younger.

'It's what you said about Fewell leaving his court summons as a suicide note.' He looked at her directly, his eyes a vivid blue. 'Did you mean that? Do you really think that's what made him do what he did?'

'I don't know about the others,' she said, 'but I believe it's what drove him to kill Mark Kirkby. After that I imagine he just lost it. But he was the only one who took the decision to go on to kill four other people – and himself – and nothing justi-fies that. He should rot in hell for that.' Recalling the row of coffins in the church, she pushed away her roll, no longer hun-gry. 'There's no explanation that makes sense of six deaths, is there?'

'No.'

Grace studied Curtis as he concentrated on stirring his cof-fee. She was trying hard not to despise him.

'I've been having nightmares about it,' he said at last.

'So it was you?' she asked.

He looked at her in wary surprise.

'Mark Kirkby asked you to smash Fewell's rear light.'

Curtis lifted his teaspoon then dropped it into the saucer and stared at the wall.

'I retrieved the broken plastic from where you pushed it under the hedge,' she said.

He made no denial.

Grace shook her head in contempt. She was tempted to wish him sleepless nights for the rest of his life, but swallowed the words as, simultaneously, a great wave of relief washed over her. She was not some crazy conspiracy lady; she had not gone rootling around that pub car park in search of UFOs; her hunch had been correct, and she'd been right to trust her instincts.

'Mark was always the leader.' Curtis's voice broke into her thoughts. 'Right from school we always did what he said, never questioned him. And we always had fun doing it too.'

'Fun?' exclaimed Grace. '*You* might've had fun. But what about other people? People like Fewell? Or his kids?' Aware of the people packed in around her, she tried to keep her voice low but refused to hide her anger. 'We're police officers. We of all people should beware of creating the kind of flashpoints that can lead to carnage. How could you do such a thing? For one of us to twist the law is never insignificant. Never!'

Curtis heaved a deep sigh. 'I realize that now. And I couldn't be more sorry for all those innocent people who died.'

Grace tried desperately to bring her fury under sufficient control to work out how best to ask Curtis what he knew about Mark Kirkby's possession of an illegal weapon. Now was the time to take advantage of his contrition, but she mustn't let her outrage scare him off. 'Do you know how Russell Fewell could have got hold of a rifle?' She asked the question as casually as she could. 'We asked Donna, but she had no idea. And we think the ammunition may have been supplied locally.'

She watched his reaction closely but was certain there was nothing, not a flicker. Curtis shook his head and once more looked directly at her, his eyes beginning to take on a flinty brightness, reminding her of the look he'd given her the night of Peter's murder when she'd asked him if he would've handled Russell Fewell's arrest any differently.

'You do realize that I'm never going to admit to breaking the light?' His tone was almost sulky. 'If you say I did, I'll deny it. Not for my sake, but for Mark, for his family. I'm not going to sell out a mate, especially not when he's no longer here to defend himself.'

'Defend himself?' jeered Grace in spite of her best intentions. 'I'd like to hear him try!'

'Yeah, well, you're not going to, are you?' Curtis shot back, getting to his feet. 'He's dead. Anyway, what would you know? From what I hear, you don't have any friends to defend!'

'Sit down, PC Mullins,' she said, trying not to let him see how much his jibe had stung. 'I have one more question to put to you.'

He hesitated, but then reluctantly slipped back into his seat.

'Why didn't you tell me last week, when you attended the scene in the alley, that you'd seen the victim before?'

He looked puzzled. 'I hadn't.'

'You didn't see Peter Burnley in the Blue Bar with DS Lance Cooper just before Christmas?'

'No.'

Grace watched as the memory slowly returned to him and he began to make sense of her question. She'd have given a lot to know his thoughts at that moment.

'I had no idea who he was,' Curtis protested. 'And, for the record, I had no idea until the Burnley murder that DS Cooper was gay either. Why would I?'

'What about your friends?'

'I can't speak for them,' he said primly, placing both hands on the table, ready to push himself to his feet. 'May I go now, ma'am?'

Grace ignored his sneering tone. 'So who were you with in the bar that night? Why would they have been in the least bit interested in Lance being with Peter?'

Curtis attempted to stare her down. 'I was with Mark, as it happens. The last drink I ever had with him. Along with his brother Adam and a couple of mates. So what is it with you? Is having friends you're prepared to stick by, no matter what, some kind of dirty offence in your book?'

'It is when you place loyalty to friends above the law. And it doesn't change what you are, PC Mullins. A corrupt officer. Don't expect me to forget that.'

'Please yourself, ma'am.'

He walked away. Grace looked down and saw that her hands were shaking.

28

Apart from dog walkers and the occasional jogger, there was no one else crazy enough to be out in such gusting weather on a dreary Thursday in Weymouth. Ivo had trailed Donna Fewell to the local primary school and then home again, and was now holed up in a steamy seafront cafe and beginning to wonder what the fuck he was doing here. Did he really intend to sit around all day in places like this until Donna picked the kids up from school in the afternoon? And then what? Stand outside the flat until they switched off the lights and went to bed? If he were honest, he hadn't really factored in how bloody cold it was going to be beside the sea.

He'd more or less decided to pack it in and return to London and was paying his bill, when to his amazement he spotted Davey walking past the window, shoulders hunched, head down and hands in his pockets. So the kid was playing hooky. That wasn't good. Zipping up his jacket, Ivo left the cafe and, staying a reasonable distance behind, followed the boy on his lonely excursion. Davey barely glanced at the closed-up play area with its sodden sandpit and empty paddling pool, but Ivo watched as, walking close to a line of terraced beach huts, he rattled several of the padlocks as if in search of an open door.

Ivo hoped the kid wasn't looking for trouble. He knew all about that. He'd been the same age as Davey when he'd taken up smoking. Sent back to boarding school after his mother's death, he'd been determined to find some way to kick against a system that had hurt him, and, as he now acknowledged, to punish himself for his own continued existence. A couple of years later, after he'd moved on to his minor public school, he discovered booze and took to it like it had been invented just for him. He didn't want Davey going down that road so was relieved when, on reaching the main esplanade, he observed him veering off to sit in one of the ornate Victorian shelters.

It contained four benches, each facing in a different direction, with glass partitions between them. Ivo didn't yet want to risk coming too close, so pretended to wait at a nearby bus stop while keeping a sharp eye on Davey. The boy's feet, in trainers, barely reached the ground, and Ivo watched him begin to shiver with cold. When Davey got up and made his way down onto the sands, walking right out towards the waterline, Ivo took the boy's place in the shelter, from where he had a panoramic view of the beach. He was ready to make a dash for it if the kid tried to do anything daft, but Davey looked around for pebbles to toss into the waves and then, seemingly bored, started walking again, still heading for the harbour and the centre of town.

There were enough shoppers in the pedestrianized streets for Ivo to blend in and remain unnoticed as he tailed the boy. In a newsagent's he observed how Davey's hand hovered over a display of chocolate bars and then seemed to rehearse the movement required to pocket one. His hesitation and the constant glances he made towards the shopkeeper caught the man's attention, and Ivo prayed that Davey, a rank amateur, wouldn't attempt the steal. The boy clearly thought better of it, and set off again on his apparently random journey, this time going back towards the sea.

The shuttered concrete cafe on the Pleasure Pier – a misnomer if ever there was one – looked across the inlet to a grim stone fortification looming above a second pier. Davey wandered to the far end of the Pleasure Pier, where a few fishing rods had been set up against the railings. Their owners were hunkered down in the shelter of the cafe's raised terrace, where Ivo suspected they were fortifying themselves with substances that young Davey didn't need to know about. As the boy leaned on the railings, staring out to sea, Ivo smiled at the fishermen.

'Catch anything?'

One of them nodded. 'Couple of bass. Not big enough to land, though.'

'Shame. Fishing good here generally?'

'Not bad.'

Ivo remembered a tube of extra-strong mints in his pocket and handed them round. By the time Davey wandered back in their direction, Ivo was as near to being one of the gang as he was ever going to get.

'Don't let the giant squid catch you!' he called out to the boy.

Davey didn't smile, but the remark did the trick of offering sufficient encouragement for him to linger, half-hidden behind one of the brick columns that supported the terrace. The fishermen were obviously tolerant of kids hanging around who really ought to be in school, and did Ivo's job for him, letting Davey bait a hook and giving him a good-natured and admiring pat on the back when not only did he fail to grimace at the contents of a plastic canister full of squirming lugworm but seemed to know what he was doing. So, when Ivo's instinct told him the time was right, he declared that he was going for a cup of nice hot tea and a bacon bap. And when the fishermen suggested a place that knew how to cook bacon to exactly the right degree of crispiness, it was easy enough to sell Davey on the idea of going with him.

Ivo was well aware that to any concerned citizen he must look like a paedophile straight out of Central Casting, but, relying on the British knack of avoiding embarrassment by pretending not to notice, he was able to steer Davey to the recommended cafe without interference. Once inside, the aroma of frying bacon acted as powerfully as a siren's song and kept the boy glued to his seat, overcoming whatever misgivings Ivo jolly well hoped any sensible lad ought to be having by now.

As Davey did justice to a bap and a chocolate milkshake, Ivo debated whether to come clean about his identity, or at least part of it. He probably wasn't going to get a second opportunity as good as this, and he didn't want to blow it by being over-cautious and losing his prey. As soon as the warmth and the food hit the boy's nervous system, he was going to come to his senses and skedaddle, so he'd better get on with it.

'So you're a fisherman, right?' Ivo asked.

Davey nodded, trying to smile with his mouth full.

'Your dad taught you.'

The boy nodded, but looked up at Ivo with troubled eyes.

'I never knew your dad, but I heard good things about him,' Ivo said matter-of-factly. 'From Martin Leyburn at the angling club that your dad belonged to.'

Davey's eyes grew rounder, and he swallowed the last bite of his bap and silently accepted the paper napkin Ivo handed him from a metal dispenser. Ivo waited for Davey to wipe his greasy mouth before he spoke again.

'He had a tough time, your dad. That's what Martin Leyburn told me. And, whatever he did, I bet he was a really good father.'

Davey nodded, his mouth puckering as tears welled up. 'I miss him,' he whispered.

'I bet you do. And now you're not even allowed to talk about him.'

'Mum made me promise not to.'

'That's OK. She's just trying to protect you. That's what mothers do. Besides, she probably doesn't know what really happened.' Ivo took a deep breath: *Christ, this was much harder than he'd expected!* 'I do. Maybe not all, but a bit. I can tell you, if you like?'

Davey bit his lip, thinking about it, and then nodded. The kid was so young, thought Ivo, his skin still peachy and his lips like rosebuds. A child. It really wasn't fucking fair.

'So do you remember where you were on your dad's last birthday?'

'At Mark's house. It was a school night and he said we'd have to wait to see Dad at the weekend.'

'So Mark knew it was his birthday?'

Davey nodded, big serious eyes clamped on Ivo's.

'Did you ever meet a friend of Mark's called Curtis Mullins? He's a policeman too.'

'Don't know. Maybe.'

'Well, Curtis and Mark were at school together. Very old friends. And it was Curtis who arrested your dad for drink-driving the night of his birthday.' Ivo allowed time for this sink in before he continued. 'Now that may simply be coincidence, but your dad thought it wasn't. Which is partly why he got so very, very upset.'

'I didn't like Mark,' said Davey, his cheeks flushing. 'He pretended to be nice but he wasn't. I didn't want Mum to be with him.' Davey's hands dropped into his lap, and he hung his head. He spoke so softly that Ivo barely heard him. 'I'm glad Mark's dead.'

Yeah, thought Ivo, you and me both, kiddo.

'It's my fault.'

'That he's dead?'

Davey nodded, looking down into his lap.

'No, Davey,' said Ivo firmly. 'That's absolutely not true.'

'It is. It is! I knew he had a gun.'

'Your dad?'

'No! Mark.'

'Mark had a gun?' Ivo was practised at concealing his surprise, but, boy, did this revelation take every last bit of skill he possessed!

Davey nodded. 'Big and heavy, just like the one Dad used to shoot him.'

Ivo had heard almost as many first-person horror stories as he'd knocked back double gins, but the natural way the kid said this chilled his heart as never before. 'Did you actually get to hold it?' he asked. 'Is that how you know it was heavy?'

Davey nodded. 'Mark showed it to me. Told me not to tell anyone. He said he hadn't even told Mum. It was a secret, just for us men.'

Fuck me! thought Ivo, recoiling in disbelief and grimacing as if he'd sucked on a lemon. *That self-aggrandizing jerk of a bully, using someone else's son to big up his pathetic macho fantasy of himself!*

And then ordering him not to speak about it. What a controlling prick! He realized too late that Davey was alarmed by his reaction and tried hard to soften his features.

'Was it exciting, getting to hold a real gun?' he asked.

'No. It was scary. Mark said it wasn't his. He was looking after it for someone, and that person would come and get me if I told anyone.'

'So *did* you tell anyone?' asked Ivo.

'Only my dad.' Davey looked up with imploring eyes. 'That's why my dad's dead, isn't it? Because of me?'

29

The grinding Friday-afternoon traffic on the hour-long drive to the prison gave Grace time to think. She felt as if she were chasing shadows. Except she'd been right about Curtis Mullins. And she believed Davey Fewell. So had Ruth Woods. And if Mark had shown Davey a gun, then that gun had to have come from somewhere. When she'd first opened the email from Duncan with the feedback from the post-sentencing interviews officer, she'd not read much further than the first paragraph outlining the officer's view that none of those recently convicted and imprisoned for offences involving firearms was likely to be helpful, as all had so far declined to assist the police with their intelligence-gathering and clear-up rates. It was only as she was closing the document that *Dunholt* caught her eye.

Warren Cox, the lorry hijacker she was now on her way to see, had lived in Dunholt before his arrest. On Christmas Day he'd already been banged up for nearly a year, and none of his family appeared to have been caught up in the tragedy of the shooting, yet Grace felt compelled to clutch at the slim chance that he might take a view on what had happened in his home town.

Even though her visit was official, the security procedures were irritatingly slow, and she was kept waiting for a further twenty minutes as someone went to fetch Cox. Grace hoped he wasn't being dragged out of the gym or somewhere else that broke the monotony of prison life, and was pleased, when at last he was shown into the room by a prison officer, to see that he seemed relatively relaxed. Warren was a muscular, intimidating man in his late twenties with a shaven head and fierce eyes. If Grace had been one of the lorry drivers he'd threatened, she didn't think he'd have needed a sawn-off shotgun to get her to do what he wanted. And Warren had been good at what he did, running a large, well-organized operation; the total value of the vehicles he had stolen ran to well over a million pounds. He had finally been caught when a police helicopter followed him to the isolated farm buildings where the trailers were unloaded and the cabs dismantled for spare parts to be shipped to Africa or the Middle East.

She thanked him for coming to speak to her and got straight to the point. 'It's about the Dunholt shootings,' she said. 'I happened to notice that you were living there at the time of your arrest.'

He nodded. 'Grew up there.'

'Did you know Russell Fewell?'

He looked as if he were going to spit on the floor but then thought better of it. 'Sick bastard.'

'I'm trying to find out how he got hold of a gun. It was a rifle, a Heckler & Koch G3, and he used soft-point ammunition.'

Warren pursed his lips. 'I've never even handled a rifle,' he said. 'That's an army job, isn't it?'

'Possibly. We think he stole it from someone he knew, someone who was in illegal possession of it. We're also fairly certain that the ammunition was produced locally.'

'So what can I tell you?' he asked sarcastically.

'Whoever made the rounds used by Fewell to kill five of your neighbours on Christmas Day has also made other calibre rounds recovered from fatal shootings in London, Manchester and Birmingham. He supplies teenage gangs, professional criminals like yourself and total nutjobs. He's not fussy. I want to know who he is.'

Warren sat back, folded his arms and gave a thoughtful sniff but said nothing.

'I went through your record,' said Grace. 'You never actually discharged a weapon on a job.'

'No need,' he said. 'Point a sawn-off at someone, and you don't get no farting about.'

'You carry a gun to make sure a job goes smoothly,' said Grace. 'Trouble is, a lot of kids these days think they're fashion accessories.'

Warren nodded. 'A teenager can get hold of an Uzi for a couple of grand. Thinks he's clever cos he's got a nine-millimetre Glock to go with his box-fresh trainers. I was offered a Sterling sub-machine gun right before I got nicked.'

'That'll use up bullets pretty quickly,' said Grace. 'I imagine ammo's where the real money is.'

'Maybe.' Warren looked at her shrewdly, and she hoped he might at least be prepared to let her plead her case.

'That's who I want to talk to,' she said. 'I'd like to take the armourer who made those bullets out of circulation. The people of Dunholt deserve some positive result to come out of this, and there's not much else I can offer them, is there?'

'Fair enough,' said Warren. 'But unless you're some punk kid who doesn't know any better, you don't just buy this stuff from a bloke in the pub who happens to have a rifle in the boot of his car.'

'Why not?' asked Grace. She knew the reasons as well as Warren did. He was far from stupid, but he had already glanced at the top button of her blouse three times: maybe, only a year into a long sentence, he'd be bored enough to be tempted into a little mansplaining.

Warren unfolded his arms and leaned forward across the table that separated them. 'You'll want to know whether it's real, converted or reactivated. You want to make sure that, if you do have to fire it, it's not going to jam or blow up in your face. And, most important, you want be absolutely one-hundred-per-cent certain it's clean. You get caught holding a gun that can be traced back to other incidents, then you'll be going away for a very long time.'

'So how do you protect yourself?'

'If you're sensible, you mean? Not like these kids who rent them out or barter them for drugs. A nine-millimetre pistol will buy you an ounce of crack, if you want it – you know that?'

'Which is exactly why I don't want someone out there selling ammo to kids like it's sweeties,' said Grace.

'Look at it from my point of view,' he said reasonably. 'If you're going to sell me some hardware, it's best all round that we know as little as possible about each other, right? So there's go-betweens, an etiquette you might call it.'

'So you wouldn't know the names of any armourers, even if you were prepared to tell me?'

'Solid ones?' asked Warren. 'Ones you can trust? No.'

Grace wasn't surprised by his answer. She'd always known this was likely to be a wild-goose chase, but she'd had to do something.

'Anyway, why would I tell you?' Warren continued. 'If the man you're looking for has any sense, he'll be keeping a record of every weapon he handles. His courier will know where they all end up. That's quite an insurance policy. No one's going to piss him off. No one's going to owe him money. And no one is going to give his name to a fucking rozzer.'

'What about selling an unlicensed gun to a rozzer?' The words were out of her mouth before she could stop them. She saw the flare of shock and anger on his face before he instinctively looked around for the inevitable security camera, as if to reassure himself that this was being monitored and was not a trap.

He gave a throaty laugh that felt to Grace more like a threat. 'You looking to buy one, darlin'?'

'No.' She decided she might as well tell him the truth. What Warren would do with the precious nugget of information once she'd handed it over was unforeseeable, but she'd have to take that risk. 'No,' she repeated. 'I want to know who sold a gun to a corrupt police officer.'

Warren whistled and looked at her in crafty admiration. 'You've got balls, lady, I'll give you that. But who in his right mind would fucking do that? Why?'

'That's what I want to know.' Grace sat very still as he thought things over for a few silent moments.

'I don't have an actual name to give you,' he said at last, 'and wouldn't even if I did. But a bent copper with a gun is something else. Armed police are trigger-happy enough for my taste even when they're on duty. Especially when they're on duty, if you ask me. Huddling together afterwards to get their evidence straight for the judge when the poor bugger they've shot is a bit too dead to tell his side of the story.' He curled his lips in distaste. 'Leaves a bad taste, if you know what I mean?'

Grace nodded, crossing her fingers tightly beneath the table. 'I don't like it any more than you do.'

Warren stared at her as if studying her face for signs of trickery or deception. She did her best to return his look unflinchingly.

'I want a promise that my name stays out of this,' he said finally. 'If you're talking about bent cops, then I don't want this going into any intelligence system other than your ears.'

'I can register you properly as an informer, if you prefer.'

'No way. This is a one-off. Just you and me.'

'OK,' said Grace. 'You have my word.'

He nodded, considering his decision one last time. Grace held her breath.

'You got a pen and paper?' He nodded his head in the direction of the security camera.

'Yes.' Grace had been permitted to keep a small notepad and a pencil in her jacket pocket. She passed them quickly across the table before he changed his mind then watched eagerly as Warren scribbled something down and pushed them back.

'This is who everyone recommends,' he said. 'It's just a nickname, but that's all I know.'

Grace read what he had written: the Lion King.

Warren must have seen her frown. 'No idea why he's called that,' he said. 'Don't know if he's local or not. He could be anywhere. Could be some fucking African ex-mercenary selling off surplus stock. That's the best I can do.'

Grace pocketed her notebook and pencil and stood up. 'Thank you.'

Warren remained in his seat, looking up at her, unsmiling. 'If anybody wants to know, we had a pleasant chat about the weather.'

'Of course.'

She went to knock on the door for the prison officer, praying that she hadn't been recklessly indiscreet.

'Oh and lady?' He called after her just as she reached the door.

She turned. 'Yes?'

'Don't ever come visiting me again.'

30

Grace left her house at first light the following morning to walk quickly down to the quayside. There was still frost on the roofs of parked cars and it was too cold to linger over her calf and hamstring stretches. Shivering as she set off at a jog along the track that led beside the river towards Alresford Creek, she broke into a quick sprint to warm up and then settled back into a steady pace. It was her regular weekend run – or as regular as she could manage for January – and she wanted space to think.

The Lion King. Leo the Lion. Leonard Ingold. Was she making the connection purely out of wishful thinking, or had Warren Cox unknowingly dropped a golden key into her lap? Had Leonard Ingold been so helpful to Duncan in order to keep a close eye on the investigation? Was Duncan corrupt even? The idea was nonsense, but she couldn't afford to be starry-eyed about anyone, not even the most unflappable and dependable member of her team. She seemed to remember Duncan mentioning he'd met Ingold through a wildfowling club: she must ask Duncan on Monday precisely how their acquaintance had come about. She was nowhere near being able to get a search warrant, but if Ingold had deliberately engineered a good relationship with the police she could play that back and make a friendly fact-finding visit to his workshop.

Across the water, the trees were leafless and the hedgerows diminished by winter. Perished ground foliage tinged the misty fields with black, and an occasional cluster of red hawthorn berries or wild rosehips was welcome relief. She could hardly be alone in hating this barren season, yet despite the horrors of the year so far she felt the first stirrings of optimism. She hoped it wasn't misplaced.

As she passed a fellow runner heading back towards Wivenhoe they nodded politely to one another, their cloudy breath lingering in the cold air. Grace suddenly recalled that Duncan had introduced her to Leonard Ingold's wife after the funerals at Dunholt. Grace hadn't been paying much attention – her eyes had been on John Kirkby – and anyway Mrs Ingold had seemed unremarkable enough. But it struck her now that Leonard Ingold – the man who may have supplied the fatal bullets and probably the gun as well – had not accompanied his wife.

She chided herself: now she was being fanciful! She had no evidence whatsoever that Warren Cox's Lion King was Leonard Ingold. And yet . . . with every pounding footstep she became more convinced she was right.

She thought about how cautious Warren had been, how little he trusted any of the people in uniform who might have access to the feed from the security camera in the legal visits room. The cameras were there for the safety of visitors, and conferences with lawyers were supposedly confidential, but prisons were notoriously leaky places. Every prison had at least one officer prepared to sell stories to the tabloids, who might well be the same officer who got paid to smuggle in SIM cards or drugs. Turf wars and vendettas among the prisoners themselves were common; add in a corrupt officer, and the network became even more toxic. No wonder Warren had wanted to know why anyone would be stupid enough to sell a weapon to a serving police officer.

Why had Mark Kirkby wanted a rifle? His motives had to be sinister. If he'd wanted it for any legal purpose, he'd have simply applied for a gun licence.

As Grace ran on beside the river, her cheeks tingling with cold, she glanced up at a skein of geese flying steadily across the featureless grey horizon. Their perfect formation and steadily beating wings ought to have lifted her spirits, but instead she felt a sudden and familiar wave of depression. Why had she not yet said anything to Colin about the difficult truth that Davey Fewell had shared with her? Why had she so inexcusably left Davey to fend for himself?

Was it simply because she couldn't face dealing with the fall-out? But if she was too afraid to rock the boat or face dealing with Colin's slippery hypocrisy, then had she stopped doing what mattered most about her job in order to feel safe?

Yet how could she expect to emerge unscathed if she took on a culture that regarded a lack of unquestioning loyalty as betrayal and championed a solidarity that bordered on corruption? The black thoughts came tumbling out. What was wrong with people? Why couldn't they aspire to the cooperative beauty of those flying birds? Why did they always have to twist and dominate and grind other people down? Worst of all, these were the very people who, if asked, would reply in all sincerity that they were in the job in order to help people and to pursue truth and justice!

But she was no better. She'd lied to Lance. She'd placed professional obedience above friendship. Maybe Peter's murder was, as Colin said, a textbook case where they just never got a lucky break. It happened. But wasn't it somehow all rather too convenient that it happened precisely when one of the security or intelligence services was involved?

She reached the point where the creek opened off the main river and stopped, hands on her thighs, to get her breath. Looking up, the freezing water and mud, the wintry grass and reeds all appeared desolate to her, and she was glad to turn back. As she ran she tried to think positively, made herself picture a comforting hot shower and breakfast. But she still had some serious thinking to do. She needed to work out how to know what she should fight for, and when. She also needed to be sure she fought hard enough, especially in the face of a consensus insisting that everything possible was being done.

Was she chasing shadows? Colin would no doubt tell her she was. She had no evidence of a corrupt conspiracy between Curtis Mullins and Mark Kirkby, let alone between Mark Kirkby and Leonard Ingold. There was no one to corroborate Davey Fewell's story, and certainly none of Mark's family, friends or colleagues was likely to step forward to sully his good name.

She longed to know what Ivo Sweatman was up to, if perhaps he'd found out anything new about Mark Kirkby, but, given the repercussions of being caught sharing information with a journalist, she dared not renew contact. She hoped he would come to the inquest, as she'd suggested, and blow some of the Kirkby family's complacency out of the water.

Meanwhile there must be something more she could do, some untried avenue of inquiry she could explore. She concentrated on her breathing and the rhythm of her feet, trying to let ran-dom ideas bounce around in her mind. It didn't take long for something to snag: if a shooter was experienced, he'd know to pick up his spent casings so there'd be no ballistics match to other incidents involving the rifle and ammunition he was using. If she searched for other shootings where a rifle and hollow-point ammunition had been used, even if no casings had been recovered, she might pick up a trail. Mark Kirkby had run the risk of being caught in possession of an unlicensed firearm for a reason, and she wanted to know what it was.

It was grasping at straws, but it was better than nothing. Grace quickened her pace, eager now to get in to work, regard-less of her weekend off. She looked ahead, gauging how long it would take her to reach home. Another runner was coming down the path towards her, and she moved to her left to give him room to pass. As he got nearer, she prepared to make eye contact and smile, but, no doubt to keep out the cold, his grey hood was pulled too far forward over his face.

At the last moment he veered sideways and bent forward to ram his right shoulder hard into her chest, like a rugby player. She gasped with shock and immediately lost her stride, giving him the opportunity to aim a kick at the most painful part of her shin and then hook his foot around hers so that she went flying to the ground. She cried out as another well-aimed kick sent her rolling down the slope towards the deep freezing mud of the river. She managed to grab at a tuft of tough grass to halt her slide and looked up to see her attacker running on towards the creek.

Frozen by terror, Grace lay still, her face against the earth, and tried to steady her ragged breath as her brain did a rapid mental stock check, assessing whether it was safe to straighten her legs and spine. Fear brought a wave of shame, and she longed to weep. As each pain slowly became separate – wrenched shoulder, damaged shin, bruised ribs where he had kicked her – the panic subsided, and she was able to haul herself up the slope on her hands and knees and then carefully stand up straight. Her shin hurt enough to make her limp, and there was a trickle of blood running down into her shoe. There was no point giving chase: she'd never catch up with him now, and, besides, there were several different side paths he could take that led to the Alresford road. She satisfied herself by uselessly screaming *Bastard!* at his retreating back.

She looked around to check if there was anyone who might have witnessed the encounter, but apart from some wheeling seagulls she was alone. She had her phone with her and considered calling for back-up, but there was no point. She hadn't seen the man's face and would be unable to identify him. Her first thought was that it had been a warning from Warren Cox not to name him as her source, but then a worse fear knotted her gut: what if the hoodie-wearing thug had been sent by Curtis to pay her back for her meddling? What if she'd just been assaulted by a fellow police officer?

31

Grace wrapped a towel around herself and opened the steamed-up mirrored door of the bathroom cabinet in search of some antiseptic for the weal on her shin. She'd allowed herself a brief cry in the shower, but now her shoulder was starting to ache, as were her ribs where the bastard had kicked her down the bank, and she was badly shaken. She had just squeezed some cream onto her finger when she heard her phone ring on her bed next door. Trying to wipe her hand so she didn't smear the cream, she registered that the call was from Lance, even though he was in Portugal.

'Hey, Lance, how are you?'

'I need to talk to you.'

'Of course.' She sat on the bed, swinging her feet up and covering her legs with the duvet so that, pretty much naked, she didn't get chilled. 'What's it like there? You got good weather?'

'Can I come round?'

'I don't understand. You're back already?'

'Yesterday.'

'Why? You've only been there a couple of days. I thought you were staying until next week?'

'I'll explain when I see you.'

ISABELLE GREY | 201

'Sure. Are you OK? Look, why don't you come over for supper tonight?'

'No, now.'

'I was planning to—'

'Please, Grace. I need to talk to you now.'

'OK, but—'

'I'm on my way.'

Lance ended the call. He'd sounded strung out, and must be in a pretty bad way to have come home so abruptly. All the same, Grace was frustrated that she couldn't now go into work as she'd planned and initiate a data search for other rifle incidents. She recognized that her urgent need to act was a displacement for her shock, and that the last thing she felt able to cope with right now was having to revisit the moral quandary she'd shelved when Lance had departed for the Algarve, but her guilt at wishing to avoid him was heavily laced with shame that she could even consider refusing him the comfort and friendship he clearly needed.

Her hands shook as she did up the buttons on her blouse. Rejecting a skirt in favour of trousers that would hide the messy wound on her shin, her tears threatened to return. Her wobbliness scared her. It wasn't like her. She hated being feeble. She needed to get a grip and not let the bastards, whoever they were, grind her down. The thug had probably just been some aggrieved idiot who'd had a row with his girlfriend and had randomly taken it out on her. She finished dressing, combed her hair and went downstairs to make coffee.

By the time Lance arrived twenty minutes later, Grace had thought through the implications of sharing her extremely sketchy new theories and had decided to keep them to herself for now. He looked stressed and preoccupied, and replied to her questions distractedly. He carried a glossy property magazine, its cover all blue sky and swimming pool against dazzling white minimalist architecture. Glancing at it on her kitchen table as she poured fresh coffee, and wondering why he'd brought it, she thought the image made her own little patio look more wintry and bedraggled than ever.

'Was it just too hard, being there alone?' she asked.

'Actually it helped in a way,' he said. 'The resort was so surreal, it kind of matched the idea of Peter being dead, which is surreal enough. But then I saw this.'

He pushed the magazine towards her, and she noticed that a sheet of paper had been inserted as a bookmark. She opened it at the marker and saw a double-page spread with photographs of an emerald-green golf course where men and women in colourful polo shirts and baseball caps posed against a background of white-capped ocean and picturesque umbrella pines.

'He never mentioned going to Portugal,' said Lance, his voice strangled and tense.

Puzzled, Grace looked more closely and recognized Peter standing in the midst of one of the smiling groups. 'But this could have been taken years ago.' She checked the front cover – the date was current – and then flicked back through the magazine, seeing page after page of luxury living and endless blue skies. 'These are just generic publicity shots, surely?'

Lance shook his head. 'No, I checked. I actually phoned the magazine to ask. I couldn't bear not knowing. It was taken last October.'

'Was Peter away somewhere last October?'

'Head office in London, that's what he told me,' said Lance

miserably. 'I went to the golf club and asked around to try and find out if he was there with someone, but no one seemed to know. Why would they?'

Grace longed to put him out of his misery. 'Maybe there was some work reason he couldn't tell you,' she said desperately. 'Client confidentiality or something.'

'You know what went through my head last night?'

'What?'

Lance laughed bitterly. 'I thought maybe he had a wife and kids, and had gone there with them.'

'Oh, Lance, no! Peter wasn't like that.'

'Some men are.'

'Not Peter. He adored you.'

'So why was he always so discreet? Why won't his family communicate with me?'

This was the moment of decision she had been dreading. What was the quote that was always used about the Cambridge spy ring? *If I had to choose between betraying my country and betraying my friend, I hope I should have the guts to betray my country.* Well, did she have the guts to tell Colin – and the security services – and the whole top-heavy hierarchy that her job had sworn her to uphold – to go to hell? Besides, could it really matter? Whatever Peter was investigating, surely it hadn't been some dire terrorist threat?

Up to now she'd managed to reassure herself that even if she told Lance the truth, it might not necessarily help him through his grief. Now she had to face the full hatefulness of her lies. She couldn't do it. She must give him the truth. Even if it meant him despising her for not having told him sooner.

'And you're absolutely sure it's him?' she asked, opening the magazine once more to give herself a moment in which to decide. But it was unquestionably Peter, wearing smart navy trousers and a short-sleeved shirt and not quite looking directly at the camera. A much older, heavier man stood beside him, leaning on his golf club, in tailored navy shorts, white polo shirt and green baseball cap; the other two were around Peter's age and undistinguished, although something about the one in cargo pants and a red shirt seemed familiar. The caption did not identify the players, only the match. 'Did you find out who these guys were?' she asked.

'Only him,' said Lance, pointing at the older man. 'A local property developer. Everybody knows him, apparently. The others were visitors like Peter.'

'Did you speak to this older guy?'

'Not directly. But I asked everyone I could. Told them Peter was dead.' He shook his head. 'Nothing.'

Told them he was dead. A memory jumped into Grace's mind: she'd met the man in the red top! It was Adam Kirkby, who'd been with his father on Christmas Day when she'd broken the news that Mark had been shot. Her mind whirred into overdrive. Hadn't Curtis told her he'd been drinking with Adam and his brother in the Blue Bar the night Lance and Peter decided to go home early? Curtis had been the first officer on the scene when Peter was killed. Adam's brother Mark had been in possession of an illegal firearm. Her shoulder gave a twinge of pain and she rubbed it. She had to think all this through properly before blurting it out to Lance. If the hoodie's attack had been specifically directed at her, then she didn't want to place Lance in danger too. Even though none of it added up to anything that made sense.

'Have you got any leads on Peter's murder yet?'

Lance's question broke into her alarm, and she strove to answer calmly. 'I'm sorry, no. Nothing. We've tried everything. I'm afraid it's going to be one of those where we may have to wait for the killer to make a mistake.'

'That's not good enough!'

'No, I know. And I couldn't be more sorry.' She took a deep breath. 'While you were away, the case was transferred to the London coroner's jurisdiction. It's out of our hands now.'

Lance was about to protest, but then covered his face with his hands. 'What do I care?' he said despairingly. 'Why should I bother about some shit who lied to me about where he was? He was probably cheating on me. He probably he went to that alley with someone, thinking they were going to fuck, and got himself killed instead.'

'He didn't go with anyone from the bar,' said Grace gently. 'He had one beer and left. Alone.'

'What about the people he'd had dinner with?'

Grace had been over this with Lance several times already, but understood his need to repeat and repeat. 'I spoke to them myself,' she said patiently. 'They were all from the Colchester office of a large wealth-management company. In fact the company advises a lot of police officers on their financial affairs nationwide. It was straightforward business, with them schmoozing a financial adviser in the hope he'd recommend their company to his clients.' Except, thought Grace, Peter wasn't a financial adviser.

'What about some army connection? There's a squaddies' pub not too far away.'

'Lance, I promise you, we've covered everything.'

'Well, I'm going to keep digging. I have to.'

'I understand. I do. But there's no point driving yourself mad over this photograph.' Grace had never felt like a bigger shit in all her life. But Lance looked like he hadn't slept in days. He was in no fit state to handle the truth, especially a truth not only complicated by her own deep but unfocused suspicion of anything to do with the Kirkby family, but now also by Mark's possible link to the Lion King. 'You have to look after yourself,' she ended lamely.

'I'll go mad if I do nothing,' he said. 'I mean, it's like he's just vanished into thin air. I never got to see him – afterwards – to say goodbye. No funeral, nowhere to send flowers or a card, nothing. Even the locks at his flat have been changed. It's unreal.'

'I know.' She squeezed his hand where it lay on the table beside the open magazine.

'You will help me, won't you, Grace?'

'Of course.' She glanced down at the magazine from where Adam Kirkby in his red shirt stared right back up at her.

32

Grace had not expected to be so thankful when Ivo called her from a public call box not long after Lance had left her house. 'I've got something for you,' was all he'd said, but it was enough, given how desperate she felt, to abandon her plan to go into work and head instead to the cafe in the ring-road superstore where they'd met last time.

She caught sight of him before he spotted her, and she thought he seemed uncharacteristically on edge, glancing from side to side as if fearing an ambush. Her own rush of warmth on seeing him again also took her by surprise, although given the way her day had gone so far, perhaps she was just glad to see any friendly face. She slipped into the seat opposite him and returned his smile.

'Thanks for coming,' he said.

'I'd been thinking about you, actually.'

'That's nice,' he said, turning slightly pink.

Grace reminded herself that this was the chief crime correspondent of the *Daily Courier*, and she mustn't be naive about trusting him.

'Coffee?' he asked.

She took a look at the grey liquid in his untouched cup and shook her head. 'I can live without, thanks.'

'Don't blame you. So, I've been keeping an eye on young Davey Fewell.'

'Oh good,' she said. 'I'm so pleased.'

Ivo looked a little embarrassed. 'I just felt for the kid, you know? I didn't like the idea of Mark Kirkby's father being the only one to look out for the family and Davey having to be grateful to him.'

'No,' Grace agreed. 'Nor me. So where is he?'

'Weymouth. In a holiday apartment owned by the Police Federation.'

Grace nodded. 'I heard John Kirkby had fixed something up for them. How's he getting on?'

Ivo shrugged. 'I caught him bunking off school.'

'Poor kid,' said Grace.

'Anyway, we got chatting.'

Grace wondered if she could guess what was coming next. 'And?'

'It's worse than we thought, about Mark Kirkby.'

'Davey told you?' Grace asked the question before she could stop herself.

'Told me what?'

She recognized his look of professional cunning and smiled. 'You go first.'

Ivo grinned. 'Fair enough.' He checked around them to see if anyone was listening, then leaned across the table. 'He said Mark Kirkby had a gun. A big one.'

She nodded. 'That's what he told me too. But then immediately backtracked. Said he'd told his dad, but was so afraid there'd be a row he insisted he'd made it up.'

Ivo looked relieved. 'So you're on it already,' he said. 'That's good.' He sat back. 'I really do hope it turns out that Mark Kirkby was shot with his own weapon. Serve the creepy bastard right.'

Grace bit her lip. 'Davey told me nearly three weeks ago, and I've done nothing.' She waited for Ivo's expression to settle into contempt and found herself grateful when it didn't.

He sighed. 'Nor me. It really went against the grain not to go front page with a story like that. Wouldn't normally have given it a second thought.'

'So why did you?'

'Because it would blow that kid and what's left of his family right out of the water. I must be going soft, but I just couldn't do it to him.'

'I can't even use that as an excuse. I bottled it, pure and simple. My boss was making all the funeral arrangements for Mark Kirkby. You must've seen how elaborate it all got.'

Ivo nodded. 'I did. You're talking about Superintendent Pitman?'

'Yes. There was no point making accusations I couldn't back up. Well, anyway, I didn't, did I?'

'Don't beat yourself up,' said Ivo.

His kindness brought a lump to Grace's throat. Her shoulder had stiffened up and was really hurting, and she still felt like crap about Lance. She struggled to maintain her composure.

'It's one thing for me to lob a grenade right into the middle of a bells-and-whistles funeral,' Ivo continued. 'That's my job. But no point you shooting yourself in the foot for nothing, is there?'

'So what is my job?' she asked bitterly.

'Keep your chin up. We can't all be superheroes.'

'I suppose one good thing is that at least Davey is telling

people,' said Grace. 'Perhaps he'll tell Donna soon too, and not keep it a secret much longer.'

'He's not likely pipe up with Mark Kirkby's father breathing down his neck. I saw John Kirkby, by the way.'

Grace was taken aback. 'Did you tell him who you are, why you were there?'

'No, of course not. I just let him bend my ear about how hard done by the brave boys in blue are these days.'

'Well, there's some truth in that,' said Grace. 'The cuts are starting to hurt.'

'I won't quote you,' Ivo said with a smile.

'I have a favour to ask,' she said, making a snap decision. She wouldn't confide in him about this morning's riverside encounter, but she had to do whatever she could to support Lance.

Ivo nodded. 'Shall we look at some dishwashers?' He got to his feet and she followed him. They did not speak until they reached an area of mocked-up fitted kitchens. Wandering into the nearest one and opening a cupboard door as he checked over his shoulder, Ivo spoke quietly. 'How can I help?'

'This is absolutely not for publication.'

Ivo held up a hand. 'Scout's honour.'

'You probably don't know,' she said, 'but nine days ago a man called Peter Burnley was murdered in Colchester. Beaten to death after leaving a bar. No witnesses, nothing.'

Ivo shook his head. 'Must've come across my radar, but I can't say it caught my attention.'

'Well, Peter Burnley just turned up in a photograph standing right next to Adam Kirkby, Mark's younger brother.'

'Well, well! Tell me more.'

Grace took his arm and led the way along the aisle between

the displays, walking slowly as if they were shopping. She checked behind before speaking softly into his ear. 'Peter Burnley wasn't his real name. He said he was a financial adviser, but in fact he was working undercover. I don't know for which service. And he'd lied to his boyfriend about where he was when the photograph was taken.'

'Which was?' asked Ivo.

'A golf resort in the Algarve. Vale do Lobo.'

'When was this?'

'Last October.'

'OK, leave it with me.'

'Really?'

Ivo squeezed her arm against his body. 'Well, shiver my timbers if I don't feel another sighting of Lord Lucan coming on. As you are no doubt aware, my dear, he's only ever been spotted in warm and luxurious climes, and it's a time-honoured tradition that every so often one's editor will agree to sign off on a few days of hot pursuit. Never know, one day we might even stumble across him by sheer accident.'

Grace laughed, though she felt more like hugging him. It was such a relief to have someone who didn't think she was crazy to believe that all these dots might join up into a significant picture.

'By the way,' he said, 'I didn't get any further with your tip about PC Curtis Mullins. My asking around in Dunholt about Mark Kirkby was brought rather swiftly to the attention of my editor, who told me to drop it, pronto.'

'Well, thanks for trying,' she said.

Ivo sighed and shook his head. 'All I want now is to put that gun in Mark Kirkby's hands so Davey Fewell can make some sense of his life.'

Mindful of Warren Cox, Grace decided it was too soon to share her suspicions of Leonard Ingold. Besides, what she really wanted to tell Ivo was that Davey was lucky to have him as his champion. But then something in the way he was looking at her made her think he might also be doing this for her. He made an unlikely knight in shining armour: a portly man in his fifties who'd gone to seed some time ago and made little effort to do anything about it since. Yet she had to admit she was happy to have him on her side.

33

Four weeks on from the winter solstice and Robyn could now reach home after school before the afternoon darkness fully settled in. It made a huge difference to her day, knowing she'd have even a few minutes to take the dogs for a quick run and to feel at home before the curtains were drawn and a long evening of homework and seclusion began. She never used to mind how remote they were from other houses or the nearest village, but since Angie's death she'd felt the need to huddle closer to fellow human beings.

Walking the last part of the track, she saw they were not alone: a car was parked outside Leonard's workshop, and the lights were on inside. Normally she would go straight into the house, uninterested in her dad's clients, but an impulse she didn't choose to question directed her to the door of the reception area, and she went straight in. Her father quickly hid his surprise – did she also detect disapproval? – and turned to his visitors.

'My daughter, Robyn,' he told them shortly.

Robyn recognized the two police officers who greeted her: DC Duncan Gregg had come to see her father a couple of days after the Dunholt shootings, and the slim serious woman in the tailored grey trouser suit had spoken to her mother at the funeral. The woman held out her hand. 'I'm Grace Fisher,' she said. 'Good to meet you.'

Robyn shook Grace Fisher's hand, acutely aware of the clear grey eyes scanning her face. Robyn backed away but stopped beside the door, where she stood against the wall, trying to remain unobtrusive yet determined to learn for herself this time why they were here and what it was they wanted with her father. But it seemed she was too late, as they were already winding up their conversation.

'I really appreciate your help, Mr Ingold,' said Grace. 'It'll be so much easier to get my head around the detail now you've shown me how a rifle round is put together. I can't thank you enough for your time and we won't disturb you any longer.'

'No problem,' said Leonard, ushering them to the door, a hand on Duncan's back. 'Duncan should bring you along to one of the visitors' days at the club. You could try a bit of duck shooting for yourself.'

'Maybe I will, thanks,' she replied pleasantly. 'You have my card if you hear anything you think we ought to know.'

Robyn slipped out in front of them into the gathering dusk and, as Leonard turned out of habit to lock the door behind him, she followed the detectives to their car. 'Are you still investigating what happened in Dunholt?' she asked.

'Just tying up loose ends,' said Grace. 'We owe it to the families to do all we can.'

Robyn nodded, her eyes on her father. 'My friend Angie Turner died. And her grandmother.'

'Oh, I am sorry.' As Grace stepped forward to place a hand on her arm, Robyn thought she seemed more shocked than the information warranted. Grace's gesture was followed by a swift, almost involuntary, glance at Leonard, who now joined them. Robyn watched as she slipped into the passenger seat and busied herself with her seat belt, leaving it to Duncan to repeat their thanks and say goodbye.

Leonard remained where he was, watching thoughtfully as the car made its slow progress back up the track. Robyn left him and went into the house, dropping her school rucksack and calling to the dogs as she kicked off her shoes and pulled on a pair of wellingtons. Bounder was keen to escape the house, and Martha, once she had staggered to her feet, was happy to do what was asked of her. Robyn was glad of their comforting presence. The light was fading and there wouldn't be time to go far beyond the first field, but she needed to gain some distance.

From the end of the garden she looked back at her home, where the lights were now on in the kitchen and living room. It looked cosy, nestled in against the rising ground, the gnarled and knotty branches of the big old cherry tree behind the house silhouetted against the silvery-blue sky. It would be cold tonight, and she should check on the hens and donkeys on her way back.

It was Leonard who'd announced they were getting the donkeys. Their owner had died, must be five years ago now, and it had proved difficult to find a sanctuary, so her dad had offered to take them, declaring that Robyn would be over the moon to have them. She'd never really taken to them, if she were honest – they were stubborn and unresponsive creatures – but they were part of the place now and it pleased her dad to think of them as hers.

The point of them was that it gave him pleasure to be the kind of dad who bestowed such delightful surprises. It didn't suit him to see that, actually, they were a chore. It was revolutionary for her to have such thoughts. She had never once questioned the goodness and generosity of her family life. It then occurred to her that the isolated spot in which they lived – chosen because it suited the needs of his business – had also always been presented to her as a special advantage, as if it bestowed something rare and commendable on them as a family.

Robyn hated herself for thinking like this. Perhaps every teenager went through this process, as the scales fell from their eyes and they began to grow up and judge their parents more objectively, but somehow this felt bigger than that. The cracks that, since Christmas, had been opening at her feet felt deep and precipitous, as if they might divide her for ever from her old life.

Martha, standing beside her, nudged a warm muzzle into her hand, reminding her that an old dog with an arthritic hip would be happier inside by a warm fire. Robyn rubbed the dog's head and stroked her back. 'OK,' she said. 'Come on, let's go in.'

She found her parents sitting across from one another at the kitchen table in earnest conversation. They both sat back as she entered, relaxing their expressions.

'Stars out yet?' asked her father. 'Should be able to see Jupiter at this time of year.'

'Not yet.' Robyn waited for him to mention the second visit from the police, but instead he got to his feet, asking Nicola if she wanted any potatoes peeled for supper. Robyn muttered about homework to do and, picking up her rucksack, shut herself in her bedroom. Waiting for her laptop to power up, Robyn made an effort to recall exactly what Grace Fisher's reaction had been when she had mentioned Angie. A look of shock, of horror even, followed by a flint-like glance at her dad.

Robyn had never looked at the online coverage of the Dunholt shootings, but she did so now. There were photographs of the town, of Russell Fewell, of his victims and their families – including Angie and her grandmother – of the locations of some of the shootings, more pictures of his victims, of a rifle and of rifle rounds and spent bullets. Staring at the images, unready and unwilling to articulate her precise thoughts, she typed in 'gun crimes' and then 'fatal shootings'. There were dozens of links: page after page of murder, guns in schools, urban gangs, domestic violence, family annihilation, suicide, armed robbery, carjacking, hostage situations, terrorism. Nearly all involved illegal weapons.

She slammed down the lid of her computer. None of this had anything to do with her or her family. Nothing.

34

Coming in to work, Grace heard the *clack* of Hilary Burnett's high heels behind her. She turned to wait for the communications director to catch up, making an effort to conceal her irritation. Grace genuinely liked Hilary and usually took pains to hide how little time she had for her role, but this morning it seemed especially hard.

'Morning, Hilary.'

'Hello, Grace. I'm glad I caught you. How are you?'

'Fine, thanks,' Grace answered, although she wasn't sure she looked it. She'd tossed and turned all night, trying to work out the best way to persuade Colin to place Leonard Ingold under surveillance.

'That's good,' said Hilary. 'Though I must say, you look a little peaky to me.'

Grace smiled at how the older woman's essential kindness always shone through whatever mission she was on. 'A bit tired, that's all,' she said. 'Nothing to worry about.'

'Glad to hear it,' said Hilary. 'Now, I don't know if Colin's had a chance to tell you yet, but the date for the Dunholt inquest has been confirmed for next month.'

'Next month? As soon as that?' Grace knew that the Essex

coroner had routinely opened and adjourned the inquest to allow the funerals to go ahead, but she hadn't expected him to reopen it for several months yet.

'Yes, it's a controversial decision,' said Hilary. 'But his view is that it will help the families and give the community a chance to heal if he speeds things up as much as possible. He's let it be known that he wants proceedings to be brief and not to stray too far from the basic requirements of who, how and when.'

Only now, feeling her disappointment, did Grace realize how much weight she'd placed on a full and thorough hearing bringing all the facts to light.

'Anyway,' Hilary continued, 'Colin thought perhaps a quick prep session might not be a bad idea.'

'A prep session?' Grace couldn't hold back a laugh of incredulity. 'Hilary, I have given evidence at an inquest before.'

'Yes, of course you have. But this one is a little different. The chief constable agrees that it's a matter of tone.'

'Tone?'

Hilary reached out to touch Grace's arm. 'I realize it may sound trivial, but small things can matter a great deal to the families at a time like this. It's important to see it from their point of view.'

Grace was tempted to point out that Donna, Davey and Ella were also among the grieving families, but thought better of it and murmured her agreement.

'There's so little anyone can do for them,' said Hilary. 'We've taken best practice from other tragedies. We had all the clothing cleaned before it was given back and returned all the jewellery in proper cases. I'm not sure whether such things really help, but they can't do any harm.'

'It's very thoughtful,' said Grace and meant it. 'I'm sorry if I sounded dismissive.'

'You're at the sharp end,' said Hilary. 'I realize that what I do can seem like a distraction, but if you could spare some time in the next day or so . . . ?'

'Of course. And I do appreciate what you do, Hilary.'

Hilary laughed. 'Thanks. It's not what you think of as policing, but it'll be a nice excuse to see you and have a chat.'

'It will.'

Hilary went on her way, leaving Grace conflicted. Of course everything Hilary said made perfect sense, but while an inquest was often about finding dignity and closure for the relatives, it could also be the only chance to put important truths on record. Grace wasn't sure she liked the idea of what had taken place at Dunholt being smoothed away by a bit of smart PR work, however well intentioned, and her resistance to the idea strengthened her resolve that the time had finally come to tell Colin about Davey Fewell. She went straight to his office and rapped on the door.

Colin looked up from his desk. 'Ah, good, Grace. I've been wanting a word.'

'Hilary just told me the date's been confirmed for the Dunholt inquest.'

'That's right. Given the unusual timing, it can only be pretty much a formality, but it'll be good to get it over and done with. And everything our end should be pretty straightforward.'

'Yes and no,' said Grace.

Colin frowned. 'You'd better sit down.'

Grace took a moment to compose her thoughts. 'Davey Fewell told me something that may shine a different light on things.'

'Davey Fewell?'

'Russell Fewell's ten-year-old son. He told me that Mark Kirkby showed him a gun, a big heavy one, and that it had to be their special secret. Davey said he told his dad about it, who was furious.' Grace waited for Colin to speak, but he remained silent so she pressed on. 'What if Fewell stole the rifle and ammunition he used from Mark Kirkby?'

'I assume Mark Kirkby had all the correct paperwork?'

'No. Nothing. But he had completed a police firearms training course, so would be familiar with a Heckler & Koch G3.' Grace knew that she had to be precise, had to build her argument brick by brick, if she was going to carry Colin along with her. 'If Russell did take the rifle, Mark wouldn't have been able to report it. I wondered if perhaps Mark's response had been to fabricate the drink-driving charge?'

'How long have you known about this?'

'A little while,' said Grace with deliberate imprecision. 'I wanted to see if I could back Davey's statement up. I haven't been able to so far. And then we had the Peter Burnley murder.'

'So why are you telling me now?'

If his question was meant as a reprimand, Grace ignored it. 'Davey may also have told other people,' she said. 'I'm telling you now because it may come up at the inquest.'

'And if it does?'

'I believed what Davey Fewell told me, and so did the FLO. But his mother knows nothing about it, and, when pressed, Davey backtracked, said he made it up.'

'So there's nothing concrete?' asked Colin.

'No, sir, but if a narrative does emerge of a gunman driven to desperation by harassment from serving officers, one of whom possessed an illegal firearm which may have been the murder weapon—'

'Do you think it's likely that such a narrative will *emerge*?' Colin's expression was inscrutable, but Grace knew him well enough to guess that he was rapidly calculating the range of available options, searching for the one that would cause him the least damage.

She gave him a straight look. 'I think it's the truth.'

He gave a cynical laugh. 'It may very well be, but that doesn't make it a good idea to go shouting "Fire!" in a crowded theatre, does it?'

'There's enough circumstantial evidence to suggest that Curtis Mullins conspired with Mark Kirkby to pervert the course of justice. Off the record, Curtis pretty well admitted as much to me. It may be strategic to refer the circumstances of Fewell's drink-drive arrest to Professional Standards.'

'Fewell never made a complaint,' said Colin sharply.

'No,' said Grace as calmly as she could manage. 'But he did shoot dead five people. The coroner is going to pay attention to the balance of his mind at the time.'

Colin glanced over Grace's shoulder out into the office beyond the closed door and then leaned forwards across his desk. For a fleeting moment Grace felt afraid of his coiled tension, as if she were facing an animal about to leap.

'What is this, Grace?' he asked quietly. 'Not payback, I hope?'

'No, of course not!'

'Because you know how sorry I am for what happened in the past. I accepted my reprimand, and I really thought we'd let it go and were moving forwards. It's why I wanted to keep you on my team, made you back up to DI.'

Grace knew it had not been Colin but her old boss Keith Stalgood who had insisted on her promotion. Besides, Colin hadn't been left with much choice: it wouldn't have looked good if he'd tried to get rid of her. She forced a smile. 'It's not payback, Colin, I promise. And I understood that I couldn't go flinging accusations around when Mark Kirkby's coffin was draped in the Essex force insignia. But it doesn't mean it's all gone away. I thought you should know.'

'I hope you're not suggesting that I'd ever place public relations considerations before an operational lead?'

He spoke lightly enough, but something in his eyes told her to tread carefully: Colin Pitman wouldn't be above twisting everything so he could put in a complaint against her. 'No. I just wanted to keep you informed.'

'Good. Thank you.' He sat back, thinking everything over. 'It's not the coroner's remit to establish *why* a death takes place.'

'Unless a coroner deems there are issues of public interest,' Grace reminded him as blandly as she could.

Colin shook his head. 'Even if Mark Kirkby was corrupt, one rogue officer who is now dead doesn't warrant that amount of attention.'

Grace said nothing – they'd been here before, and it was a waste of breath – but this time she made no attempt to hide her contempt.

Colin took no notice of her scornful expression. 'Any headway on inquiries into the origins of the rifle and ammunition?' he asked.

'Ongoing, firming up, but as yet nothing actionable.'

Watching Colin frown and purse his lips in apparent frustration, Grace decided not to name Leonard Ingold after all. The mood he was in, he might tell her to drop it, in which case she wouldn't officially be able to involve Duncan or any other members of the team. Best to stay under the radar for the time being.

'We've checked for a match on the ballistics, obviously,' she continued. 'But I also looked to see whether there had been any other homicides in the past two years involving a rifle and hollow-point bullets, even if a weapon was never recovered and no casings found.'

'And?'

'There were none until four months ago, when there were two in a six-week period.'

'On our patch?' asked Colin.

'No. The first victim was a forty-two-year-old man in Ely, an illegal immigrant from Albania thought to be operating as an unlicensed gangmaster and possible people-trafficker, the other a convicted paedophile shot near his house in Grantham.'

'Anything apart from the type of weapon to suggest they're linked?'

'No, sir.'

'Then what are you saying?'

'I don't really know. I'm gathering intelligence. Too soon to draw conclusions.'

Colin sighed heavily. 'Look, Grace,' he said, 'if you believe Davey Fewell, then fine, so do I. You know I've always trusted your instincts. But you have to admit this is verging on some kind of fixation.' He held up a hand for silence, although she'd had no intention of protesting. 'And these are very sensitive issues,' he went on. 'Very sensitive. I don't want it to look like we're somehow trying to exonerate Fewell, not unless we've got rock-solid evidence, which we haven't. And most definitely not at the cost of alienating the majority of decent coppers on the Essex force by firing an unsubstantiated barrage of accusations against a respected officer. Not when the chief constable is looking to implement further cuts right across the board. You bring me proper evidence, and I'll throw the book at whoever deserves it. But until then you must have plenty else to get on with.'

Grace wondered what Colin would say if she told him about the hoodie who attacked her yesterday morning. Or that Mark Kirkby's father had taken it upon himself to look after Donna and her children. But it would be pointless. No, worse than pointless: she didn't want to hand him anything he might use against her later.

'I understand,' she said.

'So you'll prep your evidence for the inquest with Hilary?'

'Yes, sir. We've already fixed a time to meet.'

'Good.' He got to his feet. 'I hear Lance Cooper came back early,' he said casually. 'Portugal not suit him or what?'

'Not really, no.' Grace remained in her seat, more or less forcing Colin to sit down again. 'Peter Burnley's murder has really knocked him hard,' she said. 'I think we should put him fully in the picture.'

'That's not possible,' said Colin curtly. 'I'm as sorry as you are, Grace, and I have every sympathy for his distress, but you're just going to have to put your foot on the ball on this one.'

'I think it's too late for that,' she said. 'He's suspicious. And he's a good detective. Surely it's better to tell him the truth than have him uncovering Peter Burnley's secrets for himself?' *Whatever they are*, she added silently.

Colin shook his head firmly, once again rising to his feet. 'I've received assurances that there's no connection between what Peter Burnley was working on and his death.'

'And you believe those assurances?' she asked.

'I have no alternative.'

'I'm scared Lance will crack up completely, trying to fill in the blanks.'

'I can't help. I'm no wiser than you are. They've given me no idea of what Peter Burnley was up to.'

'And if it all starts to unravel,' she said, 'have they given assurances that it won't be us who are hung out to dry?'

Colin spread his hands and gave a wry smile. 'No need for you to worry. It'll be my head on the block, no one else's.'

It went against all Grace's training and experience not to tell him about the photograph of Peter with Adam Kirkby in Vale do Lobo, but she knew that, whatever her boss might say, his job was no longer about prioritizing operational leads, and he would simply coddle her into downgrading and dismissing its significance, as he'd just done over Davey Fewell. She stood up and was heading for the door when he called after her.

'Listen, if Lance needs more time on compassionate leave, let me know. It's not a problem.'

'OK. But the simplest thing really would be to tell him what little you do know,' she pleaded. 'If it was done formally, then I honestly think he could handle it. He's party to the Official Secrets Act, after all. There's nothing he can do with the information if he's told officially.'

'Sorry, no. And that's an order.'

Grace returned to her own desk with the uncomfortable realization that she too was signed up to the Official Secrets Act.

35

There was always something cheering about the sight of a palm tree, even in an airport car park, especially when it meant that Ivo had escaped a grisly English January, and even more so when he was on expenses. It wasn't *hot* hot in Faro, but it was balmy enough to be pleased he'd dug out the baggy linen jacket that always made him feel like one of those veteran foreign correspondents. No doubt about it, he had a spring in his step today and was looking forward to a bit of old-fashioned legwork tracking down the story behind the murder of an unidentified spook in a Colchester alley.

Not that he gave much of a toss about the spook, to be honest, except perhaps that his death had upset DI Fisher; no, it was the involvement of Adam Kirkby that had really got his juices flowing and stoked up a bit of healthy outrage. Old Pa Kirkby might be a generous tipper who liked to look after his own, but Ivo had made up his mind to take a serious dislike to all the Kirkby family and was ready to embark on a mission of righteous smiting of the kind that only a great British bulldog tabloid was truly capable.

The last time he'd been in Portugal the story had been the disappearance of Madeleine McCann, which had turned into such a media juggernaut that, frankly, the fate of the poor kid often got totally overlooked. After his third trip Ivo had got fed up and headed home, leaving it to some of the junior reporters to kick their heels in the blazing summer heat of Praia da Luz. Nonetheless he still had one or two names in his address book from those days and had arranged for the best of the local fixers to meet his flight. Ever reliable, Gavin Whittaker had been waiting with Ivo's name on a card and was now escorting him to where he'd left his car.

Ivo had been a little apprehensive about seeing Gavin again: the start of the Maddie saga had coincided with Ivo's final years of drinking, when, estranged from his daughter and already well on the way to pissing away his second marriage, Ivo had not always behaved like a true gentleman. But as he and Gavin began the twenty-minute drive to Vale do Lobo, it seemed that, whatever tall tales Gavin might remember from those times, he intended to be discreet enough to spare Ivo's blushes.

Not that Ivo was about to pay him for his discretion. Gavin had been a small-time crook who'd married a Spanish girl and settled on the already fading Costa del Crime twenty-odd years ago. He'd become fluent in both Spanish and Portuguese, and hustled a living for himself finding locations for advertising shoots, acting as a stringer for a couple of news outlets, including the *Courier*, repping a couple of holiday rental complexes and acting as logistics manager for some of the drug dealers who plied their trade out of La Línea.

Gavin had immediately shuttled west to Praia da Luz when the McCann story broke, proving himself an invaluable go-between for the UK reporters and the Portuguese journalists who had the lie of the land but didn't want to be seen inquiring too deeply into the flaky police investigation for fear of upsetting the delicate balance of local politics. After all, once the great media circus finally left town, the local boys would have to pick up where they'd left off.

Not that it yet had, thank goodness, for it was not Lord Lucan but the perennial interest in the McCann story that had enabled Ivo to sell his editor on a brazenly invented rumour about child-trafficking among the golf-and-bridge community on the Algarve. He'd been tempted to trace it all the way home to some uptight enclave of leafy suburbia, but had decided reluctantly that that might be over-egging the pudding. Or maybe not. Anyway, he might yet require it as a teaser should he find he needed to stay longer than planned. And meanwhile it had got him his trip signed off, which is all he cared about.

Approaching the outskirts of the resort, Gavin suggested lunch at a little 'shack' he knew on the beach. He was already being paid handsomely, but Ivo understood that the meal was an expected perk and did not baulk at the Mayfair prices. At least, out of season, it wasn't heaving with tourists.

'So I guess you want a rundown of the local faces,' said Gavin once they'd settled at a table covered with an ocean of white linen that overlooked a row of beach umbrellas and brochure-blue water. 'Where do you want to start? Drugs, fake documents, people-trafficking, porn, money-laundering, dodgy property deals, arms?'

'I'll follow the money,' said Ivo.

'Always a sensible choice,' agreed Gavin.

'The guy I'm interested in was a financial adviser.' Ivo wasn't prepared to put all his cards on the table by telling Gavin that 'Peter Burnley' was a cover, but he had enough respect for the fixer's talents not to attempt to conceal anything that was already in the public domain, such as his death. 'This is him,' he added, digging out a colour printout of the magazine photo Grace had shown him. 'Know any of the people he was with?'

'Only that one.' Gavin stabbed a bronzed finger at the man in a white polo shirt standing beside Peter. 'That's Jerry Coghlan. Everyone round here knows him. The others, I've no idea.'

As Ivo pulled out his trusty shorthand notebook a waiter appeared and Gavin took his time discussing the merits of the different seafood on offer. Ivo's own taste buds were wrecked by years of drinking; he quickly ordered a burger and got back to the job in hand. 'Tell me about Coghlan.'

'Really? You never met him?' Gavin sounded genuinely surprised.

'Nope.'

'He was Flying Squad back in the day. Took early retirement. Very early. Several trials collapsed because of missing paperwork, and the word was that his future missus worked as a secretary next door to the CPS shredding room.'

'Yeah, that rings a bell,' said Ivo. He looked again at the photo, dimly recognizing an older version of a young detective sergeant marked out by his cleverness and ambition. 'That must've been around the time of Operation Countryman.'

'That's right,' said Gavin. 'His wife's dead now, cancer, but let's just say that the newlyweds got a pretty warm welcome when they honeymooned in Marbella.'

'But he settled here in Portugal, not Spain?'

Gavin nodded. 'He's an extremely good golfer, as it happens. Plays off scratch. Made the right connections to get in on the ground floor when the development expanded in the early eighties.'

'So now he's legit?'

Gavin was distracted by the arrival of his monkfish and prawn kebab. Ivo ate a couple of the chips from beside his burger and waited for his companion to swallow his first mouthful and murmur in approval before asking the question again.

'He plays golf with bankers,' Gavin answered. 'Don't know how legit that is in your book.'

Ivo laughed. 'Which might explain why a financial adviser from the UK would be keen to play a round with him.'

'Depends,' said Gavin. 'You heard about the Espírito Santo scandal?'

'Sounds like a search for the Holy Grail.'

Gavin sucked on a prawn and shook his head. 'Massive dynastic Lisbon bank whose investment arm went bust. Among the casualties was a big development project in the Alentejo region. Not much there except rice fields, cork trees and twelve kilometres of unspoilt beaches only an hour from Lisbon. The building is all very low impact and architecturally sensitive, but maybe not so many questions asked about where the cash was coming from.'

'So do a lot of bankers play golf?'

'They do. When they're not hobnobbing with minor European royalty or Spanish politicians taking time off from talking to their lawyers about their corruption trials.'

Ivo bit into his burger to give himself time to think. He didn't reckon the British security and intelligence services would care enough about some fairly bog-standard money-laundering, however well connected, to send Peter Burnley out to Portugal for that alone. Nor would it explain what he'd been up to in Colchester. So maybe his association with Jerry Coghlan was to gain access to his true target? Which was . . . ?

Not for the first time Ivo wished that his former assistant, the Young Ferret, had not jumped ship and, as the lad had so discreetly put it, gone 'in-house'. The nimble little poacher had declared that he couldn't see a way to keep his head above the choppy waters of Operation Elveden, the Met Police's investigation into corrupt payments made by journalists to public officials, so had turned gamekeeper and joined MI5. Ivo couldn't blame him, although, taking the long view, he didn't share the Young Ferret's belief that talents such as his would never again be appreciated at the *Courier* or her sister titles. Cleaning out the stables of the British press was far too Augean a task to reach into every nook and cranny, especially when it was not in the interests of anyone who mattered to do so.

Before he'd left London, Ivo had attempted to squeeze some kind of smoke signal about Peter Burnley out of the Young Ferret, who now graced the not-so-secret corridors of power on Millbank. But while his erstwhile protégé assured him he'd readily perform a favour for old times' sake, he insisted he knew nothing at all about a Peter Burnley, not even that he'd been murdered. Which meant one of three things: that Peter Burnley wasn't MI5, that whatever he'd had been up to was strictly need-to-know or that it was serious enough for the Young Ferret to lie to his face. Ivo could, he supposed, go back and run Jerry Coghlan's name past him as well to see if any sparks flew, but doubted that Young Ferret would know anything about Coghlan that Gavin couldn't tell him. Come to think of it, if the security services had any sense, Gavin would be on the payroll. In which case, Ivo's own visit would already have been flagged up.

Ivo pulled the photo printout back across the tablecloth, glad now that he hadn't shared Adam Kirkby's name with Gavin.

'And you're sure you don't recognize either of the other two in the photo with Coghlan?'

Gavin shook his head. 'Sorry, no. But if you want me to stay on, I can ask around?' he asked hopefully.

Deciding that Gavin's generous day rate could be better spent elsewhere, Ivo declined the offer. 'Anything else you can tell me about Coghlan?'

'He knows where a lot of the treasure is buried, but I don't think he has any ambitions to be Mr Big. I'd say he's winding down into a more-than-comfortable retirement.'

'Maybe I should be asking him for investment advice.'

'Could do worse,' said Gavin, pushing away his empty plate. 'Seriously, I think that'll be your easiest way in.' He reached for the dessert menu. 'They have a nice muscatel here that goes rather well with the chocolate tart.'

Ivo was fine with that: big fleas have little fleas upon their backs to bite 'em. He was perfectly content to sit and enjoy the view while his newspaper picked up the tab. The paper's proprietor could well afford it.

36

Robyn was so intent on her computer screen that she failed to hear her mother tap at her door and enter her bedroom. Nicola had brought clean bed linen and was mid-sentence, offering to give Robyn a hand changing the duvet cover, when she stopped and stared at the screen. 'What are you doing?'

It was too late for Robyn to hide what she was looking at, so she shrugged uncomfortably. Since the last visit from the police she had spent every free moment obsessively searching online for examples of gun crime. Last year there had been dozens of deaths, with Birmingham and the West Midlands leading the way. Many of those who died were her age or younger: a seven-year-old girl in a takeaway waiting with her older brother to buy chips; two brothers, fifteen and sixteen, gunned down walking across a park on another gang's turf; a fourteen-year-old executed after he panicked and threw away the drugs he was supposed to deliver. How had their killers been able to get hold of firearms so easily? There were so many newspaper articles, all chronicling different and unrelated incidents, that she would never manage to read them all. It felt as if they were cascading around her, cramming themselves into the very air in her room, and yet she had to keep searching and looking: if she stopped, she'd have to answer the question her mother had just put to her, and she simply couldn't face her own motives and suspicions.

Nicola reached over her shoulder to jab at the keyboard. 'Turn it off! What do you want to look at stuff like that for?'

There was no point pretending. Robyn clicked obediently onto something more benign, hunching into herself, away from her mother's anger.

'Don't you know that all your father cares about is you?' Nicola demanded.

Robyn felt her breath leave her body as if someone had let the air out of her. Fear made her angry in return. 'There is a real world out there, you know. Or don't you care about what happens outside your own little bubble?'

'What bubble?' Nicola tossed the clean linen down on the bed and folded her arms tightly across her chest. 'You think running the business and washing and cooking and cleaning and shopping is all a bubble? You wait until you have to start doing it all for yourself at uni!'

'That's not what I meant. You know that!' cried Robyn. 'But why do we have to live here like this, completely away from everyone and everything? What it is? It's almost like we have something to hide!'

Nicola slapped her across the face. It happened so fast that, had Robyn's cheek not been stinging, she might have imagined it. Her mother stood motionless with horror at what she'd done. 'I'm sorry, Birdie,' she said after a shocked silence, moving forward to try and hug her daughter. 'I'm so sorry.'

Robyn wasn't sure whether to be angry or afraid. Not afraid physically – the slap had felt like more of a gesture than an assault – but of what lay behind her mother's totally uncharac-teristic reaction. Her parents hardly ever lost their temper and had never hit her except perhaps a spank when she was little and had tried to stick her fingers in a plug socket. It had always seemed to Robyn that, perhaps because she was an only child, their relationship was far more open and inclusive than the lit-tle she'd seen of her friends' families. But now, she wondered, maybe it was only that she'd never rocked the boat.

'Get out of my room!' she cried, turning away. 'Leave me alone!'

'No, listen, Birdie. This is about Angie, isn't it?'

'No!'

'I know how fond you were of her. And it's hard the first time someone your own age dies. But, believe me, time is a great healer. And the last thing Angie would've wanted is for you to go on being miserable about her.'

'It's not because of Angie!' Robyn spun back round, but then, face to face with her mother, her courage failed and she was too afraid to raise the spectre of the truth.

Nicola sat down on the bed and patted the space beside her. When Robyn didn't respond, she took hold of her wrist and tugged her gently. Robyn sat, her head hanging, hands between her knees.

'Listen to me, Birdie. You don't want to go looking for things like that on the internet. It's nothing to do with us, nothing to do with the work your dad does.'

'He makes bullets. The kind of bullets that killed Angie.'

'That's true, yes. But he didn't kill Angie. He's never hurt any-one in his life.'

'And you don't think any of Dad's stuff ever ends up in the wrong hands, the hands of people who do kill?'

'More people die in car accidents in this country than from guns.'

'But it's possible, isn't it?'

'I suppose so,' said Nicola. 'But that's got nothing to do with us.'

'How can you say that?' Robyn felt utterly bewildered. 'Everything's connected. We're all responsible for what happens in the world.'

Nicola smiled and patted Robyn's knee. 'Everyone thinks that at your age.'

Her mother's dismissive words were unbearable. Robyn clenched her hands and turned to look hard at her mother. 'Did Dad know the gunman who shot Angie and all those other people?'

'No!' Nicola looked shocked. 'Of course not.'

'So why do the police keep coming to talk to him?'

'They've only been twice, haven't they?'

Robyn heard the sharp rise in Nicola's voice, even though she could see that her mother was doing her best to keep her expression and posture calm. 'I don't know,' she said harshly. 'Have they?'

Nicola stood up, brushing at the front of her skirt. 'That's enough. How dare you talk like this about your father!'

'Like what?' asked Robyn. 'What have I said?'

'You're not to think these things. It's so ungrateful, so hurtful. You should be ashamed of yourself.'

'What things? What am I thinking? Tell me, Mum. Say it!'

'That's enough!'

'Why do we have to live in the middle of nowhere? With locks and alarms and cameras?'

'It's security. It's what all dealers have to have.'

'There are plenty of gunsmiths in the town centre,' said Robyn. 'And why do you never like me bringing friends home?'

'We're busy. We're working,' said Nicola, becoming flustered. 'Your friends' parents probably don't work from home, that's the only difference.'

'It's not!' cried Robyn. 'Why does Dad throw things in the creek? Why not recycle or take stuff to the dump?'

'What stuff?'

Robyn saw how her mother instantly regretted her words, but it was too late to take them back.

'I don't know what was in the bags,' said Robyn, watching Nicola carefully. 'He didn't realize I'd come home early. I saw him go off with two farm shop carriers and come back without them.'

'You're imagining things!'

'No,' said Robyn. 'I've been with him when he's dumped other stuff in the creek. Casings he said were no good.'

'Nonsense. Anyway, what if he did? It means nothing. He's a good man. He's as devastated by what happened in Dunholt as you are. You mustn't think these things.' Nicola was struggling to mask her alarm.

Images came into Robyn's mind from movies or TV news footage of earthquakes and avalanches and mudslides, pictures charting the unalterable onset of catastrophe.

Nicola gripped her arm. 'You know how much he loves you,' she pleaded, giving her a shake. 'Please, Birdie. Don't break his heart.'

All Robyn could hear was a slipping roar signalling the destruction of everything she had ever known – or thought she'd known.

37

Ivo admired the manicured perfection of the putting green at the Vale do Lobo golf course from his seat on the terrace of the clubhouse brasserie. Beside him, Jerry Coghlan, tanned to a leathery brown, relaxed with his second ice-cold Sunday-morning beer. Ivo consoled himself with the custard tarts that came with his coffee.

After four nights here he wasn't entirely sure how he felt about the expat lifestyle with its endless loop of undemanding fun, whether he'd ever be tempted by the lotus-eater existence or whether he'd end up like Odysseus, rousing his men to escape. Even in his drinking days, he'd never been in search of nirvana; on the contrary, booze had only ever fuelled his indignation, his need to find a target for his anger. And now, in the shade of an umbrella pine, a fountain plashing idyllically nearby, he could feel that old anger start to rumble in his guts like an incipient bout of Montezuma's revenge.

He wasn't fooled by his companion's bonhomie either. Ivo reckoned good old Jerry was about as laid-back as a rattlesnake. His mistrust didn't merely stem from Jerry having been a bent copper. Ivo already knew plenty of those and, no hypocrite, had never held it against them, especially not when they were feeding him valuable information in return for really quite paltry sums of cash. No, Jerry was the kind of bastard who had to con you out of something, even if it was only your time or your dignity, just because he couldn't help himself; the kind of guy who insisted on calling you by some nickname of his own invention.

After Ivo had engineered an introduction, he'd clocked Jerry's frustration at being unable to find a diminutive of 'Ivo' and anticipated a backlash. He could see the gleam in Jerry's eyes now as he waited for the right opportunity, which soon came in the form of an attractive young waitress who laughed at something Ivo said to her. In a flash Jerry's arm went out, encircling her waist as she stood between them, nudging her closer when she tried politely to free herself from the grasp of a regular customer and club member, as he locked his gaze onto Ivo's, daring him to play chicken and be the first to look away.

Ivo could never be bothered with such games – Jesus, so Mummy had laughed once too often at Jerry's little winkle in the bath; so bleeding what? But Ivo knew he couldn't just throw in the towel; he'd have to give the prick a decent run for his money before letting him win. So he stared him out for as long as he could and then tried to appear suitably chagrined about losing. It seemed to do the trick, for Jerry let go of the poor waitress and ordered himself another beer, taking the opportunity to remind Ivo that he didn't drink.

'So,' said Jerry, leaning back in his chair and nodding sagely, 'you mentioned that you're looking for an investment opportunity.'

'That's right. As I told you, a few friends who, like you, were in the job, said they were very happy with their arrangements out here.' Ivo didn't dare mention either Kirkby or Burnley by name; he couldn't risk scaring Coghlan off until he'd gained a better idea of what he was looking for. 'And I know how much the boys in blue appreciate a good deal,' he went on cheerily. 'Well, they deserve nothing less after decades of service.'

'Service that you've supported,' said Jerry politely.

'Well, the *Courier* likes to do its bit. Though, what with Operation Elveden and one thing and another, none of us feels appreciated the way we used to.'

'Sad but true.'

'Still nothing beats bricks and mortar, does it?' Ivo nodded towards a distant cluster of white-walled villa apartments gleaming in the sunshine. 'Especially if there's a bit of holiday rental income to be had as well.'

'You've probably missed the boat here in the Algarve,' said Jerry. 'Although there may be some interesting opportunities opening up further along the coast, in the Alentejo, if you're interested?'

'Very much so. Although my pension arrangements are somewhat unorthodox,' said Ivo, lowering his voice conspiratorially. 'The funds might not be coming directly from the UK. Would that be a problem?'

Jerry shook his head. 'The parent company in charge of the development is based in Panama. They have plenty of experience of dealing with non-EU banking systems. All perfectly legal and above board, of course.'

'Wouldn't have it any other way,' said Ivo. 'But won't my pension pot be too small for this kind of development?'

Jerry smiled. 'That's where I come in. I wait until I can package a number of relatively small investors like yourself and then buy in under the umbrella of a single holding company. For a small commission, obviously.'

'Sounds good to me.'

'The holding company also has the advantage of providing a bit of a firewall if anyone like, say, a greedy divorce lawyer should come knocking. You won't have to share your pension fund with anyone you don't want to.'

'Suits me.' Ivo aimed for a wolfish grin. 'Two ex-wives already riding the alimony pony are quite enough for me.'

The grin seemed to convince Jerry. 'OK,' he said. 'Leave it with me. I'll talk to some people and come back to you. How long are you here for?'

'Well, I'm on expenses so I can't string it out indefinitely. But it'll be easy enough to fabricate a reason to come back.'

Jerry shook his head, though whether at the gullibility of editors or with nostalgia for his own good old days Ivo was unable to tell. He then knocked back the last of his beer and sat twisting the empty glass around on the table. Ivo waited, pretending to drain his empty coffee cup and taking a long appreciative look around at the carefully maintained grounds. He decided this place was his idea of purgatory, and he'd rather go straight to hell.

Jerry gave a loud sniff and pushed aside his glass. He appeared to have come to the end of his silent deliberations. 'You keep a pretty close ear to the ground, right?' he asked.

'I do my best.'

Jerry licked his lips, making Ivo wonder what was making him nervous. 'Ever come across an outfit called Buckingham Gate Associates?'

'No, I don't think so,' Ivo lied. 'Why?'

'Oh, nothing really,' said Jerry. 'Doesn't matter. Just some financial advisers in London who seemed keen to do business. I always like to do my homework.'

'I can ask around if you like.'

'No, no worries.'

'Well, anything I can do to help, just let me know. So what's the rental market like around here?' Ivo asked, eager to demonstrate that he had no interest in why Jerry was probing Peter's cover story.

'Pretty dire the last few years, to be honest,' said Jerry. 'But I've kept good links with the Police Federation, who send a lot of people my way. Has to be reduced rates for them, but then that's balanced by a nice steady stream of punters.'

'Any chance I could see the kind of place they go for?' asked Ivo. 'Give me an idea of what I should aim for.'

Jerry checked his watch. 'I guess we could take a gander at one of the more popular villas.' He injected enough reluctance into his reply to suggest he might almost be postponing an important meeting in order to accommodate Ivo's whim. 'Just the outside, obviously, but it'll give you a clue.' Jerry leaped nimbly to his feet. 'It overlooks the sixteenth tee. Fabulous sea views.' He looked down at Ivo. 'We can wait for the minibus if you don't fancy the walk?'

Ivo obliged with an Oscar-winning performance of lumbering up out of his chair and stretching his creaking back: he was more than happy to concede as many points as it took to win his own long game against this slimy bastard.

38

Leaving home on Monday morning, Grace felt her phone vibrate as she locked her front door. It was a number she didn't recognize, so she answered formally: 'DI Fisher.' No one spoke. Used to how often people would hesitate when calling the police, she softened her tone. 'Grace Fisher here. Can I help you?'

Her attention was snagged by a flyer tucked under the windscreen wiper on her car, and she went to pluck it out. The silent caller hung up, but then as she was getting in behind the wheel the phone went again, the same number. 'Hello, Grace Fisher here.'

'I think I need to talk to you,' said a young-sounding female voice.

'That's fine,' said Grace, hiding her exasperation that this would make her late. 'I'm listening.' She flicked open the flyer, ready to discard it on the passenger seat, and breathed in sharply. It was a folded sheet of white paper: written in pencil on it was WATCH YOUR STEP. She flung it down as if she'd been stung and then realized that she'd not heard what the voice on the phone was saying. 'I'm sorry. I was distracted for a moment. Can you say that again?'

'It doesn't matter. I shouldn't have called,' said the soft voice.

'No, wait. Really, I was just . . . Look, let's start again. You wanted to talk to me. I *am* listening.' There was no response, so Grace took a calming breath and made herself focus properly on the caller. 'It's difficult sometimes to speak to the police. I understand that. You only have to tell me what you're happy for me to know.'

After a pause, the young caller spoke: 'I think my dad might be a criminal.'

Immediately Grace had a mental image of Robyn Ingold in her school uniform standing watchfully against the wall in the gun dealer's workshop. That, and the way the girl had looked at Grace when telling her that her school friend had been among those killed in the Dunholt shootings, convinced Grace that she was now speaking to Leonard Ingold's daughter.

'That must be very difficult for you,' said Grace.

There was a second, longer pause. 'I don't know what to do.'

One half of Grace longed to be handed evidence she could use to convict the armourer. And, if Robyn were to offer such information, she would have no choice but to act on it. But the girl was young, and Grace was loath to cajole her into saying words that could never be retracted – or forgiven. 'You haven't told me your name,' Grace reminded her gently.

'You already know about my dad, don't you?' said the girl.

'Tell me your name,' Grace urged, stalling the moment when she would have to commit herself. She waited as the silence stretched. 'Is there anyone else close to you that you can talk to?' she asked. 'A relative or a teacher, perhaps?'

After another silence the line went dead. Grace cursed herself. Personal scruples had no place in an investigation, and she should have coaxed the girl into telling her more, or at least agreeing to an informal meeting. Yet, although convinced the caller was Robyn Ingold, she couldn't help being relieved. It was a dreadful thing for a daughter to testify against a parent, and it would be dreadful too for Grace to have taken advantage of a momentary impulse driven by what was most likely teenage angst.

Her gaze fell on the sheet of paper, which had fallen into the passenger footwell. *WATCH YOUR STEP.* It must surely have been left by the same person who had barged into her and kicked her when she'd been running the previous weekend. She'd gone out again yesterday along the same riverside path. Her heart had kept jumping with anxiety, making her stumble and unable to settle into a rhythm. This note confirmed that the attack had been personal, but who would want to threaten her, and why?

Robyn's call was a further indication that Leonard Ingold was the Lion King. Could this note be from him? Had he found out about her chat with Warren Cox? Or did it somehow have to do with Peter's death? It was clear that she'd rattled someone's cage badly enough to prove she was on the right track about something, but precisely what, she had no idea.

She leaned down to pick up the sheet of paper, crushed it into a ball and twisted around to chuck it behind her seat. It was no good pretending she wasn't badly upset by it. Bullying was the trigger for all her blackest thoughts, and she could sense the threatening note releasing its venom and poisoning the air in the car, making her feel trapped and vulnerable.

Her breath began to shorten and, afraid she was about to have a panic attack, she willed herself to look around in search of something to which she could anchor herself in the real world.

Across the road a narrow strip of cobbles marked the boundary between the pavement and the front wall of a pair of Victorian cottages. Poking up between the grey flints was a cluster of early snowdrops. If ever a flower stood for delicacy and survival, it was this, and it gave her the spark of hope she needed to focus on the nearest practical task.

Although her moment of defiance in scrunching up the note and throwing it aside might have felt good, it had also compromised any fingerprints or DNA that might be on the paper. Never mind, it was still evidence. By the time she'd got it properly bagged up, she was running late. Time to pull herself together and get to Chelmsford before the start of the first day of the inquest.

Once Grace had bypassed Colchester and was on the A12, she found herself arguing against Hilary's advice to stick to the bare facts, especially when doing so would coincide so conveniently with the cynical self-interest of the police service. She hadn't been in contact with Ivo since he'd left for the Algarve – she daren't risk any electronic record of communication between them – so didn't know whether Martin Leyburn, the man he'd interviewed, would be called as a witness. Ivo had said Martin was keen to come forward, but she knew it was up to the coroner to decide what evidence was relevant, and there was no certainty that he would call some random person merely because he used to go fishing with Russell Fewell. As things stood, Mark Kirkby's undeserved reputation as a gallant officer would go unchallenged. On the other hand, as Hilary had cautioned, it would be cruel to agitate the bereaved families with pointless – and uncorroborated – speculation about Fewell's motives.

Grace found a place to park and hurried into County Hall. The new facilities were comfortable and discreet, with the hushed, intimidating atmosphere that court buildings often seemed to have. She wasn't too late, and proceedings had only just begun as she slipped into the seat nearest the door. The hearings were likely to take well over a week, but she didn't want to miss the opening remarks, which would give her some sense of how deeply the coroner was prepared to probe the background to Fewell's state of mind. The first thing that struck her was that there was no jury: although not strictly necessary, a jury would normally have been expected in such a high-profile case, and it soon became clear that the coroner, as Hilary had predicted, intended to pilot his inquiries along the narrow channel between showing due respect to the dead and not needlessly reopening wounds.

Members of the victims' families sat hunched up together as if for comfort, the lines of grief making all their faces look oddly alike. Only John Kirkby and – Grace realized with a start – his son Adam sat slightly apart, both dressed in impeccable black suits. The sight of Adam made her all the more desperate to know what Ivo might be unearthing in Portugal, and she had to force herself to consider how hard the coming days would be for Mark's family.

She recognized a couple of journalists from the local papers and TV news services, but it appeared that the story was no longer of enough interest to summon any big guns from London or further afield. Maybe the coroner was right not to give Fewell his fifteen minutes of fame – not that celebrity appeared to have played any part in his motives – but Grace felt obscurely that the lack of scrutiny could only compound a failure of justice.

The coroner explained that the six deaths would be dealt with in chronological order, retracing Fewell's murderous path through the little town and concluding with his own violent end in the churchyard. Only a handful of witnesses, including Fewell's ex-wife, his manager at work and a couple of colleagues, would be called to describe his mood and intentions in the week or so prior to Christmas Day – although Grace knew that Ruth Woods, the FLO who had been keeping in touch with Donna by phone, had obtained permission for her to submit a written statement. Grace noted that neither Martin Leyburn nor Curtis Mullins was among the remaining witnesses. Grace herself would be called only to confirm that the police investigation had been completed and they were satisfied that the perpetrator, Russell Fewell, had acted alone.

It all felt completely and utterly wrong to her, but, short of breaking ranks and outlining her own private conspiracy theories, what could she do? And besides, looking at the exhausted, anxious faces of the victims' families as they prepared themselves to hear the final moments of each of their loved ones described in forensic detail, she was far from sure that her idea of truth and justice would help them in any way. Everything she had was anecdotal, circumstantial, contentious. Maybe Hilary was right, and all that could possibly matter now was to be kind.

39

When the hearing broke for lunch, Grace was able to slip from her seat by the door and get out ahead of everyone else. So she was surprised to feel a hand on her elbow as she descended the steps to the pavement.

'Lance! I didn't see you inside.'

He shrugged. 'I saw you come in. I let the coroner know that I'd come back earlier than expected, so I'll be giving my evidence later today about finding the drink-drive summons in Fewell's flat.'

'Yes, of course,' she said. 'I was going to grab some lunch. There's a kind of American-style diner over the road that's not too bad.'

'OK.'

Grace glanced at him as they rounded the corner towards the cathedral. The day was bright but with a bitter wind, and Lance's cheeks looked chafed, his eyes red-rimmed. It might only be the cold, but she thought he looked thin and not a little desperate.

'They do good ribs,' she told him, tucking her arm into his. 'You look like you could do with a square meal.'

He gave a wan smile and said nothing, but didn't disengage his arm. She was content to remain silent until they'd been seated at a corner table with a cheerful red checked tablecloth.

'How are you doing?' she asked.

'Pretty awful,' he answered with a half-smile. 'So did you talk to Colin? Are you going to use the inquest to root out the bad apples?'

'I'll be called to summarize our inquiries,' she said carefully, 'but I'm limited as to what I can say about the weapon. When the FLO last spoke to Davey Fewell, he was still claiming he made it up, that he never saw a gun. And, when we asked Donna if Mark Kirkby might ever have had a weapon, she insisted there was no way.'

'So you're not going to say anything?'

'What can I say?'

Grace explained to Lance how, although Donna was not strictly speaking a police widow, the Police Federation had stepped up and made available an out-of-season holiday flat in Weymouth. Despite this refuge, however, Donna was aware there was plenty of online abuse, including some threats, which was why she had been so reluctant to return to Essex to attend the inquest. 'It's little wonder that Davey doesn't want to add to his mother's distress,' she ended lamely.

Lance sat back, shaking his head and looking at her strangely.

'What can I say, Lance?' she said again, throwing up her hands. 'You tell me.'

'Same, I guess, as the brush-off you gave me when someone got into my flat and went through my stuff.'

He wouldn't meet her eyes, and all Grace's memories came flooding back of how it had been in Maidstone when no one would look at or speak to her for weeks except when they had to about work, and she'd begun to feel insubstantial, unreal, disappeared. Colin had been her boss then, had wrung his hands and done nothing. Was she really going to stand by and watch something similar happen to Lance?

'My flat, Grace,' he repeated. 'Where I live. And you didn't want to know.'

He was right: she'd let him down just as Colin had her. Worse. What was she turning into? She felt like she was drowning, felt the panic rise in her again as it had earlier that morning. And then something snapped. 'I do know who searched your flat.'

Now she had Lance's full attention, but instead of looking eager and alert he seemed petrified and defeated.

'Tell me he wasn't married,' he begged.

'Peter? No! No, nothing like that.' She looked around the restaurant, but the nearest tables were empty. This might not be the wisest course, yet she was nevertheless convinced it was the right and only one. She reached out to where Lance's hand lay on the red and white tablecloth and lowered her voice. 'It was the security services,' she said. 'Peter worked for them. I don't know which one.'

Lance stared at her, and then he laughed and took his hand away. 'No way. That's crazy.'

A waiter chose that moment to come and take their orders. They waved him away, requesting another five minutes.

'The reason Peter lied about going to Portugal wasn't because he was cheating on you,' Grace said, making a pretence of reading the menu. 'He lied because he was working undercover.'

'On what?' Lance asked sharply. 'Was I the target? Is that why he was with me?'

'No. No, of course not. Why would you be a target?'

'I don't know. I don't know anything any more. I really believed we had something. And now I can't trust a single thing he said, or anything we did together. Who was he? The love of my life or a total dick?'

'He was doing a job, Lance,' pleaded Grace. 'Everything else that happened between you was genuine.'

'What the fuck would you know about being genuine?' His face was suddenly filled with fury. 'How long have you been lying to me?'

'I know how you must feel, Lance, and I'm sorry. I hated not being able to—'

Lance cut her short by getting to his feet and pushing back his chair, scraping it noisily on the floor. He leaned forward, hands pressed so hard against the edge of the table that his knuckles turned white. 'You have no idea how I feel,' he spat at her. 'We're all supposed to be on the same side, but you let them kill Peter and get away with it!'

'That's not fair!' she cried as Lance turned on his heel. 'Sit down and at least give me a chance to explain!'

Heads swivelled in their direction, and the waiter peered out from behind his wooden partition to see what was going on. Lance hesitated and then returned to his seat. 'Is this what it took for you to get bumped back up to detective inspector?'

'Don't take it out on me! I've stuck my neck out just telling you this.'

'I'm sure you can look after yourself.'

'Stop it, Lance! I understand the horrible position you've been put in, but the real reason I didn't dare tell you earlier was for fear you'd react like this. You've got to calm down and start thinking clearly.'

'What, and stick to the rules? Collude in a cover-up?'

'I need to talk to you about Peter.'

He ignored her. 'Tell barefaced lies to a friend while pretending you care? Let a kid like Davey Fewell go hang? Forget it!'

Grace felt each accusation like a stab in the eye. By the time she'd gathered her wits, Lance was walking out the door. She hastily left a tip for the food they'd never ordered and followed him, but he was nowhere to be seen. It was a long time since she'd felt so alone.

She didn't blame him one bit. Everything he'd said was true. As a consequence of accepting Colin's orders, she had badly failed a friend. Failed Davey Fewell too. She wasn't sorry she'd been honest with Lance at last. Even though he might turn out to be a loose cannon, surely it was better for the truth to come out, regardless of the havoc it caused? That's what she'd always told herself before, and she'd always remained convinced, despite the deep hurt and bewilderment that never quite went away, that she had been right. Although what she could do now to limit the damage of sharing this particular truth was quite another matter.

Reaching the wide steps that led up to the main entrance of County Hall without much awareness of her surroundings, she abruptly found herself face to face with Adam Kirkby.

'Detective Inspector Fisher.' He stood directly in front of and two steps above her, his feet apart and hands by his sides as if braced against a physical threat. She was reminded that he was a prison officer, trained to deal with violent confrontation, and moved sideways and up a step so that she was on more of a level with him.

'Mr Kirkby,' she said. 'This can't be an easy day for you or your father.'

'My brother was a hero,' he said, taking a step back to regain his height advantage, 'gunned down in cold blood by an in-adequate, jealous ex-husband with a chip on his shoulder. If Fewell hadn't done the job himself, I'd've done it for him.'

'Why, do you own a gun, Mr Kirkby?' She knew her riposte was stupid, but couldn't help herself. She fully expected an out-raged, furious reaction, but was proved wrong.

Adam Kirkby laughed, his eyes veiled. 'Now, now,' he said, wagging a finger. He came closer and she could smell the meaty tang of his breath as he leaned his mouth into her ear and spoke in a tone of fake amusement. 'Take some advice: don't be such a bitch that you don't even know you are one.'

He turned and walked away up the steps. Grace was so aston-ished that it took her a moment to register that it was not her nerves jangling but her phone vibrating in her coat pocket. No number was available, and she was about to ignore it, but some instinct kicked in and made her take the call. It was Ivo, calling from Portugal. She listened carefully to all he had to say, but couldn't get out of her mind how, behind the arrogant aggres-sion of Adam's insulting words, she'd caught a glimpse of a kind of absolute confidence that seemed to her fanatical and delu-sional. Or was she becoming so overwrought that she was now conjuring phantoms out of thin air?

40

Grace had been sitting at the kitchen table with her laptop for well over an hour, trying every type of search she could think of in order to expand on Ivo's information about Jerry Coghlan and his shady property developments. All her attempts were meeting dead ends, and she hoped she wasn't busy trying to disappear down a rabbit hole.

Listening to Ivo on the phone, she'd been ready to dismiss his account of Panamanian holding companies as nothing more alarming than a bit of tax evasion until he'd told her that Jerry Coghlan had asked him about Buckingham Gate Associates. That had sent a chill down her spine and had clearly set the same alarm bells ringing for Ivo. If Peter had been murdered because of his interest in Coghlan and his financial dealings, then there must be a great deal at stake for Coghlan's beneficiaries. Ivo had promised that his old mate on the financial desk, who really knew his stuff, would eventually be able to unravel the complex fiscal structures, and that he'd get back to her when he'd got a bit further. Grace sincerely hoped Ivo's old mate also knew how to be very discreet.

Her doorbell rang. It was nine at night, and she wasn't expecting anyone, so she made sure to put the chain on the front door before opening it. It was Lance.

'I came to say sorry,' he said through the gap.

She opened up and welcomed him in. 'I'm so glad you came,' she said. 'I've been desperate to call you but didn't want to make things worse.'

'No,' he said, not quite looking directly at her. 'It's me. I've been out of my mind since Peter died, even more so since I saw that photo of him in Vale do Lobo.'

'And I didn't help. You were quite right to hate me for holding out on you.'

He shook his head. 'It sent me mad, thinking he'd lied to me.'

'I can imagine. Do you want a drink?'

'No, I'm fine, thanks.'

'Let's sit down.' It seemed incredible that the last time she had sat on her sofa with Lance like this had been Christmas Day. 'Peter was such a lovely man,' she said. 'And you two were perfect together. I'm sure he must already have been working on whatever it was he was doing when you met, that he never factored in that he would fall in love.'

Lance took a deep breath and let it out slowly, as if controlling some severe pain. 'I hope so,' he said. 'I want to know everything you know. I want to understand as much as I can.'

Grace looked at him, trying to decide how much of the truth he could handle. Although he appeared subdued enough, she sensed that his outward calmness had only been achieved with effort. Nevertheless, she couldn't deliberately withhold information from him again. However volatile he might be, she would have to give him every scrap she had.

'All Colin told me was that Peter worked for the security services, and that Buckingham Gate Associates is a cover.'

'Do you know what he was doing in Vale do Lobo?'

'Not for certain, no. But I found out the rest for myself.' Some instinct of self-preservation told her not to name Ivo. 'I have an informant,' she told Lance. 'And I'm sticking to the rules on that. You can't know who it is. Fair enough?'

'I guess,' said Lance, not meeting her eye.

'But I can tell you a bit more about the photograph you showed me.' Grace got up to fetch her copy of it from the file she'd left on the kitchen table and brought it back, sitting down beside Lance to point out the figure in a white polo shirt and green baseball cap. 'That's a local property developer called Jerry Coghlan,' she told him. 'He's ex-Flying Squad. One of those who dodged disciplinary proceedings – and probably worse – by taking early retirement just before Operation Countryman reported back.'

'I remember my dad talking about all that,' said Lance. 'Plenty of mud thrown, but none of it stuck.'

'No, the top brass managed to get it all shut down before the Met tore itself apart. Millions were spent looking at corruption, but hardly a single collar was ever felt as a result. Anyway, Coghlan took off for the Algarve at the perfect time to get in on the boom in golf and holiday resorts. A lot of the money he invests comes through a holding company registered in Panama. Apparently under that umbrella are smaller shell companies that own individual properties in order to shield them from British and EU tax authorities. The villa you stayed in is owned by one of them.'

Lance frowned. 'But it was the Federation who sorted that out. They wouldn't be involved with money-laundering.'

'They might not own it,' she said. 'It may have been lent to them.'

'I assumed it was one of the Federation's welfare properties. I didn't have to pay a penny.'

'No, I know,' she said. 'There's been a steady stream of police officers, present and retired, who have enjoyed holidays there either for free or at reduced rates.'

'So who does own it?'

'I'm trying to find out.'

'Surely Duncan would know?'

'Maybe. We can ask him, but I meant what I said about shielding my informant.'

'It was very comfortable,' said Lance. 'Three bedrooms, air-conditioned, pool, roof terrace, all mod cons.'

'I bet it was.' She pointed to the man in cargo pants and a red shirt beside Peter in the photograph, 'This is Adam Kirkby. Mark Kirkby's brother. He was staying in that villa when the photograph was taken.'

'So the Kirkby family know this Jerry Coghlan?'

As Lance looked keenly at her, Grace tried to bury the sudden fear that she was making a tremendous mistake.

'So what are they doing accepting freebies from a bent copper?' he asked. 'Let alone getting the Federation to hand them out them to serving officers like me?'

'It is pretty strange,' she admitted. 'Although John Kirkby spent a couple of years in the Met. He and Coghlan may go way back.'

'So is that why Peter went out there, to nose around about dodgy property deals? That's hardly enough to get him killed.'

'We don't know that his death had anything to do with his work,' said Grace carefully. 'Although Jerry Coghlan was interested in Buckingham Gate Associates. That suggests he had doubts of some kind about Peter.'

'But why would any of the security services give a shit about this kind of stuff?' asked Lance. 'Who cares? And anyway the Federation have plenty of muscle to front up to the Inland Revenue. I should know. My dad was a Fed rep in his time. They have the best tax and employment lawyers in the country on speed dial.'

'True.' Grace got up. 'I think I fancy a cup of tea. What about you?'

'Yeah, all right. Thanks.'

Grace was relieved that Lance remained where he was. She wanted time to think. How far did she go? Did she share her every suspicion, however speculative? She rubbed her face with her hands as the kettle came to the boil, trying to squeeze a decision out of her exhausted brain. If she told him this last thing, there would be no going back. Why was she so hesitant? This was DS Lance Cooper, an experienced MIT detective, cool in a crisis and always supportive. What was she so afraid of?

'You OK?' asked Lance. She hadn't noticed that he had twisted around to watch her.

'Yes,' she said, pouring water and waiting for the teabags to infuse. 'Tired. Been a long day.'

'Grace?'

'Yes?'

'Peter *is* dead, isn't he?'

Grace spun to face him. His look of misery was unbearable.

'I know I'm being crazy,' he said, 'but this whole thing has been so insane. Please tell me it's not just another bizarre cover story, and that he's not really still alive.'

'I saw him, Lance, at the post-mortem.'

'And you're not lying?'

'No, I promise. I'm not lying. I wish I were. I wish we could wind back to Christmas Day and have Peter here with us right now.'

Lance nodded, bereft of his last crazy glimmer of hope. Grace felt like shit. She should have remembered how her own distressed mind had filled in the blanks with unreasonable and obsessive ideas and possibilities after her ex-husband had been arrested for assaulting her. It was her fault that Lance had had to go on suffering like this: she should never have listened to Colin of all people.

'I'm so sorry.' She carried the steaming mugs over to the coffee table and sat back down beside him, giving his arm a comforting squeeze.

She was aware of how carefully he was watching her. If she tried to bluff, he'd know it and never forgive her. She took a deep breath. 'That night you and Peter went for a drink at the Blue Bar.'

Lance made the connection immediately. He went pale, lifting his chin as if preparing for a confrontation. 'Curtis Mullins.'

'Curtis told me he was there with Mark and Adam Kirkby.'

'He was the first officer on the scene when Peter was killed,' said Lance with bitter anger.

'He was on duty,' said Grace. 'He was with his partner the whole time.'

'You checked?'

'Yes, of course. I can't join the dots, Lance. I don't know what any of this means in terms of Peter's murder.'

'But you think Curtis or Adam Kirkby were somehow involved?'

'I've no idea.' The tang of Adam Kirkby's meaty breath on the steps of County Hall came back to her. 'I honestly don't see how they could be,' she told Lance. 'I've gone over and over what we had. I've not missed anything. There's been no cover-up as far as my investigation is concerned.'

Lance jabbed at the photograph. 'But here are Peter and Adam Kirkby together in Vale do Lobo.'

'But Coghlan's interest in Buckingham Gate doesn't necessarily point to anything more than him being cautious about who he does business with.'

'It's a hell of a coincidence!' said Lance.

'I know,' said Grace.

'Anything else?' Lance demanded. 'Have you told me everything now? There's nothing else?'

'Yes. That's everything.' She wasn't going to mention the hoodie or the note on her windscreen this morning, partly because she felt it would sound as if she were looking for sympathy when, if anyone was the victim here, it was Lance, and partly because, having more or less successfully boxed away her fear and vulnerability, she wasn't ready to start scratching it open again.

'So what now?' he asked, relaxing enough to sip at his mug of tea.

'My informant's digging into these shell companies,' she said. 'I'll let you know the minute anything gets flagged up.'

'And what about Mark Kirkby having a weapon? Do you think that's connected with any of this?'

'I've no idea. It's all so tenuous. Especially when we've no idea what Peter was investigating. Still, I'm pretty certain I've managed to identify our armourer.'

'And?'

'Leonard Ingold.'

Lance frowned. 'Isn't he the guy who's been helping us, who put Duncan onto the stuff about the military shell casings?'

'Yes. Smart move to hide in plain sight. He offers us intelligence that checks out, which makes him the last person on our suspect list. Meanwhile he gets the chance to explain away any inconvenient connections that lead back to him. Plus we've kept him informed of precisely where we're up to.'

'What does Duncan say?'

'I haven't spoken to him.'

'What about Colin?'

'No,' she said. 'I'm not telling anyone. I shouldn't be telling you.'

'Why not?'

'Well, for a start, I have no evidence.' Grace couldn't quite explain her reluctance to share her thinking – whether it was to avoid overloading Lance or to shield Robyn Ingold from scrutiny before she herself was entirely certain of her suspicions.

'Is it the same informant who told you about Coghlan?' Lance's question was sharp, his voice almost shrill, as if he were still in the throes of obsession.

Her heart went out to him, and she took a deep breath. 'No,' she said firmly. 'Not at all. I got a tip through a post-sentencing interview that the go-to guy for ammunition and snide guns is known as the Lion King. That gave me a hunch it could be Leo, but I only knew for sure this morning.'

'Why?'

'His daughter called me. Robyn Ingold. She didn't give her name, but it was definitely her.'

'What did she want?'

'She's put two and two together. If she hadn't realized before what her father's up to, she has now. Plus she was at school with Angie Turner, the youngest of the Dunholt victims.'

'How old is she?'

'Seventeen, I think. She's not on the electoral roll yet.'

'So how do you feel about using her to get at her dad?'

'She called me,' she said. 'I didn't go looking for her.'

'I guess there are plenty of disillusioned teenagers out there who have to grow up faster than they want.'

'I'm not wild about exploiting her,' said Grace, 'but nor do I want to see another Dunholt shooting. Or any more fifteen-year-old gang members playing with live ammo.'

'So you're happy to let her entrap her own father?'

'If she offers me information that takes a criminal armourer off the streets, then yes, I am. We're not social workers.'

Lance shook his head. 'Sometimes I wonder if I'm in the right job.'

'If she gives us enough to justify a search warrant,' Grace argued, 'then we may be able to tie Leonard Ingold to the forensics we got from the ballistics. I don't have any other strategy for moving forward on this. Do you?'

Lance remained stubbornly silent.

'And don't you think we owe it to Davey Fewell?' she asked. 'If we can tell him that Leonard Ingold supplied the rifle Mark Kirkby bragged about to him, maybe he'll start to see that his father was the final link in a chain of criminal behaviour. Fewell pulled the trigger and slaughtered five innocent victims,

I'm not excusing that, but there were other people responsible for placing that rifle in his hands.'

'So what?'

'So we're not doing our job properly if we let them go.'

Searching for some measure of acceptance in his expression, Grace realized how important it was to her to gain his approval for what she intended to do. 'So you tell me how I'm supposed to balance Robyn Ingold against Davey Fewell?' she asked. 'You can't, can you? All there is, is the job, and that means my duty is to seek out evidence that will convict Leonard Ingold, wherever it comes from.'

Lance finally gave a surrendering shrug, and with a sigh of relief Grace reached out to touch his arm. 'I don't like it any more than you do,' she said. 'But Leonard Ingold is responsible for his daughter's happiness, not us.'

Lance got to his feet. 'It's late. I'd better go.'

'OK.'

Grace rose to see him to the front door, but before opening it he turned to face her. 'I'm sorry for everything I said,' he told her. 'I've been out of my mind and—'

'Forget it,' she said. 'I handled it badly, and I'm sorry too.'

He nodded, his brown eyes no longer bright and angry, but back to their former softness. 'I'm not coming in to work this week,' he said. 'But keep in touch.'

'Of course. And Lance . . .' As he turned back, she abandoned what she'd intended to say. 'Look after yourself,' she said lamely. What she'd stopped herself asking was that he keep her confidence and not confront Colin with what she'd told him about Peter. But she had no right to ask that. She couldn't have it both ways: she couldn't expect Lance to protect her from the consequences – serious though they'd be – of having done the right thing.

Grace locked the door, suddenly overcome with a desperate longing to talk everything through with her dad. He had died a little over ten years ago, but had been a wise and good listener. As she took the mugs through to the kitchen to wash them up, she heard his voice in her head, and smiled wanly to herself. He'd always encouraged her and her sister to work out the thornier moral questions for themselves. *Some people do,* he'd say, holding up his hands with an enigmatic smile. *Some don't. You have to choose.*

41

Grace faced the barest minimum of questions when she was
called to give evidence at the coroner's court the following
morning. Despite knowing there was nothing she could weave
into her answers about how Mark Kirkby and Curtis Mullins
had contrived to torment Russell Fewell that she would be able
to back up if challenged, she left the building feeling spineless.
The inquest had been her best chance to put the record straight,
and she had failed even to begin to do so.

   She spent the drive from Chelmsford back to police HQ
thinking instead about the best way to approach Robyn Ingold.
Whatever the ethical rights or wrongs of the situation, Grace
was now even more determined that it had to be done. However,
any official contact was likely to be counterproductive, and she
knew nothing about the girl's movements and routines that
could point to any alternative way in. Grace racked her brains
for some means to waylay her casually enough to create an illu-
sion of coincidence, and in the end, lost for any better idea,
decided she'd just have to barge into her life by whatever means
she could. Her only lead was the black uniform Robyn had been
wearing when Grace had gone to speak to Leonard the previous
week. This suggested that Robyn attended one of the town's few

private schools, and also made it easy enough for Grace to identify which one.

Grace waited for the end of the school day and, judging that
it wouldn't be a good idea to invite a pupil to get into a strange
car outside the school gates, covered the half-mile from the
office on foot. Despite the murky January afternoon, Grace
could see that the entrance, marked by brick piers, led to tree-
lined grounds and buildings of mellow old red brick flanked by
modern additions. Dozens of almost identically dressed girls,
most of them well bundled up against the cold, were already
streaming out to where waiting cars lined the wide residential
street. Grace cursed her stupidity: how on earth in such a crowd
could she hope to spot someone she'd met only once before? She
looked around and noticed three school buses parked on the far
side of the road. If she stood opposite the zebra crossing, she'd
have a clear view of all the girls waiting to cross.

For all Grace knew, Robyn was occupied with sports or some
other activity and might not even be heading home at this time,
but she had no alternative strategy and was in a hurry – not
always the cleverest combination.

But suddenly there she was, emerging out of the sea of dark
uniforms, with the same watchful, thoughtful expression she'd
had as she'd stood leaning against the wall in her father's workshop. She didn't appear to be part of a group, and as soon as she
reached the pavement Grace was able to step forward and fall in
beside her. 'Hello, Robyn. You remember me, don't you?'

The girl looked terrified and very young, making Grace feel
dreadful. She had little enough appetite for what she was about
to do, but she was unlikely to get a second chance and would
just have to go in hard and hope for the best. 'I'm glad you called

me yesterday,' she said. 'I'm sorry if I didn't seem to be listening, but I'd just found a threatening note on my car windscreen.'

Robyn looked as shocked as Grace had intended. 'I don't know what you're talking about,' Robyn said rudely. 'Why would I want to call you?'

Grace kept her gaze fixed on the girl's face, which was attractive, with clear skin, delicate features and dark greeny-brown eyes. She wasn't very tall but seemed lithe and strong; the slightly too-short sleeves of her uniform blazer demonstrated that she hadn't yet finished growing. The fear in her eyes showed that her insolence was a bluff, encouraging Grace to believe that she didn't possess the ability to lie convincingly.

'This isn't a pretty business,' Grace said, guiding her around a corner, away from the buses and into a residential side street. It was nearly four o'clock, and, with the winter afternoon drawing in and all the kids milling around the buses, no one noticed them walk away together. Grace stopped under a tree within sight of the hubbub but far enough away not to be disturbed by any of Robyn's classmates. 'I'm here because you were obviously distressed yesterday,' she said. 'I'm assuming you wouldn't have called me otherwise. I came to offer you my help.'

Grace had plenty of training and experience in how to finesse forensic interviews, but this was different. When she'd spoken to Ivo the day before, he had volunteered his advice on how to tease stories out of people. *Find out what they want*, he'd said. *And give it to them in return for what you want. Keep telling them it was their idea to come to you, then block off all the exits. Never, ever offer them a choice, because that's giving them a way to back out.* She'd heard rapists and fraudsters boast about how easy it had been to manipulate their victims into submission, and it felt creepy to echo their verbal techniques like this, but she daren't indulge in self-examination or she'd end up telling Robyn to get the hell out of here and take the bus straight home.

'You're worried about your father,' she said, 'and you must feel loyalty to your friend Angie Turner too. You said you needed to talk to someone. Maybe you'll feel better if you do.'

Robyn raised her chin to stare at her. Grace could see both doubt and defiance in her eyes.

'It may be that all your fears are completely unfounded,' said Grace. 'But you obviously love your dad, and you don't want to be stuck with such an awful burden of suspicion between you. I'm sure he doesn't either.'

'No,' Robyn conceded.

'I saw Angie's parents at the inquest this morning,' said Grace. 'Her father lost his mother as well that day. Angie's grand-mother. All the relatives just want to make sure that nothing like this ever happens again.'

'My father sells sporting guns,' cried Robyn. 'That doesn't make any of this his fault!'

'But it's why we have such strict regulations around firearms. And if he's sticking to the letter of those regulations, then there's no problem, is there?' Grace couldn't help picturing herself in her last year at school, how unformed she'd been and how much her own father had meant to her, how much of her world she'd seen through his eyes. She steeled herself to keep going. 'It was you who said you were worried he might be a criminal.'

'Do you think he is?' Robyn demanded. 'Is that why you keep coming to the house?'

'A lot of people die in this country because of illegal firearms,' said Grace.

'It's got nothing to do with my dad! He'd never let anything like that happen!'

'Not deliberately, perhaps. But you know the true cause of most crime, Robyn? It's horribly simple. Money.'

'Then why don't you go after all the bankers and the people who want to frack everywhere and those sorts of people? Leave us alone!'

'Maybe we should, but that's not my job.'

'I'm going to miss my bus.'

'Think about it, Robyn. Think about the money. Think about the food you eat, and your private school fees, and probably your foreign holidays. Think about what pays for all that, and what that means. You've got my number.'

'I have to go.' Robyn darted around Grace and ran towards where the buses were about to depart. Grace couldn't bear to watch her go. She turned away, a steadying hand against the rough ridges of the tree trunk beside her, and hated herself.

42

Most of Robyn's classmates who took the same bus had shorter journeys, and so she was used to spending the last twenty minutes or so without company. The sun had not yet entirely set, but the lights inside the bus made the passing countryside appear already dark. Usually she quite liked this final part of the journey; it marked the transition from school to home, from constant noise and activity to stillness. But today she was in a state of panic. What right did that horrible interfering woman have to ambush her like that? Surely police detectives weren't supposed to sneak up on people in such a creepy way? She hated her and wished she'd never called her!

But, said the little voice of reason, she *had* called her. She had brought this avenging angel down upon herself when she'd fished the card DI Fisher had handed to her dad out of the rubbish bin and hidden it at the bottom of her school rucksack. How could she have been so stupid? How could she ever face her dad after such terrible, terrible disloyalty? Exactly what kind of damage had she done? No matter how much she now regretted her impulsive phone call, it was sinking in that it was beyond her power to stop what she – *stupid! stupid!* – had started. She had let the evil genie out of its bottle and would have to live with the consequences.

She wished she had a comforting older brother or sister to turn to, someone who had grown up seeing and hearing all the same things as she had, who could now reassure her that she was seeing demons where none existed, and that their father remained the man she so desperately wanted and needed him to be. And people like Kenny too. Surely she'd have to be crazy to suspect Kenny of being some cunning arch-criminal?

Yet what was her father doing, thinking he could bring a third person, a child, into this? The anguished question burst unsought into her head. Was the true reason she had no siblings a pragmatic move to limit prying eyes and inconvenient questions? Was any part of her life *not* moulded around her father's larger, secret concerns?

If she put her face close to the glass she could peer out at the houses and gardens and parked cars as the bus passed through a village. Lights were coming on in windows where curtains had not yet been drawn. How unknowable we all are, she thought, as her mind's eye zoomed upwards until the travelling bus became a speck, like in one of those satellite images they showed of drone strikes or in photographs taken from outer space. Only now the destructive force about to be unleashed on her home lay right inside her own suspicious mind.

Every lighted window they passed represented at least one individual life. These were people Robyn didn't know and would probably never know. Did it matter if any one of them was snuffed out? Before Angie's death, she would have said, if she were being honest, that their lives meant no more to her than the starving children and disaster victims and refugees that the charity TV ads tried to raise money for. But now that she had experienced for herself the relentless silence of death she could no longer think like that. People mattered. Every person mattered to someone. Would the crazy guy who had shot Angie and all the others still have killed them if he'd had to do it with a club or a knife or his bare hands? How many of those in the murder statistics she'd looked at online would still be alive if someone had not placed a gun in the hands of their killer? Could that person really be her father?

The bus dropped her at the end of their lane. She stood listening until the noise of its engine had floated away, and she could retune her ears to the familiar sounds of the gloaming. She was scared. Never had she stood here at the approach to home and felt afraid. Who was the Leonard Ingold the police came to visit? What was he capable of? What would he do if he found out what she had done? Was he capable of hurting her physically? Dumping her in a sack in the creek like the incriminating evidence from his workshop? For she was certain now that that's what he had been doing that day she came home early from school. Kenny had come and taken something away in his van, and then her dad had gone off down to the creek with two heavy bags and returned without them.

The thought of what would happen if she told DI Fisher about that made her feel dizzy and sick.

Robyn was convinced that, if she walked on down the track and went into the cosy kitchen and stood by the warm Aga, her father would take one look at her and read her mind. That thought was worse than anything she'd ever felt in her life. Physical torture was preferable to this, and she experienced a crushing insight into why one of the girls at school had an endlessly replenished row of diagonal scars up her left arm. But such a release of tension would not help her. Nothing could.

Only now did the full enormity of what she had done by speaking to Grace Fisher hit her. What had she been thinking?

But it had seemed impossible, just as DI Fisher had warned, to do nothing and yet continue with the gnawing suspicion, not to know the truth for sure. But, now that she had made everything so much worse, mere suspicion seemed a safe and benign state. She had turned herself into a traitor who had to go home and lie to the two people she loved most in the world.

A little voice inside her protested that she had been brought up to obey the law, to respect teachers and other people in authority, to be scrupulous about the legal constraints of her dad's business. More than anyone it was he who had taught her how to tell right from wrong, how important rules and regulations were. So how could it possibly be that he was some kind of felon, unable himself to do what was right? And what about her mum? Where did Nicola fit into all this?

Her mother spent a good part of each day in the little office that opened off the reception area in Leonard's workshop. She kept the accounts. She was not a flashy person, not the type to want expensive shoes or handbags, but there was the Aga, her new Suzuki four-by-four, the holidays in Portugal. Her parents had taken her to Disney World in Florida once, and not flown economy. Although she'd been too young then to think about the cost, she wasn't like most of the other girls at school who didn't care where the money came from as long as their parents bought them all the clothes and latest phones and shoes they asked for. But now Grace Fisher's words would haunt her every time her parents paid for anything. Until she knew for certain where the money really came from, she couldn't even accept their offer to help out when she went to uni. It would be like having blood on her hands.

Maybe her parents intended to initiate her into the reality of the family firm when she turned eighteen? But she knew that wouldn't happen. Her hand went unconsciously to the cheek that Nicola had slapped. It wasn't the physical memory of the blow that burned inside her, but the significance of the gesture: it was her mother's unintended admission that Robyn's suspicions were accurate. That was what hurt the most, what had given her a pain deep in her chest, an ache around her heart that made her feel fragile in a new and scary way.

She was getting cold and realized with a start that the last rim of the sun was about to disappear below the horizon. They kept a torch in a plastic-lined box hidden in the hedge in case one of them had to negotiate the lane in the dark, but even with the torch it was annoying to stumble about and risk twisting an ankle. The later she was, the more questions they'd ask, so, unless she was going to run away altogether, she'd better get moving.

She wished Angie was alive: she was the one friend she could have called and gone to, the one friend who would have listened without making a drama out of it, and then asked all the right questions.

Robyn's anger at Angie's futile death drove her down the track towards the lights of a home that now felt like a place of danger and distress.

But was it? Was it? Surely she must be wrong! None of this could be anything more than her ridiculous imaginings.

But there was the bit that didn't fit, the bit she knew deep down wasn't wrong. It was the insight she'd had, sitting beside her father in the Land Rover, into how he liked to be unknowable; how he derived some kind of perverse satisfaction from the performance he put on in order to evade and deflect and elide the truth. Maybe the risk of being unmasked gave him a thrill. Maybe none of it had ever been, as he told her so often, about caring for his family, about love.

Robyn pushed open the back door and, as she hung up her coat, called out to let them know she was home. She found Leonard sitting at the kitchen table, mending the torn pocket of his heavy waxed jacket. He looked up and smiled.

'Good day?' he asked.

'Not really.'

'Never mind, Birdie. No one likes January, do they?' He smiled again – the smile that usually made a bad day instantly better – and she saw that she ran no risk at all of him reading her mind. It wouldn't occur to him to guess at his daughter's inner thoughts, let alone to suspect that she was capable of betraying him. He simply failed to see her as separate, her own individual self, not merely some kind of extension of himself. It was the saddest thought she'd ever had.

43

As Grace passed the door to Colin Pitman's office the following morning, she glanced in and saw him standing in earnest conversation with John Kirkby. Colin didn't notice her, and Kirkby had his back to her, so she quickly made for her own corner of the office. It was early, and today's inquest hearing would not yet have started, but it must be something important to have diverted the retired custody sergeant from his journey to Chelmsford. She was flooded by the fear that Kirkby had somehow been made aware of her interest in his family, and was mounting a counteroffensive with her boss. She longed to be a fly on the wall, to hear what Kirkby might let slip of how much he knew about the corrupt and illegal activities of his murdered son – or what his younger son had been doing in Vale do Lobo.

From her desk she kept a wary eye on the two men, but it was not long before Colin courteously walked Kirkby to the main office door before coming straight over to Grace's cubicle.

'Poor bloke,' he said. 'Remind me, when I retire, never to come back and haunt the place like that.'

'What did he want?' She made her question sound as casual as possible.

'Nothing really. A few questions about the inquest. I reckon he just appreciates the comfort of familiar surroundings.'

Grace gave a tight smile of agreement: it seemed to her that the tense body language of the two men had suggested more than merely a nostalgic chat.

'He said Lance Cooper gave his evidence yesterday,' said Colin.

'Yes,' said Grace, again feeling the prickling of fear: just what had Ivo's trip to Vale do Lobo unleashed?

'There's no need for him to come straight back to work,' said Colin. 'He should take his full compassionate leave, if that's what he needs.'

'I'll tell him.'

Never had Grace been more grateful to a ringing phone. Mouthing, 'Sorry,' she picked up the handset from her desk. 'DI Fisher.'

After a brief conversation and some scribbled note-taking, she looked up again at her boss. 'There's been a fatal shooting at the hospital. Seventy-year-old male crossing a footbridge from the visitor car park. Single bullet to the heart. No one realized at first what had happened, so he was rushed into A & E, where he was pronounced dead.'

'Anyone apprehended?' asked Colin.

'No,' said Grace, getting up and heading past him out to the main MIT office. 'No report yet of anyone actually seeing a gunman. Sounds more like a sniper shot. Hospital security have the place in lockdown in case the shooter's still out there.' She clapped her hands and waited for the team to turn and face her.

'Listen up, everyone. Fatal shooting in the area of the visitor car park at the hospital. I want a firearms team and a surveillance helicopter with thermal imaging over there right away.

As soon as we know the area is safe, I want it cordoned off and a forensic team on the ground. I want all CCTV footage secured as soon as possible. Duncan, start a crime scene log.'

'I'll give Samit a call,' said Colin. 'Sooner we retrieve the bullet and can get started on ballistics, the better.'

'Thanks,' said Grace. 'I'll get the body secured in the hospital mortuary. It's already been moved, so we're not going to get an accurate trajectory for the shot.' She turned back to the team. 'Someone must have seen something, and I don't want anyone leaving until we've identified and positioned every single witness.' She held up a hand as she saw Duncan about to object. 'Yes, I know, it'll be a logistical nightmare for the hospital.' She turned to Colin. 'Perhaps you'd be the best person to speak to the managers, sir? Explain why they can't have their car park back until we're finished with it.'

Colin gave a wry smile. 'You spoil me, DI Fisher.'

His response broke the tension, reminding Grace of why he was to many people an effective and popular boss. He loved to be out front, rallying the troops, whenever a new case kicked off; only when the mundane drudgery of an inquiry kicked in did he tend to melt into the background, content then to let the infantry get on with the work. Which was fine by her.

'Hilary can ask the local radio stations to put something out and keep people updated,' he said. 'You'd better get over to the scene. I'll hold the fort here.'

No further shots were reported in the time it took Grace to reach the hospital, a couple of miles north of the city centre. The helicopter had scanned the area, and Ben Marrington, the uniform inspector who came to meet her in a staff car park, well away from the crime scene, felt sufficiently confident that the shooter was no longer on site to dismiss the risk that he was lying in wait to ambush the police or crime scene examiners. Although she and Ben had only worked together a few times, she knew well him enough to believe that his quiet composure was entirely natural – not like the passive-aggressive air of calm that some officers thought they could get away with – and she was content to rely on his judgement and trust to his thoroughness.

'It's possible he fled on foot,' he said. 'The car park is a pay-as-you-leave barrier system, and I very much doubt he'd have hung around to feed the correct change into the machine.'

'Which means that the weapon may still be here, stashed in one of the cars,' said Grace.

'We're talking about fifteen hundred parking spaces,' Ben pointed out.

'I realize it's a big job,' said Grace. 'We'll draft in as much manpower as we can. But I want the crime scene examiners in there first. If we can find a shell casing, then we'll have a lead on the shooter's position, and that will help narrow things down.'

'The hospital managers are already antsy about the disruption to their appointments system.'

Grace grimaced and held out her hands. 'What else we can do?'

Ben answered with a half-smile. 'Not a lot.'

'Not to worry,' she said. 'Superintendent Pitman is dealing with the hospital. You can concentrate on keeping the area safe and nailed down.'

'Will do.'

As Ben hurried away, Grace nevertheless wished that Lance

were here. She'd always valued his brisk and honest insights, and she would feel far more confident facing a task of this scale knowing he had her back covered. She'd been tempted before she left police HQ to call and ask him to come in, but her finger had hesitated too long over the icon on her phone. Lance might still be too upset and flaky to be reliable. She felt rotten even thinking like that about him, but his possible volatility would be a distraction when she needed to focus clearly. The adrenalin release in the first minutes after the initial call had offered a welcome respite from her recent hamster-wheel thoughts, but she must guard against an overreaction. It was vital for a senior investigating officer to review calmly the incoming flood of tasks and information, and she mustn't let anxiety force her into tunnel vision.

Her first priority, now that the area had been secured, was to identify the victim. It might have been a random shooting, but if not the identity of the seventy-year-old would yield valuable clues to the killer's motive. She checked her phone: Duncan had already emailed her the details of the A & E consultant who had formally pronounced life extinct.

She found Dr Mason busy with a patient in the Accident and Emergency Department and had to wait until he'd finished. He looked much the same age as her, sported a single earring and a ponytail, and appeared totally unfazed by what had happened. He took her aside, swiftly and calmly switching his entire concentration onto her.

'He was almost certainly dead before he hit the ground,' he told her. 'By chance, it was a colleague who got to him first. An ex-army medic, so he realized immediately what he was dealing with.'

'Good. We'll need to speak to him.'

'Sure. We found the victim's hospital appointment letter in his coat pocket, so we could look up his records.' He flicked through a clipboard on a cluttered desk next to a red telephone and detached two sheets of paper stapled neatly together. 'Here you go. Mr Gordon Church. Looks like his first appointment with us. Referred on from Peterborough, where he was being treated for terminal lung cancer.' Dr Mason gave a wry smile. 'Who knows, maybe this was a mercy killing.'

'OK, thanks.' Grace looked at the printed name. Gordon Church seemed somehow familiar, but she couldn't think why.

'I should get back to work,' said Dr Mason. 'Bleep me if you need me.'

The victim's name niggled at her memory, so she went out to the corridor to use her phone to check online. A page of recent entries came up straight away, reminding her of the short-lived tabloid furore sparked by the revelation of his recent release from prison. In 1981 Gordon Church, a career criminal, had shot dead two police constables who stopped his car as he attempted to flee after an armed robbery at a post office in Beckenham. He had received a sentence of life without parole but was released on compassionate grounds in order to receive proper palliative care. The tabloids had called for legislative change so police killers remained in prison for life, and had quoted the Police Federation's declaration that the release of the dying man was 'sickening and abhorrent'.

As Grace made her way back outside through the maze of hospital corridors, an idea leaped into her mind and lodged itself there: might this incident be linked to the two homicides she'd unearthed in Ely and Grantham, where the victims had also been shot by sniper-style rifle fire? Or was she finding patterns where none existed? It was unprofessional even to entertain such rapid assumptions when an inquiry had barely got under way – especially when Colchester, a garrison town, had no shortage of trained military personnel with access to weapons – but the notion had lodged itself in her brain and refused to be pushed aside. Annoyed with herself, she resorted to counting her footsteps to try to clear her mind, but the stubborn thought remained: a convicted paedophile, an Albanian gangmaster and now a double cop-killer, and all three shootings executed within a hundred-mile radius of each other.

44

The autopsy X-rays the following morning revealed bullet frag-ments, and Dr Tripathi confirmed that Gordon Church had in fact been shot twice in the heart. As Grace watched him extract bullet fragments from the mutilated muscle and flesh, and lis-tened to him explain how their limited penetration suggested hollow-point ammunition, she dared to believe that perhaps her instinctive hunch might not be so far-fetched after all.

She thanked Samit and made her way back to HQ trying not to think about the pale scrawny body on the pathologist's metal table. A prison tan, they called it. Even if Gordon Church had not been ravaged by heavy smoking and lung cancer, thirty-five years of prison food and limited exercise and sunlight had done little for the imposing thug depicted in the photographs taken at the time of his arrest and reprinted by the tabloids when he'd been released. She did not feel sorry for him: wielding a sawn-off shotgun with his face distorted by a nylon stocking, he must have appeared horribly menacing, literally the stuff of nightmares, to the couple who ran the post office, let alone the two brave unarmed officers he'd gunned down in cold blood. Yet she couldn't help but feel some pity for such a waste of humanity.

As Grace walked into the MIT office, she was surprised to see Lance at his desk. Intent on his computer screen, he merely glanced up as she passed behind him. She lightly touched his shoulder and went on into Colin's office, where she brought him up to speed on the preliminary post-mortem results before nodding out towards the main office. 'So Lance came in?' she asked.

'Yes, I called him. All hands on deck,' said Colin.

'And he seems all right?'

'Yeah, sure,' said Colin. 'He's much better off here than moping alone at home.'

She returned to her desk to fetch the rest of her notes for the daily briefing as the assembled team began moving chairs and shuffling notepads. Colin opened by thanking everyone for their hard work and announcing that the chief constable had granted his request for additional resources for the inquiry. He then handed over to Grace.

'Let's start with witnesses,' she said. 'Church was unaccompanied. No one saw the shooter, and, given that the car park was relatively busy, surprisingly few heard the shots, suggesting he used a silencer. I spoke to the ex-army medic who was the first to reach Church after he collapsed to the ground. Luckily the medic had the experience to realize almost immediately that Church had been shot and, from how and where he had been hit, instinctively noted the likely direction of fire.' She turned to Duncan. 'What else have we got?'

'Four other witnesses in the car park heard two shots, one immediately after the other,' said Duncan. 'Their statements tallied with the medic's opinion, which narrows down the shooter's likely location.'

'Which also meant we could get at least some of the area reopened to traffic,' said Colin. 'That helped improve relations with the hospital managers.'

Grace turned to the crime scene manager. 'Wendy?'

'As you know, there are two visitor parking areas, here and here,' said Wendy, pointing to a large diagrammatic map on the evidence board. 'All the witness statements suggest that the shooter was over here, at the far edge of the western car park. We made an initial forensic sweep of the eastern car park yesterday before conducting a fingertip search of the western area. This morning we recovered two spent brass casings from this point here.' Wendy's face glowed with satisfaction. 'They're from rifle rounds and have been sent to ballistics with a request to fast-track them.'

'Any other marks on the casings?' asked Grace.

Wendy nodded and smiled. 'Military head stamps.'

'Effective firing range for a rifle is up to five hundred metres,' said Grace, trying to conceal how desperate she was to know whether the casings would turn out to bear the same marks as those recovered in Dunholt and elsewhere. 'The victim was alone on the little footbridge over the water feature leading from the car park to the main entrance of the hospital,' she continued. 'The footbridge is slightly raised, giving the shooter a clear line of fire.'

Wendy pointed again to the map. 'The spent casings were found here, on the edge of the perimeter road leading in and out of the car park.'

'Two of the witnesses who heard shots recall noticing a silver or metallic-grey van, not big, with a side-opening door, head at speed along the perimeter road towards the exit to the main road soon afterwards,' said Duncan. 'He'd want to avoid having to stop at the ticket barrier, so probably never entered the car park.'

'If he was firing from the back of a van,' said Colin, 'he's not likely to have jumped out and scrabbled around after ejected shell casings.'

'No,' said Grace. 'Though that does also suggest that he might not have been alone. He could have had a driver. Which would alter the psychological profile somewhat and mean he's not necessarily a lone Unabomber type. That's something to bear in mind.'

'The descriptions of the van are hazy,' said Duncan, 'but the very fact that the witnesses associated it with what they heard makes it significant.'

'We're checking roadside cameras around the hospital within the likely timeframe to see what comes up,' said Joan, who was the team's civilian case manager.

'OK, good work. Let's move on to victimology,' said Grace. 'If Gordon Church was deliberately targeted, then who knew his whereabouts? There's been plenty of coverage about his release but not a word to link him to Colchester.'

'For the past eleven years he's been in HMP Wayleigh Heath.' Lance spoke for the first time. 'His release three weeks ago was unexpected. He was never sent to a lower-category prison first.'

'We need to know who leaked news of his release to the media,' said Grace. 'His hospital appointment could have been set up before he was let out.'

'Talk to his lawyers too,' said Colin.

'Some legal aid solicitor who thinks they're not paid enough,' quipped someone at the back of the room.

'Church actually did a lot of the legal work himself,' said

Lance. 'He's been inside since 1981. Had time to take three Open University degrees, including jurisprudence and law.'

'All paid for by honest taxpayers.'

Lance ignored the disgruntled mutter from another corner of the room. 'He started his own appeal process when he first received his terminal cancer diagnosis, and then got a barrister pro bono.'

'From some right-on chi-chi chambers in London, no doubt,' grumbled someone else.

'Good riddance. Shooter's done everyone a favour.'

'Should've been left to rot in jail.'

'With no pain relief.'

'Shooting's too good for him.'

Grace had expected this. No one liked a cop-killer, and she couldn't blame the team's resentment at having to work overtime on behalf of the likes of Gordon Church. She let them get it all out of their system before picking up the thread.

'So, he's living in a bail hostel. Apart from the people there, who else was likely to know that he was receiving hospital treatment here in Colchester?'

'We haven't traced any family or friends who are still in contact,' said Lance. 'Apart from lawyers, his last prison visit was at least five years ago.'

'What about hospital staff?' asked Duncan. 'Or his GP practice, or the prison MO who referred him?'

'And prison officers, the governor, probation services?' suggested another voice.

'They'll all have to be checked out,' said Grace. 'Though it's unlikely any of them would have known the precise time of his appointment yesterday.' She hesitated before adding to the list: 'He was out on licence. He'd have to report regularly to the local nick.'

'You mean us,' said Duncan with an unfamiliar growl in his voice.

Grace held up her hands against the immediate groundswell of hostility. 'I know, I know. But we have to be seen to be scrupulous. And in any case whoever's been dealing with him might have useful intelligence. Get me a name and I'll speak to them myself, to show respect, OK?'

'Ruth Woods handles offender management,' said Duncan.

Grace gave him a smile: she should have known his thoroughness would have got there before her. She was also relieved. Ruth was observant and smart, and unlikely to be too prickly about routine questions. 'OK,' she said to the assembled team. 'I think that's it for now. Thank you all very much.'

She waited while Colin had an extra word with Wendy, and then followed him back into his office. Now that the autopsy and the recovered casings confirmed that a rifle and hollow-point ammunition had been used in this incident, she wanted to float the idea as soon as possible that it might be connected to the other two fatal shootings. She set out her case that they might have a vigilante on their hands, playing slightly to the pleasure she knew Colin took in being the public face of any sensitive or high-profile story. He seized on the idea, welcomed her suggestion that Colchester MIT pool intelligence with the senior investigating officers in Grantham and Ely, and promised to set up a meeting with the other teams at their earliest convenience.

'I'll brief Hilary as well,' he said, already picking up the phone. 'Obviously we're nowhere near ready to go public with anything yet, but best that she's prepared.'

Grace agreed and went back to her own desk. She wanted to stop and say a proper welcome back to Lance but decided to wait for a quieter moment. First off she wanted to speak to Ruth Woods, in case she had any useful background on Gordon Church. Ruth answered her phone immediately and said she'd been expecting someone from MIT to call, not that she had much to contribute to the inquiry: Church hadn't required offender management because he was under supervision by his probation officer. As far as the police were concerned, all he had to do was turn up and sign in every week. Ruth had already consulted the record: the PC who had routinely signed him in had been Curtis Mullins.

Grace thanked Ruth and ended the call, sitting back and staring out of the window but seeing only the rain-streaked glass. The name had jolted her. Pure coincidence, but one more link in a long chain of coincidences. Impulsively she looked up the number for Wayleigh Heath, the maximum-security establishment where Church had been an inmate. She introduced herself and explained that other members of her team would be in touch regarding Church's contacts during his time there, but that it would be useful meanwhile if she could quickly check one name that might be significant: had Adam Kirkby ever worked there as a prison officer?

The answer brought a palpable wave of relief. Her suspicions had been far-fetched, and Adam Kirkby had never been at Wayleigh Heath. She would still have to speak to Curtis Mullins as a matter of routine, but she must accept this as a warning not to overreact and start imagining ominous connections where there were none.

Clicking her computer screen back to life, she saw dozens of incoming emails. She opened and read those that seemed most urgent, firing off a few quick replies before checking her phone for messages. Among them was a text from Robyn Ingold. She opened it immediately. *Can I see you after school today?* Grace was relieved that she hadn't after all bungled her meeting with the girl, and was composing her positive response when Colin made a polite show of knocking on her cubicle partition. She put down her phone.

'Good news,' he said. 'The SIOs from the Ely and Grantham inquiries are eager to crack on. They both said they can drop everything and be here for three thirty, four at the latest.'

Grace felt a whip of frustration but had no choice but to thank Colin and express her thanks for his active support for her theory, even though the meeting would be precisely when Robyn came out of school. As Colin went away, rubbing his hands in satisfaction, she thought for a moment. If she tried to postpone, Robyn might not offer her a second chance. She had to grab this opportunity. There was only one person who already knew she'd spoken to Robyn and so could deputize for her at such short notice. She got up and left her cubicle.

'Lance,' she called. 'Can I have a quick word?'

45

Ivo should have rushed off to Colchester the moment news first broke of the execution-style hit on Gordon Church, but had invented various excuses not to. Anyway, he was here now, ready for the end-of-afternoon media conference that was timed to make the six o'clock news, even if he'd pretty much had to drag himself onto the train from Liverpool Street.

He had received the same anonymous tip-off about Church's release from prison that had been emailed last week to all the newspapers. This even-handed approach – the sender had imme- diately deleted the online account – ruled out a greedy prison officer hoping to trouser some ready cash, and the hot favour- ites as the source of the tip-off became the families of the two police constables Church had murdered all those years ago. Ivo and his fellow cowboys had duly saddled up and ridden down to Beckenham, where the first victim's two sons still lived. Now strapping men in their late thirties who had both followed in their father's footsteps, they were loud and explicit in their out- rage that the secretary of state for justice had considered it neither necessary nor courteous to inform them that the low- life scum who had shot their father in the face at point-blank range with a sawn-off shotgun was about to walk free. The

Courier had run a front-page photo of them out on the beat together, but the truth was that precious few readers remembered Gordon Church or cared where he got to spend his final few weeks.

With Bobbi Reynolds at the Police Federation eager to express the organization's view that life should mean life for every cop-killer, no exceptions, regardless, end of, the story had served to whip up public support for the police, which had flagged in the light of the lies and petty conspiracies exposed by the Downing Street Plebgate row. This did of course raise the possibility that the tip-off had originated within the Home Office as some kind of ham-fisted attempt to lure the worst dinosaurs of the Federation out into the open, where they could be humanely culled. But Ivo doubted that: Gordon Church wasn't exactly a cause worth fighting over.

Which left whoever had shot the bastard as the possible sender of the anonymous email. Had the executioner been clever enough to stir up a quick hate campaign and simultaneously ensure that instead of only a handful of people with any idea of Church's movements there was now a crowd of tabloid readers among whom his killer could hide?

The conference room was already lively, and Ivo hailed a few familiar faces as he jockeyed for a seat where his line of sight wouldn't be messed up by some beefed-up camera crew and their fucking sound booms. Recognizing the kind of snarling bad mood that a few years back would have had him heading for the nearest bar, he shook himself down, hoping that Hilary Burnett's promise of a newsworthy development would provide sufficient distraction.

As he waited to see whether Grace would be part of the line-up, he finally allowed himself to examine his reluctance to be here. Since his return from the Algarve earlier in the week, he'd been busy researching the overlapping networks of property development companies that had invested in the sandy coastline of Portugal, trying to establish where their funding originated and who ultimately held the deeds to the white stucco villas with the sea views. He'd got a few names, but you had to know how to make sense of all this company structure and finance stuff, and that wasn't really his bag. So then he'd gone after Jerry Coghlan, looking back into his time on the Flying Squad, and digging deep into the oozing mud that had persuaded Coghlan to quit the job and piss off to Portugal. Not that his sins appeared all that black: money appeared to be his only motivation, and apart from a talent for losing paperwork in return for cash and a conspicuous failure to track down – officially, at least – the ill-gotten proceeds of various high-value robberies, he appeared to be a reasonably proficient thief-taker.

If Ivo were honest, he'd only gone to Portugal in the hope of impressing DI Fisher, to ride to her rescue in some way. He hadn't entirely failed, but all he'd really accomplished was to put a few names to faces and make a couple of interesting connections that still led nowhere.

Yet his researches had obviously made someone unhappy. First off, one of the associate editors had dropped by his desk to remind him that the *Courier* had some very lucrative advertisers with interests in the Algarve, so best all round if Ivo just canned this Madeleine McCann stuff, or whatever story it was he'd been chasing out there. And then, the morning of the Gordon Church shooting, he'd arrived in the newsroom to find that all his personal files had been wiped from the company system. Computer glitch, he was told, simple bad luck that he was the only one affected.

Given how careful Ivo was about never using his work computer for anything remotely sensitive, he'd decided to take it as a compliment that he'd managed to provoke one of his unseen lords and masters into showing that they cared. What rattled him was *why*? Clearly he'd yanked someone's chain, but whose? His real fear was that he'd blundered into something that would backfire on the very people he was trying to help. Maybe he should stick to simple muckraking and leave the knight-in-shining-armour stuff to people who knew what they were doing. Except that there was young Davey too. A kid in the power of adults who wouldn't let him speak about what was really going on around him. It didn't stand thinking about.

Ivo had dedicated years of drinking to the obliteration of the wounds that this cluster-fuck combination of Grace and Davey now threatened to scrape open. Self-medicating, the trick-cyclist had called it, though the chap had never been wily enough to trap him into telling tales. Nor had either of his two wives, nor even his daughter, wherever she was now. But Grace Fisher's grey eyes, sometimes they made him want to drop to his knees and sob.

Roused by the commotion as Hilary led the way to the long table set up in front of a huge image of the red, white and blue Essex Police crest, Ivo watched the door through which she'd entered for DI Fisher, but she did not appear. Instead, the communications director was followed by Colin Pitman and two men Ivo hadn't seen before, whom she introduced as Detective Chief Inspector Tony Bullen from Lincolnshire and Detective Inspector Sajiv Gupta from Cambridgeshire. More disappointed than he liked to admit at Grace's absence, Ivo settled down to hear the details of the newsworthy development.

And, he had to admit, the story Colin presented was a neat package. Not only had a similar weapon, ammunition and MO featured in all three murders, but a similar-looking silvery-grey van had also been spotted in the vicinity of each shooting. In Ely someone had noted the registration plate of a van speeding from the scene. The plates turned out to have been stolen from a metallic-grey Renault Kangoo. A roadside camera, picking up the same stolen number plate, supplied what the police thought was an image of the man they were seeking: the driver wore a hat, sunglasses and a scarf over his mouth, which while of little use to the police – at least until a suspect was detained – would make the perfect moody shot for tomorrow's front page. The photo combined with some cynical ambivalence over whether the shooter was a loose cannon or a twisted hero was going to make great copy.

Meanwhile the three murder inquiries from Ely, Grantham and Colchester would be brought together under the leadership of Detective Superintendent Pitman, who would be looking for any common elements that had led the gunman to target these three individuals over a four-month period. Hilary then wrapped up by asking the media to remember that some of the victims had grieving families and, whatever their alleged crimes and convictions, they had a right to the full protection of the law. Among his fellow cowboys, her appeal not to inflame opinion and so risk inciting copycat incidents would have about as much effect as a cattle rustler's entreaty to a lynch mob.

Ivo hung about in case Grace came looking for him. He was in no hurry to file his copy – the story was already written in his head, and he could access any images he needed from the Essex Police media portal – and he wanted the chance to tell her that he'd hit a dead end. The room emptied, and he slowly followed the rest of the pack to the front entrance, where he lingered outside, pretending to check his phone. She came out soon afterwards, passing him without a glance.

Ivo trailed her all the way to a dark and deserted park surrounding what looked like a Norman castle, but the gates were already locked. She shook her head in frustration and led the way instead to a nearby bus shelter. A bus had just departed, taking with it any waiting passengers, and they perched together on the slanted plastic bench while he told her the little he'd been able to find out about the beneficiaries of the Panama-registered shell company that held the titles to numerous Algarve villas. When he mentioned one name, her eyes grew bigger and rounder than he'd ever thought possible.

'Leonard Ingold?' she asked. 'Are you sure?'

'Yes. He effectively owns the villa where both Adam Kirkby and your friend DS Cooper stayed. Why? Is he already on your radar?'

'Yes!' she exclaimed. 'He's a local registered firearms dealer. And if I'm right about him, he's also a major supplier of illicit guns and ammunition to half the criminals in England.'

Ivo whistled through his teeth. 'And he's clever enough to implicate a steady stream of police officers eager to take advantage of free or heavily subsidized holidays in a sunshine villa paid for by the laundered proceeds of crime. Nice one!'

Grace placed a hand over her mouth. 'I just sent Lance to talk to his daughter.'

46

Grace was relieved to find Lance waiting for her when she returned to police HQ. She had spent the walk back debating with herself how much she ought to tell him, how much he'd be able to deal with. Her instinct was to offer as little as possible; on the other hand, if he'd managed to establish a rapport with Robyn – as she'd seen him do with young women before – then it was now more vital than ever to find grounds to arrest Leonard Ingold and search his premises.

'Where have you been?' Lance asked as she walked in. He was waiting by his desk, tightly coiled with impatience. Grace didn't like the look of him.

'Someone I had to see,' she said. It was late and most people had gone home, but she drew him along with her into the relative privacy of her cubicle and pulled the spare chair up close to hers. 'How did you get on?' she asked. 'Did Robyn speak to you?'

'Yes.'

'And?'

'She's just a kid, Grace.'

'A bright kid.'

'Yes, but can you imagine what she's going through?'

'She's trying to make sense of her life,' said Grace.

'And this is helping her do that?'

'She's had time to think this over.' However much Grace might privately applaud Lance's scruples, she couldn't downplay her suspicions any longer: the tenuous net of connections, with Leonard right at the heart of them all, was being pulled too tight. If Lance had access to the girl, then Grace had to carry him with her. 'Robyn chose to contact us a second time,' she reminded him. 'I didn't pursue it.'

He shook his head with a faint grimace of distaste.

'Look, Lance, she needs to be sure she's right about her father. Surely you understand that?' she asked, checking over his shoulder that there was no one in earshot. '*You* wanted the truth, didn't you? So does she. Why is it terrible to withhold it from you but not from her?'

'Because she'd be sending her own father to prison.'

'So she did tell you something?' she asked eagerly.

'There must be some other way we can get to him.'

'Oh, come on! Robyn's father may very well have supplied the bullet that killed her friend. What are we supposed to do? Tell her there's nothing we can do and we're simply going to let him get on with it?'

Grace wanted to give Lance time to come to his own decision, but as he stared moodily out at the leafless branches of winter trees thrown into witch-like relief by the streetlights below she made up her own mind: she had no choice but to press him, hard.

'I've just found out something else,' she said. 'It may make you think differently. Do you want to know?'

'What?'

'The villa you stayed in. The same villa Adam Kirkby was

staying in when that photograph of Peter, Adam and Coghlan was taken.'

'Yes?'

'Want to know who owns it?' Grace deliberately let her pause lengthen. 'It's Robyn's dad. Leonard Ingold.'

Watching the process of deduction play so plainly across Lance's face – a face that had become dear to her – Grace watched him arrive at the same conclusions she'd reached during her meeting with Ivo.

'So Peter wasn't just investigating money-laundering,' he said slowly. 'He could have been after Leonard Ingold.'

'We don't know anything for sure.' Picturing the dark gravel and brick of the alley where Peter had died, she despised herself for manipulating Lance in this way. But what choice did she have? She had a duty to too many other people.

'But if Peter had been getting uncomfortably close to Ingold, it could've been Ingold who had him killed,' said Lance. 'Or even killed him himself?'

'We don't know that,' she said as Lance rose to his feet. There wasn't enough room in her cubicle for him to pace up and down, and Grace watched him anxiously, suddenly afraid of what she might have unleashed by opening up the possibility that Ingold could be responsible for Peter's death. 'That's jumping way too far ahead,' she pleaded. 'You know what Colin would say: clear the ground beneath your feet. First we need to secure the evidence that Ingold is a criminal. Get the building-blocks in place one at a time.'

'But Ingold must be friendly with John Kirkby and his sons.'

'Possibly,' said Grace. 'Again, we don't know for certain. Could be that Jerry Coghlan acts as the lettings agent, so Adam Kirkby had no idea who the villa really belongs to, any more than you did.'

Lance's frown revealed the direction of his thoughts. 'Except that Ingold befriended Duncan at the wildfowling club, and it holds open days and stuff for Police Federation members,' he said. 'John Kirkby's a former local Federation chair, isn't he? And it was the Federation who organized my trip for me.'

'Still doesn't mean John Kirkby knows Ingold as anything more than a friendly and obliging local registered firearms dealer who is entirely legit.'

'Except Kirkby's not exactly squeaky clean, is he?' said Lance. 'He must know that Coghlan was corrupt back in the day.'

'Adam Kirkby's a piece of work too,' she agreed.

'And it would certainly explain how Mark Kirkby came into possession of a Heckler & Koch G3.'

'Yes, it would,' she said. 'But we really do need to go softly softly on this until we know more. We need to put Leonard Ingold in a position where he has to start talking to us.' She took a deep breath. 'That's why, if Robyn gave you something, we need to use it.'

Lance nodded, his mouth twisting oddly as he came to a decision. 'She said her father has dumped at least two lots of stuff in the creek out beyond their garden.' His voice was emotionless. 'I pulled up a map on my phone and she showed me precisely where. We'd probably need a dredger to get them up.'

Grace wasn't quite sure what she felt: she'd have to think about that later. 'When I went to his workshop,' she said, 'everything was pristine. He said he'd been having a long-overdue clear-out. If we find a repriming tool down there, then we've got him.'

'Good,' said Lance. 'Do you think he'll talk?'

'Who knows? He'll have plenty to say if he does. Given that he'll be facing a long sentence, a letter to the judge saying he cooperated certainly wouldn't do him any harm.'

'Unless he goes down for murder.' Lance's mouth was now set in a hard line, and Grace didn't much like the unnerving look in his eyes. She fervently hoped that she hadn't somehow placed a bomb in his hands. She asked herself how it was possible, in five short weeks, for the relaxed and joyful friend who'd played Scrabble with her on Christmas Day to become someone she feared she might not really know at all.

47

Robyn hadn't expected anything to happen quite so fast, especially not anything as noisy and large and physically present as the red dredging machine that was brought over from Tollesbury on a Saturday morning. At breakfast she and her parents had become aware of a distant and incessant engine noise, and, finishing off his mug of tea, her father had set off down the field with the dogs to find out what was going on.

Robyn hadn't accompanied him because it never occurred to her that it could be the police acting upon what she had told the young detective with the sad brown eyes. Leonard had returned, whistling to himself, and informed Robyn and Nicola that it was a dredger clearing silt. It was only after he'd disappeared into his workshop that Robyn suddenly perceived the significance of his statement. She had quickly made a clumsy excuse to her mother and taken herself off to confirm her fears.

She stopped at a safe distance at the edge of the field beyond the poplar trees that marked the end of their land. From here she could see how the big tank treads of the dredger covered the entire width of the sea wall as the operator directed the bucket out across the muddy islets to scoop deep into the sucking mud of the main creek, in the exact spot she had described to DS

Cooper. She was also near enough to make out the slim figure of Grace Fisher. The detective stood to one side of the public footpath that ran along the top of the sea wall. A couple of men Robyn didn't recognize stood nearby. She looked closely, but DS Cooper definitely wasn't with them. Grace Fisher barely moved as she watched the machine do its work. Fully exposed to the icy sting of the damp wind coming in off the water, she was well wrapped up in jeans, wellington boots and a warm padded jacket, and clearly prepared to brave the elements for as long as it took. Robyn felt sick, overwhelmed by the physical reality of what she had done.

There was no way her dad hadn't also seen the police presence, yet when he'd returned to the house he had said nothing to Nicola and shown no sign of concern or fear – nor of the anger she dreaded. His incredible skill at masking his true feelings felt more terrifying than the rage he must surely feel inside.

Grace Fisher turned briefly in Robyn's direction but made no sign of recognition. Robyn knew that they were going to find the sack she had seen her father throw into the deep mud of the creek, and maybe more besides. She assumed now that the other bags she'd watched him carry down there must contain items he did not want found: why else would he have lied to her about his actions? She was suddenly desperate to know what would happen next. Would they arrest him? And, if so, would it all happen fast, so fast she would never have to face him, never have to look at him? Have no time even to say goodbye. If not, then it would be her turn to conceal her most desperate thoughts and feelings, to hide from him what she had done, and she could not imagine how she could possibly do that for a single minute, let alone whole days.

For he must already have realized that this monstrous machine was here, its long arm stretching out to gouge deep into the mud, because of her. There was no one else who could have known to tell the police to search in this exact spot. So how had he managed to walk so calmly back into the house and tell her and her mother that there was nothing to worry about?

Robyn could never have dreamed that her father would possess the capacity to act so convincingly that, even when she could imagine all too vividly what they must be, she could not guess his true emotions. The only other possible – impossible – explanation was that he did not suspect her at all, that he found the idea of her betrayal so unimaginable that it had never even occurred to him. That thought was almost worse.

She had always loved her father more than anyone else in the world, and had always believed her love to be returned in full. But clearly neither of them had the remotest inkling of what secrets the other possessed. Unless the deeper truth was that he simply had no feelings to conceal. Or not for her, anyway. Which was perhaps as it should be. After what she had done, she did not deserve his love.

The noise of the engine eased abruptly. The bucket of the dredger, covered in slime, had swung round and now dipped down towards the footpath, like some fantasy robot monster bowing its head in submission. One of the men near Grace Fisher moved forward. Robyn could see that he wore thick black rubber gloves with gauntlets like a medieval warrior. He plunged both arms deep into the huge metal bucket and then lifted something heavy, wet and bulky clear of the machine. Standing back with arms outstretched, he turned in triumph to show his dripping silt-covered burden to Grace Fisher. The detective nodded and turned once more to look towards Robyn.

48

It was either this or the oblivion of a double gin, Ivo thought as he stared out of the first-floor window of his seafront-terrace hotel room at the windswept sands of Weymouth beach. He'd kept this crap at bay for forty-odd years, yet now it had crept up on him and was turning him into a sentimental old slob. It had been the verdict in the Dunholt inquest late on Friday afternoon that had finally got to him.

The coroner had stuck to his word and wrapped the whole thing up in a week, which had to be some kind of record. Five counts of unlawful killing and one of suicide, with a brief narrative conclusion to the effect that Fewell had been isolated and depressed since his divorce and driven to desperation by anxiety over the financial consequences of his drink-drive summons. There had been lots of the usual sort of praise for the emergency services on behalf of the three victims who survived, and that was that. Ivo doubted that anyone had given a single thought to Davey and Ella Fewell.

He had spent most of Saturday fuming, had set off for Weymouth this morning, and then spent the rest of the day freezing his bollocks off outside the development where Donna and the kids were living. He'd not seen them – they'd had more sense than to venture out on such a miserable Sunday afternoon – but he'd waited until the lights had gone on and then lingered until Donna came to the window to close the blinds. It was enough. They were safe. It seemed like the talisman he needed to voyage back to when he'd been Davey's age.

It was the housemaster of his prep school that he still had nightmares about.

Ivo had known during the Christmas holidays how ill his mother was – she'd told him herself as she'd helped him pack his trunk. He didn't really blame his father, for not coping. It was no surprise that Dad had gone into such a blind funk that he couldn't face telling Ivo that she'd died. Maybe the funeral had simply been too much for him. Perhaps he had no idea what to do about his ten-year-old son and couldn't face up to being alone with him afterwards, once everybody else had gone home. His father was a genius at solving problems of aeronautical engineering, but he'd never learned how to speak about his feelings.

Ten days before the end of term Ivo had been called to the housemaster's study. Only later did he realize that, even while he was being grilled about a maths test he'd flunked, the man had known that his mother was dead and that her funeral was taking place almost at that very moment – had known but not told him, not considered him worthy of telling. Only when Ivo went home for Easter did he discover his mother had died and it had then been decided – he was never permitted to ask by whom – that it would be best to keep it from him until school broke up for the holidays.

He should have smelt a rat when his father came by car to pick up his trunk – unusual in itself, as Ivo and it generally went by train with a group of other boys. Ivo had never forgotten the two men, his father and the housemaster, standing on the stone steps and shaking hands while he stood by in ignorance of what had happened.

When Ivo had returned to school three weeks later, at the start of the summer term, the housemaster had looked down at him sympathetically and told him to keep his chin up and he'd be all right. Only matron had ever openly acknowledged the scale of his loss. And it was only now, decades later, that Ivo saw how much that handshake, once he'd tasted the full diminishing shame of its significance, had determined the course of his life. He had never trusted any institution since: not the old school tie, not the law or the medical profession, and certainly not the family. The only flag he'd ever been prepared to defend was his loyalty to the sharp scent of ink and the aroma of warm paper that had clung to the industry back when he'd blagged his way into his first job on a local newspaper.

He'd always been proud of his cynical nonconformism, his paid-up membership of the awkward squad. As a reporter, it had helped make him lead dog. But he'd paid with two failed marriages, an estranged daughter and a decidedly dodgy liver. He didn't want any of that for Davey Fewell.

John Kirkby was a handshake man. That's why Ivo had brought himself down here to the bleak Weymouth seafront. It wasn't right that those in power got to decide what was said – simple as that. Just because Mark Kirkby had had a row of polished buttons on his uniform and a guard of honour at his funeral, it didn't mean he – or his father – got to have the last word. And if the coroner wasn't going to do the job properly, then Ivo bloody well would.

It was getting too dark to make out anything much beyond the lights on the esplanade. He thought he could hear the sea, now a huge well of blackness before the faint light of the horizon kicked in, but it was more likely just the wind. He drew the curtains and switched on the bedside lamp, feeling the well-worn mattress sag under his weight as he swung his feet up to lie on the coverlet and reached round to punch a couple of pillows into the right shape to support his dodgy back.

Ivo had been at a very different funeral two days ago, and he blamed it for leaving him in such a maudlin, retrospective mood. Once upon a time, Jock Scott had reigned over the cuttings library at the *Courier*. It had been a black enough day in Ivo's book when the old British Newspaper Library in Colindale had been demolished to make way for luxury flats, but that was a lifetime after the *Courier* had moved out of Fleet Street and the yellowing wonders of Jock's cuttings library had been chucked on a bonfire. The funeral service had been held at a crematorium in Enfield, where after the committal Ivo had hung around in the shelter of the echoing brick arches to exchange greetings with various former nabobs of the compositing rooms. He hadn't seen most of them in twenty years or more and had been ridiculously shocked by how much they'd all aged, for these were men who, in their day, had wielded unthinkable power. They too, erstwhile fathers of the chapel, had been handshake men – until Maggie Thatcher cut a deal with Murdoch.

Their old unchallenged allegiance to the trade union and the closed shop had been tribal. Some of their kids had gone to school with cousins they weren't allowed to speak to because their dads had been on opposite sides of the picket line in the Wapping dispute. Families who still didn't speak. Never would. For many, their greatest hatred was still reserved for the way

Thatcher had destroyed those bred-in-the-bone working-class loyalties.

He suspected that the same kind of tribal allegiance was at play out in Vale do Lobo. Morale in the police service was low, and with no current threat from the 'enemy within' for the government to require a paramilitary force, the fiercest loyalty of the boys in blue was increasingly reserved for each other.

Ivo wondered how far those ancient loyalties still reached. An official HMRC query on an old tax return had arrived in yesterday's post. He'd tossed it aside, but earlier today, when he'd handed over one of his credit cards in exchange for his room key, it had been refused. A quick phone call established that a stop had been put on it because of a bogus fraud warning. It was further proof that someone somewhere wanted to convince him that, should they so choose, they had the clout to seriously fuck with his life.

Trying once more to make his old bones comfortable on the creaking bed, Ivo thought about the extraordinary cross-referencing system stored inside Jock's head which had also vanished in a plume of smoke from the crematorium chimney. It was easy to recall their first encounter. Standing behind a wooden counter in his khaki storeman's coat with a stub of thick-leaded pencil behind his ear, Jock had wordlessly accepted the chit Ivo handed him and disappeared into his mysterious dominion of bulging shelves stuffed with folders. He'd returned almost immediately with a single sheet of paper to which had been pasted a solitary newspaper cutting, a single column three inches long. Ivo, still wet behind the ears, had asked indignantly if that was all there was and been stared into submission. He had learned fast to show proper respect, and in time – meaning years rather than weeks – had been rewarded with entire fold-ers, stained with coffee and reeking of cigarettes, which had prepared him for tricky interviews and backed up his riskier stories. Sometimes a note was attached to the cutting, written in Jock's stubby pencil – a correction or a coded warning that the subject of an article was likely to sue. Once in a while Ivo would be handed an empty file. Nothing was said, but this signified that the material had 'gone upstairs' thanks to a govern-ment D notice.

Jock had liked nothing better than a good conspiracy theory, and, a staunch union man, he'd kept close tabs on long-running stories such as who in Operation Countryman was aligned with whom. If anyone could have traced the connections Ivo needed between Jerry Coghlan, John Kirkby and Leonard Ingold, and between Peter Burnley and whatever he'd been up to, it would've been Jock. Back then the chains of command – or webs of cor-ruption, whatever you wanted to call them – were real, and everyone played to the same rules: honour among thieves, working-class solidarity, old boys' networks, decent honest criminals, checks and balances, rotten apples, party politics, baksheesh, you scratch my back and I'll watch yours. *Handshakes.*

And for all today's political correctness and vigilant manage-ment policies, those rules still applied. Look at what had happened to Grace Fisher back in her old job: punished for not giving a mate the benefit of the doubt, for not 'making allow-ances' for her thug of a husband. Her bullying colleagues had no doubt regarded their actions not as corruption but as upholding an essential *esprit de corps.*

Not for the first time, Ivo wondered what had driven Grace to stay in the police after her experiences in Kent. She was relatively young, had a good degree and could, he assumed, have easily found another interesting line of work. He'd also give a lot to know what kept her warm at night, what raft she clung to in the wee small hours. He'd never been much of a player, but if he'd been a quarter of a century younger he liked to think she'd have reached for his hand when the going got rough.

Ivo was amazed at how he could lie peacefully on a bed in a quaint English seaside hotel listening to the wind rattle the thin glass of a Georgian bay window and consider things he'd seldom permitted himself to think about before. His mother had loved him, yet had packed him off to boarding school telling him it would be fun to be with other boys, but in reality it was so he wouldn't have to watch her sicken and die. He hadn't been allowed to say he'd rather stay with her; he hadn't been allowed to cry or plead or bargain for things to be different; he had been honour-bound to say he loved every minute of homesickness and misery.

Something like that drove Grace Fisher too – he could feel it in his bones – something with the power to keep her awake at night, to make her not give up, to make her hold tight to her reserve. She was never going to confide in him, any more than he'd tell her about his mother, but it made them two of a kind. Not that he'd ever bought into any of that British stiff-upper-lip nonsense. His younger self had had no choice except to maintain the same front as his parents and his housemaster, but as soon as he'd been able to make good his escape he'd gone looking for his own heroes. He might now be a brash muck-raking dried-out-alcoholic reporter on a trashy tabloid with a huge circulation and the power to ruin people's reputations on a whim, but he was here on a noble quest. He was here to look out for Davey Fewell.

49

Grace was forced to spend most of Monday morning on tenter-
hooks waiting to hear back from the ballistics lab. She had
been informed on Saturday afternoon that a repriming tool
had been among the various metal objects found inside the
bags retrieved from the marshy creek a quarter of a mile
beyond the boundary of Leonard Ingold's property. Now the lab
was testing to see whether, if used to prime a new round, the
tool would leave the same microscopic scratch marks found on
primers inside shell casings recovered from Dunholt and
elsewhere.

It was always stressful anticipating the return of forensic
tests that might negate weeks and sometimes months of work
on a case, but she felt keenly that even more than usual was riding on these particular results. It was possible that, if it
transpired that Leonard Ingold was not, after all, the Lion King,
no lasting harm would be done to Robyn's relationship with her
parents. And maybe Leonard's ownership of the Algarve villa,
while of interest to HMRC, would also turn out to be irrelevant
to whatever had taken Peter out to Vale do Lobo. Yet, even without forensic corroboration, Grace knew that neither Robyn nor
Lance would ever accept that their corrosive suspicions were

unfounded, and both would forever remain haunted, mistrustful, stuck. In her instinctive opinion, they'd be right.

She tried to distract herself with work on the Gordon Church murder. Yesterday an interceptor car on the M25 had spotted a burning vehicle on a track between fields just north of the motorway. It turned out to be a metallic-grey Renault Kangoo with no number plates, which put it in the frame to be the van spotted leaving the hospital grounds immediately after Church had been shot and also the vehicle linked to the Grantham and Ely murders. Grace had arranged for it to be recovered and forensically examined, and was pushing her team for swifter results on tracking down all owners of that make, model and colour, prioritizing any vehicles reported stolen in the past four months, when Curtis Mullins appeared at the door to the MIT office.

'You wanted to see me, ma'am?'

'I asked to see you on Thursday,' she said, trying to keep her voice low, to remain cool and authoritative. She didn't like to admit to herself that it wouldn't take much to make her afraid of Curtis Mullins. He made no reply, his blue eyes sullen and resentful. Grace decided not to argue over his timing.

'Ruth Woods told me it was you who signed in Gordon Church?' she asked.

'I did, yes.'

'Was there was anything he said or did that might shine a light on what happened to him? Did he have any concerns, for instance, about being followed?'

'He came to the desk. I gave him the book to sign. He signed it and left.'

'You had no conversation?'

'No.'

'OK,' she said. 'That's it. Thank you.' She turned her back on him before her anger got the better of her and didn't turn round until she heard his retreating footsteps. She caught Lance watching her and read an even more bitter anger and frustration in his expression. She gave a shrug of apology tiny enough not to be noticed by anyone else in the office and nodded for him to join her in her cubicle.

'I know how you feel,' she said. 'It's just as galling to me to let him walk in here like that, but you can see how he's spoiling for a fight. But if we give him one, what's the next thing he'll do?'

She had already had this argument with Lance before they'd taken Robyn's information to Colin on Friday in order to greenlight a search of the creek. Lance had wanted to lay before their boss everything they knew about Ingold's villa, the Vale do Lobo connection between Peter and Adam Kirkby and Adam's friendship with Curtis, and she had struggled to persuade him to wait, to accept that it was best to take it one step at a time. She'd had no choice but to tell Colin about her interview with Warren Cox and explain how her hunch about the identity of the Lion King had taken her out to Ingold's workshop, where she encountered Robyn, but she was determined never to reveal Ivo's involvement nor, if at all possible, that she had gone against Colin's direct orders in telling Lance the truth about Peter.

'Think about it,' she told Lance now. 'If I give Curtis grounds to make a complaint of bullying or harassment against me, who's the first person he's going to speak to?'

Lance sighed. 'His Fed rep.'

'Precisely,' said Grace. 'Who, for all we know, has enjoyed

many a lovely family holiday in Leonard Ingold's villa. Or if the rep hasn't, then his local committee members have. It's enough to tie Professional Standards up in knots for years to come.'

'You're saying we let it go?'

'No!' said Grace. 'Look, I don't know what kind of rats' nest we've stirred up here, or how far or high it reaches, but what if Ingold does start talking? What if he does confirm that Mark Kirkby had possession of the rifle used by Russell Fewell, and it all comes to court, then what? If the defence can show that I've pursued some kind of personal vendetta against Mark's alleged co-conspirator, then it's all going to blow up in our faces and get thrown out of court, isn't it?'

Lance nodded reluctantly, but she could see that only half of him was attending to what she was really saying.

'Lance, please,' she begged. 'I'd bet my house that the repriming tool Ingold threw in the creek will give us the crowbar we need to lever this case wide open. Just wait until we can interview him. See what he has to say.'

Lance shook his head. 'It'll be "No comment" all the way. His solicitor will tell him we don't have enough to charge. The bag with the repriming tool was found near a public footpath. He'll say there are dozens of local amateur reloaders who could have dumped it there.'

Grace feared he was right and was trying to come up with a better argument to convince him when Duncan tapped on her cubicle partition. He was holding a sheet of paper and smiling.

'Is that the ballistics report?' Grace asked eagerly, reaching out her hand for the paper.

'On the Gordon Church shooting,' said Duncan. 'Nothing back yet on the bags from the creek. But the marks on the shell casing found in the hospital car park match those from the Dunholt murders.'

'Yes!' Grace clenched both fists and raised them above her head in elation. Duncan too was smiling broadly.

'The brass also has the same military head stamps,' said Lance, staring meaningfully at Grace. 'Almost like they came from the same batch.'

'Except that whoever is producing these bullets seems pretty prolific,' said Duncan. 'Ammo from the same supplier has already been linked to a drive-by shooting in north London, an unrelated gang shooting in Manchester, two armed robberies in Birmingham and four other non-fatal incidents across London. Now we know what to look for, a lot more may turn up.'

'Does the boss know?' she asked, trying to deflect Lance. The conversation he wanted to have would have to wait until later.

'Not yet,' said Duncan.

Lance forced a smile. 'I'd better get back to chasing down all Church's contacts around the time of his release,' he said, slipping out past his colleague.

Duncan raised an eyebrow at Grace. 'Is he OK?'

'I hope so.'

'He should have taken his full entitlement of compassionate leave,' said Duncan. 'I keep telling him to.'

'I know.' She touched his arm as she came out from behind her desk. 'Thanks.'

'Don't worry, boss. We'll make sure he gets over this.'

She was yet again grateful for the compassion beneath the detective's blokey exterior; it went a little way towards assuaging her fear that she was mishandling her own friendship with

Lance. Yet it was essential to rein Lance in until their case against the Kirkbys was unassailable.

Grace tapped on the superintendent's door, and he beckoned her in. Colin was equally delighted with the latest development in the Church case and, like her, impatient for results that would bring them nearer to Leonard Ingold's arrest.

'What about the daughter?' he asked. 'Are you intending to tell Ingold where we got the information?'

'No, absolutely not. Anonymous tip-off. He can make of that what he will, although I can't imagine he'll come up with a very big cast of likely candidates.'

'No,' said Colin. 'But if that's your strategy, then we don't want the girl getting a fit of the vapours and throwing a wobbly when we least expect it.'

'No, sir. But I'd still like to leave her father to work the truth out for himself rather than us give her away.'

'Lance is trained as a family liaison officer, isn't he?'

'Yes, I think so, but I really don't—'

Ignoring her, Colin beckoned over her shoulder for Lance to join them in his office. 'You're Robyn Ingold's confidant, right?' he asked.

'She gave me the information, yes,' said Lance cautiously, glancing at Grace, who did her best to signal a silent and urgent 'No' at him.

'Good,' said Colin. 'Then you can be her FLO. Once we arrest her father, I want you to make sure you get to her before her mother or anyone else does. Stick with her. Assure her we'll do our best to keep her secret as long as she wants it kept. OK?'

'Yes, sir.' This time Lance studiously avoided looking at Grace.

'So what's your interview strategy?' Colin asked Grace. 'Is this link to the Church murder going to help us?'

'I imagine Ingold must take pains *not* to know where his weapons and ammunition end up,' she said.

'He must regard a few innocent victims as an unfortunate side effect,' said Lance. 'If he was that easily shaken, he'd have given up years ago.'

'That's my feeling too,' said Grace. 'Although his daughter's friend was among the Dunholt fatalities. That may have shifted the balance a little in our favour.'

Colin did not appear convinced. 'What about his premises?' he asked. 'Do you expect a search to throw up anything of interest?'

'No,' she said. 'His workshop is pristine. I reckon he's already dumped anything incriminating. But his bookkeeping may give us some leads, and I'd like to look into the companies that make regular secure collections for him, and check out all the delivery addresses.'

'That'll send a clear signal that we're not going to go away easily,' said Colin. 'So what other buttons can we press? What about his profits? Now he knows we're watching him, he's going to have to lie low for a while, if not pack up completely. So he'll want to hang on to what he's got. We could always try threatening him with the Proceeds of Crime Act.'

Grace was aware of Lance once again looking at her intently, willing her to spill the beans on the Vale do Lobo villa. Looking straight ahead, she said calmly, 'We know he pays private school fees. No doubt he takes foreign holidays. As soon as we have grounds to arrest him, and hear what he has to say, then we'll start taking his life apart, piece by piece.'

She turned to face Lance and was shocked by his bitter look of disbelief. Hating herself, she willed him to understand that she was striving to find and to follow the best path to the truth.

Behind them a loud whooping cheer burst out, and they turned as Duncan hurried into Colin's office. 'Got him!' cried Duncan jubilantly. 'There's a match on the repriming tool. We've got the bastard!'

Amid the handshaking and congratulations, she heard Colin's voice. 'What are you waiting for, DI Fisher? Go and pick him up!'

50

Grace had never made an arrest without an awareness of how the act of depriving a person of their liberty was the ultimate demonstration of police power. Some people froze like a rabbit in headlights, instantly ceding control; others struggled, spitting, swearing and lashing out; Leonard Ingold appeared oblivious to the inevitability of his eventual submission. She had deliberately chosen Duncan to accompany her, hoping that the switch in power between two men who had previously enjoyed a friendly acquaintance would unsettle Leonard, and was disappointed when he greeted Duncan with unperturbed courtesy. Only the long steady look he directed towards his anxious wife hinted at any possible misgivings.

Since Nicola, as Leonard's authorized 'servant', was permitted to handle weapons and ammunition on his behalf, Grace could have arrested her as well, but she had taken the decision to wait, gambling on the notion that if Nicola were offered time alone in which to dwell on their predicament she might, when eventually brought in for questioning under caution, prove more pliant than her husband. Time would tell how much she really knew about, or participated in, her husband's criminal dealings.

Grace and Duncan drove back to Colchester without directly addressing their silent passenger in the back seat. Glancing at him in the rear-view mirror, Grace longed to know what kind of conversation had taken place between Robyn and her parents after the dredger had been hauled back to Tollesbury last Saturday. Surely Leonard must have realized that the information had come from his family or someone else close to the heart of his business? Had he really not guessed, or was he in denial? Yet he appeared to gaze out at the passing countryside without a flicker of emotion.

Once booked into custody, Grace walked with him to the cell where he'd have to wait until his solicitor arrived. As the door was opened she saw him take a quick look around and wrinkle his nose in distaste, but he walked in without hesitation and politely accepted her offer of a cup of tea.

The first move made by Leonard's lawyer – a partner in a reliable local firm that dealt frequently with the Major Investigation Team – was to seek assurances that the police would not revoke his certificate of registration as a firearms dealer unless they could immediately lay out their grounds for doing so. Grace left it to Duncan to respond, having already briefed him to lead the interview. Duncan began by reminding Leonard that this was a 'first account' interview – his chance to offer whatever innocent explanation he had for the evidence that would be put to him.

Although fully expecting him to answer 'No comment' to every question, Grace watched him closely. His face was weathered, his cheeks ruddy, and grey just starting to colour his sandy-brown hair; his body language was alert and respectful, yet she knew that, sooner or later, everyone gave something away. Often a suspect would start clowning or overdo the bravado in order to mask their true emotions, before shifting uneasily in their chair, scratching or simply failing to hide their shame or anguish. Leonard focused his gaze on a spot behind her left shoulder, just to the right of Duncan's head, and folded his hands in his lap, apparently ready to pay careful attention to everything they said.

'How can you account for the fact that we've found a bag of tools used to self-load ammunition dumped in the creek yards from your workshop?' asked Duncan.

'No comment.'

'Did you put them there?'

'No comment.'

'Do you know who did put them there?'

'No comment.'

'Do you know of anyone who would know they were there?'

Grace studied Leonard's expression, but there wasn't the tiniest flinch.

'No comment.'

'Are you aware of what tools were in the bag?'

'No comment.'

'One of the tools has been linked forensically to firearms offences up and down the country. Do you have anything to say about that?'

'No comment.'

'Have you ever used the nickname the Lion King?'

Leonard allowed himself an amused smile. 'No comment.'

'In your hearing, has anyone ever called you the Lion King?'

'No comment.'

'What's the nature of your professional relationship with Kenny Elgin, your most regular delivery driver?'

'No comment.'

For the first time Grace spotted an involuntary reaction as his pupils dilated and contracted. His hazel-green eyes slid sideways to look directly at her for a second, and – maybe it was her imagination – she glimpsed an icy coldness in their depths. She thought back to the look he'd given his wife as they'd left his house. It had seemed to suggest a degree of complicity, that Nicola well understood the need for concealment. Yet Grace had also been intrigued by how effectively Nicola's nerves appeared to have been soothed by Leonard's warning look and wondered how much she was habituated to his control. Was she a victim or a willing partner?

'What does the name Angie Turner mean to you?' Duncan's questions continued remorselessly.

'No comment.'

Grace observed a slight movement in Leonard's cheeks as he clenched his jaw.

'Angie and her grandmother were both shot dead by self-loaded bullets primed by the tool found in the creek,' said Duncan. 'The bullets had military shell casings of the type you told me could be purchased from a range warden at the Stanford Training Area. Did you know that Angie Turner was at school with your daughter, Robyn?'

'No comment.'

Leonard's chest rose and fell more noticeably beneath his faded Viyella shirt, but otherwise he did not move. Grace couldn't resist admiring the man's iron self-control. Beginning to understand how effectively disguised he was by his impenetrable ordinariness, she saw how Robyn had simply never questioned her father's actions. Her heart ached for the girl.

After her ex-husband's vicious assault, when he'd acted as though nothing much had really happened, Grace had constantly blamed herself for failing to see what was coming, for not realizing what the man she'd married was like. But she had been an adult. Very much in love, she'd chosen not to pay any attention to the warning signs. But for all her intelligence Robyn was still a child; the entire kingdom of her life had been ruled by a man who seemed to possess a remarkable ability to present himself as something totally unremarkable, as completely other than he was.

Grace couldn't imagine being able to fathom what lay behind his bland facade. Did he simply block out unwelcome realities by psychologically disassociating himself from the grisly end results of his illegal trade? Or could he be far more deeply implicated though his links with Jerry Coghlan than they yet knew?

Duncan wrapped up his final questions and ended the interview. Leonard allowed himself a deep sigh of resignation when informed that he'd be spending the night in a cell. Grace wanted to give him plenty of time in which to contemplate his possible future before she and Duncan interviewed him again in the morning – not that she expected him to change his tune.

Making her way upstairs, she checked her phone. There was a text from Lance to let her know that he'd managed to intercept Robyn at the school gates and had warned her of Leonard's arrest, and also that luckily Robyn had already arranged to stay the night with a school friend. She texted back to confirm she'd got the message, her mind on Robyn's predicament. By the time the girl finished school tomorrow, Leonard would almost certainly have been released and – at least until Grace managed to obtain the crucial but elusive evidence she still needed to charge him – Robyn and her parents could all go back to pretending they were just a normal happy family.

Except that, even if her parents never knew of the part Robyn had played, her actions would mark her for the rest of her life. Grace ought to call Lance, not just text – he would probably be at home by now – but she hesitated. Her sharpest regret was that circumstance had made him the conduit for Robyn's betrayal. No police officer could ever be happy about playing a part in that. As SIO, Grace, not Lance, should have been the one to take that burden on her shoulders. Hoping that, with all the pressure he was under, she wasn't asking too much of him, she decided she could wait to speak to him in the morning.

51

Leonard Ingold was released on police bail at lunchtime the following day. The custody sergeant informed Grace that his wife had come to pick him up. Busy the rest of the afternoon with the Gordon Church shooting, Grace was glad to get home about seven o'clock. She was just about to pour herself a glass of wine when she received a call from Ben Marrington asking her to return immediately to police HQ. He told her briefly that Nicola Ingold had called the station at six o'clock to report that her daughter had gone missing. Robyn had apparently skipped school, lied about where she'd spent last night, and her phone was switched off. Nicola and her husband had insisted on coming into the station, where they were specifically asking to speak to Grace.

Breathing through the waves of guilt and apprehension that threatened to engulf her, she called Lance to see what recent contact he'd had with the girl, but his phone too was switched off. He'd been fine this morning, and had appeared sanguine about Ingold's release on bail. When he'd asked to leave work early because he'd promised to help out a friend, she'd been happy to grant his request. Should she have paid more attention?

It took her twenty minutes to drive back to HQ. When she reached the car park, she tried Lance again: nothing.

Ben Marrington was waiting for her upstairs, accompanied by Colin. She was surprised not only that the superintendent had been called but that he had deemed the situation serious enough to come in. She soon discovered why.

'Warren Cox is in the prison hospital wing after a knife attack late this afternoon,' he said.

'Will he be OK?'

'They think so, yes,' said Colin. 'Cox is claiming it's self-inflicted, which means he's scared. What do you reckon? Is it linked to Ingold's arrest?'

'All Warren Cox ever gave me was a nickname,' said Grace. 'I'm certain that he didn't actually know Ingold's identity.' She tried to think back. 'But I did pay my first visit to Ingold's workshop shortly after talking to Warren at the prison.' She had also been attacked on her early-morning run the following day, but she didn't feel like explaining that to Colin. 'If the knife attack on Warren is Ingold's way of sending a message not to be a grass, then he has extremely fast and effective lines of communication.'

'So what about his missing daughter?' asked Colin. 'I've filled Inspector Marrington in on the background. Has she just run away rather than face her parents, or is this linked to the attack on Warren Cox?'

'I don't know,' said Grace, her mind racing. She turned to Ben. 'What have her parents said so far?'

'They think she's been snatched in order to ensure Leonard doesn't cooperate with us by naming names.'

Grace was shocked, and looked from Ben to Colin. 'Have they received any kind of communication that suggests this?' She prayed that neither Curtis Mullins nor Adam Kirkby had abducted the girl. 'Should we consider kidnap a credible possibility?'

Colin shook his head. 'Personally, I think she regrets what she's done and has run away. My daughter's fifteen. In my view, that's exactly how a teenager would react to stress. Have you spoken to DS Cooper? What's his take?'

Grace willed herself to sound totally matter-of-fact. 'I haven't been able to reach him yet. Let me try again.' She took out her phone, willing her fingers not to tremble. Lance's phone was still switched off. She shook her head. 'No joy. Maybe he's at the cinema or something.'

Ben gave Grace a level look, and she had the uncomfortable impression that he could read her mind, though there was no way he could guess at the crazy suspicions that were beginning to grip her.

'I think we must take the kidnap threat seriously,' she said. 'After all, there could be hundreds of criminals out there afraid of what information Ingold might be prepared to share with us. Not least whoever shot Gordon Church. His bullets came from Ingold's workshop, remember.'

'Well, if Ingold wants our help finding Robyn, he needs to give us some names,' said Colin. 'Time to get heavy.'

'They're parents,' said Ben quietly. 'Their daughter is missing and they came to us for help.'

Grace had to agree. If Robyn's mum and dad couldn't turn to the police to find their daughter and bring her home safe and sound, then to whom could they go for help?

'Let's go and talk to them,' she said.

Ben filled her in as they as hurried down the stairs. 'She spent Sunday night with a school friend, Sally,' he said. 'Nicola drove her there and went in for a cup of tea with Sally's mother. Robyn phoned yesterday to let her mum know she'd stay another night so she and Sally could prepare for a science presentation they were doing together.'

'That's the same as she told Lance yesterday,' said Grace. 'And I can imagine Nicola was only too relieved not to get bogged down in difficult explanations over Leonard's absence.'

'When Robyn didn't come home off the bus today,' Ben continued, 'Nicola phoned Sally's mother. Robyn didn't stay with them last night, and she wasn't in school today. No one's seen her since school ended yesterday afternoon, and both parents insist she's never done anything like this before.'

'Is there a boyfriend in the picture?' she asked.

'Not that her parents are aware of, no,' said Ben. 'Though that doesn't mean there isn't one.'

'So either they still haven't worked out that she's been talking to us, or they're not prepared to admit it,' said Grace.

'I reckon the mother suspects something,' said Ben. They arrived at the door to the soft interview room. 'Time to find out.'

Leonard and Nicola shot to their feet as the door opened. 'Is there any news?' asked Nicola.

'Not yet,' said Ben. 'I've put DI Fisher in the picture. Maybe you have some questions for her?'

'Am I still under caution?' asked Leonard.

'Not for this conversation,' said Grace. 'Our priority is your daughter's safety.'

'Then I need to know who you've been talking to as part of your investigation,' Leonard demanded. 'I was sent word about an assault on someone in prison. You know who I'm talking about, right? Well, that was nothing to do with me. Quite the opposite. I'm frightened that it was a warning.'

'Of what?' asked Grace.

'That bad things could happen. I need to know who else you've been speaking to. Who told you to go digging in the creek?'

'I can't tell you that.' Grace looked from Leonard to his wife. Did they really not know? Maybe if Nicola had been kept in the dark as much as Robyn had been, then she would have no idea why her daughter might have run away. But something about the tight set of Nicola's mouth and her downcast eyes suggested she knew more than she was saying. Leonard's eyes, on the other hand, were blazing.

'All I care about is Robyn,' he said. 'Everything I've ever done has been for her. Her and Nicola. You bring her back safe, and I'll tell you anything you want. But until she's safe I need to know who I'm dealing with.'

'Do you think Robyn was aware of your business activities?' Grace asked gently.

Leonard seemed oblivious to the way Nicola's chin shot up, and to the quick, sharp look she gave him.

'Never!' he said. 'I've always kept her out of it.'

'You're sure?'

'Absolutely. There's no way she could have the slightest idea,' Leonard insisted.

'Mrs Ingold?' asked Grace. 'You don't think perhaps Robyn heard somehow about her dad's arrest and has reacted badly? That maybe one of her friends knows where she is, and is fibbing to you?'

Nicola shook her head, not looking directly at anyone. 'We just need to find her.'

Leonard gripped his wife's hand and squeezed it hard. Grace watched Nicola move a little bit closer, shoulder to shoulder. They might have promised one another they were only doing their best for their daughter, but where had that left Robyn?

Grace could feel the weight of Ben Marrington's silence. Now, if ever, was the time for her to speak the truth, to reassure two distraught parents that the situation might not be as dark as it seemed. Except she was certain they didn't want to hear that. Besides, this whole mess was her fault. And there was someone else who needed to come out of this safely. If her crazy speculations were correct, then, once Robyn was safe, there were other people who needed – *deserved* – to hear what Leonard could tell them about his criminal connections. She had to do her best for everyone.

52

Robyn wasn't sure what she was feeling. She was used to spending time alone and had thought, when she suggested coming here, that she'd be familiar enough with this strange and daunting building not to be spooked by it, but now, after a long day by herself, she was beginning to think she must have been crazy even to think of it. Yesterday now seemed a kind of blur, as if a freak wave had carried them along. And yet it would be easy enough to tidy away the evidence of their occupation, lock the narrow door – the only entrance to this abandoned fort – return the key to the hidden key safe, and then, by torchlight, walk the mile or so along the track to the road, where eventually a bus would pass.

But she couldn't just pack up and leave without first seeing and thanking her rescuer. She didn't want him making a wasted journey all the way out here only to find her gone. If it hadn't been for him she would have jacked it in this morning and begged him to drop her off somewhere on his way to work, but he'd been so sweet last night, stoking the stove, making a treat out of cheese sandwiches and tinned soup and then talking to her as they tried to get comfortable enough to fall asleep in the fort's narrow and creaky fold-up beds. Far better to wait for his return and spend a second night here together than go back to face all the trouble she'd caused.

Yet in the end what was the point? She couldn't hide away for ever. At some point she would have to do something, go somewhere, decide where she belonged. She couldn't imagine what it would be like to go home any more than she could work out where else she could go, how on earth she would manage. And it wasn't just the immediate future she'd have to deal with; it was all so much bigger than that, too big to think about properly. She'd cried for an hour this morning after he'd left, cried until she had no more tears and her chest hurt. It had made no difference.

Her parents must have worked out by now that she had run away because of what she'd done. Last weekend, after the dredger had finished its work, had been so weird. Her dad had acted as if nothing at all had happened. And he had never – in her hearing, anyway – mentioned it to her mum. But he must have seen DI Fisher watching from the sea wall, must have realized that they'd find whatever he'd dumped there, and that, whatever it was, it wouldn't do him any good. And yet all weekend – at least until she could stand it no more and had called Sally to ask if she could come and stay on Sunday night – he had peeled potatoes and watched TV and fed the dogs as if he hadn't a care in the world. Once she thought she'd caught her mum giving her a funny sideways glance, but that was it.

Still, it was only a matter of time until someone told them or they realized, if they hadn't already, that it was she who had given them up. And, once they knew, she wouldn't have to pretend any more, wouldn't have to steel herself to be the one to tell them. They'd probably be glad she'd gone. How could they ever want her anywhere near them again?

Lance ought to be here soon. He'd warned her he might be late, but she hoped nothing had happened to prevent him coming. She didn't like the idea of spending the night here without him. She'd thought about climbing up to the roof to watch for the lights of his approaching car, but was frightened in case the trapdoor fell shut behind her, leaving her exposed to the darkness and the vicious wind off the sea.

The estuary was much wider here than on the creek at home. It was the coastal erosion that had convinced the local landowner, a farmer friend of her dad, to abandon his plans to convert the isolated Martello tower into a quirky holiday let; now he just allowed sportsmen to make use of the place on shoot days. Her dad had taken her up to the stone-flagged roof to show her where the artillery had once been mounted, ready to fire at Napoleon's invading fleet, and explained that the brick vaults at the bottom of the tower were where the gunpowder and munitions had been kept. The walls had been made up to eight feet thick to withstand bombardment, and blocked out all exterior sound.

She wondered if she'd feel differently if she'd discovered that her dad had been involved in smuggling cigarettes or importing cannabis, some enterprise where no one ever got shot or died. Maybe she wouldn't have cared or would even have admired him as some kind of free-enterprise buccaneer. But what he'd done was way more serious than making a little cash on the side. Last night, after Lance had come to meet her at school, she'd made him tell her everything. He'd explained that he couldn't give her the fine detail but had confirmed what she already feared, that the bullet that had exploded inside Angie's body had been made in her father's workshop. OK, her dad could never have imagined the nightmare Russell Fewell was about to unleash, but why the hell did he suppose anyone wanted to buy a gun and ammunition illegally? Why did the whole licensing system exist in the first place – why was it endlessly tightened and restricted – if not to deter such horrors as Hungerford or Dunblane?

Part of her, when she wasn't crying, wished Lance hadn't been so certain about the evidence – even though it was evidence she'd helped supply – but there was no way now to unlearn what she knew: Angie's murder wasn't some random, unfortunate quirk of fate for which her dad couldn't be held accountable, it was a direct result of what he did – sell bullets to people who were up to no good. How could she ever go home and pick up her old life again knowing that? How could he ever expect her to?

And yet she loved her dad. And the best thing about being with Lance was that he understood that. In the intimacy of the stove's flickering darkness he'd said that just because loving someone made you feel like you knew every fibre of their being, that didn't mean they couldn't keep secrets from you, even bad secrets. Nor did it mean that they didn't love you either. They might not love you as you deserved to be loved, but they loved you the best way they could.

It was the first time she'd ever spoken to a man about love. Boys her age didn't count, and anyway she socialized so little and lived too inconveniently far away from town to have considered anyone she'd kissed and flirted with to be a proper boyfriend. Lance hadn't really said much about his girlfriend, and, sensing how private he was, she hadn't liked to ask – not yet, anyway; maybe she would tonight – but the exhilaration of speaking and being listened to had made her catch her breath and she'd fallen asleep dreaming she was cuddled in his arms.

She wondered what her parents would do once they realized she was missing. She'd lied to them easily enough about staying a second night with Sally, but they would have expected her home today. She couldn't have lied to them a second time even if Lance had let her phone them, but he had impressed upon her never to turn on her mobile, because if she did, even just to check the time, the police would be able to track her signal. Would her parents go to the police? Lance said that if they did, DI Fisher was unlikely to tell them that Robyn had been talking to the police – though her dad must know it was her. That was also partly why Lance insisted he had to go to work today: to keep abreast of what was happening and so DI Fisher wouldn't guess he'd helped her or knew where she was.

She wished for the hundredth time she could text him, but he'd said they had to drive all the way into Colchester if they wanted to use their phones. He'd even kept to the back roads so his car wouldn't be picked up on any traffic cameras. If he said they wouldn't find her here, then she knew she was safe. And, despite the building's eeriness, she was comfortable enough. With only one small window cut into the walls, the white-washed former garrison area in which she sat was perpetually dark, but the farmer had got as far as connecting water and electricity and providing a few rudimentary furnishings, along with the stove and a plentiful supply of logs. But there was nothing to do. After a day in solitary confinement, the sheer physical bulk of her fortress felt penal rather than protective.

She supposed her father would end up in prison, but she couldn't bear to think about that. Even trying to imagine how that might be for him or for her mother left behind at home, let alone her new life at uni, made her furiously angry, not with him but with Lance's boss. Lance said DI Fisher was just doing her job, but everything had been fine until she began sending people to root out her family's secrets, to meddle in her family's life, *her* life. It wasn't fair. She'd done nothing. She was studying hard for her exams, preparing in her imagination to fly the nest and go to university. The course she hoped to do included lots of fieldwork abroad, and she had dreams of becoming fluent in a foreign language. Now she'd either have to lie to her fellow students or face up to being known as someone who only got to see her dad on prison visits. She doubted that her mum would be able to carry on alone; the house would probably be sold, and then she'd have nowhere to go in the holidays. Everything would be ruined and destroyed, and it was all the fault of that interfering bitch from the police!

Robyn suddenly felt nauseous as it occurred to her for the very first time that Nicola might also go to prison, her guilt compounded by an acknowledgement that she had never loved her mother with the same intensity that she loved her dad. If that happened, what would she do, where would she go? How could any of her plans ever hope to work out? For the rest of her life she'd be the pariah who had sent her parents to jail. She covered her mouth with her hand, trying not to cry out – not that anyone would hear her inside this stronghold. What had she done? *What had she done?*

53

When Grace got to the office the following morning she was taken aback to see Lance at his desk, having half expected him to call in sick or to have found some urgent reason to be away from the office. During another sleepless night she had mentally tossed and turned, torn between dread that she had placed Robyn – and possibly Davey Fewell too – in terrible danger and a desperate need to know for sure that Lance hadn't put his whole future on the line in the vain hope of extorting from Robyn's father some closure on Peter's death. Lance looked tired but greeted her with his usual smile and followed her to her cubicle.

'I've been trying to get hold of you,' she said, watching his reactions carefully.

'Yeah, I'm sorry. I was with a friend last night and switched my phone off, then forgot to turn it back on. I only just heard about Robyn going missing. Anything new?'

'Nothing,' she said. 'Leonard is terrified that she's been abducted by one of his criminal associates. And he could be right. Warren Cox, the guy in prison who told me about the Lion King, was knifed yesterday.'

'OK.' His gaze was steady, but Grace felt as if an invisible shield had dropped in front of his eyes, shutting her out.

'When did you last speak to Robyn?' she asked.

'Not since I saw her after school on Monday. I've texted her a few times but got nothing back.'

'What's your view?'

'Her parents must realize how much pressure she's been under,' he said. 'I mean I assume you've now told them that she shopped them?'

'Not directly,' she said. 'Besides, Leonard seriously doesn't want to hear it. He's convinced her disappearance is connected to the attack on Warren Cox.'

'So is he worried enough to admit to being the Lion King?' asked Lance.

'Both her parents are out of their minds,' she said. 'But whatever they told us last night is off the record. They weren't under caution.'

She saw his disappointment. 'You have to trust me, Lance,' she said. 'Work with me. Don't throw everything away.'

A shadow of doubt crossed his face, but he said nothing.

'Look,' she said. 'I didn't tell you before because I didn't want to make out like I was a victim in all this, but I was attacked three weekends ago when I was out running. Then, last week, a threatening note was left on my car windscreen. At first I thought it might have been a warning from Warren Cox, making sure I kept his name out of it. Then I thought it was Curtis Mullins, because I'd pissed him off. Now I'm not so sure. I'm worried too that Robyn might be in real danger. There's a sniper on the loose out there, remember. You have to help me.'

She could see that she'd reached something in him – and it wasn't concern for Robyn's safety. He completed some silent calculations and then said stubbornly, 'Her safety is her father's responsibility. It's up to him to get her back.'

'Fair enough,' she said. 'But you do understand what I'm saying, Lance? I'm trying to watch your back here.'

He held her gaze a few seconds too long and then looked away. She reached out to touch his arm, but he jerked away. She longed to shake some reason into him, but knew she'd lost him. 'Lance,' she pleaded. 'I promise we will get Leonard to talk. If he knows anything about what happened to Peter, then I will make sure he tells us.'

He shook his head. 'Peter Burnley probably wasn't even his real name! I'll never know, will I? You have no idea what it's like to live with that!'

She watched helplessly as he walked away, snatched his jacket from the back of his chair and left the office. She had failed. But, if she hadn't been sure before, she was now: he knew where Robyn was.

During the night she had nearly convinced herself that Lance, a detective sergeant, would never be so stupid as to help the girl disappear. Now she'd seen that he was too broken to believe he had anything to left to lose. It wasn't just the death of his lover, it was also the obliteration of his faith in everything that the work he did stood for. Most officers – the good ones, anyway – joined because they had an internal value system that, even if words like truth and justice sounded too overblown, encompassed a simple desire to help people in distress. Ben Marrington had voiced it last night. And when that value system was abused – as it had been when PC Mark Kirkby placed a rifle in the hands of a ten-year-old boy and PC Curtis Mullins smashed a light on Russell Fewell's van – nothing was safe. Whatever desperate measures Lance had taken, however chaotic and inarticulate his need to restore justice, she was on his side.

Meanwhile Ben Marrington would liaise with Robyn's parents and keep Grace informed while she continued to investigate Leonard Ingold's illegal activities. It was a tricky balancing act, but she still had the Church murder inquiry to pursue, and she was all too aware that the rest of the team was waiting for today's action plan. There was a message on her desk to call DI Gupta in Ely, and dozens of emails to be read. Yet she turned her back on everyone in the office and, staring out over the jumbled roofs of the town as she tried to control her panicky breathing, called Curtis Mullins.

'I want to speak to you,' she said curtly. 'I'd prefer to do so unofficially, but if you refuse, then fine, let's make it official.'

Ten minutes later she met him at the exit to the car park and led the way silently to the cafe where she'd confronted him before. It was empty after the early-morning rush and she took a table at the back where they wouldn't be overheard by the staff behind the counter. She had made up her mind to speak openly and she no longer cared about the consequences.

'OK,' she said, once they had got through the necessary business of ordering coffee. 'I don't know how much or little you know about your friends. Maybe you're in it up to your neck. But if you're not, this is your chance to put things straight. Your only chance.'

'You're out of your mind,' he said. 'One rancid fucking crazy bitch.'

'That's sweet of you,' she said. 'On the other hand, you're here, aren't you? So I can't be that crazy.'

He scowled. 'Then let's get it over with. What do you want?'

'Have you ever visited a golf resort in Portugal called Vale do Lobo?'

'No.'

Curtis looked sufficiently perplexed by the question that she believed him. It gave her some sense of the extent of his involvement. 'So how deep is Adam Kirkby's connection with Leonard Ingold?'

'Now you're really away with the fairies.'

'So why was Adam staying in his villa in Vale do Lobo?'

Once again it was Curtis's look of surprise that told her the truth. She pressed home her advantage. 'Mark Kirkby was in illegal possession of a rifle and ammunition supplied by Ingold. That same weapon and ammunition was used by Russell Fewell to kill Mark and five other people in Dunholt.'

'No!'

'What was Mark doing with a rifle? Why did he want it? Why didn't he apply for a licence and obtain one legally?'

Curtis bit his lip but then caught her observing him and sipped at his coffee. 'Don't know what you're on about.'

'Then help me,' she said.

'I'm not helping you to trash Mark's memory. No way.'

'Still having nightmares?'

He gave her a look of pure hatred, but she refused to let up. 'Mark would still be alive if you hadn't helped him to harass and torment Russell Fewell.'

'And you think I don't feel like shit about that? Let alone all the other victims? Of course I do.'

Curtis drew his lips into a tight line and stared over the top of her head. She could almost feel the waves of tension washing through him, but she sat tight and waited for him to say more.

'Mark loved Donna,' he said at last. 'Don't ask me why. She seemed pretty vanilla to me. Maybe it was the kids. One day he was eating takeaways for one, the next he had a family around him. He wanted to do his best for them. That was all.'

'And you were his friend.'

'Yes,' he said, an edge returning to his voice. 'I was.'

'Well, here's some stuff he didn't tell you,' she said. 'I just told you that his ammunition came from Leonard Ingold. Ingold also made the bullets used by the sniper who killed Gordon Church as well as two other victims. I'll ask you again: why was Adam Kirkby staying in Ingold's villa in Portugal?'

Curtis said nothing, but she saw him blink repeatedly as he attempted to process the information.

'Does Adam also have an interest in guns?'

Curtis gave an almost imperceptible nod.

'Does he have a rifle?'

'I don't know. And I never actually saw Mark with one either.'

'But . . .'

He hung his blond head. 'But they talked about it.'

'About what? For Christ's sake, Curtis, whatever's going on, it's got to stop.' Watching him struggle, she made herself recall the pain and humiliation of being kicked into the mud of the riverside path. 'Did you leave a note on my car? Send someone to assault me?'

A fine blush spread up his pale cheeks and he avoided her eyes. She felt nauseous as the shock of the violence returned to her, and she only just managed not to reach down to massage her bruised and injured shin.

'I kept the note, by the way,' she told him, managing to keep her voice steady. 'And I'm guessing it'll have your fingerprints on it, so you'd better tell me what Mark and Adam were up to.'

'They went on a trip to Arizona,' said Curtis, 'about a year ago. Their dad organized it through some links the Federation have there, like an exchange visit. They stayed with some weird militia outfit and came back full of bullshit about liberty and patriotism and inalienable rights and self-reliance. Or Adam did, anyway. I thought it was just about dressing up in camouflage gear and doing military-style fitness training. It was all so much hot air. And then Mark met Donna and had other stuff on his mind. I forgot about it.'

'What about Adam? Did he just forget about it?'

'No, probably not. He's a wannabe, Adam. Got turned down by the police so went into the prison service as second best. Always got something to prove.'

'Did Adam ever ask you about Gordon Church?' asked Grace as various pieces of the puzzle began to lock ominously into place.

'Don't think so. Don't remember. I don't see Adam much. I only ever really hung out with him because of Mark.'

'Are you sure? You wouldn't have mentioned to the guys over a beer that a notorious cop-killer had come into the nick one day?'

'I don't know.' He shifted uncomfortably in his chair. 'Maybe.'

'Has Adam ever driven a metallic-grey Renault van?'

'No idea.'

'Anything else you want to tell me?'

'Yes.' His eyes flamed an icy blue. 'Piss off and leave me alone.'

Grace gave an exhausted laugh. 'Fine. But you are not to

discuss any of this with anyone. Especially not Adam. If you do, I'll make sure the book is thrown at you. All of it. Wilful misconduct, the lot.'

'Don't worry,' he said bitterly. 'I'm getting out anyway. I've had enough.'

'Good! One last question. Are you absolutely sure there's nothing you can tell me about what happened to Peter Burnley?'

'You're the super-sleuth,' he sneered. 'That was your case, and you didn't find anything, did you, ma'am?'

'No,' she conceded. 'But Adam was definitely with you the night you saw Peter and Lance in the Blue Bar?'

'Yes. Now can I go?'

Grace nodded, glad to be rid of him. He tossed a handful of coins onto the table and made his way out, letting the door bang shut behind him. She sat on for a while in the empty café, nursing her untouched coffee. What had stopped her being immediately honest with Robyn's distraught parents or taking her suspicion that Lance was complicit in Robyn's disappearance straight to Colin? Loyalty to a friend in trouble. Yet could she honestly tell herself that the way she'd acted out of her concern for Lance was so very different to what Curtis had done for his old school friend Mark Kirkby?

54

The drive out to Leonard's workshop gave Grace a much-needed breathing space. On previous journeys she'd paid little attention to her surroundings, but now, driving over the bridge and slowing down to glance out at the long tree-fringed reservoir, she was taken almost by surprise by the empty expanse of air between water and sky, and realized how much she'd felt over the last few days as if the walls were closing in on her. She pulled over and sat for a moment, letting her mind do nothing more than take in the clouds and choppy water. Only now did it fully hit her how the enormous risk she was taking could, if things went wrong, alter the course of her life. Not only would she lose her job, but both her own and Ivo's investigations into Leonard Ingold would have been for nothing. No judge could possibly direct a jury to convict a man on evidence given under duress by the kidnap of his daughter by a police officer.

She looked out of the window and breathed in the exhilarating sense of space: she wasn't going to let any of that happen. No point ruminating over the rights and wrongs of her recent decisions, she'd come too far down the road and was determined to see it all through. She put the car in gear and drove on, relieved now that she hadn't – as the voice of correct procedure had told her she should – asked Ben Marrington to accompany her on this mission.

Leonard and Nicola must have heard her car for they rushed out of the house as she pulled to a stop. Both wore jeans and pullovers, Nicola with no make-up and Leonard unshaven. Nicola opened the car door before Grace even had time to turn off the engine.

'Have you found her?' Nicola asked, wild-eyed.

'I'm sorry, no. May I come in?'

Leonard hung back and allowed his wife to lead Grace inside. Grace had not expected the homeliness of the living room, where Nicola made a stab at removing dirty mugs from the coffee table and straightening cushions on the couch before inviting her to sit down. They'd entered through an untidy kitchen, where she'd taken note of the expensive double Aga and a big modern fridge, but the living room had certainly seen better days. Not that she had imagined bling, but there was no huge flat-screen television or designer curtains, and the well worn carpet and comfortable three-piece suite had both been made to last a bit longer with rugs and throws.

Leonard remained standing. Catching the beseeching look Nicola threw up at her husband as she sat down, Grace realized she'd have to harden her heart if she was to carry out her plan: the last thing she wanted was for Leonard to cave in and admit that he knew why Robyn had run away; she needed him to hold on to enough doubt to fear that his cherished daughter could have been snatched by people who meant to do her harm.

'I think the time has come for some straight talking,' she said. 'I've come here alone. No one knows I'm here. And if you'll hear me out, you'll understand why it has to be this way. But first you have to level with me. How well do you know Jerry Coghlan?'

Nicola's hand flew to her mouth, but this time she did not look at Leonard, whose expression reverted to its customary blankness. Grace allowed the silence to grow before she went on. 'I know about your villa in the Algarve. I know about the shell company in Panama that's supposed to stop me knowing about it. I know that a steady stream of police officers stay in that villa, often for free, all organized, at least to begin with, by John Kirkby.' She paused again to give Leonard time to think. 'Now do you see why I've come here on my own?'

'Go on,' said Leonard.

'Was it Coghlan or Kirkby who sold you on the idea as an insurance policy?' she asked. 'To ensure that no cop could ever speak out against you because they'd been compromised? Well, dream on. You're the fall guy. That insurance policy only covers Coghlan. If anyone comes knocking on his door, asking awkward questions about how you paid for your villa, then all he has to do is claim ignorance and point to the long queue of coppers taking kickbacks from you in the form of free holidays. He'd give you up, Leonard. Quick as you can say "No comment". So would Kirkby.'

Leonard sat down beside his wife and squeezed her hand. Grace wondered whether it was for reassurance or as a warning to keep quiet. He took a deep breath and let it out slowly. 'Go on,' he said again.

'Don't tell me you were really naive enough to think that a bent ex-cop would play by the rules.' She took his silence for assent and carried on. 'Not clever.'

Nicola let go of her husband's hand. 'I don't understand. Robyn will be safe, won't she?'

'Hear me out, Mrs Ingold,' said Grace. She looked back at

Leonard. 'You understand, don't you? You don't want half the police force of Essex as your personal enemies, do you?'

'No.'

'So tell me how it all worked,' she said, starting to believe that her stunt might pay off. 'It started with John Kirkby, right? When he was still a high-up in the Police Federation.'

Leonard nodded. 'He's an old pal of Jerry's. He put us in touch.'

He watched her steadily, his expression unreadable, but Grace felt a heady rush of relief: this was the first informative statement that Leonard had made.

'And Kirkby's sons got preferential rates if they wanted to stay at your place?' she asked.

'I wouldn't know,' said Leonard. 'I never needed to know. I left it all to Jerry. Arm's length. That was the deal.'

'And did you ever call in any favours in return?'

'Once or twice. Nothing much.'

'And did you do anything else for them? Like supply Mark or Adam Kirkby with weapons?'

Leonard shrugged and looked away. Beside him Nicola remained unnaturally still.

'You do know that Gordon Church was killed with two of your rounds?'

Grace watched him carefully and saw his pupils widen in alarm, a visceral reaction that not even he could control. 'John Kirkby's a pretty straight guy,' he said, a gruffness in his voice revealing an uncharacteristic note of uncertainty. 'I met his sons through a gun club. They're not hotheads, they're both in positions of responsibility.'

'Responsibilities they seem to take very seriously,' Grace said. 'What I'm hearing is that Adam, and very probably Mark too, likes to dress up as a vigilante and maybe even to run around cleansing the streets of criminal trash that the law is too weak to deal with. How does that chime with you?'

'It doesn't,' he said emphatically. 'They didn't want to go through the hassle of all the paperwork just to go hunting on private land. And they didn't need firearms licences to join a shooting club. So I cut them some slack.'

'Was John Kirkby aware that his sons were buying weapons from you?'

'I wouldn't know.'

'Are you saying these men have taken Robyn?' cried Nicola. 'What kind of danger is she in?'

'If you want to keep her safe, you need to tell me the truth,' said Grace. 'You have to trust me. It's not only the Police Federation who have a stake in this.' Grace reached into the pocket of her suit jacket and took out a folded piece of paper. Leonard's reaction to the photograph of Peter Burnley would be her final test. She smoothed it out and handed it to him, watching his face carefully. 'What can you tell me about this?'

Ingold took the paper and studied it without apparent interest. 'It's Adam Kirkby with Jerry Coghlan on the golf course at Vale do Lobo,' he said, handing it back. 'I don't recognize the other two.' His eyes were steady, his face impassive; the paper did not tremble in his hands. 'So what?' he asked. 'What's the significance?'

Grace found it impossible to judge whether his lack of reaction was natural or whether he'd reverted to his mask because she was now approaching secrets that were dangerous to him. She looked at the photograph of Peter and was assailed by a vivid flashback of his mashed-up face in the morgue. 'This man,' she said, pointing him out and trying to keep her voice steady, 'was in Vale do Lobo working undercover for one of the security and intelligence services.'

'Undercover?' Leonard's amazement was clearly genuine. 'Why? Who is he? Is he after me?'

'He's dead,' she said. 'He was murdered in Colchester a month ago.'

'Shot?'

'No, beaten to death.'

'Who by?' asked Nicola. She clung to her husband's arm. 'Leonard, tell me what's going on!'

Grace steeled herself. She was here for Lance, not for them. 'I believe that we'll get Robyn back safely if we find out who killed this man,' she said. 'Are you prepared to help me? It has to be official, under caution, or it's no good.'

Leonard disappeared inside himself again, not even glancing at his wife, who waited helplessly for him to make his decision.

'I need to speak to my solicitor,' he said at last.

'Of course.'

'We'll need protection. Assurances.'

'It can all be arranged.'

He stood up and held out his hand across the coffee table. Grace took it. If she was lucky, she might just be in time to save Lance from ending his career and earning himself a prison sentence.

55

Ivo had spent a futile couple of days trailing around after Donna Fewell and her kids, and today looked likely to be no more successful. First thing Monday morning he'd phoned his editor to ask if he could take an impromptu week's holiday – after all, he had plenty owing. When he was little, before his mother became ill, his parents had taken quite adventurous holidays, exploring out-of-the-way areas of France or Spain. He only remembered sunshine and exotic-smelling food and his parents' laughter. Afterwards, summers had meant never having enough to do during overlong visits to his well-meaning and permanently sorrowing maternal grandparents in the Scottish Borders. So Weymouth – even in early February – wasn't really that big a stretch of the imagination for him as a vacation choice. Still, even with the proviso that if a big story broke he'd be back at his desk pronto, he was rather chagrined at the nonchalance with which his request had been granted.

He should set off soon to get into position before the kids came out of school. It wasn't far from the school to their seafront apartment, and Donna walked them there and back every day. Ivo had found a small supermarket where, if he timed it correctly, he could linger without attracting too much attention, just in case the little family varied their routine and offered him the chance to make an approach. He looked out of his hotel window to check the weather: the day looked bright and blustery, with an unseasonably soft wind scudding fluffy white clouds across a watercolour-blue sky, but he wasn't going to be fooled by that and pulled on an extra sweater and made sure he had his leather gloves and cashmere scarf. The scarf, a gift from his second wife, was probably older than Davey, but Ivo still enjoyed the soft feel of it around his neck. His mobile rang, an unknown number.

'Ivo Sweatman.'

'I'm calling from a payphone on the outskirts of Colchester.'

Ivo recognized her voice immediately, but given the funny goings-on with his tax return and credit card knew better than to say her name. 'Good to hear you.'

'Where are you?' she asked. 'I was hoping we could catch up.'

'Weymouth,' he said. 'I'm taking a week's holiday.'

There was a slight pause. 'That's such a good place for you to be right now.'

'Really? There's nothing much going on here, so far as I can tell. How about you?'

'Oh, pretty busy. About to get busier.'

Ivo racked his brains to work out how to elicit the information he needed. The only thing that leaped into his mind was unbelievably cheesy, but so what? 'Hey,' he said. 'You know that film you mentioned, about the kid who might've seen something? I can't remember how the story went. Was he in some kind of danger or what?'

'Yes, that's right,' she said, her voice calm and deliberate. 'It's quite a dramatic ending. You should go see it as soon as you can.'

'Thanks, I will. Who's in it again?'

'Oh, I'm sure you know the basic plot. They're all familiar faces.'

'OK, well, it starts any moment, so I ought to get moving.'

'Brilliant. Thanks so much.'

'No problem. Take care.'

'I will. And you. Bye.'

So DI Fisher had cracked the case! Good for her, but not so bright for young Davey. Ivo would clearly have to ride to his rescue, the Ice Maiden's favours fluttering from his helmet, regardless of how clumsily it would now have to be done. No matter. He'd hustled enough tabloid stings in his time to be pretty certain of carrying the day. But the last school bell would have rung, and he'd better get a move on.

He made it to the supermarket just in time to see Donna greet both kids and, as they handed her their various bags and lunch boxes, shepherd them safely over the road. It looked as if they were heading straight home, as they usually did. Maybe Donna still felt too vulnerable to encourage play dates or make friends with the other mothers. That was good. He could exploit that vulnerability. He followed at a safe distance, only catching up as she unlocked the street door to the apartment building. She glanced at him, and he smiled and muttered a name and flat number gleaned from a late-night rummage through a rubbish bag that had been put out for the early-morning refuse collection. Donna hesitated for a second before giving a polite nod and holding open the door for him to follow her into the lobby. That was good too. From the very first moment a mark fails to say no, the con artist has the upper hand.

With the street door safely closed behind them and the button pushed for the lift, Ivo turned to Davey, who had not yet taken sufficient notice of him to remember their encounter three weeks earlier.

'Hello, there. It's Davey, isn't it?'

The boy took a moment to place him. Then the doors opened, Ivo walked the three of them in front of him into the lift and hit the button for the top floor. He gave Davey a reassuring smile and treated Donna to his best candid look.

'Davey and I had a chat one morning when he was in a bit of a quandary about something,' he said. 'It all ended happily, didn't it, Davey?' He waited for the boy to give an apprehensive nod before turning back to his mother. 'But, if you don't mind me saying, I think it's time you had a bit of background on John Kirkby.'

Ivo stepped out first when the lift doors opened and took up a position that left the family an open path to their front door. He had consulted floor plans of the building on the developer's website and knew that the only other door off the small hall led out to a communal roof terrace. Now he'd got this far, they would not be disturbed.

'I'm happy to talk right here, Mrs Fewell,' he said, judging correctly that using her real surname would prove he meant business. 'But I'd appreciate it if you'd invite me in.' He held out his business card. 'This is who I am,' he said, keeping his hand out until she took the card. 'But I promise you that I'm not here for a story. I'm here to help you.'

Donna looked at the card. 'The *Courier*!' she exclaimed. 'I don't want anything to do with the newspapers.'

'That's fine,' said Ivo. 'I've taken a week's leave and I'm here in a personal capacity. And Davey will tell you, I'm no blabbermouth.'

Davey, who had taken tight hold of his mother's hand, now looked up at her. 'He bought me a bacon roll,' he said in a very small voice. 'Took me back to school.'

'*Back* to school?' asked Donna. 'Why, where were you?'

'Life's been a bit difficult for Davey,' said Ivo. 'He went on a bit of a walkabout. No harm done. But he's probably ready now to explain what's been bothering him. Don't you think so, Davey?'

Davey looked at his feet. Ella tugged at her mother's other hand. 'I'm tired,' she grizzled.

'What do you want?' Donna asked Ivo.

'Why don't you take the kids inside?' he suggested. 'Give them their tea. Let them watch some TV or something.' He held up his hands. 'I'll wait out here if you like.'

'Mum!' whined Ella, tugging at her again.

Donna unlocked the door to the apartment and shooed the kids in. Davey went reluctantly, turning his head to gaze at Ivo, who couldn't decipher whether the look was fearful or imploring. Ivo didn't move a muscle as Donna went to shut the door. At the last moment she relented and, closing the door enough so the kids inside couldn't hear, asked quietly again what it was he wanted.

Ivo was filled with admiration for her courage and good sense. It gave him confidence that, with a little encouragement, not only would Davey tell his mum the truth, but that she would hear it.

'Your son needs to tell you something about Mark Kirkby,' he said, staying exactly where he was. 'He's kept it from you because he didn't want to upset you.'

'But he's told you?' Her tone was openly sceptical.

'He also told DI Fisher, who believed him, but then he

pretended he'd made it up, so she couldn't do anything to help him. Now it could put him in danger.'

'What kind of danger?'

'It's for Davey to tell you. I'm just here to offer my help.'

She thought about it long enough to come to a decision. 'You'd better come in.'

Ivo didn't wait to be asked twice.

56

Robyn wished she had Martha and Bounder for company. She hadn't anticipated the effect of a second day of such grinding loneliness and boredom. If this was what prison was like, then the worst punishment of all, the one that was the hardest to imagine until it had happened to you, was having too much time in which to miss the people you cared about and to think about what you'd done to them. As the time dragged past, her own thoughts became her most vicious enemy – poisonous, dark, relentless – an enemy she'd never expected to face. Now she understood repentance! Except it did no good. She could repent her stupidity and wilfulness, her short-sightedness and rank ingratitude all she liked, but it wasn't going to change a thing.

She had betrayed her family, destroyed the only world she knew, ripped to shreds the fabric of all she loved most. If she'd been at home, she'd have been tempted to unlock one of the gun cabinets and blow her brains out, if only to stop the agony.

Was that how the man who'd killed Angie and her grand-mother had felt? What would he have done instead, had a gun not been placed in his hands?

But it had been, and that was the reason she was here, why she couldn't simply go home and have her dad laugh at her and give her a hug and tell her not to be so silly. That dad didn't exist any more.

If only Lance would come! She was beside herself to hear what was happening. Her parents must have realized by now that she'd gone and be wondering where she was. It wouldn't take them long to work out why she'd disappeared. Maybe they'd even be relieved to be rid of her because now she was just an inconvenience, like the sacks her dad had thrown in the creek. She ought to feel bad for scaring them, but maybe they needed to be scared in order to understand properly what all this had been like for her.

Or had she got all this wrong? Maybe her dad could, after all, explain everything. Lance seemed to think Leonard owned the villa in Portugal where they'd had several holidays. She'd told him they'd only gone there so often because they got mate's rates from a friend, but had then remembered that was what her dad had told her, and she could no longer believe a word he said. And then she'd thought about what Grace Fisher had said, about it all coming down to money in the end, so maybe Lance was right. Last night he'd asked about her parents' friends too, and got a bit cross when she'd clammed up and said she couldn't remember when really she just couldn't bear to betray her father any more. Lance had said it didn't matter, but she could see he was annoyed, and the tiny loss in his support had felt huge and scary.

Loyalty was a strange thing. It was much more black and white than love. You could love and hate someone at the same time, go crazy and scream and yell and still be certain that you loved them. But once you'd stopped being loyal, there was no way back. And then it became the most important thing in the world to find something else to believe in and attach yourself to. Lance had never judged her for her decision to help the police. He seemed to understand that she couldn't go on living a lie, and had patiently answered all her questions while being honest about what he wasn't allowed to tell her. More than anything, she wanted to be on his side. She couldn't cope with having to make judgements for herself any more. Let him decide for her. Except she sensed that maybe his world too wasn't as simple as cops and robbers, good or bad. If she didn't understand why he'd been annoyed with her, how could she be certain where his true loyalties lay?

Like a kind of sign, a thin beam of light swept across the whitewashed brickwork of the window's tunnel-like opening. No one else could possibly know she was here, so it must be the headlights of his car. The light was quickly extinguished and she assumed he was approaching the wooden steps up to the narrow entrance to the fort. He'd ordered her not to unlock the door unless he knocked three times, and she waited impatiently for his signal. When it came, she opened up and, without thinking, flung herself at him, wrapping her arms around him.

'Hey, hey.' He disentangled himself gently. 'You OK?'

'I've had such a rotten day!'

'Well, things are moving on. You won't have to stay here much longer.'

Robyn drew back. 'Why? What's happened?'

'Your parents have reported you missing.'

'So they know what I did?'

'No, apparently they're terrified you've been kidnapped.'

For an instant she thought he looked pleased, but the light was bad, and the next moment she saw how tired he looked.

'But they must know! What about the dredger?'

He shook his head. 'Don't worry. It'll be all right. They're going to cooperate. DI Fisher told me. It's all going to be fine.'

'What does that mean?'

'Your father is going to tell us what he knows.'

'And then what happens?' Her voice rose in alarm and she brought up her hands to hide her face. 'What does he know? How bad is it?'

'I don't know yet. But this is what you wanted, isn't it? For him to give it all up?'

'But he'll go to prison. I don't want him locked up in a place like this!'

Lance laughed softly and took hold of her hands, pulling them away from her face. 'Prisons these days are nothing like this. And, depending on what exactly he tells us, he might not get much of a sentence.'

'He's doing it for me, isn't he?' Robyn asked. 'To get me back in one piece?'

'I suppose so, yes,' said Lance. He took on a guarded look, as if he were about to be angry with her. 'But it's only for one more night. Tomorrow I can almost certainly take you back.'

'I want to go now! I need to talk to him. I don't want him to go to prison because of me. This is all my fault!'

She turned towards the door, but he caught hold of her and pulled her around to face him. 'It's a bit late in the day to decide that,' he said.

'I don't care! I want to see him now, to let them know I'm all right. I want to go home.'

Lance's hold on her tightened. 'You can't. Not yet. Tomorrow.'

She tried to twist free, but he wrapped his arms around her

and pulled her close to him in an enclosing hug. 'Please, Robyn. Just one more night.'

'No, I want to go home!'

'It's not long to wait. I brought some soup and we can sit by the stove like we did last night. Stay with me, please.'

He spoke into her hair, and she could feel his breath in her ear and smell a pleasing citrussy fragrance from his shampoo or aftershave. She didn't know what to do. She was exhausted. She wanted to let him decide. His arms around her felt warm and safe, so she melted into them, raising her face to his. Lance smiled, his brown eyes kind and encouraging. He lifted a hand to stroke her hair, and she leaned her head into his caress.

'I'll go into work tomorrow morning,' he said, 'and as soon as I know what's happening, I'll come and get you, just like we planned. Of course you can never say that we were together – you must remember that – or I'll lose my job and it might mean we couldn't use anything your father tells us in court.'

She nodded, feeling his hand against her hair. 'I'll still get to see you, though, won't I?'

'Of course.' He smiled again. 'I'm your family liaison officer. We'll have lots of chances to meet.'

She sighed and looked up at him shyly. She wanted him to kiss her. If he kissed her then everything would somehow, magically, be all right after all. She closed her eyes, raised her chin and parted her lips in readiness. After what seemed like the longest few seconds of her life, he let go of her and stepped back. 'Come and sit down,' he said, taking her hand to lead her over to the folding canvas chairs placed near the stove. She followed in a kind of daze and sat down beside him. He kept hold of her hand, dipping his head to look at her until she met his eyes.

'You do know I'm gay, right?'

Robyn's mind went blank. She froze.

'You did realize?' He squeezed her hand. 'I never meant to mislead you.'

Of course she'd known! Subliminally it was pretty much the first thing she'd sensed about him – that he was not a threat as a man, he was a friend, she'd be safe if she went off alone with him and no one knew where they were. She wasn't stupid, of course she'd known.

'I'm sorry,' she mumbled. She rose to her feet, letting him keep hold of her hand. 'I'm really sorry, but I want to go home now. I can't stay here. I won't say anything to anyone about being with you.' She could hear herself starting to cry. She couldn't bear it if she did. It would be the final shame.

'No.' His grip on her hand tightened.

'Please.' She couldn't speak. What an idiot she was. Wrong about everything. She tried to tug herself free but he wouldn't let her go.

'You can't go yet,' he said. 'Not until your father signs his statement telling us everything he knows.'

'Why?' she cried out, her mouth puckering with tears. 'Why's that so important to you?'

Lance gave her a strange appraising look before coming to a decision. 'Because my lover was murdered,' he said simply. 'Your father may be the only person who can tell me what really happened, and why.'

'Then I'll ask him! I'll make sure he tells you!'

'No, that's not enough.' He gave her that same shrewd look again. 'It may be your father who killed him.'

'No!' She wrenched herself free of his grip and ran to the

door. She dragged it open and, almost on hands and knees, felt her way down the steep ladder-like steps, gasping as the freezing wind tore at her clothes and whipped her hair across her face. She felt rather than saw Lance silhouetted in the open doorway above, but the wind blew away his words.

Blindly, she started to run, stumbling on the tussocks growing among the gravel that surrounded the tower. Lance's car, parked on the rough track and only just visible in the darkness, offered some shelter, and she ran towards it. Only then did she see in the distance ahead the thin wavering beam of a torch. She looked back.

Lance was still outlined against the light from inside, presumably judging it too dark to attempt to follow her. She crouched behind his car. It was impossible to judge in what direction the person holding the torch was moving, although they were heading *somewhere*, and she knew that, apart from the tower, there was nothing but water or farmland and grazing sheep for miles around. The waning moon was covered by cloud, and she doubted she would be visible to the person walking towards her. The entrance to the tower did not directly face the track, and whoever was approaching would only be able to see a faint glimmer, but light from the single window shone out like a beacon: they would know someone was here. Robyn wavered for a moment, trying desperately to clear the haze of distress from her mind so she could decide what to do.

She turned and ran back to the tower.

Lance was shouting to her, his words still lost to the wind. She scrambled up the steps and pushed him back inside.

'Someone's coming. Shut the door. Hide downstairs,' she panted. 'You were never here. I'm going out to meet them.'

Lance tried to grab her, but she evaded him and crawled her way back down to the ground. Keeping her gaze fixed on the approaching pinprick of torchlight, she walked steadily forward along the uneven track to meet her unwanted visitor.

57

Grace saw a black silhouette against the darkness and shone the beam of her torch directly at it. She was near enough to recognize Robyn but too far away for her torchlight to dazzle the girl. It was no use shouting against the wind, and, as Robyn appeared to be walking to meet her, she pressed on. As they came together she linked her arm securely through Robyn's and pressed her mouth to her ear. 'Are you OK?'

Robyn nodded and, in turn, spoke into Grace's ear. 'I want to go home.'

'Fine. I'll take you.'

Robyn tugged at the detective's arm, pulling her back in the direction Grace had come from. 'Can we go now?'

'In a moment,' said Grace. 'Where's Lance?'

'He's not here. I don't know. I'm here on my own.'

Grace shone the torch over Robyn's shoulder, nudging the girl round to see where she'd aimed the beam at Lance's car. 'I followed him here,' she said, again leaning in close so she could be heard. 'Come on, let's go inside.'

She kept her arm through Robyn's, directing the torchlight onto the track ahead of them until they reached the steps, where she gave the girl a little push to go up ahead of her.

Once inside with the door closed it was possible to speak normally.

'How are you? Are you really OK?' Grace asked again, looking around at the whitewashed brick walls, thinking that Robyn had shown an unexpected flair for the dramatic. 'This is quite some hideout. A bit spooky being here alone, I imagine?'

'What do you care?'

Robyn sounded like a sulky teenager, but Grace was disconcerted by the vivid fear in her eyes. It was dismaying to acknowledge that she had inspired it, but she couldn't help a slight flare of anger at the girl that any of them was here at all. She swallowed it down, accepting that absolutely none of this was Robyn's fault and that, with her whole world disintegrating around her, she had every right to be afraid.

'Your parents are worried about you,' Grace said gently. 'They both love you very much. Whatever your father's done, the only thing he cares about now is you.'

'Even though I've sent him to prison?'

'You haven't. He doesn't think that either. And even if that happens, he'll have put himself there.' Grace looked around once more at the massive walls. There was no point calling to Lance; the sound of her voice barely travelled at all. 'Where's Lance? Can you ask him to come out?'

'I made him bring me here. This was all my idea.'

'Robyn, if I wanted to get Lance into trouble, do you think I would have come alone? There'd be half a dozen police cars out there by now.'

Robyn stood her ground, not altering her hostile expression.

'Listen to me,' said Grace sternly. 'I'm going to be in as much trouble as he is. More, probably. So please, just go and fetch him so we can talk.'

As Robyn hesitated, something in her face made Grace wonder about what might have happened between the two of them over the two nights they'd presumably spent together – for Grace couldn't believe that Lance would have allowed the seventeen-year-old to sleep in such a place alone. But then the girl walked over to a flight of stone steps and pointed into the bowels of the fortress. 'He's down there.'

Grace nodded and went to join her. 'You'd better stick with me,' she said. 'I don't want you running off again.'

Robyn tucked herself in behind Grace, making herself as small as possible. Lance must have heard their descending footsteps, for he appeared at the bottom of the narrow staircase before they reached it.

'You here to arrest me?' he asked bitterly.

Grace felt buffeted by the fury he projected. He seemed wound up tighter than she'd ever seen him, and some of his tension transferred itself to her. 'For Christ's sake, will you stop feeling so sorry for yourself and get a grip!' she demanded. 'If I'd wanted to arrest you, I'd have put a stop to this farce yesterday!' She waved a hand back up the stairs. 'Do you see anyone with me? Do you honestly think I'd do that to you?'

'Why should I trust you?'

'Because if you don't, then I bloody well will go and fetch reinforcements and arrest you. Your choice.' She glared at him. 'What do you want to do?'

Lance glared back, his hands clenched so hard that the knuckles were white, unable to let go of his defiance.

Grace's anger disappeared as swiftly as it had come. 'Please,

Lance. This is one huge unholy mess. We need to start sorting it out as best and as quickly as we can. Come upstairs and let's sit down and work things out.'

'I'm so sorry I dragged you into this, Lance.' Robyn's voice sounded very small, even with the dull echo from the solid stone that surrounded them. 'I'm sorry I didn't understand, that I was so stupid. I really am.'

Lance looked shamefaced. 'None of this was your fault.'

The exchange between them seemed to disperse some of his anger, and he followed Grace warily back up to the living area, where she busied herself adding a log to the stove to give him time to compose himself. But when she straightened up it was Robyn who seemed the more distraught. Lance was sitting in one of the folding chairs, elbows on his knees, head in his hands, but Robyn stood bobbing with anxiety, her arms wrapped around herself.

'Did my father kill someone?' she asked Grace. 'Not just make bullets and supply guns, but actually murder someone?'

Grace looked at Lance in angry astonishment. *What had he been saying?* His head drooped even further. 'You have to listen to me, Lance,' she said sharply. 'I showed Robyn's father the photograph, watched him like a hawk. I'm certain he had no idea who Peter was.'

'But there's no way you could ever be sure whether he was lying or not,' said Robyn flatly. 'Never in a million years.'

'I think he's prepared to tell the truth to get you back,' Grace told her. 'That really does seem to be the only thing he cares about right now.'

'Then she can't go back yet,' said Lance decisively, straightening up and looking from Grace to Robyn. 'Not until he's told us everything he knows.'

Robyn rocked from side to side as if in pain, and stumbled over to a corner of the room where Grace now saw two camp beds had been set up. She curled up on one of them, her back to them, and began to cry.

Grace turned to Lance. 'How could you do this to her?' she demanded quietly. 'You were the one who didn't want me to involve her. What the hell changed?'

'Leonard Ingold is a criminal,' he answered coldly. 'He's probably behind Peter's murder. We came into the job to take people like him off the streets, didn't we? Well that's what I'm doing.'

Grace turned to the sobbing girl. 'Like that? Is that how you want to do it?'

'You can talk! You stood in my home and lied to me about people sneaking in and going through my stuff. People who are supposed to be on our side. Is that how *you* do it?'

Grace held up her hands in surrender. 'OK, OK, let's not have this argument now. This is the shit we're in. Let's agree on that and move forward.'

'She's not going back until I find out who killed Peter.'

Grace pulled her chair closer so she could speak without Robyn overhearing too much. 'There's a reason I got you out of the way this afternoon,' she said. 'Colin's negotiating for Ingold and his family to go into Witness Protection. Leonard can give us important information on the Church murder and the other two sniper killings. I think it'll also link back to what Peter was doing in Vale do Lobo and maybe lead us to his killer.'

'You heard what she said.' He nodded towards Robyn. 'You can't believe a word he says.'

'Leonard Ingold did not kill Peter,' she said. 'I'd stake my life on that. Are you prepared to trust me or not?'

He stared at her sullenly.

'Think about it,' she said. 'Who was in the photo with Peter?'

She gave Lance time to process the information, and she could see him make the connections for himself. Eventually he nodded. 'OK,' he said. 'I think I get it.'

She heaved a sigh of relief. 'Good. So what's the best way to resolve the situation here?' She looked over at Robyn's prostrate form. 'We need to take her home.'

'Fine,' said Lance wearily. 'I don't care what happens to me, so why don't you go and I'll bring her in later? You don't ever need to have been here.'

'That won't work,' said Grace. 'Think about it. Leonard has invested a lot of time and effort in tarnishing the reputations of officers who have stayed in his villa. Including you. We don't know what loyalty Jerry Coghlan inspires among his former colleagues either. If Leonard finds out – before he spills the beans – that a police officer helped his daughter disappear, he's never going to trust any of us again.'

'You're going to lie for me?' he asked.

'I'll stay here with you tonight,' she said. 'And in the morning I'll go to work as usual and you're going to carry out whatever plan you had for Robyn's reappearance. I don't want to know what it is.'

Lance nodded towards Robyn. 'And if she tells the truth?'

'Then she tells the truth.' Grace felt her heart swoop and miss a beat, but she couldn't afford to think about the dire consequences of what she'd done by coming here. It'd had to be done. Lance was right: neither Colin nor Peter's shadowy employers had the right to lie to him. Peter should not have lied either, although that was a whole other story. But at some point the lying had to stop, and Grace wasn't about to compromise Robyn any more than they already had.

'It's her decision, Lance,' she said. 'Make your peace with her, but she has to know she's free to say whatever she wants.'

He nodded. 'She's really a very sweet kid, you know.' He sighed and, looking at Grace properly for the first time, gave her a lopsided smile. She smiled wanly back, wondering where true friendship ended and corruption began.

58

Grace arrived at work early the next morning, short of sleep but at least a little reassured that all might yet come right. Robyn had eventually allowed herself to be comforted and had eaten some soup and a sandwich. Once she had fallen asleep, Lance had persuaded Grace to go home, where she had lain awake wondering if, by the time she next went to bed, she would still have a job.

She had agreed with Lance that she would get to the office before him and make sure nothing had gone awry with Leonard's undertaking to cooperate. Her best guess was that Nicola would go along with whatever her husband decided, but one could never be certain. She was also keen to grab some time alone with Colin to bring him up to speed on the criss-crossing network of connections between Ingold, Coghlan and the various members of the Kirkby family. Her aim was to encourage her boss to make the leap himself from Peter's presence in Vale do Lobo to his murder in Colchester. She was confounded, therefore, to find Colin already in his office, locked in serious conversation with John Kirkby.

Neither man had seen her, so she moved quickly past the door into her own cubicle to give herself time to gather her thoughts.

Had Kirkby learned – through Curtis? – of Ingold's arrest? Was he here to pre-empt any accusations that would surely be coming his way once his arrangements with Jerry Coghlan were exposed? Or – far more likely in her opinion – was he here to glean as much information as he could to protect his surviving son?

That belief persuaded her of the urgent need to join the two men's discussion, and she went straight away to knock on the superintendent's door.

'Ah, Grace,' Colin greeted her. 'Just the person we need. John here has brought something rather worrying to my attention.'

'How can I help?' she asked.

Colin indicated to Kirkby to explain.

'It was my son Mark's intention to make Donna Fewell his wife,' he began. 'With that in mind, and given the dreadful situation she and her children found themselves in, I arranged for them to have use of a Federation property. They were being left alone by the media, the kids had settled in well at a local school, things seemed to be going well. Now they've disappeared – packed up and gone without a word – and I'm extremely concerned about them, to say the least.'

Grace tried to hide her astonishment – and her secret pleasure that Ivo must have succeeded in whisking the family to safety. 'Have you spoken to Ruth Woods?' she asked. 'She was their FLO and has been keeping tabs on them.'

'She last spoke to them on Monday,' said Colin. 'Everything was fine.'

Grace tried hard to read his expression, but he was giving nothing away. She turned to John Kirkby. 'Have you had access to their accommodation?' she asked. 'Was there any sign of violence or panic about their departure?'

'No, but I find it hard to believe they would have gone of their own free will without letting me know.'

Grace nodded and glanced at Colin. He returned her gaze steadily. 'I thought perhaps you could spare John a little of your time,' he said. 'Just a quick debrief. Make sure there's nothing we should be following up. Nothing that dovetails with any of our other current investigations.'

This time his look of intent seemed clear to her. 'Of course, sir. I'll see if there's a soft interview room free.'

Ten minutes later she was settled in the pastel surroundings of one of the witness interview rooms downstairs. John Kirkby seemed a little anxious but not unduly so, and Grace wondered how much he really knew of his sons' activities.

'I understand the need for tight security around Donna's relocation,' she began. 'The FLO told me Donna had been receiving hate mail and other abuse before they left Dunholt, and it was important to keep the media away from her.'

'Scum.' Kirkby all but spat.

'So who else knew where they were? Anyone in your own family, for instance?'

'I'm divorced,' he said. 'My son Adam goes his own way.'

'What about Donna herself? Was she in touch with anyone here?'

'I doubt it. She said couldn't imagine being welcome in Dunholt ever again.'

'It was fortunate the Federation was able to help her.'

'The Federation's taken a right pasting in the media recently – all from people who don't bother to find out the good we do.'

'I pay my dues same as everyone else,' said Grace lightly. 'Yet I'm not sure I really know either. Take my colleague DS Cooper, for instance. After a bereavement his Fed rep arranged a welfare break for him in Portugal. It was really helpful. I was impressed.'

She watched him carefully. He went very still for a moment and then sat back in the pale wood and upholstered chair, which, it struck Grace, belonged to a very different era of policing to the one he'd started out in. He rubbed his chin reflectively. 'I didn't know that,' he said.

'In Vale do Lobo,' she told him. 'I knew that Federation branches owned holiday properties in the UK, but I hadn't realized they'd expanded abroad.'

He gave her an unfriendly look. 'I thought we were discussing my concerns about Donna Fewell.'

She smiled pleasantly. 'We are. There must have been various Federation officials who had to sign off on Donna's use of the apartment in Weymouth. Have you spoken to any of them yet about her disappearance?'

Kirkby shuffled around in the soft chair, straightening his back as if trying to gain a height advantage over her. 'You must be one of these fast-track graduate types.'

'I am, yes.'

'Thought so. Well, I came into the job straight from school, before you were even born, young lady. There was still respect for a bobby on the beat back then. *Dixon of Dock Green* and *Gideon of Scotland Yard*, that's what my generation grew up on. We were there to protect the community, draw the line between right and wrong. And the Federation was there to look after *us*. Want to know the thing I'm most proud of, in all my years of service?'

'Tell me,' said Grace.

'That I did right by my members. All those hard-working coppers out there at the sharp end, putting their lives on the line.'

'So what was your role? How did you look after them?'

A wily look came into his eyes and he wagged a finger at her. 'Now don't go telling me you're siding with that bitch of a home secretary,' he said. 'Who does she think she is, chastising us in public, reckoning she can get away with telling us to our faces that we're not fit to decide what's best for our members? Don't kid me you're unhappy with the deals and discounts the Federation negotiates on your savings and insurance policies, your mortgage, your new car? If you want to hand all that back and pay full rates, be my guest.'

'So where do you think Donna Fewell might have gone?' Grace kept her voice level and her chin up. 'Why doesn't she want the Federation looking after her?' She paused. 'Or is it you she's run away from?'

Kirkby's already ruddy cheeks darkened, but for the first time she saw an element of doubt creep into his eyes. 'Why would she run away from me? I'm Mark's father. I'm just trying to look after her and those kids the way he would've wanted.'

'You and your family like to look after people, don't you?'

'No need to be coy with me, young lady.' He crossed his arms across his chest and planted his feet firmly on the ground, knees apart. 'If you've got something to say, then spit it out.'

Grace felt almost sorry for him. He was such a dinosaur, trying so hard to stay safely inside the ramparts of the fort he'd built around himself. 'You're very clear about what's right and what's wrong,' she said, leaning back in her own chair, deliberately not responding to the challenge of his body language. 'You and your sons are all – or were – in uniform. Three men who have no problem exercising authority, taking decisive action when they see what has to be done. Is that fair?'

'That's a good thing, isn't it?' he demanded.

'What if it extends to bullying those who don't accept your authority or even shooting someone you don't think should have been let out of jail?'

He snorted with anger and contempt. 'Gordon Church, you mean? I don't think you'll find many in this nick who'll be weeping at his funeral!'

'So canteen culture knows best?'

'Not good enough for you, eh, girl? With your fancy degree and your management-speak.'

'We're currently working through a nationwide list of owners of silver or metallic-grey Renault Kangoo vans,' she said calmly.

'Like the one you found burned out?'

Grace raised her eyebrows in mock surprise. 'You seem very familiar with my team's confidential operational details.'

Kirkby, unabashed, tapped a finger to the side of his nose. 'You really don't know who I am, do you, girl?'

'Have you or either of your sons ever owned or had access to such a vehicle?'

Kirkby laughed in disbelief. 'You asking if I shot Gordon Church?'

'Did you?'

He pushed himself to his feet. 'No.' At the door he turned back to face her. 'I deserve a bit more respect, you know.' He beat himself softly on the chest with a clenched fist. 'So you tell that guv'nor of yours not to send a girl to do a man's job in future, all right?'

Grace didn't waste her indignation on his misogyny – after ten years in the job she was used to it – but she was taken aback by the confidence with which he'd met her questions about the murder of Gordon Church. Either he possessed the same almost delusional arrogance that she had sensed behind Adam Kirkby's insults on the steps outside the coroner's court, or his sons had kept him in ignorance of their vigilante fantasies.

Either way, it was time to press her boss into action against Adam Kirkby

59

Robyn sat on one of the uncomfortable chairs in the waiting room outside the headmistress's office. The head liked dramatic flourishes, and the rather sumptuous room had been decked out like the hotel she'd stayed in once on a trip to Lisbon with her parents. The only exit from the waiting room was through the secretary's office, and she was feeling trapped.

She and Lance had packed up and left the Martello tower early that morning and then sat in a supermarket car park on the outskirts of Colchester until Grace had called and given the OK for him to drop her near her school. The plan was for her to walk in as if nothing more serious had happened than a couple of days' absence, but as soon as she was spotted by one of the teachers there had commenced a flurry of discreet alarm. She gave the same story each time: when Lance had told her about her father's arrest on Monday, she'd panicked and lied to both him and her mother about her intention to stay the night with Sally and then taken off on her own. She refused to say where she'd been, pointing out that she was back now, all in one piece, and so it couldn't possibly matter.

After an embarrassed interview with the headmistress, who seemed unsure how to strike the right tone with the daughter of a potential arch-criminal, the police had been called, and she'd been informed that her family liaison officer was on his way to collect her. Lance would then take her to her parents.

The room was hot but her hands were freezing, so she sat on them, feeling the scratchy nap of the cut-velvet upholstery fabric. She felt sick, even though she hadn't been able to eat anything for breakfast. She both longed to see her mum and dad and dreaded it. Her life of even a week ago seemed like a distant memory or something she'd read in a children's book. The process that had started with Angie's death was now complete. She was a grown-up. She could never go back to that carefree state when all she had to do if something bothered her was ask her dad's advice.

She heard voices from the secretary's office, then the door opened and Lance walked in. They went through the greetings they'd rehearsed in the supermarket car park, then he guided her along a corridor and down some stairs and out into the grounds. They drove in silence: they had nothing more to say to one another. She felt as if she were the one going to prison, not her dad, as if she were the one who deserved it.

Her parents were waiting for her at the police station in a room decorated in plain soft colours and furnished with pale wooden furniture. A box of tissues sat in the middle of a low table between the chairs. They stood up awkwardly when Lance showed her in, and then he left, closing the door behind him. Nicola started to cry as Leonard enveloped Robyn wordlessly in a big hug. She submitted rather than returned it, feeling like an unfamiliar visitor from a foreign country. Nicola then stepped forward to offer an awkward embrace. Feeling a wave of guilt that she had never loved her mum as much as her dad, Robyn hugged her back, whispering that she was sorry. Releasing herself, she took a seat opposite them and looked at the man who had lied to her all her life about who he was.

Leonard leaned over and pressed her hand. 'I'm so sorry, Birdie. I never meant for it to come to this. Although maybe it's best that it has. I don't know. Forgive me?'

She nodded. Somehow her own betrayal still felt worse than anything he had done.

Leonard looked anxiously at Nicola, who nodded her encouragement, and he sat back. 'The police have promised to arrange a fresh start for us all,' he said. 'They'll register me as an informant and write a letter to the judge, and then, once everything's sorted out, we'll go away. We'll have new documents, new names, somewhere else to live. We can start again.'

'As if nothing happened?' asked Robyn. 'Why?'

'Because it's the best way, Birdie. A new beginning.'

'But my exams,' she said. 'My university application. I can't just . . .'

She didn't know how to finish. She could see from the way Leonard was looking at her that he was still in that place where there was no separation between himself and his daughter. There had been no shift. He still believed that what he benevolently wished for on her behalf was precisely what she would want for herself. This time she felt not only sadness that he could be so blind, but also terror at the black hole of unquestioning self that he sought to draw her into.

She swallowed hard. 'I don't want to change my identity,' she said. 'I don't want to lie about who I am for the rest of my life. I don't understand why it's necessary.'

'It's the only way to keep us all safe,' said Nicola, her voice trembling. 'Your father has to tell them everything he knows.'

Robyn was desperate to ask whether what Lance thought was true – that her dad had murdered a man named Peter – but she was too afraid that they would lie to her, and of what she'd do if they did.

'You mean people will want revenge?' she asked instead.

'Yes.' Her mother, usually so capable and matter-of-fact, shrank into herself as she almost whispered her answer. 'You may not be safe if you don't come with us.'

'What about Kenny and the other drivers?' asked Robyn. 'What happens to them? Are they in trouble? Will they go to prison, or will the police help them too?'

Leonard reached out for her, but she snatched her hands away.

'It was business,' he pleaded. 'You might as well hold cutlery manufacturers responsible for knife crime, or say the car industry is to blame when some idiot crashes a stolen car and kills half a dozen people.'

'No!'

'I never made anyone pull the trigger. What about people who sell booze or cigarettes, or those payday loan companies? Or bankers' bonuses and MPs who fiddle their expenses? Britain's a corrupt society. Everyone's at it. You'd be a fool not to make it the best way you can. I was taking care of my family, same as everyone else.'

'No!' she cried. 'I never chose to be taken care of like that! I never gave my permission. How could you say you were so sorry and offer me comfort when Angie died when all the time you knew it was you? It was you!'

Nicola put her hands to her mouth as if trying to contain her distress. Leonard got up and came to kneel stiffly beside his daughter. 'Please listen to me, Birdie. You have to listen.' He paused to look over his shoulder towards the door, and then lowered his voice. 'The rifle used by that madman in Dunholt, it came from a police officer. A *police officer*, Birdie. I'll be giving evidence against gangsters *and* police officers. Where do you think we're going to be safe? Nowhere. It's our only chance, and we have to take it.'

Robyn felt as if her head were going to burst. The stress was unbearable. He was right: there was nowhere to go, no road left for her to take. But her dad would never have been arrested or had to agree to this deal, if it wasn't for her. She too was responsible for the deal he had made.

'I have to know one thing,' she said, looking down at her father, wondering how every feature could still seem so familiar and beloved. She took a deep breath. 'Did you ever kill anyone?'

'No!'

'Don't lie to me.'

'I'm not lying. I promise, Birdie. Please.'

She had to decide, but she didn't know how. She'd thought Lance would take care of her, but she'd been wrong. Her parents loved her. If she turned away from them, she'd have to put her trust in Grace Fisher. Her dad's words echoed in her head: *I'll be giving evidence against police officers. Where do you think we're going to be safe?* If she was to stay sane, she had to focus on one clear thing and cling to that: the devil who had started all this was Grace Fisher. She looked into Leonard's eyes and nodded. 'OK,' she said. 'I'll go with you.'

60

Grace had positioned herself in the superintendent's office so that she could watch out for Lance as he returned from fetching Robyn from her school. She, Duncan and Colin were running over everything they had. She suspected Colin had noted her transparent lack of curiosity over where Robyn had spent the past two nights, and she had been relieved when he appeared content to shelve the issue, at least for the time being.

He summed up the investigation as they understood it so far. Ingold had admitted illegally supplying Mark Kirkby and his brother Adam with two Heckler & Koch G3 rifles plus ammunition after meeting them through a gun club. This corroborated what Davey Fewell had said about Mark showing him a weapon. The military shell casings recovered from Fewell's lethal rampage through Dunholt had been primed with the tool recovered from the creek near Ingold's house where Robyn Ingold had witnessed her father dump another bag – also retrieved from the mud – which contained casings with the same military head stamps. Davey said he'd told his father that Mark had shown him a gun, and there was every reason to assume that Russell Fewell's weapon and ammunition had been stolen from Mark Kirkby.

'At the present time,' said Colin, 'Davey Fewell's whereabouts are unknown.'

And, Grace told herself, offering silent and heartfelt thanks to Ivo, going to stay that way until this is all safely wrapped up.

'OK,' Colin resumed. 'Moving on to the Church inquiry. The shell casings recovered from the hospital grounds also came from Ingold's workshop and also have military head stamps. It's your belief, DI Fisher, that we should be taking a look at Adam Kirkby?'

Grace was about to reply when she saw Lance walk past the door. Colin also spotted him and waved for him to join them. Grace's heart sank: this was the worst possible timing. She had hoped to be able to make a strong enough case against Adam Kirkby for the sniper killings to arrest and interview him before drawing Colin into an argument over whether Adam might also be in the frame for beating Peter to death. If Lance launched into the Vale do Lobo connections too soon – forcing her to explain both how she had come by the information that Adam had stayed in Leonard's villa and that she had told Lance that Peter was working undercover – the resulting fallout would probably persuade their boss that they should both be suspended, and so jeopardize an investigation independent of the security services.

Lance drew up a chair beside her. His face was pale, his mouth set in a thin line. He nodded to her in a friendly enough way, but he wasn't really looking at her or seeing anything. It didn't bode well.

'We're just getting on to the sniper,' she told him. 'Adam Kirkby is a prison officer, so he'd have grapevine knowledge of the releases of both Gordon Church and the paedophile shot dead in Grantham.'

'And the Ely shooting?' asked Duncan.

'Mark Kirkby was alive then,' said Grace. 'He could well have heard locker-room gossip about an Albanian mafia guy thumbing his nose at British justice. PC Curtis Mullins, an old friend of Mark's, told me that the brothers had visited a militia training camp in Arizona. When they got back, they asked Leonard Ingold to tool them up.'

'Sounds like they fancied themselves as *Death Wish* meets *Dirty Harry*,' said Colin.

'Yes,' said Grace. 'Pathetic. And lethal.'

'I heard this morning that Curtis has resigned,' said Duncan. 'Is that true?'

'Yes,' said Colin.

'But once he's gone, it won't even be possible to interview him over any disciplinary action,' said Lance.

'We can't stop him,' said Colin tersely. 'Not unless he's already subject to an allegation, and he's not.'

'Not yet!' cried Lance. 'We must be able to do something.'

Grace was equally furious. The idea of Curtis taking his pension and walking out with an unblemished record stuck in her throat. At the same time she hoped Lance would see that what mattered most right now was to let her get on with crafting her argument against Adam for the sniper killings. There would be plenty of time later to go after him for Peter's murder.

But Lance turned to her indignantly. 'You can put in a complaint, can't you? Curtis admitted all kinds of stuff to you. Get something in before his papers are signed!'

'I've got no proof,' she said gently, wishing he'd respond to her beseeching look. 'It's all hearsay. He could make a counter-claim against me for harassment. And the Federation would back him to the hilt,' she added pointedly. Steeling herself, she turned away from him, back to Colin. 'I'd like to move on, if that's OK, sir?'

'Absolutely.'

'But—' began Lance.

She spoke over him. 'Duncan, fill us in on what you've got.' She could sense Lance fizzing dangerously beside her and prayed that he'd hold it all together long enough to discern her larger purpose.

'We haven't been able to link any member of the Kirkby family directly to a Renault Kangoo van,' Duncan began, 'but a neighbour thought he'd seen one parked in Adam Kirkby's drive on more than one occasion. And we checked his working hours against the dates of the three sniper killings: he was off duty each time.'

'Good!' said Colin, rubbing his hands. 'Plenty there for him to talk himself into a nice little trap.'

'There's one last thing,' said Grace. 'Purely circumstantial, but Adam has in the past worked in the prison where Warren Cox was knifed earlier this week. Adam would have good reason to want to send a message to Leonard Ingold to keep his mouth shut.'

'But we don't think Adam had anything to do with the daughter going AWOL, do we?' asked Colin.

Grace felt as if the momentary pause, as she and Lance each waited for the other to speak, was lasting for ever.

'No, sir,' said Lance firmly. 'My view is that a friend helped her, and she doesn't want to get whoever it is into trouble. Just a bit of teenage drama.'

'Pretty understandable,' said Duncan.

'Yes,' Lance agreed.

'OK,' said Colin. 'Let's draw up an arrest plan for Adam Kirkby. We want search warrants for anywhere he might have stashed the rifle. And we don't want anyone tipping off his father, so keep this nice and tight.'

Dismissed, Grace followed Lance and Duncan out into the main office. When Lance hesitated and glanced back with a scowl of determination, she moved in front of him, blocking his way.

'Wait!' she mouthed.

He shook his head and made to walk past her. She put her hands on his chest and pushed back. 'Wait!' she hissed. 'Get Adam in custody first, then we'll do the rest. I promise.'

Duncan shot them a curious glance, and she forced a smile. 'Feels like this one has been a long time coming, doesn't it?' she said to him, giving Lance another little shove towards his desk. To her relief, this time he went.

She followed Duncan and as he sat down leaned on the back of his chair. 'Do me a favour?' she asked softly.

'Sure.'

'Check out if Adam Kirkby was working the night Peter Burnley was murdered.'

Duncan looked up at her in surprise, his gaze immediately travelling past her to where Lance sat staring fiercely at his computer screen. She nodded. 'Just between us for now, OK?'

'Absolutely.' His expression registered sympathy for Lance. 'Don't worry, boss. I'll get straight on it.'

Grace thanked him and went to her own desk, praying that Lance would get the answers he craved before he lost it completely.

61

Hilary Burnett began by apologizing that the media conference was running slightly late due to the delayed arrival of the two detectives from Lincolnshire and Cambridgeshire. They now sat either side of Colin Pitman, all three trying not to look like cats with cream-covered whiskers as the photographers jostled to take their snaps. It was a good result, Ivo gave them that, but he was pretty certain that DI Fisher had done all the heavy lifting. Besides, he reckoned he deserved at least one little pat on the back himself.

The evening news would carry the story that Adam Kirkby had been caught bang to rights with a Heckler & Koch G3 rifle in his attic – photographs and video footage helpfully provided on the Essex force's media portal – plus ammunition linked forensically to the Gordon Church killing. But frankly Ivo didn't reckon that Kirkby Junior really lived up to the hype. The arrest photos of the vigilante sniper showed an unremarkable, nondescript bloke who you wouldn't look at twice. Except when he aimed a pathetic kick at a news cameraman who came too close. It if hadn't been for the officers in bulletproof vests and snazzy black baseball caps holding his arms, he'd probably have fallen flat on his face. Poor chap must have lived permanently in the shadow of his handsome older brother and domineering father. Ivo looked forward to the pleasure he would derive from door-stepping John Kirkby for a quote about the joys of fatherhood.

He had already called Donna Fewell to let her know that Adam had been charged and that Davey's testimony about Mark would never be required. Ivo had also finessed it with the head office of the building society Donna had worked for in Dunholt for them to offer her a job under her maiden name in a pleasant but distant market town, and then organized the family's immediate relocation, making sure, thanks to a clever bit of accounting, that the *Courier* stumped up their first three months' rent along with any additional costs. Yesterday he'd taken them to the station, where, managing not to blub, he had insisted on shaking Davey's hand. The boy had looked a little bemused, but Ivo didn't care. Hoping that the kid now had a fighting chance, Ivo had felt the cares of the world slipping off his shoulders.

He looked at his watch. All this self-congratulation, both on- and offstage, was pleasant enough, but he was eager to get on with the mysterious meeting that Hilary had requested once the conference was over. He assumed it was the Ice Maiden's doing, and he would just have to take his lead from her.

Twenty minutes later, as all the other cowboys saddled up for the ride home, the communications director gave him the glad eye, and he followed her through a door with a security keypad, along corridors and upstairs to a suite of offices that had secured a far bigger furnishing budget that the squad rooms he'd glimpsed on their way. He was overjoyed to see Grace Fisher already there, standing beside a window. It was dark outside, and as Hilary went to close the vertical blinds, he shook Grace's hand warmly, amused when she smiled and raised a warning forefinger to her lips. Clean cups, a coffee Thermos and a neat plate of biscuits sat waiting on a low table between two executive sofas.

Hilary invited them to sit, but remained standing. 'Thank you for coming,' she told him. 'DI Fisher asked me to set up this meeting. She thinks you may have information pertinent to an investigation and wants this to be both informal and officially logged.'

'I'm glad to be of help,' said Ivo, 'although I'm sure you realize that I'm not at liberty to reveal any of my sources.'

'Of course.' Hilary smiled. 'Coffee?'

'Thanks.' He turned to Grace. 'So how can I help?'

'Oh dear,' said Hilary. 'They've forgotten to give us any milk. I'll go and see if I can find some. Won't be long.'

She closed the door quietly behind her.

'Sorry about the amateur dramatics,' said Grace. 'But I might have to go on record with some of what you've given me in the past, and I couldn't think of any other way to make it official.'

'It's fine,' he said. 'And I take my coffee black, thanks.'

'Good. How's Donna Fewell?'

'All settled,' he said. 'Snug as a bug. I don't know how Davey and Ella will ever really manage to come to terms with what their dad did, but at least they all now know the full story.'

'Thank you – for Davey and for me.'

Ivo cleared his throat and helped himself to a biscuit. 'So why am I here?' he asked through a mouthful of crumbs.

'It's for my colleague, Lance Cooper.'

Ivo wasn't expecting that, but he was happy to sit back and listen to anything she wanted to say.

'Do you remember I told you that Peter Burnley hadn't even told his boyfriend that he was in Vale do Lobo when the photo of him with Coghlan and Adam Kirkby was taken?'

'Yes, I think so.'

'Well, Peter Burnley's boyfriend was Lance Cooper.'

'Right.'

'And Lance won't rest until we find out who killed him,' said Grace. 'I mean, really won't let it go. I had it all figured out that it was Adam Kirkby, and that we'd finally get the case wrapped up and Lance could move on.'

'But . . .'

Grace sighed heavily. 'But Adam Kirkby was at work that night, in a prison, logged in and logged out. You don't get a more cast-iron alibi.'

'So what made you put Adam in the frame in the first place?'

'Because of Vale do Lobo. You said Coghlan asked you about Buckingham Gate. Well, if he suspected that Peter was there to investigate their connections to Leonard Ingold, then Coghlan probably told Adam. A month or two later Adam and Mark saw Peter having a drink with Lance in Colchester. They'd have had no idea that Lance and Peter were a couple, so maybe they jumped to the wrong conclusion – all they saw was the guy who'd been asking questions in Vale do Lobo talking to a DS from the Major Investigation Team. Neither of them would want to be caught in possession of illegal weapons. Not long afterwards Peter was dead.'

Ivo didn't get it. 'But so was Mark,' he said. 'And you're saying it can't have been Adam. Who's left?'

'If it's about Ingold, then there's nothing,' she said. 'That's the trouble. I've been over and over the case, but Lance simply won't accept that there's no big secret that we're all keeping from him. And I can't blame him. But it's like he's gnawing his own arm off over this.'

'How do I fit in?'

'Only that I know you've been digging into Coghlan. I thought, if I can put everything I know in front of Superintendent Pitman and demonstrate to Lance that there's no cover-up, no hidden agenda, then maybe he'll finally be prepared to let it go.'

Ivo shook his head. 'There's nothing new to tell you about Coghlan.' He couldn't bear the disappointment in her solemn grey eyes. 'I did, however, turn up a juicy bit of gossip that, at a stretch, might explain what Peter was up to, though I'm not sure I see it leading to murder.'

'Tell me anyway.'

'I've got a mate in MI5. Let's call him the Young Ferret. Used to be my junior on the crime desk. He's never heard of your so-called Peter Burnley, but when his fur was stroked the right way he did relate some rather entertaining in-house rumours to the effect that after Plebgate and the forced resignation of a cabinet minister, the home secretary let the secret squirrels loose on the Police Federation with orders to dig up some useful dirt.'

'You're saying the home secretary was spying on the Police Federation?'

'Told you it was entertaining. Know what a number two account is?'

'No. Should I?'

'Bear with me,' he said. 'So, each of the local Federation branches negotiates a whole range of offers for its members, everything from broadband deals to bridal gowns. They're billed as rewards for the brave and difficult things the police do on our behalf. Anyway, a lot of these member services attract administration fees, which are paid into so-called number two accounts, the point being that half the time head office can't be arsed to keep tabs on them, regarding them rather as petty cash for the local branches to dip into.'

Grace frowned, and Ivo paused to find out what was bothering her. She took a deep breath and gave him a straight look. 'You know John Kirkby was a local branch chair?'

Ivo whistled. 'No. I knew he'd been a copper, but that's all.'

She nodded, evidently still running through everything that was in her mind, checking what other connections might jump out at her. Suddenly she opened her eyes wide and stared at him. 'Oakmoor Wealth Management does a lot of business with Federation members,' she said. 'Peter had been taken for dinner by people from the Colchester office the night he died.'

'Yeah, but they'd have no reason to worry,' said Ivo. 'It's what happens to the fees once they've been paid to the Federation that counts.'

'But what if Peter was following the money trail? What if John Kirkby was in charge of the number two account and asked Jerry Coghlan, his old pal from his first nick, for a good investment rate via his Panamanian banking connections?'

'Are you suggesting that Kirkby was skimming his own members?'

'No.' She shook her head vigorously. 'That would be theft. Kirkby's far too self-righteous for that. But he might have played his cards close to his chest in terms of the bookkeeping he presented to his branch. As long as he turned a healthy profit, he was probably given a free hand to get on with it.'

'I didn't like the man,' said Ivo. 'But all the same, I don't see him as the type to beat someone to death.'

'I'm not so sure,' said Grace. 'When Peter was killed, it was only a fortnight after Mark's death, remember. Kirkby's a zealot. Imagines he's patron saint of all the boys in blue.'

'A grief-stricken zealot,' said Ivo. 'One who'd kill to protect the best interests of his members?'

'I think he might, yes. Especially after the horrors of that Christmas Day in Dunholt. His own son gunned down in cold blood. And now Peter Burnley was out to take away everything he'd worked for. I've talked to him. In his own eyes, John Kirkby *is* the law. If he thinks it's right, then it is right.'

'Certainly what he taught his sons,' Ivo agreed. 'And lovely creatures they turned out to be.'

'No wonder we kept hitting dead ends in the investigation,' she exclaimed. 'I always felt like the killer got lucky, but John Kirkby had a lifetime's experience as a police officer to guide him past the obvious mistakes. He could've been stalking Peter for days before the right opportunity presented itself.'

'He was a bitter man,' Ivo reflected, thinking back to his own conversation in the Weymouth curry house. 'He thought the police weren't properly respected any more, resented all the budget cuts. If he found out the government had sent someone to spy on him, well . . .'

'This is awful,' she said. 'Peter was such a lovely man. I couldn't bear it if he died just because of some tawdry political point-scoring.'

'You can be sure no one on either side is going to thank you for bringing it to light. I mean, how much of this are you prepared to share even with Hilary?'

Grace wasn't listening. 'How do I tell Lance?' she cried. 'If this is really true, it'll destroy him!'

Her distress made Ivo squirm at the invidiousness of his profession. For the truth was that he lived for just this kind of scandal, for the stories that proved him right about his fundamental view of the world. It was the glee he took in exposing the pettiness of the so-called great and good, in bringing shame and disgrace on hypocrites and liars that got him out of bed in the morning. He'd like nothing better than to run with the Young Ferret's gossip about the Police Federation. He couldn't even honestly say that he cared much about poor dead Peter Burnley; Lance Cooper's boyfriend was merely part of a good story in which the home secretary waged a clandestine war against the Police Federation and John Kirkby thought he was above the law. But the Ice Maiden cared, and her distress made him remember just how deeply this stuff could hurt. The image of Ivo's father and housemaster shaking hands over his mother's death had distorted everything that came afterwards, just as this would surely do for Grace and her friend. And he couldn't do that to her.

62

Colin sat tilted back in his executive chair, elbows bent and fingertips touching, as he listened impassively, his expression unreadable. At least he had heard her out, thought Grace. He hadn't called a halt to her insane ramblings about the political misuse of state resources. Nor had he yet tried to defend John Kirkby. She finished laying out her theory of Peter Burnley's murder and waited.

'As you know,' he said after several long moments, 'the security and intelligence services stick rigorously to their policy to never confirm or deny. You're not going to get anything out of them.'

'Even in a murder case?'

'The only time the principle can be overridden in court is when disclosure of an informant's identity is required to prove a defendant's innocence. That's not the case here.'

'But then equally the defence won't be able to prove that Peter wasn't working for MI5.'

'True. But there's also the inconvenience of your having no witnesses, no CCTV and no useful forensic evidence to tie anyone to the murder scene. And if the spooks are sitting on anything we don't know, they're not about to share it.'

'What about Kirkby's Panamanian investment accounts?' said Grace. 'We can at least investigate them.'

Colin regarded her levelly and in reply raised his eyebrows in an ironic question.

'You're saying that because they were Federation funds he's above the law?' she demanded.

'I've not said anything. Look, even if the rumours you've heard are true, and the home secretary has been looking for a stick to beat the Federation with, it doesn't mean she wants to beat them in public. That's not how politics works.'

'We're not politicians.'

'You don't think, these days, that's being a little naive?'

'I don't need your permission to make a complaint about the Federation's financial affairs to the IPCC.'

Colin laughed. 'Be my guest! The Federation has fought tooth and nail from the start to water down the powers of the IPCC. And even if they could investigate a retired officer, the first person Kirkby would consult would be his Federation lawyer. He's going to get the best defence money can buy.'

'If we do nothing, our hand may be forced by the *Courier*,' said Grace. 'I think Ivo Sweatman is planning to kick off with a big story about Jerry Coghlan's financial operation in the Algarve.'

'If he does, then I assume he'll find a nice fat D notice on his desk, strongly suggesting he spike the story,' said Colin. 'Besides, the *Courier*'s proprietor supports the current government, and even without a D notice, he isn't about to run a story that's going to embarrass the home secretary.'

'You're the head of the Major Investigation Team!' she said. 'I've brought you a strong argument that John Kirkby is involved in money-laundering and murder. What are you going to do?'

'Fine,' said Colin. 'Arrest him, bring him in for questioning. He'll give a "No comment" interview with a Federation solicitor by his side. Then what? You think the chief constable wants to start a fight with the local Federation branch? Effective policing in Essex would grind to a halt tomorrow. And you can kiss good-bye to counting on backup ever arriving in time to save your skin.'

'Lance isn't going to let this go.'

'That's the same DS Cooper who accepted free foreign hospi-tality from a criminal armourer, correct?' Colin sighed. 'Believe me, Grace, I'm not trying to be deliberately obtuse or obstruc-tive, but I am telling it like it is. You're a good officer, with the smarts to take you a long way. If you want to run with this then I won't stop you, but until you've got more to go on than a theory, it's career suicide, and my strong advice is to drop it, and to persuade Lance to drop it too.'

'I can't do that, sir.'

Colin shrugged. 'OK. Keep me informed.'

Grace got up to go. At the door he called her back. 'One other thing to remember, DI Fisher,' he said. 'Anything you were told about Peter Burnley's true identity was in your capacity as a police officer. That means your knowledge is subject to the Official Secrets Act. You might want to read up on that before you go tilting at windmills. Especially if it comes out that you shared that knowledge not only with DS Cooper but also with a journalist.'

Grace managed to walk out of his office, but then, afraid she was about to vomit, rushed to the toilets. She didn't throw up, but she felt dizzy and light-headed with anger and frustration. How dare he threaten her like that! She'd have more respect for him if he'd gone ahead and suspended her for an offence he knew she'd committed. Her overwhelming desire was to march back into his office and resign. But if she did that, John Kirkby would have won. His sort would take over the service, and slowly, bit by bit, all the unchallenged lies would become the truth.

She washed her hands and splashed cold water onto her face, avoiding her eyes in the mirror above the row of sinks. She had been here once before with Colin Pitman. When he'd been unwilling to take action against a popular officer, everyone's best mate.

Was Colin's pragmatism merely the tribal knee-jerk reaction that looks after its own or the worst form of corruption, the kind that muddies the waters to such a degree that all hope of truth or justice is lost in the silt at the bottom? Is that what she wanted for her career, for her life? She wished her father were still alive so she could ask him what to do.

There was a tap at the door, and Lance came in, glancing at the cubicles to check she was alone.

'What did he say?' he asked.

'He didn't tell me to bury it,' she said. 'But he did throw every kind of spanner in the works, including the Official Secrets Act.'

'Then we'll go over his head,' said Lance. 'Take it right to the top.'

Grace shook her head. 'It won't work. He blocked off every gap I tried to run through. And in the end he's right. We don't have enough physical evidence to persuade the CPS to charge John Kirkby with murder.'

'That doesn't stop us bringing him in, though? At least so he knows he didn't get away with it. We can tell him we know what he did, even if we can't prove it. We'll get him in the end somehow, won't we?'

'We can bring him in,' she said wearily, unwilling to repeat all of Colin's caveats.

'Then what are you waiting for?'

She hung her head, too tired to move.

'Grace?' He was already at the door, holding it open.

All her life she'd believed that justice, however difficult, however hard-won, restored order. For the first time it struck her that perhaps there was no order. She wondered where that left justice.

'Hang on a moment,' she said to Lance. She dug into her handbag and with a shaking hand combed her hair and applied fresh lipstick. She was as ready as she'd ever be.

63

Lance drove. John Kirkby's address was near the golf course. A small detached house with an integral garage and wide driveway, it may well have been new when he bought it but now looked in need of updating. The front door was inside a glazed porch, and they heard chimes when they rang the doorbell. John opened the inner doors but, recognizing them, stood his ground and spoke through the closed outer door.

'What do you want?' He suddenly gripped the frame, looking frightened. 'Is my boy all right? Nothing's happened to Adam? No bastard's got to him in custody?'

'It's nothing to do with your son,' said Grace. She tried the handle of the porch door, but it was locked. 'Please can you let us in?'

'I don't have to,' he said. 'What do you want?'

'It would be much easier if we came in.'

'Open the door, Mr Kirkby,' said Lance. 'If you don't, then we'll have to force an entry.'

Kirkby stared them out.

'We are here to arrest you on suspicion of the murder of Peter Burnley.' Lance began the formal caution. 'You do not have to say anything, but it may harm your defence if you do not mention when questioned something which you later rely on in court. Anything you do say may be given in evidence. Now please open the door.'

'Just give me a minute or so,' said Kirkby.

'No. Now.' Grace tried again to open the porch door, even though she knew it was useless, as Kirkby quietly closed the inner door and disappeared.

'Round the back,' said Lance, already heading off.

Grace went to the nearest window and peered in at an untidy lounge with an unused fireplace and a scratched leather three-piece suite. She remained where she was in case Kirkby decided to make a run for it through the front while Lance looked for an open back door. She looked again at the interior: little sign of a woman's hand. A couple of opened beer cans, a paperback thriller, the *Daily Mail* open at the crossword. This man had one son murdered, the other facing life imprisonment. He had little left to lose. She ran back to the porch and put her shoulder to the door, holding down the handle and trying to force the lock. But the double-glazed PVC was strong and wouldn't give. She was just about to call for backup when from deep inside the house she heard, loud, the blast of a shotgun.

'Lance,' she screamed.

He came running back as she put in the call to the emergency services. 'No entry at the back,' he said.

She pointed to the garage, and he sprinted off. She watched as he managed to push up the overhead door and edge his way past the big saloon car inside. She ended her call and followed in time to see him open the inside door that led into the house. 'Wait!' she called. 'It could be a trap. Wait for armed response!'

But he either didn't hear or didn't listen. She waited anxiously until he reappeared, ashen-faced. He nodded in response to her silent question and went to sit on the low garden wall, his head in his hands.

'Any chance he's still alive?' she asked.

Lance shook his head. 'Brains all over the wall.'

She sat beside him and rubbed his back. 'You OK?'

He nodded and then turned to her, a sour, contorted look on his face. 'They'll spin it that he's some kind of hero like his son Mark, won't they? Killed himself because he couldn't live with Adam's dishonour.'

'We've done what we can,' she said. 'And it's still justice of a kind, I suppose. At least now we know the truth.'

'It doesn't matter,' he said. 'The truth is what you read in the newspapers, what they tell us on the news, what the bobby on the beat believes. They'll never know why Peter died.'

Grace could hear an approaching siren. Lance stood up, reached into his coat pocket for his warrant card and tossed it on the ground. 'I'm sick of it,' he said. 'Had enough. What about you?'

What about her? She didn't know. The siren came closer, joined by the wail of another emergency vehicle. She thought of the bloody mess the paramedics would find inside the house. Was this what she really wanted to do with her life? Yet, if this kind of disorder was ultimately all there was, someone had to be here, someone who cared about the things that mattered. She looked up at Lance. 'I think I'll stick around for a bit longer.'

ACKNOWLEDGEMENTS

First of all I must thank my brother Allen who altered the course of my original idea by saying that bullets are far more interesting than guns. Any mistakes I have made about the pathology of gunshot wounds are mine. For invaluable specialist expertise, my grateful thanks to Mark Mastaglio and Andrew Perks. Again, all errors are my own. And I am indebted for other local knowledge to Duncan Campbell, Vicky Hayward, Jeff Edwards, Robert Wilson, Kathrine Smith, Jackie Malton, Merle Nygate and Lisa Cohen. Lines from E. M. Forster's 'What I Believe' are reproduced courtesy of the Provost and Scholars of King's College, Cambridge and the Society of Authors as the E. M. Forster Estate.

My heartfelt thanks as always to my wonderful editor Jane Wood and her team at Quercus, and to my equally wonderful agent Sheila Crowley, and also to Rebecca Ritchie, at Curtis Brown.